The author was born in Yorkshire in the market town of Malton, and now lives in Suffolk. Retired, she enjoys walking, her head always abuzz with stories. In 2002, she wrote her first fantasy tale. The sequel followed almost two decades later. And now, *The Disappearance of Amaryllis August,* is her debut novel.

To all those who have walked this journey with me.
And to Anne, "my eagle eyes."

PJ Holmes

THE DISAPPEARANCE OF AMARYLLIS AUGUST

AUSTIN MACAULEY PUBLISHERS™

LONDON ∗ CAMBRIDGE ∗ NEW YORK ∗ SHARJAH

A CIP catalogue record for this title is available from the British Library.

ISBN 9781398443211 (Paperback)
ISBN 9781398456211 (ePub e-book)

www.austinmacauley.com

First Published 2022
Austin Macauley Publishers Ltd®
1 Canada Square
Canary Wharf
London
E14 5AA

NINETEEN FIFTY-SEVEN

AMARYLLIS

Chapter 1

It is the 21st of June. The longest day. The first day of summer. It is also Amaryllis August's birthday. The sun filters through her curtains, paints her room in pastel hues. She jumps out of bed; flings open the curtains and looks down into the garden below.

It is a large lawned garden with sculptured flowerbeds full of bright flowers. There are a lot of geraniums. Her father loves geraniums. Charles August is a doctor. He is tall and handsome with curly fair hair and twinkling blue eyes. Charismatic. Her friends think he is dashing.

His surgery is in a big house set back from a pot-holed un-tarmacked road. Amaryllis passes it on her way to school. In the winter she likes to hear the ice in the potholes crack when she jumps on them. Dr August does house calls in the small market town where they live. He also attends at the local cottage hospital where he does minor operations and deals with emergencies. So, Amaryllis sees little of him. Yet it is always her father who disciplines her. Any misdemeanours are saved until he is home.

Amaryllis is naturally clumsy. She is always breaking things. But Charles August does not see accidents. It is crass stupidity, he says. His retribution is to be feared. So, although she loves her father, she is also, at times, afraid of him. One day Amaryllis will ask herself if you can truly know and love a person you spend so little time with. If a surprise birthday present can ever live up to its promise.

The lawn is always perfectly mown, dark green stripes next to pale green stripes. And not a blade of grass betwixt. Amaryllis wonders how Garden man does this.

When she asks him, he says, "Oh Miss Amelia…" He always calls her Miss Amelia. She never corrects him. "Doesn't tha know, curiosity kills the cat?" She laughs.

Amaryllis knows she's not a cat. But she does like to potter about with him, asking endless questions. He does not read or write but he does know a lot about plants and flowers. About trees and shrubs. The insects that share them. Garden man is old and gnarled like the Old Oak Tree at the bottom of the garden.

High up in the tree, on its broad lower branches, hidden by foliage when he (Amaryllis always thinks of it as a man tree because it is so big and strong) is in full leaf, is a tree house. Her Uncle James builds it on one of his visits. There is a rope ladder so you can climb up. The rope ladder twists and turns so you need to hang on.

Amaryllis likes to sit in the tree house and read. She is reading THE FOLK OF THE FARAWAY TREE. It's by Enid Blyton. She loves this book. She wishes that the Old Oak Tree is the Faraway Tree. That Moonface and Silky are her friends. That she can visit all the different lands that come to the Faraway Tree. Dodge Dame Washalot's dirty water.

There is a pulley wheel fixed to a branch with a long rope that reaches the ground. Amaryllis can put her book and some sweets in a basket, tie it to the rope and haul it up when she has climbed up into the tree house. She thinks if Garden man put a pan on his head, he would look like Saucepan man.

At the side of the lawn, behind a tall hedge is a greenhouse. It is full of tomatoes. There is a boiler in it which feeds on coke. It keeps the greenhouse warm in winter. The greenhouse smells of soil and old tools.

"The tomatoes does talk," Garden man tells her, "in the warm dark when there be no-un about."

One night, she thinks, she will sneak out and creep down the path to the greenhouse and listen to what the tomatoes talk about.

Opposite the greenhouse is a shed. It is where the coke is kept. Amaryllis does not like the shed. Once she manages to get padlocked in. It is dark and dusty. There are spiders. Big spiders. And rats that scuttle amongst the coke. When Garden man opens the creaky padlocked door, he is mighty surprised to find her. "Why, Miss Amelia," he says, "whatever be you doing in this dirty dark hole." She never goes in the shed again.

As Amaryllis looks down onto the garden from her bedroom window on this day, the day of her birthday, when the sun is shining and bubbles of excitement burst in her tummy, she sees the huge tent her father put up yesterday. It's for her party this afternoon. Nine of her school friends are coming. One for each year of her life. There is to be a magician. He will perform magic tricks and make animal balloons. There will be paper hats and Barratt's Sherbet Fountains with sticks of liquorice. It's going to be super.

The dining room doors will be opened out. The striped awning will be pulled down. Under the awning there will be two tables. One will have plates with paper doilies. These will be stacked with triangular sandwiches: chicken paste, beef paste and egg. On the other will be a glass jug of home-made lemonade and bowls of jelly. Blackcurrant and strawberry jellies. There will be bread and butter. Amaryllis does not understand why she can never have jelly without bread and butter. But she does not ask. Children should be seen and not heard, she is always being told by grown-ups.

This is the front of the house. A large red brick Victorian house. There is a bay window with a bench under. A grassy slope leads down to the garden where the tent regally sits. Amaryllis likes to roll down this in the summer and sledge down in the winter when the garden is covered in snow. She uses a cover on top of the gas cooker. It is made of enamel and is square. Perfect to slide and spin down the slope. She is not sure her mother agrees.

If her father is home, he builds igloos with her. And they have snowball fights. But he kneads his snow until it is hard. His snowballs are balls of ice. Not soft like hers. He is a better shot too. Laughs when they hit her. Sometimes she wonders if he knows how much they hurt. But she does not cry. She will not cry.

It snows often in Yorkshire. Cloaks the garden with a deep soft layer. A carpet of snow covered with eerie shapes as the plants, shrubs, bushes and ornaments lay, not quite buried, beneath. The big house is very cold. There are coal fires in the lounge and dining room. And in some bedrooms. But in the kitchen the icy winds blow up from the cellar and you can see the floor undulating.

Amaryllis sits by the Aga which is always stoked and warm. It's what her mother cooks on. And in. Her father cooks too. But only at Christmas. He takes over the kitchen. Banishes her mother. Boils pig's trotters on the hotplate. Makes the pie crust and filling for a stand pie. Stuffs the turkey front and back. The stuffing is a secret recipe which he shares with no-one.

He prepares all the vegetables. Does all this on Christmas Eve. And whilst Columbine and Amaryllis go to St. Michaels evening service, he puts the turkey in the Aga to cook slowly overnight. On Christmas Day the house is filled with delicious aromas. Christmas, she thinks. I love Christmas. I love my birthday. But Christmas is six months away. And my birthday is TODAY.

She skips down the red carpeted stairs in her nightdress. Across the tiled hall, down a corridor and into the kitchen where smells of baking assail her nose. The sound of beating alerts her ears. The smell of baking comes from the aga. The sound of beating comes from the scullery. It's a room off the kitchen which has a door that opens into a back yard.

A small back yard with a coke bunker near the door. The rest of the coke is stored in a shed. One of three sheds in the back yard. They all have green painted doors. Coal for the fires is stored in another. Men covered in black dust deliver it in sacks. As they do the coke. The middle shed houses a porcelain toilet. The bottom corner is gnawed. By a rat. She knows there are rats in the yard. In the coal bunker. So, Amaryllis never uses the toilet. She is scared her bottom will be bitten. A door from the back yard opens out to steps which lead down to the driveway. There is a stepped rockery to the side.

The scullery has a sink. And a table behind which is an old disused fireplace with a mantlepiece. All sorts of bits and bobs live on the mantlepiece. At the side of the fireplace is the gas cooker, its burners covered by Amaryllis's enamel sled. There is an adjoining larder full of pans and trays and chilled foods.

On the table there will be a big brown stone bowl tipped on edge, whilst her mother, sleeves rolled up, will be beating the sweet, gooey, cake mixture with a wooden spoon. Amaryllis cannot wait to lick out the bowl. She hopes her mother is making fairy cakes. Fairy cakes with sponge wings and butter icing. Her mother makes the best fairy cakes. She also makes the best scones too.

Gladys is in the kitchen. Gladys is Garden man's daughter. But you would never guess. She is not old and gnarled with soil under her fingernails.

"Happy Birthday, Miss Amaryllis," she says and takes three tubes of pastilles out of her apron pocket. Puts them in a row on the wooden kitchen table. Amaryllis loves the blackcurrant ones best.

"Thank you, Gladys," she says, pulling out a chair and sitting.

Gladys, who is not exactly a maid but comes to the house every day except Saturday and Sunday, boils her an egg. Toasts her a slice of bread on the hotplate. Butters it and cuts it into soldiers.

"Don't you be eating them sweets all at once mind, Miss Amaryllis," she says as she puts the plate and egg cup in front of her.

A small square parcel also lay on the table. It is wrapped in pink tissue paper. A red ribbon tied around.

"Mummy?" Amaryllis calls as she dips a soldier into the runny egg.

"Just a minute," Columbine August calls back.

She is always saying this. Her mother is a busy person. She is a seamstress. In the war she was a nurse in a field hospital. She sewed up wounded soldiers. Amaryllis thinks it must have been truly awful. Because now her mother only sews clothes. Right at the top of the house, up the beige carpeted stairs, there is an attic. There are four rooms. Once upon a time they were the servants' bedrooms. There are no carpets. Just painted wooden floorboards. When you walk, your shoes make clip-clop sounds, like a horse's hooves.

One room has a long wide-topped cupboard. On this is a sewing machine. There are drawers stuffed with patterns. Rolls of materials and ribbons. This is where her mother measures, cuts and sews. Amaryllis never sees the ladies her mother makes clothes for. They use the back stairs. Stairs that the servants used when the big house belonged to gentry. They climb up steeply behind a door just off the kitchen. Gladys uses the main stairs. So Amaryllis decides that is why she is 'a part of the family not exactly maid'.

Another bedroom is used as a fitting room. It has a long tilt mirror so the clients can parade in their attire. The mirror has fancy filigree round it. Sometimes Amaryllis puts one of her smocked dresses on and twirls, this way and that way, in front of it. No criticism. It will be several years before she becomes conscious of figure and fancy.

One is still a bedroom. It has a double bed, a dressing table and a desk. Amaryllis sleeps here when she is seven. There is a round porthole window. On a clear day you can see all the way to the coast. This is where there are two doors on a wall. Behind each is a closet. One houses a huge bath with a ball cock. Her mother tells her it is a water tank that supplies all the water they use. Amaryllis likes this closet. She sometimes hides in it and reads.

The other is a sort of walk-in wardrobe with mothball smelling clothes on wire hangers. The dresses are long and elegant. The coats have padded shoulders. One is off-white, made from the fleece of a sheep. Another is a fur jacket made from a baby seal. It is soft and silky. Amaryllis likes to stroke it. Some many years later she will decide what a heinous and cruel fashion this is.

But Amaryllis likes the fourth room the best. It is crammed with all sorts of things. There is a post war gas mask, which looks very scary. A tin of a peachy coloured powder. Her mother says it is face powder which was difficult to obtain in the war. Amaryllis wasn't alive in the war, but she knows there were bombs. That people had to hide underground. That there were shortages. Ration books for food and sweets. In fact, she thinks she was five when sweet rationing ended.

There is a box of vinyl discs. An old wind-up gramophone with a turntable and a big, fluted horn. You put a disc on the turntable. There is an arrow to set the speed. Amaryllis always sets it at forty-five. Then you pull this arm down. The arm has a round head with a needle poking out. The needle scratches round and round the turning disc. Crackling music and singing sound out of the horn. It is absolutely smashing.

"Happy birthday, Amaryllis," says her mother. She comes into the kitchen with floury hands and hugs her. "Do you want to open your present now?"

"Yes, please."

"I hope you like it. This is from me."

"Where's Daddy's present?" Amaryllis asks. "He hasn't forgotten, has he?"

"No sweetheart, he hasn't forgotten. Your father said it's a surprise. So you will have to wait until he comes home," Columbine August says this, knowing full well that patience is not one of her daughter's virtues. But it is one she will have to embrace sooner than expected.

"Do you think it could be a pony?"

Amaryllis lifts the pink package. Oh how she would love a pony. Her best friend, Penelope, has a pony. It is white with a long flowing mane and tail. She calls it Tonto, like the horse in the Lone Ranger, a television programme that they both watch and love. Although it's in black and white, they can see that the Lone Ranger's horse is white. Sometimes Amaryllis dreams *she* is the Lone Ranger, galloping across the country saving people.

She peels away the pink tissue paper.

"It's not a pony, Amaryllis," says her mother.

Amaryllis also knows that it will not be a puppy, or a kitten, or a rabbit. Or anything furry come to that. Columbine Amaryllis has an allergy to fur. Her eyes swell and water profusely. Her lips swell. She coughs and sneezes until she chokes.

Inside the pink tissue is a fancy box.

"Do *you* know what daddy's present is?" Amaryllis lifts the lid of the box.

"Hush on you. It's a secret."

Amaryllis knows all about secrets. That you must keep them. That is why she never tells her mother what her father sometimes asks her to do when he comes into her bedroom to kiss her goodnight. Or what he sometimes does to her when she is in the bath. He says she must never tell anybody. That it is their little secret. He says it's because he loves her. That she's special. That it's just for her. That her mother would be angry and jealous if she tells. Amaryllis doesn't understand why. Because what he does hurts. Makes her feel sick. Does it mean her mother isn't special then? That he doesn't love her?

She peers into the box. Gasps. There, nestled in black velvet, is a wristwatch. It's rose gold and sparkly. Very grown up. The best present ever. Next to a pony or a puppy. The watch is all wound up and set at the right time. She lifts it carefully out of the box.

"I love it mummy," she says slipping it over her hand onto her wrist. Then she tightens the strap as far as she can.

Her wrist is slim so it's still a little loose. Jumping up, she flings her arms around her mother. Columbine is short, round and cuddly like Miss Tong, her class teacher. Except Miss Tong has dingy brown hair, whilst her mother's is a shiny raven black.

Amaryllis loves Miss Tong even if she often sends her out of class for talking. Miss Tong says that she is a bright pupil, despite. She is sure that when Amaryllis takes the eleven plus in two years, she will easily pass. Then she will go to the local Grammar School, which is just up the road. Unless her parents send her away to boarding school. There is one at Bridlington which is not far away.

Although she will miss her mother, it will be exciting to go away and board. To sleep with other girls. To talk in the dark. To giggle. Amaryllis looks at her beautiful watch. It is Miss Tong who taught the class how to tell the time. The hands on the dial tell her it is 9 o'clock. She counts on her fingers…ten, eleven, twelve, one, two, three, four. Seven fingers. Seven hours until her party. Why is time so slow?

"Now I must get back to the scullery," her mother is saying. "You can lick the bowl, Amaryllis." She pauses. Thinks. "Then go upstairs and get washed and dressed. But not in your party dress, or your lacy white socks," she says.

Amaryllis's party dress is a stiff pink cotton. Her mother sews it on her machine. It is very pretty with lots of petticoats layered under a flared skirt. There is a pink sash around the waist. The dress and new lacey white socks are hanging in her bedroom ready for the party. Underneath is a pair of silver slipper shoes.

"Now Gladys," Columbine says, "can you come and make the jellies. The kettle is on the simmer plate. It will soon boil."

"But then what shall I do mummy?" Amaryllis asks as she runs her finger round the brown bowl.

"Well since you are not going to school, why don't you watch out for your Uncle James. He says he's driving over when he's finished his ward rounds. So I don't know what time he'll arrive. And I think he might have a surprise present for you too."

Uncle James, who, like her father, has been in her life forever. He is tall and handsome too. Has curly auburn gold hair. Brown eyes like her mother. And he is also a doctor. But he works in a big hospital in a city. She thinks it's called Sheffield. It sounds an exciting place. Uncle James says there are trams. Amaryllis would love to ride on a tram. Perhaps one day he'll take her back to Sheffield so she can.

Under the oak tree with the tree house there is a big blue swing. Uncle James made this for her too. A long time ago. When she was little. He is a fun uncle. Playful. He'll say, "Give me your hands, Amaryllis." And she does. Then he starts to whizz round, faster and faster. She keeps her legs straight. Her feet take off and then she too is flying round. Round and round like an aeroplane.

Uncle James is always playing with daddy too. They playfight and roll about on the grass. Tickle each other. Hug. She thinks they must love each other as much as she loves them. So, on this bright June day, her ninth birthday, Amaryllis sits on the wall that runs from the backyard door to the big gates on either side of the driveway.

She is wearing blue dungarees, plain white socks and plimsolls. From the wall she can see up and down the road below. She will be able to see Uncle James in his red Austin Healey. It's an Austin Healey 100. Amaryllis know this because both her father and uncle are crazy about cars. And so is she. Her father has a Triumph TR 3. It is a glossy dark blue colour. She always knows when he comes home as he screeches into the large driveway, scattering stones. Her mother complains that one day he will chip her Morris Minor.

In Amaryllis's bedroom are boxed dinky toys of cars. She does not really like dolls. They are made of hard stuff. Not cuddly like real babies. Uncle James drives fast. Sometimes he takes Amaryllis for a 'spin', he calls it. They zoom

14

round the country roads, and her hair flies out all ways. Her father very seldom takes Amaryllis for a 'spin'.

But Amaryllis will not have her party. She will not see the birthday cake decorated with dolly mixtures. Nine candles pushed into the butter icing for her to blow out. She will not sit in the tent and watch the magician do magic tricks. She will not get an animal balloon. She will not eat jelly. Bread and butter. Eat fairy cakes with their little sponge wings. Drink homemade lemonade. She will not sit her eleven plus in two years.

Because this day, the 21st of June. The longest day. The first day of summer. The day that she is nine years old is also the day that Amaryllis August disappears.

Chapter 2

Tyres squeal round the corner as James pulls into the driveway of Oakwood Drive. He parks next to Charles's car, switches off the engine. Opens the door and climbs out. James is casually but smartly dressed. A white Cuban collar shirt. Brown chinos. A tan leather jacket. His feet comfortable in brown Penny Loafers. An expensive Rolex Oyster watch with a tan strap on his wrist. He glances at the time. Three-thirty. *Done it*, he thinks. Got here in time.

He strolls up the steps from the driveway, through the open porch and into the tiled hall. There is an air of disquiet.

"Charles? Columbine? Amaryllis?" he calls.

The hall remains silent.

Gladys appears. She is wringing her hands. Her face is etched with distress.

"Oh Mr James," she says. "Summat terrible 'as 'appened."

"What?" he asks. "What has happened? Where are they?"

"Dr August's gone out looking," she says.

"Looking for what?" he asks. "Charles is expecting me. They all are. For Amaryllis's party. And I see his car is in the drive."

"Oh lordy me, Mr James," says Gladys, wiping her hands on her apron. "Dr August's out looking for 'er, Miss Amaryllis. When Mrs August goes to tell 'er to get ready for 'er party, she's nowhere to be found. Now where'd the lass go on this day of all days? She were that excited. Mr Kirby ain't seen 'er neither. Mrs August's in the lounge. She's in a right state, Sir."

James enters the lounge where Columbine stands in front of the bay window, staring down the garden.

"Columbine," he says softly.

She turns. Tears have streaked the powder on her face. He doesn't want to hug her. But he feels he must. He knows Charles won't. They are not exactly a loving couple. And he knows why. Columbine buries her face in him. Sobs copiously. He prays she's not putting snot on his leather jacket.

16

"I gather Amaryllis is missing," he says when she turns from him and goes back to the window. Stares down the garden. Does she honestly believe Amaryllis will suddenly appear? "Have the police been up to the house yet?" he asks.

"I don't…don't…No." She sobs. "They said something about most missing children are found within a few hours. Or they just turn up." She sniffs. "Charles couldn't wait. He's rounded up some of the neighbours and some of his patients. They're looking in sheds, outhouses and garages. Mr Kirby's checked the greenhouse, the coke shed, the tree house."

She weeps loudly. "But why would she go in *any* of them? Why would she go off anywhere?" She wipes her nose with a damp handkerchief. "Today of all days, her birthday. She was so looking forward to her party…" More sobbing, "…and I didn't send her to school."

Columbine wonders that if she had, would the day turn out differently? The way it is supposed to.

The lounge door suddenly opens. "New car, James?" Charles enters, walks across to him and they hug. Really hug. Then he places a hand on Columbine's shoulder. Squeezes it. Hard. She does not turn round.

"I sold the Healey. I did tell you. Thought it's time I got a bigger car. More room."

"It's an MG, isn't it?"

"Yes. An MG-YB saloon. This is its first long run. Drives like a dream. And what do you think to the colour? It's called Sunbronze Metallic Brown."

"Smart. A good choice."

Is that envy James hears in his voice?

Columbine turns. Faces them.

"For God's sake, how can you? How can you talk about cars when our daughter's missing?" she wails.

"Just trying to lighten the mood, my dear," Charles says. Shrugs his shoulders at James.

"Sorry, I'm a bit late, old chap. You know how these things are." He smiles at Charles. "But all sorted now. And here I am? How can I help?"

"I just came back to use the toilet," Charles is explaining. "Then I'm going back out. I've organised a search party for Oaktree Drive. I'm the commanding officer."

As to be expected, thinks James.

"So, it's all under control. Come and join us. The more, the merrier."

Columbine follows them out to the front door. Stands in the porch and watches them go down the steps to the driveway and out. Before she goes back inside, she spends a moment or two looking at James's new car. The sun catches the metallic crystals, so it shines like spun gold. Amaryllis will love this, she thinks. And quietly begins to weep.

4 o'clock approaches. No sign. So, it's not one of Amaryllis's jokes where she'll jump out at the last minute and shout 'Surprise!' Columbine cancels the party. The magician. Gladys and her carry everything back into the house. Columbine fusses with the party food. Sets it all out like a buffet. Surely someone will eat the sandwiches, the fairy cakes. The jellies she puts in the fridge. And the birthday cake with its nine candles stays on a plate in the cupboard. For when Amaryllis comes home.

Darkness falls. It's the longest day of the year, so it's well past 10 o'clock when Charles and James return. Without Amaryllis. She is not in anyone's shed, outhouse or garage. She is nowhere.

Columbine does not go up to her bedroom when Charles and James retire. She can't sleep. Doesn't want to. So, she curls up on the settee. Listens to the ticking of the grandfather clock in the hall. The lounge door is ajar.

In the early hours of the morning, before the sun is up, she hears first a click, then the creaking of the stairs. A shaft of brightness creeps under the lounge door and cuts a narrow ribbon of light across the carpet. Columbine, her eyes puffy from crying, swings her legs to the floor and stretching, gets up. The hall light is on. And there is James, fully dressed, his overnight bag by his feet.

"Are you going already?" she asks.

"I've had a call from the hospital…"

Strange, thinks Columbine. She doesn't hear the phone ring.

"There's an emergency. I'm needed in theatre."

Now Charles, his feet slippered, a dressing gown tied about his waist, descends the red-carpeted staircase. He yawns. Rubs his eyes. As if he's just woken up.

"I've got to go, Charles," James says. "What about the police? Didn't you say after twenty-four hours they'll take Amaryllis's disappearance seriously."

"Yes," Charles replies. "They'll be here later this morning."

James hugs him. Tight.

"I can't be here. Will you square it with them? And let me know if, no, when they find her."

"Yes, of course. They'll be here later this morning." And then, "Don't worry, I'll make sure Columbine doesn't mention your presence yesterday. She knows better than to disobey me. And Gladys and her father won't. Not if I tell them not to. They're loyal to the bone. You'll be no use to the police anyway." He hugs James. "Best you just get on your way. Then you can do what you need to do," he adds.

His words are so deliberate, thinks Columbine. Is it a staged speech just for her? But remembering that the police will shortly invade her home, dismisses the notion.

And then Charles is hugging James again. Whispers in his ear. "Safe journey, old chap. Good luck. And keep in touch."

They part. Look into each other's eyes. Mouth 'I love you'.

James tosses the overnight bag onto the back seat. Opens the driver's door and gets in. Dons a hat and enormous sunglasses. He just knows the sun will rise, bright and beautiful. Mocking what will be a harrowing day. For Charles. For all of them. Neatly manoeuvring a three-point turn, he revs the engine and, raising his arm in a farewell gesture, zooms out of the driveway.

Later that same morning police finally arrive. Gladys shows them into the kitchen.

"Good morning, Dr and Mrs August. I am Detective Chief Inspector Moulton. And this is Detective Inspector Foster," he says as they hold up their ID wallets.

Columbine looks. DCI Moulton is an ordinary looking chap in an ordinary looking grey suit. But his shoes are well polished. The DI wears a navy linen suit. Has a notepad and pen.

"Terrible business this," says DCI Moulton. "A missing child case always is. I'm not normally involved with cases in the North. I'm at Scotland Yard but was up at York Headquarters on other business when the call came in. Missing persons, especially children, is my raison d'etre. The circumstances of this disappearance are most unusual. I'm intrigued, so I've cleared it in London that I can lead the case."

He looks at Columbine's ashen, tear-stained face.

"And I want to assure you, Mrs August, that in all my years of policing, I have found most missing persons. Now DI Foster will take and record your statements. Whilst Sergeant Stockhill…" A stocky man in blue uniform steps forward. "And Sergeant Gibson…" A young fresh-faced police officer with enormous, booted feet, stands next to him. "Will accompany some of the police constables and search the surrounding area."

The immediate area, the kitchen, which always seems so big, shrinks as police constables, helmeted and uniformed, crowd the space. Three are from the local constabulary and the rest from neighbouring constabularies. It's a missing child. They all want to help. And it means, between them, they can conduct a thorough search.

"We've already searched the local vicinity," says Charles. "Thoroughly. Gardens, sheds, outhouses and the like. Columbine telephoned all Amaryllis's friends."

Columbine nods.

"None of her friends have seen her. And we found nothing. Nothing."

Charles frowns. Rubs his eyes.

DCI Moulton knows that in most cases of missing family members, one, or both, of the parents are somehow involved. But his gut tells him it isn't Mrs August. He's not so sure about the husband.

"Now, Mrs August, I know this is all very distressing for you. But I have a warrant," he says, digging about in a jacket pocket and producing said signed document, "to search your home. And even though you say you have searched your garden and outbuildings, we will recheck. Just in case." He smiles at her. "It's normal procedure in these circumstances."

"And I wonder, Mrs August…" Columbine is wondering too. "It would be useful if we had a photograph of your daughter." He smiles at her again. Tries to engage the distressed woman before him. "Do you perhaps have a recent one of Amar…?"

Columbine nods her head. She does not speak, only sobs. She finds she has lost her voice as well as her daughter.

"Amaryllis," says Charles. "We do. This was taken last year during the summer holidays. She hasn't changed much."

The Inspector takes the photo. It is not in black and white as he expects but in colour. He knows it is expensive to process a film in colour. The family has money. But he feels the despair in this room. What matters if you have all the money in the world but do not have your child? He studies the photo. The face of a beautiful, brown-eyed, blonde child beams out at him. A face it would be hard to forget.

"A very bonny lass," he says. "Now two constables…"

Nine, thinks Columbine, counting. Nine altogether. One for each year of her daughter's life. Panic bubbles. She tries to focus on the detective's voice…

"…will cover the house and grounds and both sides of Oaktree Drive. Whilst seven…"

Her mind jumps back to Amaryllis's seventh birthday. They went to Peasholm Park in Scarborough. Rode on the miniature steam train. Got drenched on the water splash. Ate candyfloss and cream waffles. A lovely day. A moment in time when Columbine is happy. But time plays tricks. She's back in the kitchen. Her eyes alight on the leather straps of truncheons. She knows each constable has one. Kept in a special deep pocket in his trousers. Truncheon in the right, handcuffs in the left. She wonders if they will have cause to use them. Wonders what sort of biscuits the Inspector likes.

"…will search farther afield," the Inspector is saying. "All will search until the light fades."

His words pierce Columbine's daydreaming. What is she doing? Her beautiful daughter disappears and here she is, filling her mind with inane trivia. What use are truncheons, handcuffs or biscuits? But her mind does not want to dwell on this terrible happening.

"I would like you and Mrs August to remain here, in the house," she hears him explain. "In case your daughter should return." He does not say that, in view of the circumstances, he thinks this is highly unlikely. Instead he says, "Now, after Detective Inspector Foster has taken your statements, why don't we sit down with a cup of tea, and you can tell me all about Amaryllis. Everything and anything. You never know, something you mention might help us to find her."

Sergeant Gibson, Sergeant Stockhill and the seven PC's leave the kitchen. Although helmeted (they are not allowed to remove these whatever) and fully uniformed, the Chief Constables at both stations have decreed that, because of the heat, they can wear open-necked, short-sleeved shirts. The kitchen suddenly seems small. Shrinking, thinks Columbine. Like my life.

But the day does not shrink. It stretches and stretches. Even after the warm June sun sets.

Gladys makes a big pot of tea. She puts cups and saucers, spoons, a milk jug and sugar bowl on the table, round which Charles, Columbine and Inspector

Moulton sit. Fetches a plate of pink and yellow iced biscuits. Columbine stares at them. They are Amaryllis's favourite. She takes a deep breath. Holds in a howl. She's been howling a lot since…Deep, guttural howls, like there's a wolf in the house. Charles is talking about…She doesn't know. She can't concentrate. Dislikes his constant aggressive glances.

Suddenly, she finds her voice. Animated by memories of Amaryllis, she talks and talks. A tirade of words. Rants and raves. It borders on hysteria. Charles slaps her.

Says, "I'm sorry." But does not sound very apologetic.

"Difficult times, Dr August," the Inspector says, eating a biscuit.

He detects little from the wife's ramblings. No clues that will be of any use.

Sergeant Gibson, Sergeant Stockhill and the seven PCs return in the gloaming, footsore and weary. It is 11 o'clock. The night is still warm. They have not found Amaryllis. But they have found something else.

Chapter 3

Columbine August stares at the rose gold watch that the sergeant places on the kitchen table. Gladys has stayed on. She makes more tea for everyone. But Columbine can't swallow. She can't drink. She can't eat. She can't see through the tears clouding her sight. But what she does see through the blur is the glint of the gold. The joy in Amaryllis's face as she slips the watch over her wrist. How long ago? Only hours. Hours that feel like years. Nine years. She dabs her eyes with an already wet handkerchief.

"Do you recognise this, Dr August?" asks Inspector Moulton.

Charles shakes his head. "I've never seen it before," he says.

The Inspector wonders at this. But does not pursue it.

"Mrs August?"

Columbine nods. Cries copiously. Loudly. Charles August squeezes her shoulder. Digs his fingers in. Hard. It stops the tears.

"Where did you find it?" he asks in the sudden quiet.

"It was found in the grass. Through that plantation at the end of the lane…"

Columbine knows instinctively which lane he refers to. Which plantation. Oaktree Drive is lined with large Victorian and Edwardian homes. Homes of solicitors, teachers and doctors. No trade folk. How demeaning that would be they say. There is an entrance to the cottage hospital up the road from Oakwood and on the opposite side of the Drive is the grammar school. The school where the clever children go. The school that she knows her bright and beautiful daughter will attend when she passes her eleven plus. But then she wonders on this. On anything that speaks of a future.

She has no tears left. Holding herself erect, she concentrates on breathing. On mapping Oaktree Drive all the way up to where the tarmacked road ends and a rutted farm track leads out into the countryside There is a small plantation before the lane leads to fields and an old disused farm. The abandoned farmhouse and barns, in dilapidated neglect, cling to a past they will not see again. The farmyard is overrun with weeds. It will be sold eventually to create a modern housing estate. But why would Amaryllis…? Surely she can't be?

"We searched the plantation and all the farm buildings," Sergeant Gibson is saying. "But we found nothing. Not a clue or a sign that your daughter or anyone else, was or is, there. Looks like it's been empty for years. All we find is the watch on the way back."

"What happens now?" asks Charles.

"Well, I believe that now, in view of what you have told us about her. The lead up to her disappearance. The fact that we have not found a body, there are two possibilities."

Columbine holds her breath. Tenses.

"She has either been kidnapped or abducted."

Columbine wails. She jumps up from her chair and paces round the kitchen. Pulls at her hair. Slaps her head.

"What's the difference?" She is agitated now. "Whichever it is, we've lost her."

"Not necessarily, Mrs August." Inspector Moulton coughs. "If it is a kidnapping, you will receive a ransom note, asking for money for her safe return."

"Which we would pay, wouldn't we, Charles?" Columbine, hopeful, turns to her husband.

"Of course." Charles inclines his head. "However much." A furrow flits across his brow. "Within reason," he adds.

Chief Detective Inspector Moulton acknowledges this. He has seen the size of the house and the garden. The cars in the driveway. The antiques. He knows they can cough up the cash. But thinks perhaps Dr August's assent is not as genuine as his wife's.

"And if we don't receive a ransom note…?"

"Then…"

Inspector Moulton does not get to finish his sentence as Columbine bursts into yet more wailing and sobbing. Her world, her wonderful world with the big house, the handsome husband and the beautiful daughter is imploding.

"She has been abducted."

There it is said. Charles rubs his chin thoughtfully.

"A kidnapping would be the best outcome," says Inspector Moulton. "At least then we have a chance to return her safely home."

But, in the ensuing days, a ransom note does not come. And despite posters nailed to telegraph poles, pinned on noticeboards round the villages, no-one comes forward. Despite her picture appearing in the local Gazette & Herald, not a sniff of a sighting. Despite her cherubic face beaming out of the national newspapers; months of media coverage, not a lead or clue comes. Despite a large reward that Dr and Mrs August offer for any information, the only calls come from people presenting false facts for hopeful monetary gain.

Despite Scotland Yard's involvement, nobody comes forward with any real evidence as to what could have happened to her. Apart from the rose gold watch, not a trace of her is found. A body is never discovered. Amaryllis August has vanished off the face of the earth. After seven years she is presumed dead. Abducted by person or persons unknown.

It is the one unsolved missing persons case (The beautiful blonde, brown-eyed child who never saw her ninth birthday) that haunts Detective Chief Inspector Moulton throughout his career, until his untimely death at the age of sixty-two.

Chapter 4

Charles August stares at his wife. Tries to remember the smiling, vibrant, raven-haired beauty who enters his life in those last two years of the war. His mind wanders back. Back to those war-ravaged years. She's a nurse. A nurse in white scrubs which are blood-stained within minutes as wounded soldiers are brought back from the front line. Brought back in ambulances or whatever way the constant shelling and bombing allows. They're in a hastily erected field hospital in Italy. Canvas tents. Crude lighting. Portable drugs and surgical apparatus. So they can pack up and move when the order comes in.

The casualties are triaged. Those with lesser injuries are hastily patched up and returned to the front. Burns and mustard gas victims are given emergency aid and transported to specialist hospitals farther back behind the lines. Those requiring surgery are operated on. A conveyor belt of unrecognisable charred and bloody bodies. Once stable, some will be shipped back to hospitals in England. The war will be over for them.

He is a doctor. Due to the war, fast-tracked to be a surgeon. Takes things out which should not be there. Puts things back where they should be. The shifts are long. Twelve hours. But often run longer. Twelve hours faced with the most horrific injuries he has ever seen. And never wants to see again. Twelve hours listening to strong men reduced to shrieking in unbearable pain. Young lads crying like babies. Calling out for their mums. Their sweethearts.

Columbine joins the team. Brings renewed vigour. And deft fingers. Fingers that sew folds of skin together over gaping holes. Sews up post-operatively. The neatest stitches. The least infection. She stays calm in the face of hell. Her fingers never falter.

Columbine is funny and chatty, unlike the other nurse in the team. He forgets her name. She has horsey teeth. Is unremarkable to look at. But well-schooled with administering anaesthesia. Not too much. Not too little. Enough to create a pocket of temporary peace. A space for him to operate in. Under the swinging lantern light. Columbine always close by. Waiting.

And then there is James. A newly qualified doctor. If he had only three words to describe him, they would be…Raw. Competent. Beautiful. James tells him, in their last few months together, that he will go back to Sheffield. Specialise in orthopaedics. Oh James, he thinks. With his big brown eyes. Big hair. Big smile. And big heart.

What a team they are! Between them, they try to patch up the ghastliness. The horrific burns. The shrapnel-torn flesh. The broken, dismembered bodies. Try their best to save someone's father, brother, uncle. Son. So many lives lost. So many lives changed. He's seen young lads, terrified, trying to escape. Go back to their mums. Shot for desertion. This war will change people forever. But not me, he thinks. It only confirms what I've always known. There are some people who don't deserve to live.

He is fond of Columbine. He respects her. She's a hard worker. Never complains. But he does not love her. He loves James. Bodily and spiritually. Always will. But it is not their time. He knows that, in the eyes of the law, homosexuality, under the 'Offences Against the Person Act 1861' is the abominable crime of buggery. Punishable with life imprisonment. Something neither of them can contemplate.

Charles has always been a pragmatist and a planner. And so he lays in his makeshift bed whilst the war rages around them and makes plans. Plans for a future that James will always be in. But until their predilections are acceptable and they can truly be together, he will marry a woman. To appear respectable. Ordinary. A woman who can bear him a son. Once the war is won by the allies, a certainty he is now sure of, and they return to England, he will ask Columbine to marry him.

****

At last, they are in London after weeks of completing paperwork in a demobilization centre. After weeks of travelling through chaos on overcrowded trains. Everyone trying to get to the ports. Secure a passage to England. To London. But this is not the London they knew. Bomb damaged. Craters. Houses with perhaps a bit of a wall standing here, cupboards hanging there. The lives of its occupants exposed for all to see. Or homes completely flattened. Streets and streets obliterated.

He takes Columbine to dinner at The Ritz. Presents a ring. Now, as the past invades, he cannot recall where he purchases it. Hatton Garden he thinks.

"Will you do the honour of becoming my wife?" he asks, taking one of her fine-fingered hands.

The left he assumes. Places the ring on the fourth finger.

'Vena Amoris', he says. "The vein of love. Did you know the Ancient Romans believed this finger has a vein which leads to the heart?"

He leans over and places her ringed hand on his heart. Her eyes are wide. Full of love. "So..." He waits. Holds his breath. Does he think she will? Yes. He knows she will say yes because...

Columbine's home is one of the flattened ones. Her street is no longer there. Her parents are no longer there. Bombed in the Blitz. She has nothing and no-one. And, sure enough, "Yes, Charles." She smiles. "I will marry you."

"You've made me a very happy man," he says.

She knows she hasn't. She knows she can't. But she loves him. Thinks he will treat her kindly. Give her a good life.

"But where will we live?" she asks. "What will we do? I am leaving nursing. This I do know. These past few years have filled my head with images I want to forget. I never want to sew human skin again." She laughs. "But I find I am good at sewing. I know I want to sew seams. Make clothes. They are less bloody. Do not need anaesthetising. And do not shriek and scream."

"I can't remember if I told you," he says, taking no notice of her conversation, excepting that one word 'yes'. "I have a three storey, eight bedroomed, house in Yorkshire. A Mr Kirby and his daughter have looked after it while I've been away. It will be marvellous to go back up there. It's a beautiful place. Peace and quiet. It was bequeathed to me by my mother. She died whilst I was at medical school."

"And your father?"

"I never met him. He joins the army when the First World War starts. Is killed in action at Ypres in 1915. My mother is pregnant when she hears. She never gets over it," he says. His piercing blue eyes stare at her. "I believe this is what finally kills her." Not entirely the truth he thinks. But she doesn't need to know what really happened.

****

"Stop staring at me like that, Charles! Please."

A jolt back to the present. Away from his meanderings. He hears her voice worming its way into the here and now.

"I know I have let myself go. That I eat too much. That I'm fat. That I should have tried harder to lose the pregnancy weight. And I know you don't love me. Not in that way anyway. I know you love James. But I married you. I gave you a child. I loved you, Charles." She pauses for breath. "I still love you." And she does.

"Don't!" Charles slams a hand down on the table. Columbine jumps. "I can't listen to you. I can't do this anymore."

Do what, wonders Columbine.

"I'm not sure what you mean," she says.

But somewhere at the back of her mind, she thinks she does.

"Live in this house with constant reminders of her." He does not say a name. He does not need to. "It's too full of memories."

Memories, Columbine echoes in her head. Happy memories. So many.

"What's the point of any of it?" Charles sounds distressed, yet it does not reflect in his demeanour. "And now I know I can't have a son." He looks at her with distaste. "I can't do that…that…with you again."

Columbine dies a little inside. She knows exactly what he means. She also knows that Charles is used to getting what he wants. And now, for the first time in his life, he hasn't got what he wants. A son. James. She doesn't tell him that she always wanted a little girl. And Charles, despite his disappointment, does not tell her that the moment he holds his daughter, looks at her exquisite little face, he thinks perhaps one day she will redeem this error. Slot nicely into his plan. That he will love her. In his own way.

"I'm leaving," he says.

Columbine's mouth gapes. Her eyes are round with shock. She feels like she is drowning.

"I've already sold the bottom one and a half acres of the garden. A property developer bought it. He has planning permission to build three bungalows. There'll be a side road for car access. I've put a deposit on one." He clears his throat. "For you."

Now, it is Columbine who is staring. Unable to comprehend the speed of it all.

"I've sold the practice to a colleague of mine."

Another shock. What *is* he doing?

"Once the house is sold," he continues. "The antiques. The silver. The furniture. Everything. There should be a tidy sum. Enough to see you well looked after for the rest of your life. I don't want to be unkind."

Unkind, thinks Columbine. Does he even know the meaning of the word? He's been unkind to her since the birth of Amaryllis. Cruel at times. She thinks the war and the horrors he witnesses; the fact that it is war that takes his father only enhance his inherent desire to cause pain. To control. Perhaps a throwback to the childhood he never speaks of. But she knows better than to argue. To plead. Charles makes plans. Carries them out to a T. This must be a plan he has considered for months. Perhaps years. So, what use is there in trying to make him change it.

"I suggest," he is saying, "you start to pack the things you want to take with you. But most of the furniture will be too big to fit in a bungalow," he adds. "Perhaps the odd bureau, footstool, lamp, wall mirror…"

Is this what he thinks of her? She thought they were good together. Despite.

"And you," she says, hearing the wobble in her voice, the weakness. "What will you do?"

"I've always wanted to travel," he replies. "Not Europe. No, I've had enough of Europe. Africa. Asia. Australia. Anywhere. A fresh start. New beginnings, eh? For both of us."

New beginnings, she thinks. Maybe that will be for the best. A new life. She wonders if Charles even considers that she will only be a stone's throw away from the three storey, eight-bedroomed house and wonderful life he tempted her with. The home and life she is happy in. Until…A tear wanders from the corner of her eye. Trickles down the side of her nose. Salts her lips. That she will be reminded every single day.

Chapter 5

Columbine sits at the kitchen table. In her new kitchen. In her new life. She gazes through the glass patio door at her small rose-bushed garden. There's a light dusting of snow on the patio. It will soon be Christmas. Her seventh since…She recalls that first one without her. The pain. And it's not getting any easier.

She would be fifteen now, going on sixteen she thinks. Tries to imagine what she would look like. But can't. Her fingers, no longer fine and deft, idly tap the lid on a bottle that sits in front of her. There are five bottles. Each full of sleeping tablets. They were prescribed for her after Amaryllis's disappearance. To numb the pain. To help her sleep. But, back then, she does not want to sleep. She wants to stay awake. Alert. To remember.

She doesn't take the tablets. Five bottles she counts. Enough to kill an elephant. And she is certainly one of those. And as she looks at the bottles lined up, a tall glass of gin and tonic next to them; she thinks, now it might be good to simply go to sleep. Sleep forever.

Someone stole her daughter. Her heart. Charles stole her home. Her life. This new life is not as she expects. She has lost most of her clients. Readymade clothes are now widely available and affordable. She hides from the world. She hides from herself. Hides in food. Eats and eats. Drinks too much alcohol. She is enormous. Columbine stops tapping the bottle. Instead, she unscrews the cap. Snow is softly falling now. Watching a robin hopping about on the shrubs, she tips out the tablets. They roll randomly across the table. Fumbling, she picks one up.

ISLA

Chapter 6

She is curled up like a foetus, cocooned in the sheets which are starched white and prickly. A blue blanket is on top of the bed. She can hear the click-clack of knitting needles. A dumpy little lady sits in a chair by a fire. The fire is damped down. Glowing embers cast a little light. Before she turned into this chrysalis, she notices that her bed is not alone. There are others, all with blue blankets atop. They must be occupied, she thinks, as snoring, both gentle and guttural, irks her ears. She wraps the sheets tighter round her. Wonders if she stays like this long enough, she will turn into a butterfly and flutter out of the window. Into the wide blue sky.

But no. After time which she has lost and cannot find, there is a slap on her bottom. The sheets are torn from her. A face, kindly enough, hovers over her.

"Up you get, Isla."

Isla. Is that her? Say it. What is your name? A man's voice. But whose? She winces.

"My name is…Isla," she says out loud,

"That's right dear," says the disembodied voice. "And no screaming and shouting like yesterday."

Screaming and shouting? Had she? She cannot recall. They put a needle in her arm. And then she is in this bed. And the darkness cloaks her.

"Dr Zircona will be coming to see you on his rounds," the lips in the face are saying. A doctor? No. NO. Isla struggles. Tries to curl back up into a ball.

"Come along now," the lips are saying, "let's not be having any fuss."

Isla sees a fine line of hairs above the top one. Fuss. No, she must not fuss. Bad things happen when you fuss. So she will do as she is bid. She is to go to the toilet. Wash her face and hands. Brush her teeth. A washbag is put on the bed. Isla does not recognise it. But it is pretty and packed with all she needs. She is still feeling very confused, so let's the body that belongs to the face show her where to go. The body is dressed in green. A metal brooch is clipped above a pocket. Isla reads 'Nurse Coverley'. So, she is in a hospital. But where? And why? And when will this fog that is her brain clear?

Isla sees that she wears a blue, lacey, nightdress with a ribbon that ties above her breasts. It has a matching gown. She cannot recall buying it. St. Michael, it says on the label. Who is St. Michael, she wonders? "She'll be a fine buxom woman." Who say this? The nurse's lips are not moving. Besides, Isla is not buxom. Her breasts are small. The nightdress is loose and floaty. She swings her legs to the edge of the bed. They are long and thin. Her arms are long and thin too.

"Well, look at you. You're like a stick insect." Nurse Coverley scoffs. "Take three of you to make one of me."

Stick insect, she thinks. A voice, faint in the mists of her mind…Look at your arms and legs, Isla. They're like twigs. Why are you doing this to yourself? You'll never be a real woman. No man wants to bed a stick insect…She shudders involuntarily. Sticks and stones may break my bones, but words will never break me. Her voice.

Is this something she says to herself? But why? Unbidden she rubs her left wrist. She can't remember. Just jumbled fragments of a time before. Before she wakes up in this bed. But the whole is lost. Perhaps, in time, she will find it. There are two fluffy slippers at the side of the bed. Isla puts her feet in and stands up.

"Your husband made a good choice," says Nurse Coverley, "to fetch you here. The Sanctum is one of the most renowned institutions in the country. We'll soon have you better and home."

Home. Where is home? Better? Is she ill then? And a husband? Has she? She can't remember. Her psyche is out there, floating in a sea of twisted strands. Ribbons of fractured memories. She can't make sense of anything.

"He must love you a lot to buy you all this pretty stuff," Nurse Coverley is chattering on. "Oh and your rings. They are beautiful."

Rings? She lifts her hands. Spreads out her fingers. There are no rings. Just a voice, a man's. Fragmented in the muddle of her mind…

"They're a perfect fit. I knew they would be. Your fingers are just like hers."

Nurse Coverley sees the girl's rising distress.

"The rings belonged to my mother," Isla suddenly cries out. Punches her head with her fists.

"Now, now, we'll have none of that. Your rings are locked up safely. Best that way. You can have them back when you go home. You'd like to go home, wouldn't you?" Nurse Coverley smiles. "They all want to go home," she says.

Isla stays silent. Believes that sometime in her past, the past she forgets, she is told to speak little. Keep her own counsel. So without a word, she follows the nurse into a small annexe. There is a toilet and two wash basins. Nurse Coverley hands her a towel and a rough cotton flannel. Hovers outside, whilst Isla performs her ablutions.

A metal trolley clanks into the big room with the beds and the fire. Isla now sees that there is a small square table beneath a window. She is told to sit there. Three other young women join her. One is clutching her head.

"Got a headache, Jennifer?" asks another lady in a green dress. Her brooch says Nurse Bradley. "I'll get you an aspirin."

Four bowls of porridge are put on the table. A bowl of sugar and a jug of milk. There's a metal rack stacked with slices of toast. A pat of butter on a plate. The porridge is sloppy. Isla watches it dribble off the spoons. The toast looks undercooked. Isla does not eat. She does, however, drink the cup of tea which is poured out of a big metal teapot. The other three tuck in. Especially the girl called Jennifer. Jennifer is a large girl with big breasts. She has piggy eyes, greedily looking out from folds of skin on her face. But she is smiley. Friendly.

"We want you to eat," Nurse Bradley is saying. She pushes a bowl toward Isla. "Your husband tells us you don't." A sigh. "No wonder you're so skinny."

Isla doesn't see herself as skinny. She is slim. She is fit. Her muscles are well defined. A memory…Swimming. A loch of cold, crystal-clear water. Walking. Along sandy beaches. Through conifer trees. Up craggy hills. Standing atop…? A hill. Windy Hill. A name. A name without a picture. The memory fades. Eludes her. Nurse Bradley cannot be described as slim. She is well padded. Sturdy. Has a lop-sided gait. She does not look very fit.

"If you don't eat, we've been told to give you an insulin injection. And then you'll have to eat, you'll go into a coma."

Isla understands what she is saying. But she does not want to eat the porridge. She does not want to get fat.

Now, Isla sees that there are three other women still in bed. They are not being forced to get up. To eat a bowl of porridge. They don't even have a cup of tea. She wonders.

The aspirin girl's piggy eyes see Isla looking.

"That's Cat, Peg and Margot. They're not allowed anything to eat or drink," she explains. "It's their treatment day."

Isla glances at the three women. One looks about her age. Another older, maybe a decade or so. And one just looks old. Isla's too fuggy headed right now to fit a face to a description.

"I'm Jennifer by the way. But you can call me Jen. Me, Caro and Bea had our treatment yesterday," the girl called Jennifer continues. She gestures to a young woman sitting next to her. "This is Beatrice. But we call her Bea. Leastways, I do." Bea or Beatrice, remains quiet. Stares into space. "And this is Caroline." Caroline manages a smile. "Otherwise, Caro." Jen laughs. "I always shorten names," she says. "So what's your name?"

Isla freezes. That voice again in her head... "Say it for me."

"My name is Isla," she says.

"Not much I can do with that, is there?" Jennifer laughs, her open mouth displaying crooked, worn-down teeth. "Can't do much about the thumping heads either. Always have 'em after the treatment, don't we girls?" Jennifer rattles on. "Always gives me a huge appetite too."

Isla watches her scoop the last spoonful of her porridge up Wipe her finger round the bowl, so there is not a smidge left. Lavishly butter the last piece of toast. She decides Jennifer has a huge appetite all the time. Isla's head is thumping too. Yet she has no appetite at all. Hopes she will not be having this treatment. She wants to ask more but reserves her curiosity.

Isla eats a spoonful of porridge. Feels guilty. Whilst Nurse Coverley and Nurse Bradley make the beds, she tips the rest into Jennifer's bowl. Jennifer smiles at her with crooked teeth. Shovels it down so they will not notice.

She's back in bed. Curtains are pulled around. They don't quite meet. She hears voices murmuring and then the gap in the curtains widens. A tall, white-haired man walks up to her bed and looms over her. Beside him is a slim, pretty woman in a blue dress. She has a white hat on her head. A fob watch on a pocket. There is a brooch pinned above the pocket. The brooch says Matron. The tall man has a white beard and a moustache. He is reading notes through round spectacles. Isla can't see his eyes. The lenses are thick.

"I am Dr Zircona," he says. "Your husband has given me a history of what has been happening…"

Isla stares at him, wide-eyed.

"So, Isla, I will be planning your course of treatment. How you co-operate and how you respond will determine the length of your stay with us."

Chapter 7

Isla walks up the red carpeted slope from Naomi Ward, past the hairdressers, past a porthole window. It's like she's in a ship. On holiday. But she knows she's not on holiday. She's had three treatments. That is why.

When she has the first one, she is terrified. They give her something early in the morning. It dries her mouth out. Makes her feel floppy. It's a muscle relaxant she is told. So she doesn't damage herself during the treatment. A male nurse, Nurse Mulligan, takes her to the treatment room. She likes Nurse Mulligan. He's Irish. She loves the lilt of his voice. He makes her laugh. Has a twinkle in his eyes. Yet Isla feels no threat from him. Only from what is about to happen.

Nurse Mulligan tells her she will not feel anything. She will be put to sleep. Isla likes the sound of this. In fact, she loves the swimmy, rushing feeling as she is told to count back from ten. She seldom gets below six before a warm velvet darkness engulfs her. When she awakes, she is in the recovery room. And there is a cup of tea waiting for her.

Later she learns that they put a pad against either side of her head. Then shoot an electric current through her brain. Her body convulses. It is called Electroconvulsive Therapy. ECT. She has no idea what it is supposed to do. Except shock the brain.

Now Isla eats in the dining room on Naomi. There are round tables with tablecloths. It is all very civilized. She meets other young people but is reluctant to engage. It does not come naturally to her. She tries to sit with Bea or Caro. Cannot stomach Jennifer's gluttony.

Isla only eats protein. And vegetables. She might eat an egg or a rasher of bacon at breakfast. But no toast. At lunch she likes the mince. Especially the chicken mince. The kitchen always sends her the burnt bits round the edges of the cookpots. They have been told that Isla loves this. But she never eats the potatoes, the apple crumble and custard or any of the puddings. Even though she is tempted. And always leaves more on her plate than is eaten. She must not get fat.

Up the sloping red carpet into a foyer, a reception area behind the main doors of the Sanctum. The core of the asylum from which all avenues lead. Yes, Isla now knows that this is a place for the mentally ill, the insane. In the foyer there is a café for visitors and patients. Isla loves the smell of the freshly brewed coffee. She drinks hers black and strong. The café sells crisps and packets of biscuits. Cans of Coca-Cola. Cigarettes.

Isla is encouraged to work in the café a few hours a week. She finds she enjoys it. Setrak will be there. He's from Beirut. But he is not an Arab. He is Armenian. His family are wealthy. They have sent him all the way to the Sanctum. Setrak limps. He also drinks more cans of Coca-Cola than Isla could drink in a year. They say it's all in his mind. They give him ECT. But still he limps. Setrak gives Isla a red rose every day. She thinks he pinches it from the gardens.

Isla is also smoking now. Everyone here seems to smoke. She buys Dunhill. She likes the elegance of them. The red and gold carton the cigarettes are in. As she puffs out the acrid smoke, she feels sophisticated. Tries to recall if she has done this before. Thinks she hasn't.

Naomi Ward is split. A left side where the women's dormitory and single rooms are. A right side where the men's dormitory and rooms are. At night both sides sometimes meet. Sit on the carpet in the corridor and play cards. Wait for the hot drinks trolley before bed and the night staff come on duty. Isla listens to the chatter but does not contribute much. She sketches with a pencil. She plays patience. All the while she is mentally doing a jigsaw of her life. So far only the outline is completed.

During the night, when she does not sleep, Isla helps the night nurses with the older incontinent patients. They are rolled from side to side. Their sodden nightdresses removed. Their backs washed. The rubber pads they sleep on wiped. A fresh nightdress put on. All this without awakening them. Because every night they are given sleeping tablets. As is Isla. But, unbidden, Isla squirrels hers away. She wants to stay awake, in case she finds more pieces of the jigsaw. The jigsaw she is making in her mind. When it is complete, she will know everything.

The Sanctum introduces exercise and art classes to accompany the traditional methods of drugs and ECT used in the treatment of mental health. So, every weekday morning Isla and Bea go to keep fit. Sometimes Peg and Cat come too. Never Jennifer. It's held in the physiotherapy department.

Robert Howard is the instructor. He is a long-haired, slightly wild looking chap with muscles and charm. He's flirtatious. Isla likes him. Really likes him. But she thinks he prefers Bea. Bea has such an attractive personality. Isla is just attractive. Beautiful in fact. But she doesn't see this. She only looks in the mirror when she must. Thinks she is fat and ugly.

When the exertions come to an end, they are told to grab a mat off a pile stacked in a corner. To lie on it. Robert tells them it's important to cool down after exercise. To stretch. Isla lays on her mat and listens to his droning voice. She stares up at the ceiling. Finds it strange that although she knows they are there, she cannot see the corners of the room.

Isla is encouraged to attend the art classes. The idea is that it's her subconscious which will speak, not her lips. That she will express her inner self through abstract painting. She doesn't know that each will be scrutinised by Dr Zircona. Isla's creations are dark. Mostly of brains. Spirals. Spiralling brains. Spiralling eyes. Macabre. Disturbing. The painting of them, although it whiles away the time, doesn't make her feel any better.

But exercise does. Robert sees this. He begins by playing tennis with her. He's sporty. Competitive. And much to Isla's surprise, she discovers that so is she. She wants to win. Hits the ball hard. Feels each anxious thought fly away with every shot. He usually wins. Just. But she does manage to beat him a couple of times.

There are squash courts. Isla has never played squash. So Robert teaches her. She's a natural, he tells her. It's the ultimate work-out. The ultimate endorphin releaser. Isla loves it. She slams the ball hard. Watches it bounce off the walls. Imagines the ball is smashing the ice that covers her frozen mind.

Robert flirts with her. Takes an interest in her. Talks to her. In her naivety, she believes he loves her. Thinks she loves him. Which is why, when one day he takes her to his 'den', a concealed nook at the back of the Physiotherapy Department and asks her to suck his penis, she does. It's what you do when you love someone. You do whatever they ask. No refusal. You never refuse. Bad things happen if you do.

It is only through the passage of time that Isla realizes she cannot be the only one who performs sexual favours for him. That he doesn't love her. He doesn't love any of them. He has a wife and two sons. She meets them one day. They are nice. It is also later, years later, that she knows, should Robert Howard have been exposed, genitals and all, he would have lost his job and possibly his family.

The way he behaved was reprehensible, she thinks. We were all vulnerable. Mentally unfit. I was so naïve. The forbidden fruit he bites. Yet using physical exercise, he helped me a lot. He was engaging. Kind. And despite his predilections, I will remember him fondly for the rest of my life.

And so the weeks and months pass by. Isla has several courses of ECT. Takes her medication. Her feet walk on air. Her eyes cannot see corners. Her brain does not sleep. Whirls away through the night. Yet still only the odd, random glimmer of her past presents. Nevertheless, she does as she's told. Makes no waves. Until…

Chapter 8

Mary. Mary Locke. She comes onto Naomi with her beautiful smile that hides the pain she is in. Mary has a husband. Children. But they put her here, in the Sanctum, to mend her. They think her mind is broken. But it's her arm. Her dangling, useless arm which she cannot lift. Her fickle fingers.

Isla is writing poetry now. Reams of verse full of angst. Depressing. But it's her way of pouring out the feelings inside which she cannot express in spoken words. She will keep them. Whether she ever reads them again she does not know. She does know that they are poorly written.

The words pour out. A tirade of verbal diarrhoea. But they are her words. A reflection of how she feels at the time. This is the poem she writes for Mary. After she dies. It is not her mind that is sick. It is her brain. Something nasty grows there. Gradually eats her. Swallows her being. Isla writes this in 1969. She has been incarcerated for two years.

To Mary Locke: She came and was but is no more. Her enigmatic smile no longer lights the world of those who knew her. And she tried. Standing before the mirror: "Raise the arm!" The will was there, but only the smile came through and the arm hung limply by her side.

She came and brought her youth; her zest for life, fading just a little then; gently ebbing back and forth as every day she tried a little harder the world grew more unpleasant.

She was just a girl, and yet a mother, a wife who wanted to take and give all that life and time had to offer. A girl with a smile who wanted to live. But time stood still and leaves only a memory for those who knew her. How great was her grief seeing a body, once supple, losing feeling, not responding, only the smile.

Crying only in the lonely hours of night when she must have known the truth, though others told her, "it's just in your mind."

And so she smiled.

Coming and going; living and knowing her secret.
Alone.
She came and was but shall be no more. But her smile will live on. And surely some small comfort that though she failed, she tried.

This is the straw that breaks the camel's back. Isla's grief encompasses her. She wants to scream and shout at the injustice of it all. But not here. She cannot do it here. So one night, when the nurses are busy, she goes to the toilet. Puts the toilet seat down. Stands on it. Opens the top window. Isla is still very tiny. She cannot believe that she can slip through such a small gap. But she does. And then she is running down the steps. Down through the garden, past the tennis courts. All the way to the very bottom of the grounds.

There she drops to her knees. And erupts. A volcanic spewing of her guts and grief. The despair of a life she believes warrants this. Eventually, the loquacious lava flow stops. She is purged. Spent. Isla clambers onto her feet and slowly walks back up the garden toward the place that is now her home. She is calm. Absolved. Isla knows the drop from the toilet window is too high for her to reverse her exit. She has no idea what she is going to do.

In the event, the decision is taken from her. As she approaches the doors that open onto the gardens, she sees them. Three figures in white. There is no time to run. What would be the use anyway? There are two burly blokes. Male nurses. And the night nurse of Naomi. She must have raised the alarm when she found Isla missing. They do not give her time to explain. Her arms are grabbed. She feels the prick of a needle. And then the beautiful satin black darkness envelops her.

She emerges from this lovely cocoon with a dry mouth. Her eyes are sticky. The lids stuck together. She has no idea how many hours she has lost.

"That was a very silly thing to do," she hears a voice saying. Thinks it is Nurse Stanley. "You're to get up, get dressed and go to Dr Zircona's Office. He wants to talk to you."

Talk *to*, Isla thinks. Not talk *with*.

"Actions have consequences, Isla."

She wonders what they will be.

"Now then, Isla."

Dr Zircona peers at her over the top of his spectacles. His grey-white hair sticks up. Messy. Not combed. Her case file lies before him. She can just see her name before he opens it. Flicks through.

"Can you tell me how you are feeling now?"

She can't.

"Can you tell me then." He does not look at her. Keeps reading her notes. "How you were feeling when you tried to escape…"

Escape? Is this what they think she was doing? She has been here two years. With no thoughts of escaping. She is waiting for someone to come and rescue her. Someone on a white horse. She will sit behind him. Wrap her arms about his waist. Ride off into the sunset. Yet in all this time no-one visits her. No-one rescues her. Not the elusive 'husband'. Not a mother or father. An uncle or aunt. Nobody.

"I…I wasn't trying to escape," splutters Isla. "I just wanted to…"

She tries to explain about Mary Locke. Dr Zircona does not look up. Is he even listening?

Before she even finishes, he is saying, "You're obviously very depressed, young lady. And we can't have that, can we? I am going to increase your medication. Try something else. It's relatively new and its results promising. If there is no improvement, then we'll try more ECT."

With that he dismisses her. Isla goes back to the ward. Climbs into her bed. Pulls the covers over her head.

The new medicine is called Largactil. It's a liquid. She swallows a thimble full. Likes the syrupy taste. Likes the way she feels afterwards. Light-headed. Woozy. Sleepy. Calm. It's very addictive.

Three days later Isla goes shopping in the city centre. She goes with Janet, the Occupational Therapist. They catch an orange and brown bus. She can't remember riding on a bus. And the many streets bearing strange names and packed with shops confound her.

"Look," says Isla, pointing at some bell-bottomed trousers. They're mustard coloured with a wide waist band. "Do you like those?" she asks.

Janet nods. So, Isla takes them to the fitting room and tries them on. They are in St. Michael's. It is full of such pretty clothes. And oh, the lingerie. Isla is besotted with everything. The trousers fit perfectly. She buys these and a few tops. Some new underwear. And then they go for coffee and cake in Bettys. Isla thinks it's the best place in the world. She wonders, as they ride the bus back to the Sanctum, why her elusive 'husband' still pays money into an account for her but never comes to see her. Wonders what will happen when the money stops.

The Sanctum sits on the top of a hill outside the city centre. Dr Zircona, in one of their fortnightly sessions, tells her that once it was surrounded by fields. "The god-fearing folk do not want to share their space with, I quote, 'the criminally insane'. But as the city grows, the asylum and its undesirable inmates are swallowed by the urban sprawl into the stomach of the community. A place where the mentally ill will be seen and treated with a new concept. Compassion."

Compassion, thinks Isla. Does not believe that shooting electric currents through a brain is the slightest bit compassionate. But does not speak it.

Instead she asks, "How long has it been here?"

"Oh, since the late seventeen hundreds," he replies, pleased that she shows interest. "It was commissioned by Quakers." He clears his throat. "So called, did you know because they were said to 'tremble in the way of the Lord.' It's been run by Quakers ever since."

"No, I didn't know," she says. "I thought Quakers were porridge oats." And embarrassed by her ignorance, she gets up and leaves his office.

****

"Want to play tennis later, Isla?" Robert Howard asks her as he comes onto Naomi for a quick check on the patients who need physiotherapy. "Say after lunch. I'm free all afternoon. Got to win my position back." He grins at her. "After you beat me twice last week."

"Sure," Isla replies. On another trip to town, she buys a pretty tennis dress, frilly knickers, lacy topped socks and white tennis shoes in a large department store called Browns. It's on a street called Davygate. As she fingers the lacy-topped socks, it is like 'deja vu'. She feels quite strange for a moment. Something niggles, then is gone. Another piece of the jigsaw? She also purchases a new tightly sprung racket. All to impress Robert. Yet, she cannot think why. Nevertheless, that afternoon, she plays the best tennis ever.

Time passes. It's now June. Beautiful blooming June. And it is. The gardens are splendid. The smell of the lavender and roses pungent.

She still plays tennis with Robert. Goes to keep fit. But Bea is leaving soon, her obsessional behaviour apparently cured. Isla will miss her bubbliness. Setrak, too, leaves. He goes back to Beirut. He is still limping. Margot is moved off Naomi. So, now only two of her partners in crime, remain. Cat and Jen.

Isla wonders, why she thinks of them as partners in crime. Have they committed any? Well Bea and she do once take their shampoo to the swimming pool. It's an outside pool. Square. Small. No-one seems to use it. They wash their hair. Laugh…Yes, Isla laughs. And once she starts, she can't stop. They laugh and shriek. Splash and frolic in the suds and froth.

Isla does also put joke soap on the basins in the dormitory. It looks like ordinary soap. But when you wash your hands or anything else, your skin turns black. She finds it in a Joke shop in town. Isla has no idea what a Joke shop is. Intrigued, she enters. Buys the soap and a cushion that farts. The cushion, she thinks it is called a whoopee cushion, Isla puts under Dr Zircona's seat pad when he gets up to fetch a file out of the filing cabinet. She's in his consulting room. Her fortnightly session. Are these crimes? She doesn't think so.

"Now how are we feeling today, Isla?" He sits back in his chair. The most enormous fart explodes into the room.

"Oh dear," Isla says, trying her best not to laugh. To look innocent.

"Er, yes. Well. That is…Hmm…Most unfortunate. I do apologise." Dr Zircona is discombobulated. He squirms in his chair. This causes more lesser farts.

Unbidden, spontaneous, Isla's laughter is unleashed.

Flabbergasted would be the word to describe the look on Dr Zircona's face. In all the time Isla has been in the Sanctum, he never sees her smile. Never hears her laugh. Is this a breakthrough?

Unfortunately, it is not. A month later, he receives a call to say Isla is missing. No-one can find her in the house or the gardens. No-one knows where she might have gone. What she might do.

Chapter 9

Isla is walking. Fast. Furiously. Along a busy main road which says it goes to Selby. There is an Abbey at Selby. Isla knows this because when she is in the library, she reads a book about Cathedrals, Abbeys and Churches of England and Wales. She reads that Selby Abbey was founded by a monk, Benedict Auxerre, in 1069. He has a vision sent from God. Is called to St. Germain, who tells him he is to start a new monastery at 'Selebiae'. Three swans will mark the site. So Benedict sails from France to England. Confuses 'Selebiae' with 'Salisbury'.

Here, a man called Edward gives him a beautiful wrought golden shrine. In this he puts the relic, a finger of St. Germain, which he is told to take with him. Passing through Kings Lyn, he walks until, resting at a bend in the river Ouse, three swans alight on the water. 'Selebiae', the site where he must build the monastery. Now, Selby Abbey. And three swans have been the Abbey Arms ever since.

Isla is entranced by this story. So decides she will walk there. She will go in the Abbey and search for peace. She wears her mustard trousers. The bell bottoms slap against her ankles. It's been raining, so they are wet. Dirty. Isla doesn't care. And the lorries, vans and cars don't seem to care either. No-one stops. No-one worries. But the nurses on Naomi worry. This does not look good for them. They have no idea where she is. Or what she is doing. The police are notified. A description is given. But it is not the police or the public that find her.

As Isla leaves the outskirts of the city, she begins to see the odd field. There are some black and white cows in the distance. Milking cows, thinks Isla. Cows are a gentle benign presence. They have beautiful eyes. How does she know this? Has she lived on a farm? She feels she has. But it's only a feeling. There are no images to accompany it.

Isla's feet eat up the road. Worries eat up her thinking. She worries about Caro. She too has been moved off Naomi. Isla doesn't know to where. No-one will tell her. New faces are appearing on the ward. New patients. But Isla does not want to start all over again. Make new friends. It was hard enough the first time. And Jennifer is too pre-occupied with food. And ironically, her health. They don't chat much. Not like Isla and Caro do.

"When I am eight," Caro once tells her. "An uncle…"

Uncle. The word shoots through the misty clouds of Isla's brain. And out the other side. She pales. Feels sure it means something. Another piece of her jigsaw. A peripheral piece. But nevertheless, significant. When the outer edge is finished, Isla will work to the centre. But it is taking such a long time. Sometimes, she thinks she will be a dotty old lady when it is complete. And she discovers the truth.

"Rapes me," Caro is saying. Isla listens. "I tell my mum. She doesn't believe me. Nobody believes me. They are angry with me. I am bedwetting. I am naughty. A nuisance. The rape continues. Until I leave home. Go to Art College. But I never speak of it again."

Caro paints. Chain smokes. Her laugh is deep and throaty. Her paintings are phenomenal. Flora and fauna. In intricate detail. She even paints on ties. The sort of ties men wear. One day, Isla will ask her to paint a bird on a tie for her husband. A Whooper Swan. Unbidden, the name pops into her mind. Isla has no idea what a Whooper Swan is. But perhaps, once, she does.

"So, how do you end up here?" asks Isla.

"Once I am away from home. Away from that situation, I am so angry. Angry at my family. Angry at myself. I go a little crazy." Caro laughs her deep throaty laugh. "Drink too much. Smoke too much. Same old same old. When I start painting, I pour all that angst into abstract pictures. At first it helps. And then it's just not enough. One day I am chopping onions. The knife slips. Cuts through a finger. Oh, the blood!"

Blood, thinks Isla. I saw a lot of blood once. There was blood and screaming. Was it my blood? Was I screaming? But the image flashes away as fast as it comes.

"I watch it drip, drip onto the chopping board," Caro says, "painting the onions red. And the shock of the pain afterwards. But it is a good sort of pain. Suddenly, I feel calmer. Absolved." Isla knows this feeling. "That time is an accident," Caro says. "The next time…"

"So, you start cutting yourself," Isla states, "not to punish yourself, but to turn one sort of pain into another."

Caro nods. "Yes, I suppose."

47

"And somebody notices?"

"My tutor. He contacts my parents. They send me here. They can't deal with it. Don't really want to know. I think deep down they knew I had been telling the truth all those years ago."

Caro's arms and legs are a patchwork of angry scars. Sometimes, her arms are bandaged. Isla has never seen her legs. Caro wears long, voluminous gypsy skirts. She tells Isla that when she is at the dining table, she squirrels a piece of crockery away. Conceals it under her skirt. The odd saucer, cup. Finds a quiet spot. No-one about. Smashes it. Cuts.

But now there is no Caro to chat with. Isla thinks she must have cut herself so badly she's in a hospital somewhere.

She walks faster. The pumping of her heart, the rush of blood to her head, invigorate her. She's been walking for over two hours. Has no idea how much longer it will take. I'm going to do this thinks Isla. I'm going to sit on a pew in Selby Abbey and pray.

Do I even know how to pray, she wonders? Or to who? It doesn't matter. I will pray for Bea, Cat, Caro, Peg, Margot, Jennifer, me. All of us. That we will each leave the Sanctum. Be whole. And...Yet she cannot imagine a life without walls, an unmapped life without routine. But I will, she thinks. One day.

She follows the A19. A road that says it goes to Selby. And it does, without deviation. Isla finds the Abbey. She has been walking for four and a half hours. Selby Abbey is magnificent. A beautiful behemoth. Its great doors are open. Tentatively, she walks through. It is glorious inside. Quiet. Meditative. Peaceful. Some candles are lit, their flames flickering.

Isla sits on a pew. She stares at the huge arches. The ornate carvings. That strange feeling of deja vu floods her being. Has she been here before? Or somewhere similar? She feels sure it is another piece of her past. The past she can't remember. Isla weeps. Why and for what, she doesn't know.

"Are you alright, my child?" A voice asks.

Isla looks up. Wipes the back of her wrist across her dripping face. Nods. Snivels.

"I am the Reverend Canon John de Vere," says the voice. It is a lovely voice. "But you can call me Vicar John. And you are?"

"Isla," she replies.

"Can I help you, Isla?" he asks. He thinks she is not well. She is so dishevelled. Dirty and unkempt. "Where are you from? I don't think I've seen you in the Abbey before."

"No." Isla replies. "You won't have. I'm not from here. I read about your Abbey. I want to come here. Sit on a pew and pray. So I walk. I walk all the way from the city."

Vicar John is thinking. The nearest city is York. Surely this child has not walked from there. Why, it's almost fifteen miles.

"You've walked a long way, Isla. Why did you not go to the Minster? You could pray there. God will listen wherever you are."

"No!" Isla snaps. "It has to be here. I read about Saint Benedict. I want to walk. However far. Walk until I find the Abbey. And now, I have." She wipes a hand across her face. "Walking helps," she says.

"Helps with what? Are you troubled, child?"

"I'm trying to do a jigsaw," Isla says. "In my head. My life is in bits and pieces. I can't remember where I was or what I did before. Sometimes I think I do. A thought. A feeling. An almost memory. But then they float away."

Vicar John does not interrupt. He sits next to her on the pew. Listens. Isla doesn't know why she can let her lips fly with him. Yet not with Dr Zircona. The words pour out. Like a tipped-up teapot she thinks. But there is something about Vicar John. An essence of pure goodness could it be?

"I come to pray for my friends," Isla says. "I can't remember my old friends. Before. But I feel their loss. And I come to pray for my new friends. Do you think if I pray to Saint Benedict, he will bless us? Make us whole?"

"Whole," echoes Vicar John. "What makes you think you and your friends are not whole?"

"We can't be. Because we are all incarcerated in the Sanctum. Do you know of it?" Isla asks. "It's an asylum for the mentally insane. Therefore, we cannot be whole, can we?"

Vicar John does know of the Sanctum. It is one of the most renowned institutions in the country. Insane? Surely not. He turns his head and looks at the pretty young woman beside him. Really looks. She is not mad. A great sense of sadness emanates from her. He believes she has been wronged. That the past she forgets is too terrible to remember. But he cannot leave her here.

"Why don't you come back to the Rectory with me? Freshen up. I can get the housekeeper to make you something to eat. Perhaps a glass of homemade lemonade."

Isla jolts. Her face is ashen.

"What is it?" asks Vicar John. He is concerned. She is as white as his collar. "Are you alright?"

"No. Yes. Something. A flash back. But it's gone now. Like they all do," she says.

He stands up. Offers her his hand. "Come then, my child. Come to my humble abode."

"No." Isla does not take his hand. Does not budge. "I want to stay here. I like it. I feel safe." Isla smiles at him. She has the most beautiful smile, he thinks. Angelic. "And you don't need to worry about me," she says. "I will go back. To the Sanctum. I promise." A tiny hiccup of a laugh. "After all, where else can an insane person go?"

"You are not insane, Isla. Far from it. But you are greatly troubled. Stay here then, my child and pray. Find your peace. I will go to the Rectory myself and fetch you back a sandwich and cold drink. In truth, you must be both thirsty and hungry."

"I am thirsty." Isla acknowledges. "But not hungry." She is. But this, she will not acknowledge.

Vicar John leaves her sitting in the calming quiet of the Abbey where she feels safe. But the afternoon is waning. She will be walking back in the gloaming. She will not be safe. Once back in the Rectory, he picks up the telephone. Speaks quietly into the receiver. As if she can hear. Feels he is betraying her.

"There you are, my dear." He hands her a tall glass.

Isla wraps her fingers round it. Revels in its coolness. Revels in the cold liquid as it cascades down her throat. And as she sits on this pew in Selby Abbey, a serenity surrounds her. She finds her peace.

And then they come for her.

"Is that necessary?" The Reverend Canon John de Vere asks as Isla is manhandled. Jabbed with a needle. Put in a straitjacket.

"Yes," replies one of them. There are three. Three burly nurses in white. The straitjacket is white. As is Isla's face.

Purity, thinks the vicar. Isla is as pure as virgin snow.

"You never know what they're going to do. Dangerous some of 'em are."

Not this girl, he thinks. And in the last glimpse he has of her, as they drag her out of the Abbey, he sees her eyes. They overflow with his betrayal.

Chapter 10

Isla wakes in a different bed. In a different room. She knows this because the ceiling is different. Her limbs are stiff. Sore. And then she remembers. She walked to Selby Abbey. A long way there. A short way back. Yet, where is she? What day is it? What time is it? A drugs trolley clatters into the space around her bed. She recognises the noise the wheels make.

"Isla?"

She recognises the voice too. It belongs to Nurse Coverley. So, she is back on Naomi. Nurse Coverley hands her a thimble of Largactil. Watches Isla swallow it. Watches too closely thinks Isla.

"You had us all worried, Isla," she says. "We found your stash of sleeping capsules. And then you go and disappear on us."

"I didn't disappear." Isla's voice is croaky. Dry. She feels the Largactil working its magic. "I just went for a walk."

Nurse Coverley snorts.

"Rather a long walk, eh? Well, you won't be doing that, young lady. Not for a while. You're on Hannah now."

Hannah. The locked ward. The hidden ward. Up the winding carpeted staircase. Out of sight, as are its inhabitants. The deranged. The demented. The wanderers. The forgotten. A place Isla is told some of its inmates are locked in a bare cell of a room. Their only companions a bed and a commode. A place no-one wants to be. Yet, to her horror, she now finds herself.

"There's been a staff reshuffle. Me and Bradley were moved up here too," she's saying. "So, no monkey business, young lady. Not on our watch!" But the words are kindly spoken. There's a twinkle in her eye.

Isla gets up to use the toilet. There is one opposite the dormitory her bed is in. There is no lock on the door. In fact, Isla discovers there are no locks on any of the toilet or bathroom doors. The only locked doors are the dispensary and those of the violent patients. The inmates who spend most of their time in a cell.

She later learns that often a nurse unlocking one of these doors gets a pan full of excrement thrown at her. The other locked door is, of course, the ward door. So, they can never escape. It leads into an enclosed office where the Staff Nurse sits at a desk behind a glass door. There is a black telephone on her desk and piles of paperwork. Isla notices all this as she crosses the corridor and opens the toilet door.

There is someone in it. Horrified, Isla stares at the old wrinkly-skinned woman that sits on the toilet. Her hair is a yellowy white. Wispy. Long. Unkempt. Some is piled on top of her head. Some hangs down. Curtains half her face.

"Oh. I'm so sorry," says Isla. Tries to close the door. But the woman stops her.

She's gesticulating wildly. Her fingers are long and thin. The nails overgrown. A buttock lifts off the seat. Aghast, Isla watches as she claws at her bottom from which a fat brown sausage is dangling down. The woman is distressed. Without thinking Isla grabs some toilet paper.

"Here, let me help," she says.

Grabs it. Pulls. There is a loud 'plop' as it drops into the pan. The woman grins at her. Her mouth is crinkly with one fanged tooth and small yellow teeth, which look like they've been filed down. She scrambles off the seat. Wipes her soiled hands on her dress. And, leaving brown matter on the toilet seat, walks down the corridor with a lop-sided gait. She trails her dirty fingers along the wall.

Isla sees Nurse Coverley, her arms full of sheets and pillowcases. She chases up the corridor after her.

"Can I clean the toilets?" she asks. "I can't use that one." She points back. "And I've just checked all the others. They're all pretty much the same…Disgusting."

"My, oh my!" exclaims Nurse Coverley. "I don't think I've ever had a patient make a request like that." She thinks on it. "Just let me have a word with Staff Nurse Bernadette."

She bustles back to the office. Isla watches the movement of their lips. Wishes she could lip read. It doesn't take long, the conversation. Does that mean it's a 'no'? Nurse Coverley, her arms still full of sheets and pillowcases bustles back.

"There are some cloths and Ajax in the sluice," she says. "And a bucket and mop if you need one."

Isla grabs them all. She scours the toilets and basins. Wipes the walls. Mops the floors. And then she decides that she will not feel safe to use the baths until she has scoured them too. She uses the whole container of Ajax. All this is done in her nightdress. A long and blue nightdress with little flowers on it. A cotton velour. Like a proper dress really. But it's a winter nightdress and she's all sweaty when she finishes.

Puts everything back in the sluice. Then fills a bath with hot water. The bath is not exactly sparkling. But it is much cleaner than it was. Isla strips off and climbs in. The bubbly bath water cossets her bony frame. But Isla doesn't see bones. She sees fat. She will not eat today.

Isla tries to relax. But every now and again the door is opened. A face peeps in. She supposes they are making sure she doesn't decide to drown herself. It seems that privacy is no longer something she can enjoy.

The weeks and months take their own time. Sometimes fast. Sometimes slow. Isla cleans. A lot. She hoovers the long carpet down the corridor. Mops the linoleum at the sides. She wipes the nasty plastic high-backed armchairs in the lounge where the old ladies, some incontinent, are put. She cannot sit in one unless she does.

The ward cleaners become Isla's friends. At least their conversation makes sense. Isla likes to listen to them chat. About normal stuff. About boyfriends, family. Trips to the cinema. The latest films. Fashion. What clothes they have bought. A world outside the Sanctum. A world Isla yearns for yet fears greatly.

There are two cleaners. They do alternative days. But it is Annie, Isla looks forward to being on shift. Annie reminds her of a little sparrow. Flitting here. Flitting there. Busying about like a tiny bird. And it is Annie who runs it past Sister Bernadette, the more lenient of the ward Sisters, whether Isla can be allowed to help in the kitchen.

"Would you like to, Isla?" Staff Nurse Bernadette asks her. She has a liking for the girl. Does not think she should be incarcerated here. Yet cannot think where the right place could be.

Isla nods. She finds cleaning and washing therapeutic. Is she trying to cleanse herself, she wonders? The kitchen has two huge porcelain sinks. One for washing the pots and crockery. One for rinsing. Then there is a large draining rack to slot them until they are dry.

So, Isla helps Annie wash up after lunch. There are a lot of plates and dishes as three separate courses are served. The waste, of which there is also a lot, goes into special bins. It will be used to feed pigs. It's called pig swill, Isla learns. She has a notion pigs are intelligent. But thinks they cannot be, to eat such a mishmash of meats, potatoes, vegetables, custard, pies, rice pudding, gravy and cold tea.

The cleaners and nurses are all fond of Isla too. She is really the only patient they can have a yarn with on Hannah. And although Isla speaks little of herself, she is a good listener. Always has an answer. And her help makes their jobs less stressful. Easier. It will be a shock when she leaves. When they must take it all upon themselves again. Nevertheless, they all wish she is not here locked up. A pretty, vibrant young girl whose life is being stolen.

And thus, a pattern develops. In the morning Isla cleans and helps in the kitchen. In the afternoon she lays on the sofa outside the dormitory. It's not covered in a soft plush fabric. It must be wipeable. So it's hard and uncomfortable. Nevertheless, Isla sleeps for exactly two hours. She wakes up when the afternoon tea arrives. And then she helps with that.

In the evening, after supper, when she has wiped all the high-backed chairs again, wiped and stacked the dining room chairs, she watches television. The picture is not brilliant but there is never anyone else in the lounge. All the old ladies are tucked in their beds. Dentures in the sluice. Sleeping medication and laxatives in their bellies. The dangerous locked in their rooms. Isla can choose which ever programme she wishes. Stay up until the small hours. I am part of the furniture she thinks.

But every evening, late, after the night nurses have arrived, a dumpy little lady in a long nightdress emerges from her room. No-one ever takes her back. She is not dangerous. Just walks the long carpet, which runs down the centre of the corridor. Up and down. Down and up. Chunters and laughs to herself. Sometimes, when Isla finds it hard to concentrate on the television, she walks with her. Isla calls her Juddy Buddy. It's just a name, but it suits her.

And then one afternoon, something alters the symmetry. Annie needs the afternoon off. A family emergency. There is no-one to cover for her. Annie asks Isla if she can do the afternoon teas. All on her own! Isla assumes Annie has run it past a Staff Nurse because there she is, filling up the urns to boil the water. Getting out the big teapots. The cups and saucers. Teaspoons. Sugar. Milk. All the things she has done so many times before, she doesn't have to think. As she waits for the cakes or whatever the main kitchen sends up, Isla fills one of the porcelain sinks with soapy water.

Years later, though vague of recollection, Isla will liken this afternoon to 'Who ate all the pies?' Because when the trays arrive, they are not filled with cakes. But scones. Warm, buttery scones with jam and cream. Isla stares at them. Tastes a memory. Unbidden, she lifts one off the tray and puts it to her lips. Bites into it. And something snaps. She can't stop herself. One after the other she devours their sticky sweetness. Until the trays are empty and Isla is replete. Stuffed.

Horrified, she now stares at her gluttony. She must assuage her greed. Her shame. Without thinking, she gets a glass. Fills it with warm water and salt. Downs it. Drinks another. And another. Then whilst she waits for the salty water to assault her stomach, she lifts the tap on the urn. Puts her arm under. Grits her teeth whilst the boiling hot water cascades onto her skin. Yet Isla does not move until the urn is empty.

The kitchen floor is flooded. Her arm is a deep shade of red. Scalded. Now she runs to the farthest toilet on the ward, pulls back her long hair, drops her head over the bowl and spews and spews. Only stops when her stomach and self-abhorrence are spent. And she thinks, this must be how Bea feels when she cuts.

Isla runs to her room. Yes, she has her own room now. Near the end bathrooms. It has a bed, a side table and a small wardrobe. Basic. Isla hides under the bed. Wonders what Annie will think. Wonders what Staff Nurse Bernadette will think. Wonders if the old ladies will notice there is no afternoon tea. Many years later when Isla recalls this afternoon, she wishes she can remember what happens after. But she can't. It's just a story to tell.

But then something wonderful happens. Caro suddenly appears on the ward. She too is now locked up on Hannah. A different pattern is created. Caro and Isla commandeer a bathroom. They bath the old ladies. Scrub-a dub-dub them until they are clean, towelled and talcumed. A conveyor belt of wrinkled bodies. Cleaning the bath with Ajax between each one. Re-filling the bath with fresh hot water. It is steamy, sweaty work. But far outweighed by the benefits the girls receive in kind.

They get to know the inhabitants of Hannah. Their quirks. Who doesn't like their hair washed. Who is terrified of being submerged in a bath. Their trigger points. And Isla and Caro gain a sense of belonging to a community. As mad and bizarre as it is.

"We're the naughty ones. The rebels," Isla says as she and Caro sit in the corridor smoking. "Locked up for our sins."

They both stay up late. Isla writes poetry. Caro paints. Her chair is always surrounded with paints and brushes. Turpentine and carrier bags of paintings. Intricate paintings of flowers: roses, harebells, columbine. An ashtray, always full. Two chairs. Two needy people. They smoke, drink black coffee and natter. It's easier to talk, really talk, if your fingers are busy and you don't have to see the pain in the other person's eyes.

The night nurses are used to them being there. Pay no heed. And then one evening Staff Nurse Susans, who alternates with Staff Nurse Bernadette (Isla loves them both) says, "There's a dance downstairs tonight. Would you both like to go? Get off the ward for a while."

"What sort of dance?" asks Isla. She's not sure if she can dance. And what would she wear?

"Oh, the Gay Gordons, The Highland Reel. Quick Step, Polka. The Waltz. Those sorts of dances. The ones they remember."

And suddenly Isla remembers. I can dance the Gay Gordons, Highland Reel, she thinks. I can dance them all. But how? Where did I?

Caro doesn't want to go. Isla is about to say she doesn't want to go either. But then she thinks maybe she would like to dance. Get off the ward. Have some fun. Or not. She decides that if she doesn't go, she will never know.

And this dance. The dance she almost doesn't go to, in hindsight, is the dance that maps her destiny. Her future.

Isla finds the holdall that comes with her. A commodious bag with the colours of the rainbow striped across. She rummages in its deep corners and pulls out an all-in-one trouser suit that has remained buried there. A catsuit she thinks it's called. There's also a pair of shabby white ballerina pumps.

But just as she lays them on her bed, she spots something else. Two things which must have also been secreted away in the holdall and now tumble out onto the floor. She reaches down and picks them up. Gasps.

What? There's a tiny white sock, the size of a toddler's foot, and a teddy bear. The teddy is well worn. One arm hangs by a thread, as if it has been lovingly carried everywhere. 'Mammy'. She hears the voice in her head. Tries to conjure an image to accompany it. But her memories are a jumble. Jostle to find a place to slot in. Make no sense. Whilst she is engulfed by an inexplicable sadness.

"Smile and the world smiles with you," These words she speaks out. "I will not let melancholy be my partner to the ball."

And so saying, Isla puts a smile on her face, smooths out the creases and puts the catsuit on. It's white too, smudged with tiny smears of green as if she's skidded in wet grass or algae. She doesn't know. Can't remember wearing it. Is it even hers? But it fits. The legs are wide and floaty. There are tiny translucent pearls embroidered on the bodice. They sparkle in the light.

"Stunning!" exclaims Caro as Isla floats down the corridor towards her. "And very on trend." She exhales a cloud of cigarette smoke that shrouds her with an acrid grey mist. There are probably forty butts in her ashtray.

"It's a bit difficult to go to the toilet," says Isla. "There's only one way in and one way out. I won't have to drink much." She twirls and the floaty legs fan out. "Are you sure you won't come? I could do with some moral support."

Caro laughs. "From me? I'm the least moral person I know." She lights another cigarette. "Want one?" She offers the packet to Isla.

Isla shakes her head. She's left her hair loose. It's long and shiny with a slight curl. "I don't want to go smelling like an ash tray do I." She smiles.

It's a beautiful smile, thinks Caro. She's a beautiful girl.

"Why, are you looking for your Prince Charming? I'm sure he won't notice. The whole place probably smells like an ashtray." Caro snorts. "The Sanctum is the tobacco industry's answer to monetary heaven."

Caro's words are not far from the truth. Because an ethereal mist of cigarette smoke cloaks the dance hall. And someone does see her float into the crowded space. Sees her hesitate on the fringe. Thinks her beautiful.

The floor is covered with shuffling slippered feet. The feet of old ladies who dance together but can neither recall who they, themselves, are, nor even if they know each other. Yet they can recall the music. Stomp to the rhythm. Sometimes sing a few words. Whilst their stockings roll down to their ankles.

Isla is suddenly uncomfortable. Feels that eyes are watching her. She looks up. Sees him. Thinks him beautiful. He stands out as he dances with a middle-aged woman whose face is smothered under layers of foundation, rouge and lipstick. She looks like a clown. Whereas he does not. Neither does he look middle-aged, nor old. Does not appear to be deranged. And in fact, is not.

He turns out to be a nurse training in psychiatry. A year or so older than her. Isla learns this later. But just now her heart is racing. Butterflies flutter in her stomach. Her lip-sticked lips are wet as her Prince Charming drifts toward her through the spiralling cigarette smoke.

The music for the Gay Gordons suddenly plays. A voice whispers in Isla's ear. "Would you care to dance?" It's a nice voice. He has a nice face. A beautiful face. It smiles at her through the smog.

And Isla dances with him. She gets the turns right. The feet right. The twirls right. However and wherever, Isla knows this dance. For the first time in a long time she feels wonderful. His name is Eric Skeldergate. He's supposed to be dancing with those patients who have no partners. Yet, somehow, he ends up dancing with Isla through the Foxtrot, the Highland Reel (risible as no-one else knows the footwork except her), the Gay Gordons again. And all the way through to the Last Waltz.

Then, even more wonderful, her Prince Charming, her knight in shining armour, escorts her back up to the ward. As they climb up to the top of the stairway, Isla spots a piano sitting at a junction between the locked side of Hannah and the unlocked side. She pulls out the seat. Sits. Lifts the lid. And plays. Eric squeezes beside her. Is captivated.

"Where did you learn to play like that?" he asks as classical, ballads, jazz and popular tunes punctuate the sombre soul of this place. A place that is easy to enter. Yet seems impossible to exit.

"I don't know," replies Isla as she runs her long fingers up and down the keys. "But I will do, one day." And she tells Eric Skeldergate about the jigsaw she is putting together in her head.

"That's an excellent idea. And I hope...No, I'm sure..." He smiles at her. "You will succeed."

She wants to stay with him. Sit here side by side on the piano stool. Smoke a cigarette. Talk all night. But already he is putting the key in the lock. Turns it. And hands her over to the night staff.

"Goodnight, Isla. I enjoyed tonight. You turned a mundane evening into something magical. You're a real dancing queen." Isla glows. And when the Swedish pop group, Abba, release Dancing Queen in 1976, it becomes one of her favourite songs.

"Why thank you, kind sir." Isla bows. Her long hair sweeps the floor. But when she throws back her head, Eric Skeldergate and the magic are gone. And she is standing on the thread worn carpet, the door locked behind her.

There is Juddy Buddy treading the boards, chuntering to herself. There is Caro with a cup of black coffee on the floor next to her feet, a cigarette dangling from her mouth. And as the smells of Hannah envelop her, Isla wonders if it has all been a dream. That she never dances the light fantastic at all.

She tiptoes toward Caro. The cigarette's tip is a bright glow, almost burnt down to the stub. She's had her meds thinks Isla. Strong meds that make her very sleepy. Carefully Isla removes the stub which is stuck to Caro's lips. Drops it into the ashtray. Then she walks back along the corridor with Juddy Buddy until she reaches her room. There, without putting the light on, without getting undressed, she kicks off the white ballerina pumps, flops on to the bed. And dreams of Eric Skeldergate.

Chapter 11

The next morning, Isla and Caro sit in their chairs smoking. Mugs of black coffee on the floor.

"So," says Caro, "what was the dance like. Were you the belle of the ball?"

Isla is about to reply when she espies Staff Nurse Bernadette and Staff Nurse Susans in the office deep in animated conversation. The door opens and they come on to the ward.

"Caroline, Isla," says Staff Nurse Bernadette. "We wanted to tell you in person that we are both leaving. Pastures new…"

She does not look well, decides Isla, her heart a well of regret. Of sorrow. Because Staff Nurse Bernadette believes in Isla. Trusts her. Comforts her when the tears flow. And Isla tries so hard. For her. And now she is leaving. They are both leaving. Her beautiful birds of Eden. Isla jumps up. Spontaneously hugs them.

"I won't forget," she whispers to Staff Nurse Bernadette. And she doesn't.

"You will get your memory back, Isla. And leave this place. You both will. You will find your peace. Believe in yourselves. As we are doing," she whispers back. And this is the last time Isla sees either of them.

She writes more poetry. Poems of loss, love and hope. For it is to be not her but Caro, who leaves first.

"I'm going back to Sheffield," she's telling Isla.

"Wh…Where?"

"Sheffield," repeats Caro.

Sheffield. A flash. A snapshot of a face. A face she loves. Or does she?

"Trams," Isla blurts. Bumping along. Busy streets. Not Sheffield. So where? "I know," she says. "When I get out, I'll come to Sheffield. Find you. And we'll ride on a tram."

Caro laughs. "Silly moo. We can't. They stopped running in 1960."

"Oh yes. Of course. I know that," Isla says to cover her ignorance. Because she does not know. She does not know anything. "Do you know what you want to do? Are you going to paint?" she blurts out instead.

"I'm going to breed dogs."

Caro draws on her cigarette. Exhales its pungent aroma of Turkish tobacco. Caro smokes Camel cigarettes. Once Isla tries one, but the smoke is too intense. Too strong. She knows Caro is intense. She believes she will be strong too.

"What sort of dogs? Big ones?" Isla asks.

"No, small ones. Chihuahuas."

Isla watches intense joy light up Caro's face. She will succeed she thinks. She will be OK. She can't let Caro know how much she will miss her. That for the rest of her life when she smells Turkish tobacco, she will remember her. That the empty chair she leaves will be synonymous with her. Long gypsy skirt trailing, the ashtray on the floor, the paints, turpentine and carrier bags. Her presence. For as long as Isla remains here, on Hannah.

Caro leaves in the October.

"When Autumn leaves drift by my window. Autumn leaves of red and gold," she croons.

Isla feels hollow. Empty. Hopes so much Caro will find happiness. She deserves it. Picking up a pen, she writes a poem. Calls it 'The Empty Chair':

A ticking clock, a long and silent corridor with windows opening to the night and here a chair; empty; bare. Was it only this afternoon we made our goodbye, it seems a thousand years and more and I just cannot envisage before; before your coming, when this same chair was in its place but no-one sitting there… And more lines in similar vein until its poignant end:

Oh yes, I miss your graceful spirit, the night just lingers on and yet I'm selfish because I should be glad that you have gone. Perhaps soon all these chairs will be empty. And we will be some other place; free and happy.

And now, it is Eric who becomes her salvation. One morning he comes up to the ward. Isla espies him in the office. Her heart begins to race. He is in animated conversation with the new Staff Nurse. Staff Nurse Magdalena. 'Maggie', Isla secretly names her. She watches their lips mouthing words she cannot hear. Wishes she could lip read. Thinks perhaps one day she might learn to. She watches his hands gesticulate. Those same hands that hold her at the dance. The smile that flits across his face.

And then the office door opens and Eric is there, standing in front of Isla's chair where she sits smoking a Dunhill. Drinking a cup of milky coffee, instead of her usual black. She finds she quite likes it.

"I've come to collect some of the patients that are normally locked in their rooms," he begins to say, "to take for a walk around the gardens. Get some fresh air. I could do with some help. Care to come? Stretch your legs. It's a beautiful Autumn day."

Isla is still in her nightdress. She doesn't get dressed any more. What's the point? She's a prisoner. Nowhere to go. But now she does have somewhere to go.

"Just let me go and get washed and dressed," she says. And freezes.

A voice in her head again. It's not hers. Something clicks. Those words. Spoken in her mother's voice. Isla is certain. But when? Where?

"Isla?" A note of concern.

The memory is gone. Isla stubs out the cigarette and weaving between the pacing slippered carpet wearers, runs to the nearest bathroom. A quick wash, then into her cell where she dons corduroy jeans on. They're a plummy colour. She wears a light blue jumper and casual shoes. She ties her long blonde hair up in a ponytail. Likes to feel the swish of it as she walks. Likes to hope Eric notices. He does.

"You look lovely," he says. "Can you walk beside Arnie, please. I don't think she'll be much trouble."

Arnie. A giant of a woman who is reputed to strangle Alsatians. Isla is not so sure of this. Wonders if it's children she strangles. Or her family. She knows Arnie is capable. As she tries to strangle Isla. One evening, as Isla is bent over, fiddling with the TV buttons, Arnie comes behind her. Jumps on her. Isla feels the woman's hands about her throat. They are strong. But Isla is strong too. She struggles. Almost gets her off when nurses come rushing in. Sedate her. Take her back to her room. Someone has forgotten to lock the door.

But now, out in the Autumn sunshine, Arnie presents no threat. True, she is over seven feet tall. Towers over Isla. Her hair is as white as driven snow. It drifts across her scalp leaving barren patches. Arnie does not speak. But lopes along with big strides.

The leaves on the trees and shrubs are turning. Wonderful vibrant reds and gold. They look like they are on fire. There is a smell in the air. Isla knows it. The smell of Autumn. She can smell all the seasons. Except summer. Summer is odourless. Colourless. Desiccated. Eric talks to Isla as they wander through the dry leaves which are just beginning to fall.

"I want to help people," he says. "Eventually, I want to train and work my way up to be a Psychiatric Staff Nurse. Either here or at Bootham Park."

"Where's that?" Isla kicks a pile of leaves.

"In Jorvik. Now known as York."

"So you live in York?"

"Yes. With my mother, Doris. Did you know that there is a street in York called Skeldergate? It's a Viking name. Street of shield makers."

Shield makers, thinks Isla. Knights in shining armour have shields. Will Eric Skeldergate shield *me*, she wonders. When I finally confront the truth.

"And the only street so named in Great Britain," he says.

Isla laughs. "No I didn't. And you live there?"

Now Eric laughs. "You'd think so, wouldn't you, having the same name. But no. I live in a house in Peasholme Green".

Peasholme, thinks Isla fleetingly. The name fills her with joy. But she can't think why.

"It's about a twenty-minute bus ride from here," she hears Eric saying.

"Do you live on your own?"

He shakes his head.

"With my mother, Doris and a mad puppy called Rafferty."

Puppy, thinks Isla. She shivers. No joy this time. Something terrible worms its way through her past. Then stops. Does not surface. She walks on. But there is white noise in her ears. She feels odd. Light-headed. Strange.

As the next few weeks pass, there are changes in Isla's life. In her mind. Her body. Buried feelings are unearthed. Feelings she thinks she's had in her past. Feelings she does not understand. But can she express through her poetry.

Eric writes poetry too. They are written in a small book with a red cover. He gives her this when they have coffee together. His are full of broken promises. Broken hearts. Isla does not know the girl he writes about. But she feels his pain.

Isla's poetry is about the people she meets. The people that affect her. Mary Locke, Bea, Caro, Staff Nurses Bernadette and Susans. Eric. Her life as it is. Why she even writes one called 'The Physiotherapist'. About Robert Howard, the Sanctum's favourite physiotherapist. Oozes praise and admiration for him. There is also one called 'The Shit Shoveller' which makes Isla smile. It is the only one remotely light-hearted. Describes what she does on Hannah. There are countless more. Badly written verses. Full of grief and loss.

Isla does not go to Keep Fit now. She still plays squash with Robert. And tennis when the weather permits. Still must be escorted from the ward, escorted back. Like the prisoner she is. And Robert teaches her to fence. The footwork is intricate. It's like a dance. But not a dance of closeness. Of love. It's a dance of avoidance. Of hate. Sparring and dodging. You need to concentrate. No mistakes. And this helps Isla both physically and mentally.

Robert even manages to take her to his house one afternoon. She forgets how. There she meets his wife and sons. Knocks back a glass of white whisky, believing it is wine. Gets very squiffy. Robert is good company. She likes him. But not in the same way she likes Eric.

Isla is now permitted to assist Eric on his ward. Odd jobs. Basic stuff. Anything. She doesn't care. It means something to look forward to. A temporary parole from the ward. Just to be with him enables her to cope. Because sometimes, she feels she will be left to rot in that place. 'Hannah'.

The name which epitomizes the stink of old ladies' incontinence. Of smelly slippers. Mince and custard. Of dentures all in a mix up. Forgotten people. That she will never be pardoned. Be forgotten too. So, Isla works hard. She is quick to learn. And quick to love.

One afternoon when Eric is not on duty, he comes up to Hannah and signs Isla out.

"I'm taking her into town," he tells Staff Nurse Magdalena. "With a couple of the men. To do some shopping. Be a few hours."

Staff Nurse Magdalena is also fond of Isla. Does not like to see her cooped up. She also sees the light in Isla's eyes whenever Eric comes on to the ward. Hopes it will not end up in tears for this young woman who desperately wants to find her way.

"Fetch her back before Dr Zircona's round. 5 o'clock," is all she says.

Isa skips down the stairs fleet of foot, light of heart. She loves to ride on the bus. They leave the large frontage of the Sanctum. Just her and Eric. Isla is so happy she does not notice there is no-one else with them.

And they do not bus into town. Instead, they catch a red double decker bus. Eric steers her up the stairs to the top. They sit right at the front.

"This is awesome," Isla says. "It's like being on top of the world. You can see so much more up here." She does not ask where he is taking her. She trusts him.

They have only been riding about ten minutes when Eric grabs her hand. Pulls her to her feet. "Come on," he says. "This is where we get off."

"Oh, it's where you live!" Isla exclaims, spotting a sign which reads Peasholme Green.

"Yes, I thought you'd like to meet my mum. I know she wants to meet you. Come along." Eric takes her hand in his. "We live at number eleven."

They walk through a small gate, up a short path to a green door. It's wooden with a brass knocker. But Eric opens the door. Beckons Isla in. A furry bundle, barking and waggy tailed, charges down the hall. Jumps all over them.

"Down, Rafferty," commands Eric. Rafferty takes no notice.

Isla drops to her knees. He jumps on her thighs. Licks her face. She wraps her arms around his neck. I've done this before she thinks. And in that one moment, the ominous cloud which hovers over her when she thinks 'puppy' is blown away.

"Mum?" Eric calls out.

"In the kitchen," a voice carries through. It's a welcoming voice, Isla thinks. She'll be nice, like her son.

Eric kicks off his shoes, so Isla does the same. Follows him into the kitchen where a small wiry haired woman is reading a newspaper. A mug of a steaming beverage lays next to her.

"Mum. This is Isla."

Isla moves tentatively toward her.

"Isla. This is my mum, Doris."

Doris smiles at Isla. It's Eric's smile.

"I see you've already met Rafferty," she says. "He seems to like you."

In fact, Rafferty will not leave her alone. He is removed to the back garden, whilst they have tea and cake. Doris notices that Isla drinks the tea. Guzzles it. Cup after cup. But does not touch the cake. The girl is very thin. She watches Isla as she chats to Eric. She watches Eric as he chats to Isla. Easily. Freely. She sees the love that is blossoming. Wonders where it will lead. Or end.

Isla tells Doris as much as she can about herself. About her life before the Sanctum. But it's so jumbled. Huge chunks missing. Doris cannot make sense of it. And she soon realizes that neither can Isla.

"Eric's told me quite a bit about you. How you help on your ward. And on his. The three of them sit and chat. Doris tells Isla that she is an archivist in the City Library. It sounds important, thinks Isla. She has no idea how important this will prove to be.

"Eric wants to climb all the way to a senior position," Doris is saying. "And he will. He works so hard." There is such pride in her voice. But Isla is distracted. She sees a piano in the corner of the kitchen.

"May I?" Isla asks pushing back her chair and walking over to it. Gasps. "Oh, it's beautiful!" she exclaims. "A Steinway Vertegrand. Nineteen twelve, I think…" I've played one of these before, she thinks. But she can't recall when or where.

How does she know that, wonders Doris, nodding her assent.

Isla sits in front of the glossy walnut cased piano with reverence. She would like to run her fingers over the glossy veneer but knows better. There are beautiful carvings of strapwork and beading.

"It's been rebuilt I think," Isla murmurs. "Cabriole style legs not Sheraton."

Eric is dumbstruck. Where did that come from?

"It was my mother's," says Doris. "She was an accomplished pianist. Sadly, I only tinker."

Isla lifts the lid. Sits. And plays beautiful haunting music. Doris knows that whatever Isla's past, she has been well schooled. And when she remembers, she will be able to take on the world.

Eric stands. Hugs his mother.

"We've got to go," he says. "I must get Isla back to the ward by 5 o'clock. I promised Staff Nurse Magdalena."

Doris hugs Isla. "I hope you'll come again," she says. "I'd like to help. Talking might trigger more memories."

"More pieces for her jigsaw," Eric tells her. He does not tell her that Isla should not be here. Or that he will bring her again despite.

Autumn sings her swan song. The trees stand stripped. Bare. Fragile. The earth is brown. Everything is brown, dead, empty, thinks Isla as they bump along on the top of the bus to Peasholme Green. But not my heart. She glances at Eric beside her. He turns and kisses her. His lips are warm. Just enough pressure to make her shiver. No, my heart is full, she thinks. Blossoming. It's like I've slept through winter and awoken in the spring.

This will be their fifth visit. Each time Isla plays the Steinway Vertegrand. Feels the ivory keys beneath her fingers. Feels the piano's persona. Its soul. Both are all encompassing. It plays like a dream. And Eric and Doris love to listen.

Now Isla sits on the kitchen floor with a boisterous Rafferty dropping a well chewed and loved toy on her lap. He wags his tail. Barks with anticipation. Isla throws the scabby toy. Rafferty bounds after it. Brings it back. Again, and again.

Eric laughs at them. "He'll do that forever," he says. "Come on. We'd best get going or we'll miss the bus."

Neither of them knows that this is the last time they will ride the bus to Peasholme Green together. That these unauthorized visits have been noticed. Noted.

Isla scrambles to her feet. Grabs her bag and coat. She hugs Doris. And as she's putting her shoes on in the hall, she hears Doris say, "You don't want to stay in that place forever, my dear. And you don't have to."

Isla's ears prick up.

"You can't find a future until you find what it is you don't want to face." She taps Isla's head. "There's a space in here where it's locked away. Only you have the key. Use it. Unlock that space."

Isla turns to face her, eyes wide. They glisten in the hall light. Doris sees the fear etched there.

"I know you're scared. But better to know than live in the disjointed, topsy-turvy world you inhabit. To live in an asylum when you are as sane as the next person." Doris hugs her. "And when you do discover the truth, my advice would be to only tell someone you trust. Tell a few fibs if need be. You will be discharged, I am sure. And when you are, come here. You can stay for as long as it takes."

Doris sees Isla's lip tremble. A solitary tear rolls down a soft downy cheek.

"I mean it," she says. "For as long as it takes."

Chapter 12

For three days after this visit Isla is on cloud nine. Staff Nurse Magdalena even hears her singing as she scrubs out the toilets. Cleans the baths. It is a joyous, uplifting sound.

And then the letter comes. Addressed to Miss Isla Duncan.

Not a letter with a stamp on. Someone writing to her. Who would anyway? No-one knows where she is, except the phantom 'husband'. The elusive Mr Duncan who pays the fees, her spending money. But never visits. No, this is an internal letter. Eric? But why would Eric write to her when he sees her almost daily. Besides her name is typed. Bold black print on a snow-white envelope.

Isla takes the letter off 'Maggie' and takes it to her tiny room. Sits on the bed. Pulls up the flap. Tentatively removes the single sheet of paper. Unfolds it. Reads.

And her new, bright and beautiful world implodes. Explodes. A rage erupts inside her.

"No! NO! NO! NOOOOO…" Isla jumps off the bed. Flings open the wardrobe. Pulls out her favourite blouses. And rips them. Tears them apart with her bare hands. Hands through which all the anger, the injustice, the unfairness of it all channels. The letter falls back onto the bed. Its typewritten, devastating words disclosed.

Dear Miss Duncan,

The Policy of this establishment is that there should be no fraternizing between staff and the patients in their care. This is for the safety of both parties.

To this end, the impropriety of the developing relationship between yourself and a trainee nurse, Eric Skeldergate, has been noted. Mr Skeldergate has been duly notified that such association must cease, or he will be removed from the Sanctum's staffing forthwith. Such removal would, of course, jeopardize any future career in mental health nursing.

We trust you will understand the importance of your compliance.

Yours sincerely
The Board of Trustees.

Now Isla lights a cigarette. Draws on it a few times. Waits until the tip glows red. Stubs it out on her arm. Twists it so the scorching heat gouges. She tells herself there is no such thing as pain. But there is. Yet, this is a better pain than the one she does not want to feel. She lights another. And another. Stubs them out by grinding the hot tips in. A smell of burning skin assaults her nose. Who will notice? Not the old biddies. Isla waits awhile. And then, pulling the sleeve of her jumper down, calmly leaves her room.

But Staff Nurse Magdalena sees the red-rimmed eyes. She knows. After all, she is informed too. She thinks perhaps Isla will talk to her when she is ready. There is a degree of trust between them. But Isla does not talk. She cleans. Furiously. In between she sneaks to her room. Stubs more cigarettes out on her arm. Relishes the pain. Thinks of Caro.

That night Isla sits in her chair, next to the empty chair and thinks. She thinks how come it is alright for Robert Howard to fraternize with the patients but not Eric Skeldergate. Is it because Robert Howard holds a position of authority and Eric is just a junior? It is all so unfair. They are not committing a crime. They are not hurting anyone. And now one letter destroys something beautiful. Turns it into something sordid. Something to be ashamed of.

But Isla is not ashamed. She is angry. For less than a minute, the drugs trolley is parked on the corridor outside the dormitory. Unattended.

Without thinking, Isla grabs it. Tears off down the corridor toward the dispensary. The trolley jolts on its rotatable wheels. Glass bottles clink and clank. The noise alerts the nurse who is dispensing the drugs. She rushes out of the dormitory. Sees Isla. Gives chase. But Isla is light on her feet. She reaches the dispensary. The door is not locked. She opens it. Drags the trolley in and shoves it behind the door to wedge it.

There is hammering on the door.

"Isla. Open the door. Don't do anything stupid."

Isla thinks she knows the voice. But she is fired up with adrenaline. Too afraid to stop. She starts opening bottles. Shovels tablets into her mouth. Runs the tap and filling a glass container, swallows them.

70

The hammering and banging on the door grow more insistent. More voices are shouting. Telling her to come out. She recognizes one of them. Robin, the chirpy young night nurse who chats to Isla. Robin, who witnesses her daughter being knocked off her bicycle by a hit and run. Yet still puts a smile on her face. Comes to work. Listens to other people's moans and groans. And just before Isla's limbs start to misbehave and her brain begins to shut down, she thinks, I've betrayed her. And in the worst possible way.

Without saying a word, Isla opens the door a fraction. Wide enough for her tiny frame to squeeze through. And she runs. Fired by guilt and fear of what she has done, she hurtles down the rest of the corridor before they can catch her. Plunges her arms through a window at the end. Glass shatters. Someone grabs her before she can jump through.

There is blood everywhere. It drips on the shards of glass strewn across the corridor. Runs down her arms. Ribbons of red. There's a red ribbon tied around thinks Isla as she lapses into unconsciousness.

Isla is rushed to York County Hospital. Her stomach is pumped. Her cuts are roughly stitched. No finesse. They are tired of young drama queens. Time wasters. Isla has just missed the arteries in her wrists. She sleeps for two days.

And some time, during those two days, a stamped addressed envelope arrives. It's addressed to, Isla Duncan, Hannah Ward, The Sanctum. The handwriting is neat. The letters looped and even. It lays amidst a pile of unsorted post on Staff Nurse Magdalena's desk. But as she enters the office, her cape sweeps the letters off. Scatters them asunder.

Hurriedly, on hands and knees, Staff Nurse Magdalena gathers them together. But one letter remains underneath the desk. Upended, flat against a side, there it lays, concealed. The handwritten letter for Isla Duncan.

Chapter 13

As soon as Isla is semi-awake and out of danger, she is discharged from the hospital. The men in white come for her. Bundle her into the hospital van. She is too weak to protest. At last, fully conscious, she opens her eyes and sees 'Maggie' sitting beside her bed. I'm back in the Sanctum, she thinks. Back in the dormitory. No more privacy.

"Oh, Isla," says Staff Nurse Magdalena, "whatever were you thinking? You almost died. And your poor arms. We know what you've been doing. There's to be no more of that. Dr Zircona wants you to have more ECT. Starting on Friday."

"NO!" Isla sits up. "I don't want any more. Please, Staff Nurse Magdalena. Please."

"It's out of my hands, Isla. Pulling such stunts has consequences."

"But I won't do anything like that again. I wasn't thinking. I'm sorry. Really sorry."

"Not as sorry as the night nurse. She has been suspended."

"I'll apologize to her. I'll apologize to everyone. I will. I was just so angry, so upset."

"Because of the letter." It's a statement not a question.

"Yes, because of the letter. It's not fair. We weren't harming anyone."

"It might not be fair. But it is not permitted. If you really want to pursue a relationship with Eric Skeldergate, Isla, you need to do it outside these walls. But to get there, you need to be well enough to leave. But right now, your behaviour does not inspire such confidence."

Isla stares at her mutely.

"Have the treatments, Isla." Staff Nurse Magdalena takes her hand. Squeezes it. "I'm here when you're ready to talk."

But Isla is not ready. She presses the self-destruct button. Stops talking. Stops eating, Stops cleaning. Stops doing anything. Keeps stubbing cigarettes out in places where the burns will not be seen. Realizes she has the power to do this. But not the power to stop the electrocutions. The frazzling of her brain.

Well, I don't have much choice, do I? she thinks. Yet, she wonders why there seem to be so many this time. Wonders, when it will end. Whilst at the same time, she relishes the oblivion the anaesthetic gives. Wishes that could last for ever. Then after each treatment she lays about. On top of her bed. On top of the sofa. Stays in her nightclothes. Smokes like a chimney. Suffers the pounding head. The exhaustion.

And every night, as her brain, all in a whirl and a twirl, refuses to sleep, she recites a poem. A poem both she and Eric read and love. It's by Rupert Brook: *All the day I held the memory of you. And wove it's laughter with the dancing light o' the spray. And sewed the sky with tiny clouds of love.*

It is her memory. Her love.

At first, she does not notice what else is happening. As the cycle of ECT rides its course, chunks of the cliff face that Isla is always trying to climb break off. Each chunk is a memory. Many chunks. Many memories. Jumbled. Out of sequence. But nevertheless there. She has time. All the time in the world to sort them. Put them in order.

And day by day, little by little, Isla works from the periphery inwards. Puts each piece of the jigsaw where it fits. Belongs. And on the shortest day of the year, 21 December 1973, Isla puts the last piece in place.

What to do? Who to tell? "My advice would be to only tell someone you trust." Doris's words on that last visit. And suddenly Isla knows exactly who that someone is.

She has a bath. Washes her hair. Gets dressed. And knocks on the office door where, behind her desk, Staff Nurse Magdalena faces a pile of post. She unlocks the door and beckons Isla in. Although taken aback by Isla's transformation, she keeps her counsel.

"There's something under your desk," says Isla, bending down. "It looks like a letter." She wrestles a white envelope from where it has been wedged. Turns it over. Gasps. "Oh, it's addressed to me!"

"It must have fallen there," says Staff Nurse Magdalena. "But I've no idea when. Is that what you came to tell me?"

"No." Isla says. "I came to tell you that I've remembered. Everything. And I want you to listen. But it's going to take a while," she adds.

"That's not a problem, Isla." Staff Nurse Magdalena closes the door. Pushes the pile of post to one side. "I can deal with this later." She beckons Isla to sit in the chair opposite her. And then she listens.

There are a few interruptions as staff come into the office to report things. Ask for things. But Staff Nurse Magdalena does not interrupt Isla's story. Not once. It is Isla who pauses when someone comes into the office. Interrupts. Whilst she waits, she opens the letter. Reads. It's from Eric.

Dear Isla, I expect you received an official letter, as did I. So we cannot see each other anymore. My future is too important. I can't throw it away. But you are important to me too. Very. I love you, Isla Duncan. So, you must get better, my darling. Get out of the Sanctum. Come and live with us until we can sort something out. Try and get an annulment of your marriage (if there ever was one). And then, I will ask you to marry me. Hope your answer is 'yes'. Stay strong. All my love, Eric xxx

A smile big enough to light up the world beams across her face. Transforms her. And Isla Duncan sits there, nursing the letter. An ethereal beauty shining with hope. Whilst the cigarette she lights, lays smouldering in the ashtray that always sits on Sister Magdalena's desk.

She is loved. She has a future now. Something to work toward. Had she received the letter when intended, would she have pressed the self-destruct button? Probably not. But then there would have been no need for the ECT. She would not have found the key. And perhaps her past would still be just that, her past. And she would not have learnt the truth. Discovered her true self.

Picking up the cigarette, she twiddles it between her fingers. Then stubs it out in the ashtray. This will be the last cigarette Isla stubs out on herself. The last cigarette she will smoke.

The office door closes. Isla folds the letter and still clutching it, resumes. Staff Nurse Magdalena is shocked, yet entranced. But does not doubt the veracity of her words. No-one could create such an intricate story of a life unless they have lived it. And she also realizes the strength of this girl to survive. To come out smiling. It is no small wonder that she didn't want to remember.

Finally, a few hours later, Isla purges her past. Faces its perpetrators head on. Knows she has a fight on her hands. Knows that with Staff Nurse Magdalena, Eric and Doris on her side, she will win. Nothing can justify his plan. What he does to her. The beginning, all those years ago, gives her no justice. Not then. Not today. But now, at the end, she knows tomorrow it will be hers.

"And you say you have a son?" says Staff Nurse Magdalena, her eyebrows arched.

Isla nods. "Williain," she says.

****

"He's two. I must leave. I think perhaps I'll go back to Yorkshire. Find my mum. If she's still alive. I never believe that I will be brave enough to do this. Leave on my own. Escape. But I am." Isla smiles. "And I do. He tells me they are going to a livestock sale," she continues. "That they will be out all day. So, I wait for them to go. There's a holdall in my wardrobe. I fill it with some clothes for both of us. Williain's favourite teddy. The money he gives me. A little food. Drinks."

Isla pauses as she remembers.

"Then we walk, my son and me. We walk all the way to the town. It's a long way. Because I know a safe way. Where we will not be seen. But he only has little legs. He cries because he is tired. I keep carrying him. Tell him we are going on a boat. On an adventure. The ferry goes from the town. Across to the mainland. To a bay. Wemyss Bay, I remember. And from there is a train to a big city. A place called Glasgow. And we would have escaped. We would."

A solitary tear tracks down a cheek.

"But there is a storm. The ferry is postponed until it's over." She gulps. "But he finds us. Tries to snatch Williain. I struggle with him. Try to stop him." Isla is crying quietly now. "But he hits me. Shoves me so hard I fall. Bang my head. And suddenly, it is night. When I awake, I am in a bed in a hospital. I've never been in a hospital before. Not even when I give birth to my son. And never in one like the Sanctum."

Staff Nurse Magdalena pushes her chair back. Stands. And walking around the desk, takes Isla in her arms. Holds her tight. An embrace which needs no words. Speaks its own language. And Isla knows that her trust is not misplaced.

Isla is moved from the locked side of Hannah to the unlocked side. She has her own room. Privacy. Is allowed a measure of freedom. Goes to a gym with Robert Howard. He shows her how to use the equipment. Tells her what foods are good to eat. To get her fit. So her physical health matches her newfound mental health.

She gets a part time job in a charity shop a short bicycle ride away. Borrows a bicycle off Staff Nurse Magdalena's daughter. Isla helps sort the donations. Serves in the shop. Discovers she is good with numbers. Does the accounts. The staff know she resides in an asylum but find her quite normal. A delight to work with. All this positivity is fed back to the Sanctum.

Dr Zircona is pleasantly surprised when he hears. More so when Isla attends what will be her last session with him, entering his office full of smiles and vigour. She tells him little; except she is feeling wonderful.

"I was reluctant to have the ECT," she says. "But I believe it helped. A lot. And I'm not taking any medication now," she adds. "I don't need to."

Dr Zircona knows this. He gazes at her. Can hardly reconcile this beautiful young woman with the wreck he first saw on her admittance. He strokes his chin thoughtfully.

"You do know that you are no longer sectioned, Isla. That you are free to go. And have been for some time."

Isla does not know this, but she is not going to demur. Does that mean she could have walked out months ago? Somehow, she thinks not.

"Have you somewhere to go?" Dr Zircona is asking her.

"Tell a few fibs if need be." Doris's words again.

And Isla tells the first fib.

"I have telephoned my husband. He and my son are coming to collect me. Meantime, he's paid for me to stay in a hotel…"

"Ah, your husband and son," echoes Dr Zircona. "In all our sessions you make no mention of either."

"Because I had forgotten. All of it…But I remember now."

Now, she tells her second fib.

"Oh yes. Before I forget, Dr Zircona, my husband says there's no need for you or the Board of Trustees to contact him. He asks that you just cancel future payments for my stay here." She laughs. "Because in the future, I shan't be staying."

"Of course. Consider it done." His brow furrows.

"Oh and before *I* forget…"

He gets up and skirting round his desk, walks across to a metal safe. Turns the combination dial. Isla hears the click. Watches as the door opens and he retrieves something.

"Your rings, I believe," he says ands hands her a small box. A label that has been pasted on reads—Isla Duncan/July 1967.

Isla stares at the label. Tries to look joyful as she slips them on her finger. Yet, Dr Zircona can see that she is anything but. He is not going to ask. Isla Duncan is no longer his patient.

"Thank you," she says. "For everything. I feel reborn. It's like a miracle."

"Indeed it is. When you were brought here, I was told that, after the birth of your baby, you develop a form of psychosis. That you do not sleep. Do not eat. Try to kill yourself and the child."

"How interesting," says Isla. "It's not quite how I recall it," she adds mysteriously. "But never mind, isn't that what you would expect from someone not quite right in the head."

Dr Zircona smiles. Peers at her over the top of his spectacles as he has so many times over the years.

"I think, Isla, you are a remarkable young lady. And are as right in the head as anyone."

"Well, that's comforting to know," she says, smiling back. "He'll be nine now. My son." The significance of this does not elude her. "I've missed him growing up." She tells her third fib. "I can't wait to see him. But they have a long way to come."

"From Bute, I believe," says Dr Zircona. "I've holidayed there. It truly is a beautiful island. You are fortunate, Isla."

"Yes, I am. And it is," Isla agrees. And then she tells her fourth and last fib. "It will be so good to go back home. To the farm."

Dr Zircona gets up from his chair. Walks round his desk. Shakes her hand.

"You've come a long way too, Isla. I wish you well for the future."

Isla tries not to skip out of the office. Her feet are light as thistledown. Her heart sings.

And in the April of 1974, Isla packs her few possessions and steps out into a new beginning. A new future. But before she leaves what has been her home for the past seven years, she must ensure that her new home will not be revealed to anyone. Because once they discover that she is discharged. Out there. Free. He and his partner will know she remembers. Everything. Will worry that if she tells, they and their lives will be exposed for all the world to see.

Hopefully, the fibs will give her a little time. Time to gather and collate all the information she will require to take them to court. To get that justice. For her lost childhood. Her lost son. And all the lost years.

"They won't hear it from me." Staff Nurse Magdalena assures her. "Whoever turns up here asking questions. My lips are sealed." They embrace.

Isla leaves the Sanctum with no regrets. Heads for the bus stop. And throwing the rings into the first bin she sees; thinks, I am free, finally free. And freedom tastes wonderful.

And as she bounces along in the bus to Peasholme Green, she's imagining a different embrace. Eric's. Can hardly contain the fizz of anticipation that bubbles inside her. Disembarking at the stop, she walks up the road, through the little gate, up the path. Raps the brass knocker against the green door. Hears Rafferty barking. And throwing back her head, shouts to the heavens above, "Thank you, Saint Benedict. Merci beaucoup."

Chapter 14

They sit round the kitchen table, Doris, Eric and Isla. Steaming mugs of coffee in front of them. A bowl of brown sugar in the middle. Rafferty lays underneath, a toy by his side. He nibbles their toes. Licks their legs.

Isla narrates her story. Not quite as she told Staff Nurse Magdalena. She omits the very beginning. Starts on the Isle of Bute. But there is something she tells neither Staff Nurse Magdalena, nor Eric and his mother. Something, she learns. Something, he tells them one night. When they play Monopoly in the parlour. When the whisky he drinks loosens his tongue. When he narrates a story too awful to believe. To comprehend. A story she remembers. A story she will only tell the police. When the time is right.

The kitchen is quiet. Just the odd gurgle from the fridge. The hum of the heating. And as they listen to the words, sure and steady, that pour out of Isla's mouth, they too are both horrified and entranced. Yet do not doubt their veracity. Do not doubt Isla.

"So, you were never actually married," says Eric, trying to keep the relief he feels hidden, whilst Isla relives her torturous memories. Memories neither he nor his mother can conceive.

"They want people to believe it," she says.

Picking up a teaspoon, she stirs the coffee round and round. Her mind meanders into the past as she watches the whirlpool in her mug.

"When I am sixteen. When I wear a wedding band. When I am out and about. And do you know what he tells folk to avoid them chatting to me. Asking questions?"

Doris and Eric hold their tongues.

"He says, I've had an accident. That I find it hard to talk. That it's left me not quite right in the head." She smiles wryly. "Ironic, isn't? When I actually end up in an Asylum."

"It's cruel," says Doris. "He was cruel. He *is* cruel. To abduct you. Drug you. Brainwash you. Imprison you. Deprive you of friends…"

But I had friends, she thinks. Even if they did have four legs…And I thought I had him.

"And to rape you." Doris sobs. Dabs her eyes with an already wet handkerchief. "Let you give birth on your own."

"I am not my own," says Isla recalling the pain. Her screams. The blood. "They are both there," she says. "And they know what to do."

"That's beside the point," says Doris. "None of it is for the right reasons."

"They want a child, a boy." Isla places her hand over Doris's. She's the strong one now. "His partner can't give him one. But I can." She pauses, lost in memories. "And I do."

And should the baby have been a girl, what then? Doris thinks. But does not voice her thoughts.

"And in fairness, I think perhaps my acceptance of this time helps me cope with my incarceration in the Sanctum. It becomes a way of life. The norm. I don't know any different way of living. And I think I love him. I think he loves me. But his partner has different thoughts. Thoughts poisoned by the past. The War."

Doris sniffs. "I know the war changed people. Some for the better. Some for the worse. But…"

"Don't make excuses for them!"

Eric slams his hand on the table. Rafferty yelps. Runs out. Jumps in his bed.

"Nothing can justify what they did. Surely you can see this."

"I can," says Doris. "I do. I just…"

"It's alright." Isla squeezes her hand. "I give birth to a beautiful boy. And I do know that what they did, for whatever reasons, is wrong. But it's the writer of the play I really want punished. The engineer of peoples' lives. There are things that really need to be told." Her beautiful brown eyes gaze at Doris. "In my own way. In my own time. Can you understand this?"

Doris nods.

"And I want my son back." Isla asserts. Williain, she thinks.

All the day I held the memory of you. And wove its laughter with the dancing light o' the spray. And sewed the sky with tiny clouds of love.

But will he have memory of me? Will he still love me?

"They're evil excuses for human beings!" exclaims Eric loudly.

"Eric." Isla grabs his hand. "I believe there is evil in all of us." She entwines her fingers with his. "Most of us keep it locked away. Beneath a veneer of niceties. Charm. Charisma. Present to people the good side. But sometimes if two people get together. One more forceful than the other, the weaker one can be persuaded to break that veneer. Let the bad side out. Do things they would not normally do."

"Don't, Isla. Don't." He pulls his hand away from hers. Jumps up, knocking the chair backwards. Calls Rafferty out from his bed with, "Coming for a walk boy?" Puts on his lead. Kisses the top of Isla's head. Pats his mother's arm.

"I need to get out for a bit. Clear my head. I'm just so tanked up with anger." And with that he walks down the hall, Rafferty wagging his tail behind him. They hear the front door slam shut.

"It's because he loves you," Doris says, smiling. "Can't bear to think what they did to you."

"I know." Isla smiles. Her mind is back there again.

"But it isn't all bad. Because now I am expecting they are so happy. And I walk. Swim. They say it will be good for me. Good for the baby. The island is incredibly beautiful. Its air and water so pure. He takes me into Rothesay. People smile at me because they see the burgeoning bump. But of course, believing me not quite right in the head, do not engage in conversation.

We go to church where I pray that the baby will be healthy and strong. We walk on the pier. And he takes me on the big paddle steamer to a magical place. He's always with me. His partner can't be. So it's just me, him and the bump. I feel like we are a proper married couple. That when the baby's born, we'll be a family. And I think perhaps he does care. Does love me. As I love him. Those are my magical months. But I am a fool."

Isla smiles ruefully.

"Because, in the end, he doesn't choose me."

"You're far from a fool, dear," Doris says. "For so long, there is only ever him. It's not surprising your feelings are so intense."

Isla looks at Doris. "Yes. Because now there is Eric. And I can see the love I feel for all those years is not real. But born out of dependence. That it's the love I feel for Eric which is free and true."

"What will you do now?" asks Doris. "Go to the police surely."

"I will. But not yet." replies Isla. "I have to try and find my mother."

"And your father?"

"Ah, the orchestrator. The puppeteer who pulls the strings for thirty years," she says.

"But I have all the time in the world now. And I know where he is. So, first I'd like you to do something for me."

"Anything. I said, I'd help."

"The newspaper archives," says Isla. "Can you go back to 1957. Find local and national papers with articles on missing children."

"I can try," replies Doris.

"Good. And then I will tell you what I am going to do."

A few days later Doris and Isla are in the kitchen. The table is covered with newspapers. Eric has an early shift at the Sanctum. So it's just the two of them.

Doris is looking at a copy of the Gazette & Herald. It's dated the 22nd of June 1957. There's a photo of a girl on the front page. In fact, the same photo is on the front of all the papers. A girl with a beatific smile. And even though the photo is in black and white, you can see that she has long fair hair.

A girl who goes missing on her birthday. Doris picks up the paper. Looks from the photo to Isla. The similarity cannot be coincidence, she thinks. Isla's long blond hair. Large brown eyes. Button nose. Even if now that child is a woman. Her cheekbones more enhanced. Her lips fuller. Her face more defined. She is sure it is her.

"It is you, isn't it?"

Isla nods. "Yes," she says. "It is me."

Doris's hand flies up to her mouth.

"Oh my!" she exclaims. "You are not Isla Duncan, are you? You never were."

"I am Isla for sixteen years." Isla rifles through the papers. Stares at the photo of the child who beams out from all of them. Remembers when it was taken.

"But that is not who I am," she says. "That is not my name."

Her eyes glance from that happy, smiling girl, to Doris.

"My name is Amaryllis. Amaryllis August."

AMARYLLIS

Chapter 15

Amaryllis sits astride the wall, swinging her legs back and forth. The wall drops down in stages, flanking the steps that go down to the driveway. She's quite high up so she can see down the road. Her eyes watch for the red Austin Healey. Her ears listen for the roar of its engine. Uncle James. Oh, where is he? Why is time so slow?

The rose gold watch dangles loosely on her wrist. She can't tighten it any further. Perhaps Uncle James, or her father, can do something. Take some links out? It's 12 o'clock. Noon. Four hours to her party. As she thinks of it, she feels butterflies flutter in her stomach.

There's a car driving up Oaktree Drive now. It's not a convertible. It has a roof. And it's not red. But it sparkles like gold in the high noon sun. Amaryllis watches as it creeps past the gates to the driveway. Doesn't turn in. She waits for it to pass by. But it stops immediately below her. The engine ticks over.

"Well hello, birthday girl!" calls a voice.

Amaryllis looks down. A window is wound open and she espies a face swamped by enormous sunglasses looking up at her. But she knows it's Uncle James. Wonders why he is driving a saloon, not his open-topped Austin Healey.

"Coming for a spin before the party?" He smiles up at her. Oh he is so handsome.

Amaryllis jumps off the wall. Runs down the steps. Out of the gates. He opens the passenger door and she climbs in to sit beside him. He hugs her.

"D'you like my watch?" she asks, jiggling her wrist in front of him. "It's fabulous, isn't it."

"It's very pretty," he says.

"It's a present from mummy. I love it. But it's a bit loose," Amaryllis rattles on. "She says daddy's present is a surprise. And yours might be too. And I love your new car, Uncle James. It is so shiny and sparkly. Like my watch."

"And your mother is right. That is where we are going now," says her uncle. "To collect your surprise. But first we're going to play a little game."

"Super!" cries Amaryllis.

"You have to get down in the footwell. Close your eyes. And don't peep till I tell you. Can you do that?"

"Yes," she replies.

The car speeds up. She hears the rushing of the road beneath her. But the engine is much quieter than the Healey. And there is more room.

"No peeking, remember?"

"I'm not. Promise."

She is crouched like a stretching cat, head down, bottom up. Hands over her eyes.

Suddenly she feels the car reversing. It stops. The engine dies.

"You can get up now," says her uncle.

Amaryllis uncurls. Stretches. Sits back on the seat. Does not recognize where they are. It looks like someone's driveway. She sees a house farther back. But all the curtains are closed.

"Should we be here?" she asks nervously.

"Don't be such a worrywart." He laughs. "They're friends of your father. And they're on holiday. He told me. So, c'mon. Out you get."

Slowly she opens the passenger door. Gets out. Closes it quietly. "Don't slam the car door Amaryllis," her father tells her. She's not sure why. But she never does. Now she walks round the car to where her uncle waits. He takes her hand and then he is walking. Walking with big strides up a lane. There are fields stretching out to either side. Amaryllis skips beside him.

"Oh, we're in the countryside!" she cries animatedly.

Yet wonders how a birthday surprise can be out here. In the middle of nowhere. Suddenly the lane peters out. Becomes a small, wooded plantation with grass verges.

"Where are we going?" she asks.

"You'll see," he replies. "It's just through here and up a farm track."

"Are we going to a farm then?" she asks.

He laughs. "You're such a clever girl," he says.

She's excited now. They're going to a farm. Does that mean?

"Is it a horse?" she cries. Farms have horses she thinks. Why else would they come all the way out here unless it was to?

"It is, isn't it? That's my surprise birthday present."

Amaryllis jumps up and down with excitement. Does not notice the rose gold watch slip off her wrist and slip into some grass, leaving only a sparkly bit of bracelet showing.

"Sorry, poppet." Uncle James smiles wryly. "It's not a horse. The farmer's dog has just had a litter of…"

He doesn't get to finish because Amaryllis is hugging his legs. She can hardly believe it. Not a horse. But the next best thing.

"A puppy," she sighs. "Oh, thank you. Thank you." And then she pauses. Releases her hold and looks up at him. "But what about mummy?"

"Your mother knows. She's fine with it. Because you see this farmer's dog has fur that is hypo-allergenic."

"What does that mean?"

"It means, sweetheart, that the puppy won't make her sneeze and choke."

They have left the plantation now and are walking up a rutted farm track. Toward the buildings. Amaryllis stares at the weeds. The barn with no roof. The dilapidated farmhouse with its peeling paint and broken windows. There is not a soul about. No-one. Just her and Uncle James. Suddenly, she is afraid. Something does not feel right.

"I want to go home, Uncle James," she says, dropping his hand and turning about.

They are the last words she utters. Something pricks her arm. And the world goes dark.

Chapter 16

She tries to move her legs. But can't. It's dark. So dark. She reaches out with her arms. Tentatively, her fingers crawl up and down. Side to side. There's little space around her. She's enclosed in something. It's hard. Has a familiar smell. A bit like her father's whisky. Where is she? What happened? She can't remember. Only that she is going to get a puppy. And then...

She struggles. Twists and turns her body. But it's no use. Wherever she is, she is trapped. Something brushes against her lips. She uses her fingers to define it. A straw she thinks. A paper straw. The sort they are having at her party. Oh her party! It's not going to happen. What will her mother do she wonders? Her father? When they realize she's not there?

"UNCLE JAMES!" she shouts. "Uncle James, I'm in here."

The dark and the silence stay.

"HELP!" she shouts. "Somebody help me." But nobody comes. Perhaps something bad has happened to her uncle too. Nobody knows where they are. Nobody will ever find her. How long does it take to die? Will it hurt?

"HELP!" she screams again. But her cries ricochet in the container that traps her. Now she is terrified.

Panic pervades. Nausea rumbles inside her. Threatens to erupt. There's a horrible taste in her mouth. Her lips are dry. Without thinking, she grabs the straw with her teeth and sucks. An acrid tasting fluid fills her mouth. Floods it. She has no choice but to swallow. And then the blessed relief of sleep envelops her.

Something rouses her. She has no idea how long she's been here. But she's stiff. Cold. Half awake. And has an overwhelming desire to go to the toilet. Oh, no! She mustn't go now. Not in here. But again, she has no choice. A warm liquid dribbles down her dungarees. Onto her socks. Into the white plimsolls. Amaryllis sobs.

She is wet and ashamed. Her beautiful rose gold watch is gone. She has had nothing to eat since breakfast. Was that this morning? Or yesterday? Or days ago? She has lost all sense of time. And she is very thirsty. So, horrid though it is, she sucks up more of the liquid. Wonders what it is. Wonders where it's coming from. And then wonders no more. Sleeps. Dreams. Dreams of the party she never has. And the puppy she never sees.

Noise intrudes her slumber. Disturbs her troubled mind. Loud noise above her. Whatever she is enclosed in begins to rattle. Judder. Amaryllis stirs.

"HELP!" she shouts. "Get me out. Please."

Something is sliding. There's a gap. A shaft of light shines down. It's direct and bright. The beam of a torch. Someone is there! She's going to be rescued. But her eyes, unaccustomed to the glare, are blinded. Cannot see who it is.

"So there you are," says a voice she recognizes. "I've been looking for you."

"Oh, Uncle James," she cries. "I'm so glad you've found me. So glad you're alright."

He can see her large doe eyes, wet with tears, looking up. But she's alive. No harm done then.

"Come on. Let's get you out of there. Can you reach up your arms?"

He grabs her hands. Holds them tight. Pulls. Slowly, steadily, Amaryllis emerges. Into greyness. Not exactly night. Not exactly day. Twilight. There is the faint sound of birds singing outside. The dawn chorus.

"I didn't know we are playing hide-and-seek," he says, hugging her. Then nipping his nose, he laughs. "And you're a bit whiffy, poppet."

"Because we aren't," she says, affronted. "How could I climb into that?"

She sees that she has been packed in a wooden cask. A large wooden cask. With a lid. She later learns it's a large barrel called a 'Hoggie'. The name amuses her. But being stuffed in one does not.

"And just suppose I did." Amaryllis pouts. "How could I put the lid on? No. I don't climb in. Someone put me in." She glares at her uncle. "It wasn't you, was it?"

"Now why on earth would I do that, eh?" He laughs. "To my favourite girl."

"Then who?"

"Ah now, that is the brainteaser."

"I don't want to tease my brain," retorts Amaryllis. "I want to go home. I want to see mummy. I want a bath."

"Then that's what we'll do," he says in a jocular manner.

Amaryllis looks into his eyes. Sees into his soul. Something there she can't reconcile. Yet she can tell from his voice, from the expression on his face, that it was him. He put her in the cask. He slid the lid across. But what she cannot tell, is why. And now she is too afraid to ask.

They are outside the barn. Daylight creeps above the horizon. The MG-YB saloon is parked on the track. Its sun-bronze colour muted in the gloaming. Amaryllis is cold. She's shivering. Her uncle opens the boot. Takes out a large horsehair blanket. Wraps it round her. Then tells her to get in.

"No. Not in the front," he says as she walks round to the passenger door. "I can't drive sitting next to something that stinks like a sewer rat." He opens a rear door. "Hop in there. You can lay down on the back seat."

Amaryllis tries not to cry. Why is he being so horrid? He never speaks to her like this. She doesn't understand. Neither does she demur. Stiffly, awkwardly, she and the blanket step on the running board and climb onto the back seat.

"Uncle James," she calls. "I can't lay down. There is an enormous suitcase on the seat. And a bag next to it."

And there is. A tan leather steamer trunk. And an overnight bag. No room for her. Uncle James leans in. Lifts the bag out and throws it onto the passenger seat. Lifts the lid of the trunk. Amaryllis sees that it is beautifully lined. That there is a cushion at one end.

"In you get then," he says, not unkindly. "You can lay down in that, can't you? Just imagine it's a bed."

The blanket slides down into the footwell as she climbs into the trunk. Luckily, Amaryllis is small for her age. Fine boned. She lays down. Just fits. Doesn't even have to bend her knees.

"You're not going to shut the lid, are you?" she cries.

"No, silly," he replies, smiling down at her. "Now give me your arm like a good girl."

She doesn't want to give him her arm. But what can she do? "You're a bright pupil Amaryllis, despite." Miss Tong's words when she is expelled from the classroom for talking. *But it doesn't matter if you're 'bright'*, she thinks. *When you're only just nine. And a grown man asks you to do something.*

There is a syringe in his hand. Amaryllis looks up at him wide-eyed. It's her Uncle James. He loves her. He is not going to hurt her.

"Just a little prick, poppet. Something to help you relax. On the journey."

A journey, she thinks. Then he is not taking her home. So where is he taking her, she wonders? And why?

Amaryllis surrenders her arm. Surrenders her thoughts. What choice does she have? A short sharp jab. She yelps. But it is done. Whatever he gives her now flows through her veins. She can still hear. She can still feel. She can still see. But it's all through a dreamy haze.

She hears the slam of a car door. The start of an engine. The rev of a motor. Feels movement as they bump along the rutted farm track. She can see the branches of trees as they pass back through the plantation, the light flickering as the sun rises in the sky. On. Off. On. Off. A soporific rhythm. She closes her eyes. And it is night-time again.

James stops the car. Covers her with the horsehair blanket. And closes the lid.

Chapter 17

James is tired. He has been driving a long time. Up the Great North Road. The gateway to Scotland. If he drives steadily, he can get forty miles to the gallon out of the MG. But it still means a few pit stops to refuel. Luckily, the Great North Road is the main road used by lorries transporting wares from the south to the north. This means there are plenty of transport cafes. James knows the route well. Knows the best cafes.

The three years before Amaryllis's ninth birthday are difficult. He leaves his orthopaedic consultancy at the Northern General. Leaves Sheffield. Sorts out where they will live. A farm. It's remote. On a beautiful island. An island where they can live their dream. Be together. Then in the August of 1954 his parents sell Simmental. The farm where he is born. The farm he grows up in. His mother and father grow old. The long days and hard work without respite, coupled with the Depression, break them.

James, born at the end of the first world war to a returning soldier and a woman entering her forties, is their hope for the future. A future he fails to give them. They remain in Buxton. Yet enjoy only a few months of an easier life before both dying within days of each other with the flu.

And as James drives towards his future, a future with Charles, he feels great sorrow, compounded with guilt, that for his own selfish reasons, he leaves Simmental to go to Sheffield. Never returns to run the farm. Perhaps his parents would still be alive if he had. He sorts their funerals. Clears the bungalow they live in for those few months.

And then, whilst Charles lives in pretence with Columbine, it is he who secures a dilapidated farm on Bute. Gets it up and running with the help of local folk. Hires a helper. Someone capable of managing the farm, whilst he is away. Prepares the farmhouse. A room for Amaryllis. Yet he still drives the long and tiring journey to Oakwood for Charles's and Columbine's birthdays. For Christmas. And on that fateful day.

The day Charles decides, he drives all night and day to get to Oakwood before lunch. To abduct Amaryllis. Secrete her away. Arrive at her party as if he knows nothing. Charles's plans. Always Charles. A strong and forceful man who does not care to be thwarted. Yet irksome though Charles can be at times, James loves him. Wants to be with him. And Amaryllis. A family.

Now, however, on this final journey, he has Amaryllis to consider. He can't take her in the cafes. He can't let her use the toilets. She must not be seen. He cannot think of the consequences if she were. He buys bacon butties for them to eat in the car. Gets a flask filled with tea. There's one café which does the best mince and mash. It's in a green tin shack with a corrugated roof. He takes a copper pan in and asks them to fill it. He has spoons in the glove box in the car. Then he pulls into an empty layby, rouses Amaryllis.

Sometimes, she is sick after she eats. He wonders if it's because of the medication he gives her. But he needs to keep her in that twilight world. Half awake. Half asleep. She's less of a problem. Should she need the toilet, he opens the door away from the road. Lifts her out of the trunk. And then she must squat where she can. He gives her strips of newspaper if she says, "Uncle James, I need to do a number two." The first time she says this, he has no idea what she means. Amaryllis gets distressed. Cries. He doesn't like it when she cries.

He knows a quiet, remote place to stop when night closes. They have covered a lot of miles, but it is too far to drive in one day. He has slept here before. Knows it is safe. Getting onto the back seat, he sits beside the trunk. Holds her hand. Dozes. But Amaryllis hardly stirs. Now, in the beautiful early light of a June dawn, he drives westbound from Scotch Corner, their last pit stop.

It's a trunk road. Ironic he thinks. He is driving along a trunk road with a trunk in the back. Two more large cities to get past before Glasgow and the ferry from Wemyss Bay to Rothesay. They can stop at Gretna Green for fuel and food. Once on the island he will drive the last leg of their journey to the farm.

Farm…The word conjures memories. And so, with little traffic to worry about on this long, quiet stretch of road, James reminisces. Simmental. Simmental Farm. It's near Buxton. His parents and their parents before, farm it for years. It's not a large farm, but it's lively and productive. They have a small herd of Simmental cows which provide both milk and meat. His mother makes cheese from the milk.

James recalls the two breeding pigs, Boris and Betty. They produce piglets to fatten for pork, gammon, bacon and ham. A small flock of sheep keep weeds at bay, their lambs sold for meat, their fleeces for wool. Hens lay eggs in an open-ended barn where there is straw and places to roost. They wander in and out. Peck up grit from the courtyard. Wander into the orchard and peck at fallen fruit.

There are Perry pear trees and apple trees in the orchard. His father makes Perry from the pears. Cider from the apples. Near the farmhouse are rows of potatoes, romanesco and carrots. There are three fields to maintain. One for oats. One for hay. And one for corn.

And there is Bilbo. A large, strong, white shire horse who pulls the plough. Pulls the cart laden with produce to deliver to the surrounding villages. To the pubs. To the outside markets.

So, James knows all about life on a farm. As soon as he can walk, he is helping. Gathering the eggs. Feeding the chickens. Bottle feeding the lambs should ewe have triplets. He likes this job best. Taking care of something. Nurturing. When he is older, stronger, he helps groom Bilbo. Walks with him beside the plough. And then in 1923 his father buys a John Deere tractor.

James longs to drive this. And he does when he is ten. It makes ploughing and setting much easier. But Bilbo still pulls the cart. They will never part with him. He is part of the family. And as the MG eats up the miles, he wonders why he did not fulfil his parents' dream. To take over Simmental when they are too old to manage it.

He loves everything about the farm. Where he lives. As a boy he loves to walk through Grin Low woods to Solomon's Temple. From the top of the tower there is a panoramic view. Why does he leave all this to go to a busy city where space is rationed? Coveted.

There are two reasons he can think of. He is a bright boy. Attends Harper Hill primary school where his class teacher tells him he is clever enough for further education. So, instead of leaving when he is fourteen to join his parents on the farm, he is persuaded to aim for grammar school. It's the Depression. His parents cannot afford the fees. So at the age of eleven he wins a scholarship to attend the County Grammar School, formerly Buxton College. 'Sic Luceat Lux Vestra' chants James, amazed he can still recite the school's motto. 'Let your light shine forth'. And he hopes he did. Hopes he does.

His parents are proud of him. Yet still believe he will leave at the age of eighteen, better schooled, better able to run all aspects of Simmental. Then in 1937 James is offered a place at Sheffield University. To study medicine. And now that he realizes his sexual orientation, he fears that, if he stays, the farm in its loneliness will devour him. That his chance of meeting a man with the same predilections is slim. That his parents could never understand. So, much to their disappointment, he accepts.

A whole new world opens for him. He studies hard. Plays hard. Meets like-minded men. Finds it liberating that there are certain bars where they can gather. Where there is no stigma. But in the confines of the university, it beholds to be discreet. He falls in love with a man who attends his tutorials. Karl Muller. He's German. Blonde haired. Blue-eyed.

James smiles wistfully as he recalls the eighteen months they spend together. Before disquiet unleashes. Talk of war. With Germany. Karl goes back to his homeland. To fight for his country. James never sees or hears from him again. So, grieving at the loss of his first true love, he throws himself into his studies. Qualifies. And in the last two years of the war volunteers to help in the field hospitals behind the enemy lines. It's where he meets Charles, Columbine and another nurse, Eleanor Dingle.

Eleanor tells him she grew up on a farm too. Went to Harper Hill primary. James does not recall her. But he does remember a Dingle Farm. Small world.

Wrapped in his memories, he begins to feel sleepy. Keeps yawning. Decides to stop at the next lorry park that has petrol and a café. He'll buy another newspaper or two. Yesterdays' papers make no mention. He doesn't expect them to. Too soon. But today, the 22nd of June, most feature the disappearance of Amaryllis August. Her photo. So, he is anxious.

He will have to keep the trunk lid closed. Keep her doped up. He regrets how he treats her. It is not who he is. But he is stressed. It is even more important now that she is not seen. Charles. All part of his plan which James believes originates in the war. In the field hospitals. And germinates in the years after. All to an end.

Charles's vision of the future. Where the demons of the past are put to bay. But I have no idea how to look after a nine-year-old girl, thinks James. One that is distressed. And although he is careful, he fears that her slight body might not cope with the sedatives he gives her. To keep her asleep. Until they reach their destination. And what then?

Chapter 18

Amaryllis stirs. She is rocking. Ever so slightly. It reminds her of being a baby. Being rocked to sleep. Where is she? Her eyes shoot open. Darkness. He has shut the lid! And he said he wouldn't. She punches it with her fists. But they are small fists. Make little noise. No-one comes. Resigned, she sleeps.

Now the rocking motion stops. She hears the hum of the motor. There's a clunking sound. And then they are once more driving. This time the journey does not seem so long. The car stops. She holds her breath. Hears his footsteps. The car door opening. The lid lifts. Amaryllis scowls at him.

"You said…"

"I know," he interrupts. "No more trunk, poppet. We've arrived. So, come on. Out you get."

Amaryllis stretches. Sits up. Stretches again. Then, climbing out of the trunk, she steps onto the running board and hops down onto the ground. They're in the middle of nowhere. Hills in the distance flank an enormous expanse of water. Its surface glints silver white in the long afternoon rays of the sun. She hears the bleating of lambs. The low mooing of cows. Hens wander round her feet. Pecking. Scratting. Clucking.

"It's a farm!" she exclaims.

"It is," says James, smiling. "And it's ours. It's called Lochfrein Farm. Welcome to your new home, Amaryllis."

Amaryllis pouts. Folds her arms.

"I don't want a new home," she cries. "I want my old home. I want mummy and daddy."

"All in good time. They will join us soon."

He thinks of Charles who will have Oakwood and its encumbrance, Columbine, to sort. And, to avoid suspicion, he will not be able to do that for a few years.

"When they can," he adds. Half a truth he thinks. Half a lie. Will it be enough to pacify her? It is.

"See that…" Her uncle points. Amaryllis follows the direction of his finger. There's a stony track with a strip of grass running down the middle. Small banks of greenery either side. At the end, a vast expanse of water.

"Is it the sea?" she asks, gazing out. In the distance green and purple tinged hills flank one edge.

"Well," he says, "the sea isn't far away. But that is called a loch. And see the two white birds on it? They're called Whooper swans. They fly from Iceland to winter here. Scores of them. The sky fills with a ballet of white. A thrum of a thousand beating wings is their music. You'll get to see them, Amaryllis."

She's beginning to listen. He can tell.

"But a small number of pairs, swans, mate for life, you know, they stay on Bute. And they breed." He laughs. "Not quite like rabbits. But they hatch their eggs here. They like the wide, open space of the lochs."

Amaryllis tries to grasp what he means. She's busy staring at the white birds.

"We also get Hen Harriers, Peregrines and Osprey. They're birds of prey," he explains, seeing the puzzlement on her face. "I'll point one out when I see one."

Amaryllis peers. "I want to see the swans properly," she says. "But they're too far away."

"Stay there," he says. "I won't be a moment."

He goes back to his car and fetches a pair of binoculars out of the glove compartment. Loops them round her neck.

"Put them to your eyes, Amaryllis. You'll have to twiddle until you can focus."

"I know how to use binoculars," she says grumpily. She's tired. Wonders why. All she's done is sleep for what seems like days.

Nevertheless, curious, she puts the binoculars to her eyes and adjusts the lens. Zooms in on the two large white birds which sit out on the loch.

"What long necks they have," she says. "They look as if they might snap."

She watches as one plunges its head and neck down into the water, leaving what looks like a pair of frilly white knickers wiggling side to side.

"Let's get you inside," her uncle suddenly says. "And out of those pongy clothes. How does a nice hot bath sound?"

A bath, she thinks. Yes, that sounds good. So, meekly, she follows him into a long, low-roofed farmhouse. It's clean. A stone floor. A few mats here and there. She can see an Aga, like at home. A wooden rack on a pulley fixed to the ceiling above it. Clothes draped over, airing. Another wooden rack from which copper pans are strung. A wooden table with two spindle-back chairs at one side, two at the other. And one at each end.

A large dresser owns one wall. Lots of shelves. All full. Books. Plates. Glasses. Cups hanging on small hooks. Sprigs of dried Lavender everywhere. Amaryllis breathes its calming scent. There's a butcher's sink under a window that looks out onto the yard. Flowery curtains. She can see the hens. And is that a dog? A dog with a man following behind.

"Uncle James," she says, pointing.

"Go!" he suddenly snaps. "Up those stairs. Hide. And not a peep, you understand. You can't be seen or heard."

She doesn't understand. She's scared. But catching the fear in his voice, she does as he says. Light-footed, she flies up the few stairs. They lead to a landing. And two doors. She can hear voices now. Uncle James's and a lilting voice. A cadence she can't comprehend. Quickly opening the first door, she steps through.

"Oh!" she gasps, taking it all in. She's facing a wall papered with cars. Every sort of car you can imagine.

There's a single bed. A lamp on a bedside table. A desk. And shelves and shelves of books. Books on mathematics. English. History. Geography. Biology. Religion. Science. And so many more. She even spots some Enid Blyton, A.A. Milne and Beatrix Potter books. Anna Sewell's Black Beauty. All her favourite reads.

She's looking from one thing to another. Tries to work it out. Whose bedroom is this? Does another child live here? One who likes the same books as her. One who loves cars. A boy perhaps? Oh she hopes so. It will be so good to have a friend. Guiltily she opens the doors of a big rosewood wardrobe. Why, it's full of clothes. Smallish clothes. Some dungarees, jumpers. A jacket. A thick winter coat.

She can't see any shoes. Now she opens each drawer in a chest of drawers that has been crudely painted cream. Plain white pants, vests in one. Socks, long and short in another. Pyjamas in the third. No bras, girdles, slips or garters. A child's room then. But not a boy's room. So, a girl's?

And then, as Amaryllis looks from the cars to the books, she realizes. It's all for me, she thinks. This is my room. Uncle James. He does it. And mummy. She must have told him what clothes to buy. What my favourite books are. So she really must be coming! She closes her eyes. Wraps her arms around herself. Imagines. It's a hug from her mother. But why couldn't I have my party first before we set off? Why didn't she tell me? Why can't I find any shoes?

So many unanswered questions wander through her mind. She can only take comfort that Uncle James remembers her love of cars and all books. Knows her. What she does not know is how or when, he could do all this. Neither can she know that she will have all the time in the world to read every single volume.

The bedroom door is ajar. She hears a door shut. The patter of paws. The sound of running water. She ventures onto the landing. Looks down. There is a large black and white dog in the kitchen. Uncle James is putting food in one dish, water in another. He looks up and sees her.

"Bath's nearly ready," he says. Oh, the bath, she thinks. "That was Scott McGinty," he is saying, "the farm helper. And this is Chad." He ruffles the dog's fluffy coat. "Keeps an eye on the sheep. We have a couple of feral cats too. They keep an eye on the mice and rats." He grins. "Wouldn't want them running around the kitchen now, would we? Now let's get you out of those clothes."

Amaryllis follows him into a room off the kitchen. Steals a stroke of the dog. His fur feels so silky, like velvet. She spies a porcelain bath on legs. Steam swirling from its bulbous belly.

Uncle James undoes a strap of her dungarees. She flinches.

"I can do it," she says. "I'm not a baby. I can undress myself."

"I'm sure you can. But I am doing it today. And I am washing you too. I can wash your back. And your hair."

Horrified, Amaryllis stares at him. Her bottom lip trembles.

"But…"

"No buts. No argument. Naughty girls get punished." And then, wondering if that's a bit harsh, "But you're not naughty, are you? You're a good girl. And besides, I'm a doctor. I've seen naked bodies before."

Not mine, she thinks. And paralysed with embarrassment, lets him undress her.

The water is hot. Lovely. He gives her a flannel to hold over her eyes whilst he shampoos her hair with carbolic soap, filling a jug from the bath and pouring it over her head. Down her back, which he scrubs with a long straw-coloured loofah.

She begins to relax. Finds she likes it. Likes the feel of his fingers massaging her head. His nails scratting on her scalp. Like the claws of the chickens, she thinks, scratching in the farmyard. The prickly scrub of the loofah against her back. And when he washes between her legs with his hands, she feels a tingling. A tingling that makes her want more. He's gentle. Not like her father when he does it.

"Do you want me to do something for you now?" she asks.

"No," he replies. "Why would I?"

"Daddy does. He says, it's because he loves me. It's our secret. Do you love me, Uncle James?"

Charles? Surely not. Her own father. And for the first time James begins to doubt the decisions he has made. The decisions he makes.

"Of course I love you." And he finds he does. She has been through so much. Yet is still Amaryllis. The sweet little girl with the beaming smile. The girl he has known since her birth.

"Come on," he says. "I think we're done. You can pull the plug out now." Amaryllis pulls the plug out. Watches the dirty water swirl down the plughole, gurgling and belching. And then he turns on the tap, fills the jug with fresh hot water and rinses her hair. Pours it over her body.

There's a rickety old chair with a large, yellowy white towel draped on the back. She stands up and he wraps her in the towel. It's rough and scratchy. Not like the lovely soft fluffy towels at home. And then she sits on the seat whilst he rubs her hair. Dries her body.

"Uncle James," she says as the towel scrapes across her skin, "if lots of swans is a ballet, do you know what lots of buzzards is?"

"A wake," he replies. "A wake of buzzards."

"I like it. Do you know any more?"

He's drying between her legs. The towel is rough. But he is gentle.

"I know enough," he replies. "It's a parliament of owls. A murder of crows. Oh, and a mustering of storks."

"I don't like the murder one," she says. "Tell me more."

"Not now. Stay there," he says. And leaves.

Has she said something wrong? Is he going to punish her? That underlying fear and panic is ready to surface. But then, there he is, back in the bathroom, carrying a pair of pyjamas, a smile on his face.

"Forgot them," he says. "Can't have a nuddy buddy running about."

He laughs. Like the old Uncle James, she thinks.

"Did you find your room?" He's drying her feet now. In and out of her toes like her mother teaches her.

Amaryllis nods.

"Do you like it?"

Amaryllis nods.

"Good. Because you'll be spending a lot of time in it."

"Why? I want to explore the farm. See all the animals."

"Well you can't!" And hearing the tone of his voice, says a little kindlier, "Not for a while, poppet."

"That's not fair," she cries.

They're in the kitchen. Amaryllis sits in front of the Aga like she does at home.

"Who says life is fair."

"I can help that man, Scott Mc…"

"He must never see you!" James's voice is loud. Brooks no argument.

"But why?"

"Why do *you* ask so many questions? Why can't you just accept. And do."

"Daddy says if you ask questions, you get answers. And then you get clever."

Charles again, he thinks. Damn Charles.

"Garden man always answers my questions." She's looking at him questioningly.

He's caught on the hop. Has no time to concoct an answer. The best he can do is, "Curiosity kills the cat, Amaryllis. Mr McGinty is good with animals, machinery and crops. But he is not good with children…Especially little girls."

"Why? What does he do to them?"

"Terrible things," he says. Watches as uncertainty clouds her eyes.

"What sort of things?"

Mother of God! He slams a hand down on the table.

Amaryllis jumps.

"That's what daddy does when he's cross with mummy. Or me," she says. "Are you cross with me, Uncle James?"

Tread carefully James thinks. "No, I'm not cross, Amaryllis. I'm…I'm tired," he blurts out. Then realizes that he is.

"Like me, Uncle James," she says, yawning.

"Yes, like you. But it's best you don't know what McGinty does. And if he sees you…Well then…"

James feels bad. Scott McGinty is not a child molester. Far from it. He's a decent chap. A hard worker. A family man with, "Leor loons and lasses tae ha' ma aun feutbal team," he tells James.

Amaryllis finally bites her tongue. Decides. She will not let this McGinty see her. Ever.

"Perhaps I can take you out at night and show you around," he says to appease her.

A funny time to look round a farm, she thinks.

"Now, why don't you go to your room and read." He suggests. "Whilst I rustle us up some food."

"I'm not hungry."

She gets up and begins to walk toward the stairs. Tries to avoid treading on Chad, curled up by the Aga on a hairy mat.

"It's your favourite," he says.

Amaryllis turns. Locks her big brown eyes on his. She's not going to ask any more questions.

"Sausages, mashed potato, onion gravy and apple sauce. That's right, isn't it?" He's putting a frying pan on the hotplate of the Aga. "Columbine told me." Another half-truth. It was Charles. But she doesn't need to know this.

Amaryllis climbs the stairs. Grabs an Enid Blyton. The Famous Five. The whole series sits on a shelf. As does the entire collection of The Secret Seven and Malory Towers. Many she hasn't read. She chooses 'Five On A Treasure Island'. Throws herself on the bed and opens the first page.

She's a good reader. Devours several chapters before she hears her uncle call up the stairs.

"Tea's ready!"

Amaryllis carries on reading. And then a delicious aroma wanders through the open door and fills her nostrils. Sausages. Onions. Perhaps I'll try some after all, she thinks. Just to see if it's as good as mummy's. She rolls off her stomach onto her back. Sits up and slides her feet onto the floor.

"There you are," he says as she descends into the kitchen. Chad wags his tail. Amaryllis watches her uncle put two sausages and a dollop of mashed potato on a plate. Pour a thick, rich-smelling gravy over. And place it in front of her. There's a glass of water on the table. A bowl of apple sauce. A silver dessert spoon beside. Chad sits and watches all of this, saliva drooling from his mouth. But he does not move from his mat.

"He'll wait until we've finished," James says. "He knows he'll get any leftovers."

Amaryllis slices a bit of sausage off. Pops it in her mouth. Chews. Delicious. Even better than her mother's. She finds she is hungry after all. But does not clear her plate. Wants to leave some for Chad.

And so, the first day in her new home passes. She feels like she has been nine for a long time. Not just a couple of days. Uncle James brings a mug of Ovaltine into her bedroom. Places it on the bedside cabinet. Kisses her goodnight. She always has Ovaltine at home. So when the steam stops rising out of the mug, she picks it up and sips. It doesn't taste the same. Nevertheless, she drinks it all. And as she falls into a deep and dreamless sleep, she wonders when her mother and father will arrive. She so wants to see them.

Outside, in the farmyard, there is a large metal drum. It's what James burns rubbish in. Amaryllis's clothes and the plimsolls sit in a heap beside it. Fetching a pitchfork out of the barn, he scoops up the pile and thrusts it into the drum. Pokes it down to the bottom. And pouring a little petrol over, sets it alight. Watches the flames devour any evidence that she is here.

Chapter 19

In the ensuing days and weeks Amaryllis learns four things.

Firstly that Uncle James is not her uncle at all. But a friend of her father's. A dear friend. The significance of this she is yet to discover.

Secondly, he tells her that she is no longer Amaryllis. Amaryllis has disappeared.

"Is that why I can't be seen?" she asks. "Am I invisible?"

"Not to me," he says. "But you must be, to everyone else."

"Oh." Amaryllis ponders. "Then if I'm not me, who am I?"

"From now on you are Isla."

"I don't want to be Isla. I want to be me. When can I be Amaryllis again?"

"Never!" he says. "So say it. What is your name?"

"My name is Amar…"

He slaps her. Repeats. "What is your name?"

"My name is Ama…"

Another slap. She bites her lip. She doesn't want to be Isla. Not for ever.

For the third time, her uncle grabs her arms. Pulls her close. So close she can smell his breath.

"What is your name?"

He digs his fingers in. Watches her eyes fill with tears. But she does not cry. Will not cry.

"Come on," he pleads. "It's not that difficult. I don't like hurting you. But it's important. Say it for me. I'll keep asking you until you do."

Amaryllis sniffs. "My name is…" She falters. But not wanting another slap or worse, says, "My name is Isla."

It will be many years before she hears her real name spoken again.

And then one day, out of the blue, he asks, "Can you cook, Isla?"

"Can you?" she replies.

"Don't be cheeky!" But his voice has a lightness to it.

"It's fun," she says. "I'm not allowed to be cheeky at home. Daddy says children should be seen and not heard."

"Well, I don't want your parents to think I've been remiss in my care of you. When they come," he adds.

Isla only hears 'miss' and 'come'.

"So, you miss them too," she says in her naivety. "Well, I can boil an egg," she tells him. "I know how to make toast. And porridge. I can make an omelette." She thinks a bit more. "Oh and I can bake a cake. Is that enough?"

"That's enough for now," he says. And then, "I know, we'll have cookery classes. At night."

A funny time to have a cookery class, she thinks.

Which is when she learns the third thing. That even as Isla, she can be neither seen nor heard. It is not only Scott McGinty who cannot see her. No-one can see her. Not even the woman who comes to clean the kitchen, bathroom, and parlour once a week. Isla later learns that she is Mr McGinty's wife. On these days James tells her to be 'even quieter than a mouse'.

By day she is a prisoner. Locked in her bedroom. James leaves her bread and butter. Biscuits. A jug of water. He's up early. Out early. Looking after the farm and the animals. Animals she would love to see in daylight but is not allowed. There's a white porcelain chamber pot in the corner, patterned with pretty flowers. Isla hates it. Tries so hard not to use it. But the days are long. She can't always manage.

There is nothing else to do but read. Sit at her desk and do the written exercises he sets for her when he's out and about on the farm. Because when Scott McGinty goes home to his wife and brood, James schools her. It's these times when Isla misses Miss Tong. Penelope. Her other friends.

In her mind she sees them, sitting at their desks, Miss Tong at the blackboard, a piece of white chalk in her hand. She sees them in the playground. Skipping. Playing hopscotch. Playing tag, pigtails flying as they chase. She wonders what they think about her sudden absence. Do they think she's dead? Do they miss her as much as she misses them? But they still have each other, she thinks. I have only myself. And James. Yet she likes it when he is teaching her. When he reads the non-fiction books with her. Explains what she cannot understand. And opens a whole new world to her.

Geography and History become her favourite subjects. She loves looking at the different countries. Their landscapes. Their people. How they dress. What they eat. The exotic animals that share their habitats. And she loves to learn their histories. How it influences their development through the years.

She especially likes English history and religion. Both of which she finds fascinating, yet gory at the same time. And in her loneliness, she grows more and more dependent on James. For company. For clothes. For food. For everything.

James teaches her chess. Is amazed at how quickly she picks it up. It's not long before she's checkmating him every time. They play cards, draughts and dominoes. And in the evenings when the animals are fed and bedded, she is allowed down into the parlour.

"It smells fusty," Isla says, sitting on a brown settee filled with horsehair that faces a fireplace. Two high-backed chairs, which have seen better days, sit either side of the hearth. There's kindling in the grate.

"That's because the fire's not been lit for a while."

Isla looks round the somewhat barren room. Apart from the chairs, there's a battered old sideboard. It's dust free. Home to a tray of cut-glass decanters and glasses. Oh and tucked in a corner she spots an upright piano. It's brown and shiny. A polished mahogany. She has piano lessons when she lives at Oakwood. Her mother teaches her.

Jumping off the settee, she goes to look. It's a Steinway Vertegrand. That's what it says. And Isla realizes the music she hears when she is in bed, before she drinks the Ovaltine and falls asleep, must be James's fingers flying over the keys.

"Will you teach me to play?" she asks. "I can do the scales." And lifting the lid, she sits on the piano stool. Runs her fingers up and down. "But I want to play proper music. Like you do."

So James does. And again is amazed at how quickly she learns. Learns to read the notes. Recognizes the different cadences of them. He finds her bright. Enthusiastic. Enjoys teaching her. Not just the piano. But reading through the books with her. She's like a giant sponge. Absorbing everything. Facts and figures. People and places. Yet, unlike a sponge, she holds on to it all. Remembers.

In the gloaming when the curtains are drawn and the evening draws nigh, they cook. He knows she will need this skill when her life changes. But Isla knows nothing of such change. She falls into the pattern of her new life. Imprisoned in her room by day. Set free at night.

It's late. A balmy early summer night. All is quiet. Darkness cloaks the farm. They are in the parlour playing chess. Suddenly James gets up.

"I said I'd show you around, didn't I," he says. "So, come on. Are you ready for some exercise?"

Isla stops wondering why so much of her life is conducted in darkness. It must be about not being seen she decides.

There are waterproof boots in a cupboard. Her size. A waterproof jacket. And from thereon, whatever the weather, he takes her out. Sometimes there is moonlight. But often it's pitch black… "Black as the Earl of Hell's Waistcoat" as McGinty would say. James tells her the very first time he takes her out. When clouds obscure the moon and all sleeps in the deepest dark. In case she's afraid. But Isla is not afraid. She likes it best when they walk round the meadow, fields and outer hillier pastures in the pitch black. Just her, James and Chad. Following the beam of the torch.

"What's that?" she cries, clutching his sleeve, as one night it catches the eye of something.

"It's alright. Don't worry. It'll be one of the sheep. We've got nine," he explains. "They're good outside so they live out on the hills."

"Don't they get cold in the winter?"

"No. They have warm white coats. And they eat the winter cereals which, when they next grow, are more hardy, more resilient to pests."

"Are they tame?" she asks. "Can I stroke one?"

James whistles to Chad. Even though there is only a smudge of light from a harvest moon, the beam of the torch, he singles one out. And then, there it is, right in front of her. A creamy white sheep.

"It's Bethan," he says, as Isla runs her fingers through its woolly fleece. "They're Lleyn sheep. They come from Wales. McGinty had them shipped over. They make good mums. I've named them all," he tells her. "Welsh names, of course. I'll write them down for you if you like."

"I like," Isla says.

"Oh and mustn't forget the ram, Gruffyd." He laughs. "Gruff by touch. Gruff by nature. You'll get to see his new lambs next Spring."

Isla digests this. Ponders. "What happens to the old lambs?" she asks.

"They are killed. McGinty sees to that. Takes them to a butcher in Rothesay. Their meat is sold for meat." He shines the torch in her face. Sees a tear wobbling in an eye. "Come on now," he says, wiping it away. "You eat roast lamb. Where do you think it comes from?"

She doesn't think. Just eats it. But from thereon Isla decides that perhaps, she won't.

"We have a small herd of ten milking cows. They are right out on the farthest pastures. We won't go that far tonight. Besides, they have calves…"

"That means babies, doesn't it? Oh, can't we go? Please, Uncle James." She calls him uncle for so long it's too hard to call him anything else. "I want to stroke them." She stops. "Oh no, you don't kill them too, do you?"

"Not the heifers. We add them to the milking herd. But the bullocks, yes they go for slaughter." He laughs. "Don't tell me you don't know what a steak comes from. Or the beef in your stews."

"Well mummy doesn't tell me. Or Miss Tong. All they tell me is that cows have calves. And sheep have lambs. I never think they end up in my belly," she cries.

"Well, you live on a farm now. Have a lot to learn. And your first lesson is not to startle animals in the dark. Especially cows and their calves. The mothers can be very protective. So, we'll give stroking calves a miss. Come along. We're going back now."

Resigned but disappointed, Isla trudges back to the farmyard. As they pass the barns, byre and milking shed, her ears catch a different sound.

"Pigs," she says. "I can hear pigs."

"Boris and Betty." James shines the torch into a sty where two big brown spotted pigs snuffle and grunt. He swings the beam round to an empty sty. "Hopefully, we'll have piglets," he adds.

"Oh, I love piglets!" exclaims Isla. "Not that I've ever seen a proper one. I love Piglet in Winnie the Pooh. And I've read Charlotte's Web. And all the Pig Tales." A horrid thought intrudes on her joy. "Do you kill those too? Please say you don't, Uncle James."

"Not the piglets," he replies. Isla is leaning over to stroke one.

"Oh!" she exclaims. "It's all rough and scratchy. I was chased by one once," she says.

"Do you like bacon?" he asks suddenly.

"I love it! It's the best thing ever!"

"And do you think it grows on a tree?"

Isla ponders. Realizes. And decides she will not eat lamb or beef again. But she is not quite ready to give up bacon.

"Don't worry we shan't be sending Boris and Betty to slaughter. They are named in honour of Simmental. The farm I grew up in. We had a Boris and Betty there."

"So are you a doctor or a farmer?" she asks.

"I thought I was a doctor," James replies. "But I guess you can take the farmer out of the farm. But you can't take the farm out of the farmer."

"Oh look. A cat!" It's emerald eyes sparkle in the dark. Before he can stop her, she runs across. The cat hisses. Spits. And yowling, swipes a clawed paw at her. Isla withdraws. Steps back.

"They're feral." he tells her. "Not nice cuddly pets." There's blood on her arm. "Are you alright?" he asks.

"It's just a scratch," she says. And thinks she won't do that again. She'd rather cuddle the lambs next Spring. Pick up a piglet with their soft pink skin and funny little curly tails. Just as she's seen them in her books.

"Well, we'd better get you back. Disinfect it. Cats have a lot of nasty bacteria in their mouths."

And as they walk back to the light and warmth of the farmhouse Isla thinks, 'I'm like a vampire'. She's just finished reading Bram Stoker's 'Dracula'. Shut in my coffin all day. Coming out when it's as black as the Earl of Hell's waistcoat. Except I don't have two pointy teeth. And I don't suck blood'.

The fourth and last thing she learns is that her parents are not arriving any time soon. Because the months pass. The first Christmas passes. And they don't. Who does arrive, once a week, is Mrs McGinty. She clatters into the farmyard on a horse drawn cart. Isla hears the snort of the horse. The champing on the metal bit in its mouth as James loops a sack of food over its ears. So it will stand patiently. Waiting for the cart to be unloaded. And loaded again.

She can watch all this. There is a window high on her bedroom wall. It's covered with a venetian blind. So she repositions her bed under the window. Then, standing on tiptoe, she can peer through the slats down into the farmyard.

"That's Bilbo," James tells her. "He's a shire horse. Just like the one we had at Simmental. Damn good workers. McGinty stables him. Takes good care of him. But he belongs to me." And someone else he thinks.

Isla wishes Boris could be stabled here at the farm. So she can groom his splendid coat. Give him a carrot. Only at night, of course.

On Thursdays. The day of the weekly clean, Mrs McGinty takes James's dirty laundry. Brings it back, washed, dried and folded She also brings two loaves

107

of freshly baked bread. Mrs McGinty is always baking bread. She has a lot of mouths to feed. In return, James gives her two dozen eggs a week. The odd cut of beef or gammon. An occasional lamb shank. And pays her husband a weekly wage, which is more than he could earn anywhere else.

He can't let Mrs McGinty take Isla's dirty laundry. It would raise too many questions. Create suspicion. So James washes her clothes in the butcher's sink. Wrings each item out by hand. He makes a wooden clothes horse to stand in the fireplace in the parlour. Drapes the damp washing over. Lights the fire. And makes sure every Thursday that there is nothing of Isla's on the clothes horse. Or anywhere else.

Chapter 20

Christmas. James does his best. Each year, twelve days before the twenty fifth, he drives to the ferry. Then from Wemyss Bay to Glenbranter Forest where he chooses a tree. Buys tinsel, baubles. The very first Christmas they spend together he brings home lights shaped like bells, each with a different nursery rhyme character on. And even though Isla is not a child anymore, every year they decorate the tree with them. Isla likes them. As does James.

And that first Christmas at Lochfrein, which she will never forget, she hears the arrival of the Whooper swans. Sees the sky fill with 'the ballet of white' as they arrive on Bute for winter.

For the first three years they share a simple meal together. James prepares a chicken, puts bacon on its back. There are sausages and roast potatoes. Isla prepares these. And the vegetables. Helps him decorate the tree. And on that third Christmas, when Isla is eleven, he lets her have a glass of wine. Whilst he has one or two.

This is also the Christmas they first dance. On Christmas Day, they sit at the kitchen table and eat by candlelight since the daylight fades early. There is always a big bowl heaped with everything for Chad. Whilst Isla washes up, James suddenly pushes the table and chairs right up against the wall.

"Would you care to dance Miss Isla?" he says, taking the drying cloth out of her hands and hanging it over the Aga rail.

Isla goes to ballet classes when she lives at Oakwood. But she doesn't think it's ballet James means. And it isn't. He's jigging about. Twisting. Throwing his arms every which way.

"It's Jive," he says. "All the rage."

She watches his fancy footwork. Copies it. And then he grabs her hands and they are whirling and twirling. Leaping and kicking all around the kitchen. Chad, unable to understand their dissemblance to sheep, shoots under the table, drops on his belly and head on paws, watches their un-sheeplike behaviour.

"This is so much fun!" screams Isla, putting in a few of her own moves.

"Wahoo! Anything goes," shouts James. "Just a minute…"

He dashes out. Comes back with an old gramophone that is kept in a cupboard in the parlour. Puts a vinyl on. And loud jazz music fills the kitchen. And their feet. They dance until they drop. When Chad emerges from his hideout and licks the sweat off their faces. This becomes their custom each Christmas Day. Over time, he teaches her the Waltz, the Foxtrot. And two Scottish dances, the Gay Gordons and the Highland Reel.

"How do you…?" Isla once begins to ask.

"Sheffield," he answers. "I go to dance classes, whilst I'm at university. Something, I always wanted to learn."

And this is the year. The year before she is twelve in the spring, that she looks out of her window and sees the new-born lambs frolicking. Boris and Betty's piglets trotting and squealing round the farmyard. Just as she imagines.

****

It's at Christmas she so wants to buy him a present. But she never goes to any shops, so can't. James always buys her something. He drives into Rothesay. Takes the ferry. Makes his way to Glasgow. Visits his favourite book shop and purchases her one. One he knows she'll like. Gets them to wrap it up. In a bustling city he can lose himself.

No-one questions a man shopping on his own. For female clothes. Personal female things. Because now, this fourth Christmas, Isla is twelve. Soon she will be thirteen. She is blossoming. He can see the outline of small breasts beneath her clothes. Although still small in stature, she nevertheless, grows out of her original dungarees, t-shirts and jumpers. Needs new underwear. Bras and sanitary towels, which he talks to her about. A mother's job, he thinks. But there is only him.

And this fourth Christmas Isla's young life takes yet another turn. Everything will change. And not for the better.

It's two days before Christmas Eve. They are in the parlour. The tree stands in a large green pot, the nursery rhyme lights and festive tinsel trailing between its branches. Isla makes paper chains which they hang round the room.

Now she's at the piano, playing Christmas Carols. The whole gamut. James sits on the sofa. He marvels at her. Sings along to the well-worn festive tunes.

Chad, gently snoring, lays beside him. The fire crackles and sparks in the hearth. Spits burning bits of wood onto the fireside rug. James leaps up and stamps on them. A smell of pine pervades the usually fusty parlour.

Isla's Christmases are nothing like the ones she remembers from Oakwood. When her father cooks a turkey. When the nicely bronzed bird rests on a tray, surrounded by crispy brown potatoes and bacon wrapped round sausages. Bowls of vegetables. Gravy, made from its giblets and juices, steaming from a gravy jug. All set out in the dining room on the long ornately carved table. The best silver and finest plates used.

But then she thinks, there is a similarity. Because her and James will dine alone. And it is only she and her mother who sit at that long table. Use the best silver. Eat off the finest plates. Her father never joins them. He is always bad-tempered throughout the festive season. A curmudgeon. She doesn't understand why. But never asks. Neither does she understand why he always insists on preparing and cooking the entire meal yet does not join them. But she and her mother must always remember to thank him. Profusely.

"That was the best meal ever, daddy," she says.

"Thank you, Charles," says Columbine. "It was wonderful. Even better than last year's," she adds.

They both know that he creeps down in the dark. And eats.

So in a way, thinks Isla, it isn't dissimilar. And as this fourth Christmas draws nigh, when she is twelve. When she notices her body is changing. Her feelings. When her dependency is complete, she whispers quietly to herself, "I love him. I love the touch of him. The smell of him. The all of him."

****

She's in her bedroom. The door is no longer locked. James trusts her. And she, so embedded in her new identity and way of life, feels no intent to try and escape. Go anywhere. The card with the names of the sheep he gives her sits on her desk. She almost knows them all by heart. Angharad. Bethan. Carys. Dwynwen. Elin. Fflur. Glynis. Hafren. And Iona. Oh and mustn't forget Gruffyd, she thinks.

Her ears are now accustomed to the comings and goings of the farm. Recognize the different vehicles. The tractor. James's pick-up truck. The vehicles that go back and forth. The clopping of Bilbo's hooves as Mrs McGinty arrives.

Yes, she recognizes each different sound they make. But this wintry day, the twenty-third of December 1961, a new sound invades the farmyard. Filters through her open bedroom window. It's a sound she doesn't know. Curious, she stands on the bed and carefully widening the slats, peers down into the farmyard.

A large blue van has driven in. Comes to a stop. The driver's door opens and a figure steps out. It's a man. A tall distinguished looking man with pure white hair. The colour of the snow which now begins to fall. And then there is James. He comes tearing out of the barn and running towards the man, throws his arms around him. Hugs him tightly. Something about the stranger's stature. His stance. Something about the embrace.

"It's my father!" she exclaims.

But only the empty room hears her.

Tingling now, with anticipation and excitement, straining to see, she waits for the passenger door to open. For her mother to step out. He says they both will come. She believes him. Yet never dreams it will take this long. But the passenger door stays shut. Instead, her father and James open the rear doors of the van. Start unloading crates, trunks, packing cases and suitcases.

Mr McGinty arrives in a plume of exhaust smoke. He's driving James's pick-up which needs an overhaul. He switches off the engine and jumps out, followed by Chad. Chad rushes up to James. Fusses all around him. He does not fuss around Charles. Goes nowhere near him. But drops down. Flattens his belly into the straw, the dust, the debris, strewn across the farmyard. And head on his front paws, fixes both eyes firmly on him. Snowflakes fall on his back, his head. But he doesn't budge.

Isla hears the murmur of voices. Sees her father grasp Mr McGinty's hand and shake it. McGinty says something. Laughs. Isla just catches, "Is the cat deid?" Wonders which cat, and why he finds it funny. It will be a few years later when one of the McGinty offspring tell her it's a Scottish saying for when trousers are a tad short. Now, one by one, McGinty takes the crates and packing cases. Stacks them in a disused shed. Meanwhile James and her father heave the suitcases and trunks across the farmyard. Carry them through the kitchen door and deposit them on the stone floor.

Isla hears the kitchen door shut.

"Isla," James calls. "Come on down. I've got a surprise for you."

112

Not exactly a surprise, she thinks. She grabs a new tartan skirt and pretty, fitted jumper from the wardrobe. Discards her dungarees and the jumper that is too small. Too holey. A quick brush of her hair and her slippered feet are on the landing. Then she descends the stairs. Carefully. One by one. Ladylike. A girl on the cusp of womanhood.

Charles looks up. It is surprise which now crosses his countenance. He hasn't seen her in four years.

"You've done a good job, James. She'll be a fine buxom woman."

Buxom? That means plump and busty. No! I will never be either of those she vows. And from that moment Isla stops eating as much. Stops clearing her plate. Stops eating extras. Charles and James, so engrossed in each other, do not notice. At first.

"Well come on then, Isla," says her father, smiling up at her. "Come and give daddy a hug."

"Where's my *mother*?" she asks, pausing half-way down the stairs. Does not say 'mummy' to show that she is not a child anymore.

"Hell if I know," snaps Charles, turning to glance at James. "Probably topped herself by now. She turned to drink. After you disappeared. Just let herself go. Always crying and moaning. A nightmare to live with. I couldn't stand it."

No wonder, thinks Isla. *My poor mother. She doesn't know I am still alive. Yet her father does. He also knows the name she answers to. But how?* And then, as she steps down the last two stairs, she realizes. This is all him. He is the puppet master. He plans all this. They are just puppets. James and her. Dancing to every string he pulls.

She's afraid now. He is not the father she once adores. Wonders why he plans all this. But, of course, does not ask. Instead she lets him hug her. Tries not to recoil as his hands wander. Squeeze where they shouldn't. He is still very handsome. But there are creases at the corners of his eyes. Round his mouth. His lips have lost their fullness. Are thin. And mean.

"Well let's get your cases upstairs, Charles. And then Isla will rustle up some food. Once McGinty has gone. She's a half decent cook." He looks at her. "You'll go to your room now, won't you, Isla?"

He tries to smile at her reassuringly. This must all be such a shock. The sudden arrival of her father. Without her mother. He's sorry. But cannot revolt against Charles's plan.

"You can finish that essay on the slave trade," he says.

113

The irony of this does not escape her.

Isla is glad to flee. Bolts back up the stairs to her bedroom. Wishes now that the door is locked. Is he going to creep in during the night like he did sometimes at Oakwood? But he doesn't. And she soon finds out why.

That night, after she cooks bacon and eggs. After they sit at the kitchen table, the three of them. After she pushes the food aimlessly round her plate in pretence of eating, whilst her father and James give each other lingering looks, they go into the parlour.

"Will you play for us, Isla?" asks James. "You'll be amazed, Charles. I've been teaching her. She'll soon be better than me."

Isla plays Beethoven's Moonlight Sonata. Note perfect.

"Bravo!" Charles claps. Gets up and pours himself another whisky. He's had four already, thinks James. He never thought of him as a drinker.

"Again!" he says.

Isla plays it again. And whilst her fingers float over the keys, finding their way to each note, Charles lurches across the room to James. Grabs him. Kisses him. They moan. Groan. Isla stops playing and swivels round on the piano stool. Cannot believe what she witnesses.

"That's disgusting!" she cries. "You're both disgusting!"

She doesn't expect the blow. How fast her father moves. His face, ruddy with rage, right in front of her.

"Don't you ever, ever, speak to me like that again!" He spits at her. Slaps her. "Do you understand?"

Isla remains mute. Looks across at James. He lays on the sofa, mouths 'I'm sorry', a sheepish expression on his face. How could he? How could they?

"Answer me!" orders her father.

She does not answer. Prepares to leave the room. Then two things happen in sequence. With consequence. Firstly, Charles grabs her. Twists her arm. Isla shrieks. Which is when Chad rushes in from the kitchen and seizing a trouser leg between his teeth, shakes it. Growls.

Charles immediately releases Isla. Kicks out at the dog.

"Get that bloody cur off me!" he shouts.

"*He's* not a cur." Isla remarks. "It's you who is the cur."

And with a withering backward glance, she leaves the parlour. Slams the door behind her. She's shaking. But she knows Chad will not let her father come after her. Will protect her. He's a good judge of a man's character. Their innate nature. She wishes she were.

Now she hears them arguing. James and her father. Arguing over her. Over Chad.

"I expect you've been soft with her. Well, you obviously feed her well. But discipline? She needs discipline, James. Or she'll never give us what we want." Charles.

What is it they want she wonders?

"I haven't needed to discipline her much. Only at first. She behaves. Is a joy to be with. She's clever. Kind. I love her. As I always have." James. His words warm her.

"Not too much, I hope." Charles laughs. But it is not a laugh of amusement. "And that dog. That dog loves her. Too much. Well it's not to come in the house anymore. It's a farm dog. It can live in one of the barns. It has taken a dislike to me. And I have taken a dislike to it!"

"But Chad has always lived in the house. He's part of the family. He won't understand." James again. Defending.

"He's a bloody animal, James. He doesn't need to understand. We've both risked a lot to get to this point. We can't let it all fall apart because of a damn dog." Charles. Defensive.

She's heard enough. Runs to her room. Sobs. No more cosy evenings with James and Chad. No more walks in the gloaming. And all Chad's done is see behind the charming veneer. See what lurks beneath. Why couldn't she?

That night when Isla is in bed there's a tapping on her door. Not her father she thinks. He would just come in, invited or not. So James then.

"It's me," she hears him say as the door creaks open.

Isla shuffles up the bed. Emerges. It's so cold she's cocooned herself in the blankets. Pulled the eiderdown over her head.

He's carrying a glass of Ribena in one hand. Two capsules in the other.

"Take them," he says.

"But I thought…"

"It's your father," he says ruefully. "He wants you to have them every night."

Isla wonders why. But has a sneaky feeling she knows.

Taking the capsules out of his hand, she pops them in her mouth. Sips the Ribena. Swallows. And closing her eyes, slips back down into the warmth of her cocoon.

James switches off the light and softly closes the door. Locks it.

Isla spits the capsules out. She knows just how to secrete capsules and tablets into the pouches of her cheeks. Swallow yet keep them in her mouth. And like a hamster, disgorge them. Hide them in a safe place. She creates a hidden pocket in the lining of an old jacket that no longer fits. Sews two buttons, one on the flap, one on the pocket. Uses a piece of knicker elastic to wrap round the buttons. Close the flap. Her father will never think to look there. Why should he? He'll believe, like James, that she takes them. Sleeping tablets, she imagines.

And that first night, because she is wide awake, she hears their rutting animalistic noises. Buggery. Bestiality. Isla reads all about it. Cannot believe it of James. Yet the more she mulls over it, the more she realizes it's not about that. It's about the love between two people, irrespective of gender, sex or age.

She has no idea then that decades later society will accept such liaisons. That in the twentieth century man will marry man. And woman will marry woman. That one of her favourite singers will be Elton John. That he will 'come out' as a homosexual. Marry his lover. Have a son. Be happy. It's all about love. Like the love she feels for James. Despite knowing he is almost as old as her father.

She wishes he hasn't come. Wishes James doesn't love Charles. At least not in that way.

But this fifth Christmas everything changes. On Christmas Eve Charles brings a turkey out of the van. Plucked and ready to stuff. He asks James to fetch potatoes and vegetables. Isla to show him where everything is kept. Then orders both out of the kitchen. Like Oakwood, thinks Isla.

"Don't worry," she says. "This is what he does. But I have no idea why. He probably will not dine with us either. Just drink too much." She smiles at him. "But he'll likely creep down in the night and eat…A lot," she adds.

Another facet of Charles he doesn't know. And wonders how many more aspects of this man he forsakes all for he will find.

And it is just as Isla says. On Christmas Day the farmhouse is filled with mouth-watering aromas. And they are banished to the parlour. James lights the kindling in the grate. Neither comment that the lights on the tree have all been removed. That the only present under the tree is for Isla. From James.

It's a book on the Human Body. He hopes it will help Isla understand hers. She hugs him.

"Thank you," she says, her small breasts pushing against his chest. He feels aroused. And confused and disgusted at himself, pushes her abruptly away.

"Look," says James, trying to atone. He pulls a battered looking box from under the tree. "Your father bought a new game for us all to play."

Monopoly, Isla reads on the lid. Shows no interest. He's hurt her. More than her father's fist ever could.

James pushes it back under the tree.

"Why don't we go and see Chad then?" he says. "I'm sure he'll be pleased to see you."

He fetches her a coat and some boots. And opening the front door, steps out, Isla behind him.

"Oh!" she exclaims. "It's beautiful! A winter wonderland."

And it is. The farmyard, the barn roofs. The trees and hills in the distance, are all blanketed in snow. Even the loch has a dusting. It lays on a thin veneer of ice.

"If the temperature drops below freezing for a few weeks," James is saying, "which it will, the shallow parts of the loch will be frozen enough to skate on. Have you ever skated before?"

"Only on roller boots," says Isla. "I'm pretty decent."

"I'm sure you are." He pauses. "Very decent indeed."

His feet make virgin prints in the snow as they cross the yard. Isla tries to hop in and out of them, so it looks like only one person walks. It feels good to do something childish. Inane. They go past the cow byre where the few milking cows are stalled for the winter. Are passing a large barn which houses straw, hay and fodder, when Isla pauses. Something glints in the bright winter sun.

"What are you doing?" James calls back.

"Just looking," she replies. "Is that your car?" She goes closer.

It's covered with sacks, but part of the bonnet, the headlights and large wheel arches are visible.

"Yes, it is! I remember. I remember the lovely sparkly bronze colour."

She reads the number plate, JDZ 777. Of course she thinks, JD, James Duncan. And commits this to memory. Senses it may, one day, be of importance.

"Not much use as a farm vehicle," says James. "That's why I got the pick-up. Much more practical. But I don't want to part with it..." He's pushing a door of an old, disused outhouse. An old wooden door with iron fitments which creaks and groans as it opens. "Come on, Miss Nosey Parker," he calls. "I know you love cars. But I thought you wanted to see Chad."

Isla trudges through the snow. Catches him up.

Inside the outhouse it's cold but not freezing. Charles's boxes and crates are stacked up against a wall. There's straw on the floor. A bowl of dirty water. And in the corner a couple of bales, on top of which lays Chad. The shiny black coat is less shiny, but much denser. His thick winter coat. He leaps up when he sees them. Isla drops to her knees. His raspy tongue licks all over her face.

Wrapping her arms around his fluffy neck, she whispers into his fur, "I'm sorry."

"He's alright. Aren't you, boy?" James says. "Don't worry. I'll bring him a big bowl of Christmas fare for his supper." He ruffles the dog's fur. "He'll scoff the lot, won't you buddy?"

Something he notices Isla no longer does. In fact, despite Charles's sumptuous Christmas dinner, he notices she only eats the turkey and the odd sausage. "And he'll be out with McGinty and the sheep tomorrow," he adds. "That's what he loves best."

"I never knew my father was so cruel," Isla says. "He's changed. Or maybe, he was always cruel. And I never spent enough time with him to see it."

James remains silent.

It will be the year that Isla turns fifteen when they both will learn what Charles is truly capable of.

Chapter 21

That winter is fierce. Bitter winds blow across the loch from the hills. The cows are brought into the barn. Fed hay cut and baled in the summer. James, McGinty and Chad are constantly out, monitoring the sheep. McGinty puts up a crude shelter where Gruffyd and his harem can flock together to keep out of the wind and rain. Keep each other warm. As long as it keeps dry, their thick fleecy coats protect them against the elements. But snow and ice can be a hazard. If ice forms on their coats, their hooves, they cannot keep warm. Cannot feed. And illness can settle like the snow.

Charles goes with them. At first just to be close to James. But then he starts to help. Takes warm water to put in the water troughs. Fodder should the snow lay too deep, and they are unable to ruminate. Removes the ice from their hooves and coats.

"They're rumen-based," James explains to her.

"What!" exclaims Isla. "They've come all the way from Rome?"

He laughs, not knowing if she is joking or genuine.

"Rumen," he says. "Not Roman."

Isla laughs now.

"Two stomachs. I know. And they rely on their rumens being active to produce enough heat to keep them warm."

"You do actually read all those books in your room then," he says, grinning at her.

"Why, James. Don't you know I'm a veritable mine of information?" And she is.

Over the weeks and months of the new year Charles becomes more involved. He learns to milk the cows. Enjoys squeezing their udders and watching the creamy white liquid fill the bucket. He gathers the eggs from the coop when the hens are let out to range free. But strangely he will have nothing to do with Boris or Betty, or any of their piglets. The farm seeps into his psyche. Files away the sharp edges. Spring which heralds new life, new beginnings, drowns his sometime melancholy.

The physical toil on the land when Summer announces herself, when there is so much more to do, mutes his angst. Snuffs out the fire in his soul. They are quite a team, James, McGinty and he. It's almost like being back in the field tents, he thinks. But without the bombs, the screaming. The blood and gore. Chad, however, is another matter. Perhaps something he will have to deal with one day. It is not just some people that don't deserve to live he thinks.

But as Isla keeks through the slats, sees the bond between Chad and McGinty. The dog's constant avoidance of her father. She realizes the core of Scott McGinty is good and kind. That he is devoted to the farm and his family. That it is her father who is bad. Has the rotten core.

Chapter 22

Time marches on. Where it goes Isla does not know. It's now 1963, her fifteenth year. She knows this because at the beginning of each new year she adds a year to her age. Her birthdays come and go without acknowledgement. She's glad. Doesn't want to remember. Six years on the memory of her ninth birthday still lays raw. Is too painful to dwell upon.

Home schooling by James stops when her father comes. So, Isla schools herself by studying every volume of every book that languishes on her shelves. Then tests herself. Her grasp of mathematics is on a par with a university student. Something she knows she will never be.

Instead, her father and James put this skill to use. She now does the farm accounts and any other paperwork. They buy her a new desk. It has a red leather top. More drawers. An ink well. Places for pens, rubbers and pencils.

There is a beautiful, embossed ledger which lies open on the red leather top. And there she sits, surrounded by a tidy order of cheque books, stubs, orders and invoices. Enters each transaction in her neat penmanship. Adds and subtracts each column so they all balance. Whilst the sounds of the farmyard float up through the window. And the pungent aroma of the animals she loves fill her room.

In the Spring she hears the lambs bleating. Wishes she could go out and frolic with them. Dwynwen, a calm and gentle ewe, is prone to having triplets. It's a problem that fortunately doesn't happen very often. Sheep only have two teats. Enough to cope with a single lamb or twins. Sometimes the third one or an orphan lamb, is brought into the farmhouse. Warmed on straw in a wooden box, which is placed by the Aga, the simmer door left open. And is bottle fed, using milk expressed from a ewe birthing a single lamb.

In the night, Isla gets to do this. It's her favourite thing in the world. Even though the lambs are messy. Produce a thin, yellowy excrement that she needs to clean up. During the day when she must not be seen, Mrs McGinty mothers the lambs. If Isla hears they don't survive, she sobs her heart out. James comforts her. Says it's not her fault. It was meant to be. But Charles just tells her to shut up.

"You can't have life without death," he says. "And you can't have death without life."

This summer is unusually hot. Her bedroom, with the door shut and the window only able to open a fraction, feels like the saunas she reads about. So she doesn't dress. Lays on top of the bed naked. Reads. I'll dress later she thinks. When it's time to go down. Get the dinner ready. She doesn't expect any visitors. But this particular day, she has one.

Since Charles's arrival two years ago she has been locked up again. By day. And night. Her father's edict. Not to be flouted.

Lunch time. She hears the key turning in the lock. And before she can cover herself or wedge something behind the door, it opens. And there he stands. Her father. A look of distaste on his face as his eyes rove her nakedness. He's carrying a tray of food.

"Look at your arms and legs, Isla," he says. "They're like twigs. Why are you doing this to yourself. You'll never be a real woman…"

I don't want to be, she thinks. Knows what is expected of a real woman.

"No man ever wants to bed a stick insect."

Isla clamps her hands over her ears. "Sticks and stones may break my bones, but words will never break me," she chants over and over. A mantra to block out his cruel words.

He yanks her hands away.

"You'll eat this," he barks. "All of it. We're not blind you know. We watch you getting thinner. Gaunter. And we need you fit and well."

"What for?" she dares to say. "So I can be a puppet and dance to your tune."

He refrains from slapping her. Instead he says, "You will eat every little bit. I mean it. Leave one morsel and you will be punished. Is that understood?"

Not waiting for her reply he spins on his heels and departs. The key turns in the lock.

Isla stares at the heaped plate of bread and butter. Cheese. Slices of ham. An apple.

She waits until the farmyard is empty. Breaks the bread into buttery crumbs. Crumbles the cheese. And standing on her bed, stretches up and throws it out of the window. The chickens will find it. Peck it all up. And then she eats the ham and apple. Nothing there to make her fat.

Her father looks pleased when in the evening he unlocks her door and sees the empty plate.

"And empty that chamber pot too," he says. "It stinks."

Isla carries it as carefully as she can, trying not to let its contents slop over the top. Down the stairs, through the kitchen, all the way to the bathroom where she empties it down the toilet. Washes her hands. And begins to prepare their dinner.

Afterwards, when they have eaten and the dishes are cleared away, Charles goes to the parlour. Comes back with a decanter of whisky and three crystals glasses. The box containing Monopoly tucked under his arm.

They have played it several times. But Isla always bankrupts her father. Charles does not like to lose.

"Come on," he says. "Can't let my beautiful daughter trump her father. Or you James," he adds.

They open the windows. And the kitchen door. The front door. So a breeze can blow through. Charles fills two of the glasses a quarter full. Pours a couple of shots into the third. Gives it to Isla.

"It's whisky," he says. "The best. A 1960's 'Longmorn'. I brought it with me. Sip it slowly. Savour it."

But Charles does not sip his. He slugs it back in one swallow. Pours some more. Meanwhile, James takes the Monopoly board out of the box and puts it on the kitchen table. Along with the houses, hotels. Chance and Community cards. The Title Deed cards for each property. The paper money and the metal tokens. He watches Charles and wonders where this night will lead.

Isla takes a sip of whisky. It slips down her throat like liquid fire.

Charles picks up the top hat token. He always insists that he has this. That he is the banker. James takes the car with driver. And Isla has the Scottie dog.

And so, shaking the die, they begin. In the small hall between the kitchen and lounge there is a grandfather clock. Isla hears the sound of the pendulum as it ticks away the minutes. Chimes on the hour. It's 11 o'clock. Dark now. But still warm and muggy. A thunderstorm is brewing. And Charles is on his fourth glass of whisky. James and Isla have barely touched theirs.

"Rent please!" cries Isla as Charles lands on Mayfair.

The rent is high as she has a hotel on it. James is already bankrupt and out of the game.

Charles starts to count the rent. Then stops. Stares at the money he is counting. The board.

"You know this game is about property, money," he slurs.

They nod.

"Well, I'm going to tell you a story…"

Story? Hah! Thinks Isla. *He just wants to stop the game. He knows I am going to win. Again.*

But then he says, "It's a story that must never leave your lips. Or the farm."

He staggers to the dresser. Puts another shot of whisky into his glass. Sits clumsily back at the table. The glass swipes the houses off Isla's properties. The money flutters to the floor.

"My mother." He laughs. "My loving mother…" Another swig of whisky. "She'd have left me with no property, no money. Not a farthing to my name…"

James and Isla glance at each other.

"Did I tell you my father is killed, 1915…" He doesn't wait for a reply. "That I am born at the end of 1917." He leers at them. "Do the maths."

"Does that mean…" James begins to say.

"That I'm a bastard? Yes, I am. She spends my whole life telling me. Though she has the decency to put my father's name on the birth certificate." He scoffs. "For propriety's sake."

"Do you know who your real father is?" Isla asks naively.

"Oh yes. She is always fond of telling me. Of likening me to him."

James and Isla hold their breath. Wait.

"It's the pretty, pink-faced butcher boy. He gives her extra meat rations. Steaks and gammons. In return for favours. But when she tells him she's pregnant, he doesn't want to know. And she hates him. Just as she hates me. From the minute I come screaming out of her womb. To the minute I snuff out her life."

Snuff out? Have their ears heard correctly? James takes a glug of whisky. Isla knocks hers back in one. Somehow, she thinks she'll need it.

"D'you know," he slurs. "She never shows me one ounce of affection or love. Oh yes, she feeds me. Scraps." He grunts like a pig. "Makes me eat them off the floor. Baths me…" He grimaces. "In water that is too hot and scalds my skin. But gets me out before any reddening will last." A slight pause.

"Or water too cold, I freeze. And sometimes, just for her added pleasure, she pushes me under. Holds me there until I think I am going to drown. Then, at the last minute, pulls me up. I am her punch bag. She knows just where to aim each blow, so no bruising will be seen. To send me to school in clean clothes, hair neatly brushed so no-one suspects. I am just this weedy little boy who doesn't fit in."

James and Isla are horrified.

"Charles," James says, putting his hand over his, "you don't have to tell us."

"I damn well do."

He is finding it hard to get the words out. But the magma, beneath which his chilling childhood has been kept, has burst. And lets the lava flow. He can't stop it.

"There's a cupboard under the stairs…"

Isla remembers this. It's just inside the hall. It's where she and Penelope make dens. Have midnight feasts.

"She locks me in it. For hours. Sometimes days. When she comes back, I've usually soiled myself." He shudders with the memory. "She makes me take my clothes off. Uses a belt to thwack my bare bottom. Calls me a filthy bastard. As I get older, she says I look just like him. A pretty, pink-faced pig."

Charles tries to get up. Lurches. Slumps across the table, knocking everything off the board. A crystal glass shatters on the stone floor. Shards glisten amongst the tokens, houses, hotels, cards, and money.

"And Christmas!" He scoffs. "Want to know why I don't like Christmas?"

They don't. But fear he's going to tell them anyway. A gust of wind blasts through the open door. The air changes. Thunder rumbles over the hills. But they close neither the door nor their ears.

"From the moment I can stand, I watch her cook," he is slurring. "I take it all in. And, oh, on Christmas day Oakwood is full of delicious smells. I am hungry. Always hungry. But she locks me in the cupboard. There is no food for me. No present. She sits at the long table in the dining room, surrounded by antiques. With the finest silverware and best crockery. Dines on her own.

She knows I will sneak down to the kitchen in the night. And I do. There are scraps of turkey, perhaps a potato or two, a sausage, some stuffing, strewn across the floor. Blobs of gravy poured over. A note on the table. It reads 'FOR THE PIG'. And because I am starving, I drop to my knees and shovel it all down, like the pig she calls me. Lick up the gravy. For should a morsel be left, the floor not completely clean, I am severely punished."

"That's horrible," says Isla.

"You poor chap," says James. "Was there no-one you could confide in? No-one you could trust?"

Charles spits.

"How? I'm not allowed friends. She hides me away should anyone call. Which they seldom do. I am alone. With her." This paradox does not elude either James or Isla. Charles suddenly smiles. "But I get taller, bigger, don't I? So the physical abuse stops. A kind of blessing perhaps. Yet the verbal tirades she keeps up until I leave Oakwood. Because, despite her treatment of me, I am clever. Get into Grammar School. And then Medical School in London. I am free of her. Or so I think."

He's rambling on. Back in that time. That life. James and Isla do not interrupt. They are both focused on those two earlier words he mutters, 'snuff out'.

"So what happens?" Isla tentatively asks. She needs to know now. Despite James shaking his head at her.

"I get a telephone call. She's ill, she tells me. Her diabetes is worse. Her kidneys and liver are failing. I need you son," she says. "It's urgent."

"Son?" Now Charles laughs out loud. "Never do I hear that word leave her lips. Need? Never does she need me. But her flattery and *my* need. Well, they beguile me. I go…"

He grabs James's glass, which still has some whisky in.

"I think you've had enough, my love," James says, putting his hand over the top of the glass. Hopes the 'my love' will soften him. It doesn't.

"Don't you tell me what to do!" Charles shouts.

The curtains billow. Lightning flashes in the darkening room. Etches Charles's angst-ridden face.

"Nobody tells me what to do! She tries. And I get rid of her. Some people don't deserve to live."

But she's his mother Isla thinks, horrified. Could he have gotten rid of her mother too?

"Why?" Isla asks.

"Because when I get to Oakwood, there she is, sitting under the awning. A glass of gin and tonic beside her. Like the Lady of the manor."

"Well, well," she says, peering over the top of her sunglasses, "the prodigal son returns! Her voice is weaker. I can see she's frail. Ailing."

"What's so urgent?" I ask.

"I need you, Charles. I need you to look after me."

My name. For the first time she speaks my name. I look at her. Her eyes are rheumy. Bloodshot. Her skin has a yellowy hue. Waxy and crinkly.

"Like good sons do," she says. "Look after their mams."

"I'm almost through medical school," I say. "I've worked hard to get where I am. And I am not going to throw it away for a woman who does not deserve the name 'mother'. As I do not deserve the names 'bastard', and 'pig'. Or any of the other names you call me."

"Well then," she says, getting up and walking slowly through the open dining room doors into the house. "You've made your bed. Best you lie in it. But it will not be here." She cackles like the witch she is. "Tomorrow I shall go to the Solicitors. And make a new Will. You can kiss goodbye to Oakwood, Charles. I shall bequeath the house, its contents and all my assets to the War Veterans. You're just like your biological father. Gutless. A pig! And you're no son of mine."

The smell of sulphur seeps into the kitchen as they listen. Scores his story with its acridity. So it's not the war that changes him, realises James. Creates this cruel streak. The anger he tries to hide. It's this. His abusive dreadful childhood. But he never dreamt that his lover could be capable of murder.

Because this is what Charles tells them. Between the cracks of thunder, the flashes of lightening. That it's this, his mother's final spite what breaks him. He's a doctor. Knows how to tamper with her medication. His mother injects herself with insulin three times a day. He replaces her next syringe with one he puts a lethal dose in. Unsuspecting, she injects herself. Then, turning the taps on in the bathroom, fills a bath.

He waits until she climbs in. Lays there. And then he enters. Looms over the bath. She's already sleepy. Her eyes when she sees him say it all. She knows. Without a pang of conscience, he pushes her under. Water flows into her lungs. Drowns her. It's so easy. She's old and ill. No-one will notice. And they don't. Death by misadventure is written on the Death Certificate. Only he knows the truth. But now they do too.

"I watch as her life ebbs away," says Charles. "It's hypnotic. Cathartic. And a far better death than she deserves."

Then, with his demons set free, he slumps across the table in a drunken stupor.

"What a night!" exclaims James. And he's not referring to the storm. "At least I know why he doesn't even look at Boris and Betty. C'mon, give us a hand. Let's get him to bed."

So they take an arm each and drag him across the floor. He's a dead weight. And the effort of lugging him up the stairs, culls any conversation. Once in the bedroom, they drop him onto the bed. James turns to her.

"I'm sorry to ask you this, Isla. But could you clean up downstairs. I'll see to Charles. He's going to wake up with one hell of a hangover. And I bet you he won't remember this night. And what he's told us."

But I will, Isla thinks. I will never forget.

She goes back down to the kitchen. Sweeps up the broken glass. Picks up all the Monopoly bits and pieces and puts them back in the box. Replaces the lid. Washes up the two remaining glasses. Takes them, the decanter and the game back to the parlour. And then shutting the doors, turning out the lights, she climbs wearily up to her bedroom.

Strips off her clothes and collapses onto her bed. There she falls into a deep sleep. A sleep full of dreams. Dreams of monsters and ogres. All with her father's face. And neither the thunder nor the lightening as the storm passes over disturb her.

What does is the creak of her bedroom door as it opens. The storm has passed. The world is quiet again. And the air blows through her open window fresh and clean. Half asleep, Isla feels a body climb onto her bed. Slide under the covers beside her.

"It's only me," she hears James whisper in her ear. "I can't sleep with him tonight. He's been sick. He's snoring. And that sofa's too damn hard."

Isla spoons her body into his. Feels the warmth of him. Feels the comfort of his arms about her. And falls back to sleep. A dreamless sleep. All monsters and ogres vanquished.

When the cockerel announces a new day, she awakes. There is nobody in the bed except her. She is alone again.

Chapter 23

Just as James predicts, Charles makes no mention of the night before. The confession he makes. And he does have a hell of a hangover.

What he could not predict, is the change in Charles. He is more loving. Appears brighter. Lighter. More like the man James remembers. He even allows Chad back into the farmhouse. And Charles, seeing the work Chad does about the farm, learns to respect him. Whilst Chad, providing Charles does not threaten his 'flock', learns to tolerate him.

The months of July and August are filled with harvesting, gleaning, baling. It's been a long hot dry summer. The bales of straw are brought into the barns. The cowshed. The pigsty. The hen coop. There are plenty of bales of hay for fodder in the winter. The three men work the farm together. Each pulls their weight. Isla hears them whistling. McGinty whistles directions to Chad. James and her father whistle tunes from bygone days.

Autumn arrives in all her glory. Mists swirl on the hills. Across the loch. The light is golden. The leaves red. A new pattern develops. One of co-operation. Symmetry. But Isla's life remains the same. With its own pattern. Until...

But first there is Christmas. A poignant reminder to Isla that another year is about to pass. That it's almost seven years since she saw her mother. The mother she misses every single day of this twilight life she leads.

But this Christmas is different. Charles still takes over the kitchen as usual. Makes his mother's special stuffing. Her secret recipe. Which now only he knows. When he leaves Oakwood, he takes all his mother's recipes. Even though he could cook each one blindfolded, so many times did he stand and watch. The recipe for the stuffing is amongst them. He hopes, one day, to leave all her scribbled notes to someone special.

As Isla sets the table. Not with fine silver or china plates but with whatever she can find. Charles comes through the outside door.

"Set another place," he says, brushing snow off his overcoat.

She arches an eyebrow. He stares at her. His daughter. Not buxom but nevertheless, a beautiful young woman.

"That's wonderful, Charles," says James.

He's squatting down by the Aga, brushing Chad. The turkey and all its trimmings lay on a large oval dish behind the simmer door. The sprouts, carrots and gravy in their respective dishes and jugs on the top. A perfect meal waiting to be served.

Isla finds an extra plate, glass and cutlery. An extra napkin rolled up in its polished bone ring. She lights the candles. Sees in their flickering light the joy on James's face. Whilst the light in her goes out.

They pull crackers. Wear silly hats. Read silly jokes. Drink Babycham, which bursts with Somerset fruits. Isla eats little. She wants this Christmas to be like the others. Just her and James. Her father is drinking too much again. Is leery. She doesn't think there will be any dancing tonight.

But there is. James says to him. "Charles?"

"Present and correct, Sir."

Charles raises a glass to him. Lights a large fat cigar. James watches as the tip glows. He has never seen him smoke. Not even a cigarette.

"After the Christmas meal, which was, as always, splendid my love, we, that is Isla and I, usually dance."

"Don't let me stop you, *lover.*" Charles emphasises. And lounging back against the chair's spindles, puffs smoke up into the kitchen's aura. Like the nuclear bomb dropped in the war, it blossoms out. Pervades each nook and cranny with its pungent aroma.

So, James pushes the table up against the wall. Chad, anticipating, shoots under. Whilst Isla fetches the gramophone and some vinyls. She's not sure about this.

As Charles polishes off the Babycham, they are dancing Bebop. A variant of jazz that originates in America. He watches their fancy footwork with little interest. Lounges back in his chair. Smokes and drinks. Until the music for the rumba begins. James teaches Isla this when she is fourteen. And she's good. Loves the intimacy of the dance. The feel of James against her. The strange sensations that course through her body.

Charles sits up. His eyes narrow. He does not like his daughter's seductive closeness to James. Her sauciness. He gets up. Pushes them apart. Shoves Isla out of the way. Grabs the man he loves, and dances a highly charged, sexually frustrated, salsa with him. Another seductive dance which originates in New York.

Isla cannot watch. She's embarrassed. Finds it hard to believe she has a father so disgusting.

"Time you were abed, Isla," he says when it finishes. "I've had enough of watching you and James. He's *my* partner. He is not supposed to get intimate with you…Yet," he adds oddly. "I want him to myself. So, run along. James, will you go up with her, lock her in." He kisses him. "Then you and I can really party."

"You don't need to bother." Isla snorts. She wants to cry. But she won't. Not yet. "As if I would ever want to watch what you two do together. It's not right."

She turns her back on them and leaving the kitchen, climbs the stairs to her bedroom. James follows her anyway.

"Merry Christmas, Isla," he says, standing on the landing, the key hanging off his finger.

"Is it?" She slams the door in his face. Listens to the key turn in the lock. And throwing herself onto her bed, weeps. Her father spoils something special again. James hears the sobbing and with a heavy heart, walks back down the stairs to Charles. But what can he do? He has no say in the matter. Dare not deny his lover's needs.

Chapter 24

It's early morning. A morning like every other. Isla waits for her bedroom door to be unlocked so she can go downstairs to the bathroom. Perform her ablutions. Get dressed. And like every other morning, she wedges the chair under the door handle. Just in case.

As she finishes and prepares to go back to her room, her father calls out, "Isla! Wait!"

She waits. Notices that he sits at the kitchen table whilst James stands at the Aga, holding the handle of a large frying pan. She can hear fat spitting. Smell bacon. She also notices that there are three plates on the table. Three sets of knives and forks. Three mugs.

"Sit!" He barks. Like a Sergeant giving a military order, Isla thinks.

She sits.

"Will you," he says, nodding at a milk jug and large teapot on the table.

Isla puts milk in the three mugs. Picks up the teapot and fills them with tea. Just as James fills the plates with three slices of crispy bacon. Two fried eggs. Two slices of toast. There is a butter dish. The butter is churned from their own cows' milk.

Isla looks down at her plate. There's too much, she thinks. I can't eat all that. She pokes and prods at it. Moves the eggs around. James sits next to her.

"Just try," he whispers. He now knows full well Charles's wishes.

Isla waits for her father's reprimand. It doesn't come.

Instead he says, "You'll soon be sixteen. You're a young woman now, Isla. You don't need to be locked up. You're free."

He smiles at her. Despite his white hair and visible ageing he still presents a handsome face. How her friends used to envy her Isla recalls. If only they knew.

"Free?" she echoes. "I don't know how to be free. You've both made sure of that."

"Well, you're a clever woman," Charles says. He taps his head. "Brains, Isla. You've got plenty. You inherit them from me I'm sure." He wipes his chin where egg yolk dribbles down. "Use them. Work it out."

"You can help with the animals," James says. "Feed the chickens. Milk the cows. Work with Chad and the sheep. McGinty will teach you. And you can go with Mrs McGinty to the market. On the cart. Sit astride Bilbo. You can come into town with us. Look round the shops. You can come to the Highland Games with us. Dance. Have fun. You can walk. Swim. Get fit. You can do all the things you've wanted to do…"

"Whoa! Slow down, James." Charles is buttering some toast. "Perhaps, she doesn't want to do any of those things."

I did. But not anymore. Because you'll spoil it. Just by being there. I want it to be how it was. Before you came. Just me and James. But Isla's lips do not move. These thoughts will have no voice. They must remain unspoken.

She nibbles a bit of bacon.

"And how will you explain my sudden appearance?" she asks instead. "Won't folk find it odd?"

"We've already sorted that," says her father. "You don't think freedom comes without a price, dear daughter."

We've? Isla ponders on this. Waits to hear what the true cost to her sudden liberation will be. She does not believe for one moment that it's James who sorts this out. No, it's her father. The man who pulls the strings. Who has always pulled the strings.

"Give me your hand, Isla," he orders. "Your left…"

Isla turns to look at James. He nods.

She holds her hand out above the plate of congealing fried food.

And, like a conjuror, her father produces two rings out of somewhere. Just as he does when she is a child, when he conjures silver sixpences out of her friends' ears. And they all think he's marvellous.

One ring is a beautiful sapphire surrounded by diamonds. But it's the other he puts on first. Slides it over the knuckle of her fourth finger. It's yellow gold. A split wedding ring. Then he puts the sapphire engagement ring on top of it.

Isla spreads her fingers. Bends her hand up. Admires them. The light catches the diamonds making them sparkle. They really are very pretty.

"You are now Mrs Isla Duncan," he says. "James's wife. Quite respectable. Quite acceptable."

"And quite sudden." She scoffs. "Quite laughable actually. Where has my husband been hiding me then? Surely not locked in a bedroom with a chamber pot."

"Don't be so damn insolent!" snaps Charles.

He slaps her. Isla flinches but does not cry out.

And then, "They're a perfect fit," he continues. "I did wonder. But as soon as I saw your hands, I knew they would be. Your fingers are just like hers. You see the rings belonged to my mother."

Isla stares at them aghast. She no longer thinks them pretty. After what she knows, she finds them hideous. Whenever she looks at them, she will remember what he did to his mother. But she dare not take them off.

"Oh look," says Charles. "Here comes McGinty now."

Chad jumps up and all waggy-tailed bounds across the kitchen to the door.

The look on Scott McGinty's face is priceless. He's come for his mug of tea and bacon sandwich. Expects to see Charles and James. Not a member of the female species. The prettiest lass he's ever seen. Just sitting at the table as if she's always been here.

"This is Isla," Charles says. "James's wife."

He watches the wonder, the disbelief, in McGinty's expression and before he can ask questions, rushes on.

"They meet on the mainland. She works there. Lives there. But after they marry there's a terrible accident. They don't think she'll survive. She is in hospital for many months. Then rehabilitation. But now she is back where she belongs. On the farm. With my brother."

McGinty doffs his cap. "Guid mornin. Nice tae meit ye," he says. "Yer a bonnie wee lassie."

"Unfortunately," Charles says, lowering his voice, "the accident damaged her brain. She finds it hard to talk. Not quite right in the head." He adds as an aside.

"Pur wee hinnie," says McGinty.

How could I ever have believed him bad? Thinks Isla, hearing the genuine concern in his voice. Seeing the kindness in his eyes,

"Well, say hello, Isla."

"Hello, Isla", Isla says.

Charles glares at her.

James smirks. Despite all, she still has a sense of mischief.

"Well aw'd stay," says McGinty, slugging the mug of tea back with the last morsel of bread and bacon. He whistles Chad. "But A maun awa. Dwynwen, Bethan and Glynis are aboot tae ha' lammichies."

"English, McGinty." Charles reprimands. "If you please."

"Isla knows he refers to the ewes," says James. "I told her their names. I think she can guess what a 'lammichie' is. Why don't you go with him, Isla?"

"Aye. Come wi' us," says McGinty.

Isla pushes her chair back and going to the scullery, finds herself a jacket and boots that fit. Without saying a word, she follows Scott McGinty and Chad out of the door.

****

"Are you sure I won't be in the way?" she asks as she trots behind him. He's a big man. With a big step.

"Dinna fash yersel lassie. But can ye coorie up."

I know what that means, thinks Isla. And tries to match her stride with his.

They go all the way to the outer pastures where both the sheep and cows are grazing. There's a shepherd's hut and a wicker lambing chair where a less robust lamb can be placed out of the wind and rain temporarily. Unless it requires to come into the farmhouse.

McGinty shouts "Come-bye" to Chad, who immediately circles to the left. Then it's, "Awa tae me" and Chad goes to the right. He's rounding up a large sheep with horns. Gruffyd, thinks Isla. "He's gittin in the wa," says McGinty. "A reit crabbit."

Isla tries to remember the commands. Perhaps, one day he will let her handle Chad.

Chad keeps his eye on the ram whilst McGinty scans the pastures for the ewes.

"Ane, twa, three, fower, five, sax, seven, aicht, nine."

Isla hears him count whilst, awed, she just stands, gazing all around. Breathing in the beautiful pure air. All she breathes through her bedroom window is the smell of the farmyard. The animals. She hasn't been outside in the day for so long. When her father arrives, even the night walks around the farm stop. She can no longer leave her coffin. Fly out into the velvet dark.

"Can ye gie's a haund lassie," McGinty suddenly shouts.

Isla snaps out of her reverie. She knows he doesn't really need any help. He's just trying to be kind. But she goes across to him. Sees he's trying to get one of the ewes up on her legs.

"'Tis Bethan," he says. "She maun hae the lammichie noo. She's tackin tae long."

Isla helps him support Bethan. Once up, things happen quickly. A large bubble appears out of her back end. It breaks, expelling a watery liquid, 'amniotic fluid', James tells her later, which spurts all over their feet. But Isla is entranced because, at the same time, she can see the tip of a nose and two front feet, and Bethan's first lamb slithers out into the world. Isla watches as Bethan cleans it and then there it is, on its wobbly little legs, ready to suckle.

"She'll be awrite noo." He grins at her.

Isla knows there will be another birth soon. That Bethan will eat the placentas. It's nature's way. And it seems that the other ewes are doing perfectly well on their own.

"Taphadh leat hinnie," he says. "Thenk ye."

"You're welcome," Isla says shyly.

And then he's calling Chad, "Awa laddie. That'll do. Come wi's," he says to Isla. And she follows them. Her new-found friends.

This day, her first taste of freedom, feels surreal. Strange. Special. And it is Scott McGinty and Chad who teach Isla how to 'be' again. Her legs cannot quite catch up with her desire to explore further. They have been side-lined for so long. But gradually, day by day, she walks with him. Helps when she can. Exercises. Gets fitter. And, full of her newfound confidence, begins to explore farther afield.

"Where have you been today?" asks James.

"I walked to a village called Port Bannatyne," Isla says. "It's by the sea. Can you believe they actually have trams here? Right until 1936. Now it's just an empty track. I walk along it, all the way to a bay which has a glorious beach. Ettrick Bay, it's called. Oh it's beautiful James…"

As are you, he thinks. Her hair shines. Her eyes sparkle. Her cheeks glow. Blushed by the wind and the sun.

"There's absolutely nobody about," she says. "So, do you know what I do?" She giggles at her audacity.

James has never heard her giggle. It's joyous.

"I take of all my clothes. I wade out. And I swim. The water is wonderful!" She grins. "And I don't sink. I remember the strokes Miss Tong teaches us. She takes us swimming to the local baths once a week. The water is always cold and has a funny smell." Isla laughs. "Someone says it's because it's built over an old graveyard." She shivers. "But this water is warm. Smells like the sea. And it is so clear. I want to swim forever. To the end of time."

James wishes he could be there too. Swim to the end of time with her. Perhaps, one day he can. If Charles permits it. If work allows it.

"I'm going to find Windy Hill," she is saying. "Did you know it's the highest point on Bute. I'm going to walk to the top. And just stand. Let the wind blow through my hair. I haven't felt the wind in so long." She flexes her muscles. Laughs. "See, I'm getting stronger, James. Fitter."

He can see this. As does Charles.

She finds Windy Hill and it is as blowy and beautiful as she imagines. Then her feet take her along many paths to many hidden gems around the island. She walks miles. Seldom meets a soul. If she does, she nods and says, "Hello, isn't it a lovely day." Or. "Hello, isn't it a windy day." And other weather-related phrases which give no rise to conversation.

One day, on her travels, she comes across St. Ninians Bay where an old church is open for prayer. Isla goes in. And just sits. It's so quiet. So still. As if the world has ended and this is all there is. Absolute peace. She leaves with a spring in her step. Her heart uplifted.

In the August of that year, Charles suddenly announces.

"Look sharp! We're away to the Highland Games in Rothesay. Get your glad rags on, James. You too, Mrs Duncan," he adds.

Isla digs out a white catsuit and some white ballerina pumps from her wardrobe. She buys them in town on one of her trips with Mrs McGinty. She likes the floaty white material. The tiny pearls embroidered on the bodice. They are translucent and when the light catches them, they glow. At the time she has no idea when she will wear these. But thinks now will be the perfect time.

They go in Charles's new toy. A blue quad cab. He sells the van he arrives in. Splashes out on what is, in effect, a large jeep. But this has more space. Can tackle any terrain. Isla likes it because you sit up high. She has a scenic view of the island. James likes it because it's fun to drive. And it certainly causes a stir when they arrive in town.

When they reach Rothesay, Isla hears the haunting music of the pipe bands. Stands awed as she watches row after row of marching kilted men. Each impeccably attired. Matching. Each in himself anonymous. The whole, a glorious parade of blue and red skirted clones.

There is so much to see. She spots Mrs McGinty with two of the older girls and three little ones hanging onto the pleats of her skirt. The older McGintys work on the farm now. Two laddies, Donald and Hamish. Two hinnies, Fiona and Caitlin. They are all hard workers. Boisterous. Good fun. Kind. And they speak to her in English, with just a hint of a Scottish accent. Isla loves them all. She waves. One of the girls runs across to her. It's Fiona. She's breathless with excitement.

"Oh you must come Isla." She grabs Isla's hands. "Donald and Hamish are playing shinty," she cries, "they were picked for the team. And me and Caitlin will be dancing later."

Fiona looks at James. "Don't worry, Mr Duncan," she says. "Ma told us. We'll take good care of her." And before Charles can create a scene, Isla skips merrily away with Fiona. She has no idea what shinty is.

There are two teams. She spies Donald and Hamish. They are running, carrying curved sticks. Fiona tells her they are called camans. They're made of wood, the curve slanted on both sides so they can hit the ball either side. It's a small leather ball. But oh, they hit it so high. Up into the air. All over.

Isla is entranced. Cheers and claps with Fiona. And then her eyes alight on them. Her bodyguards she thinks. Coming to check. James takes her hand. So they look like a proper couple. And, reluctantly, she leaves the match and goes with them.

"By the bye, Isla. You look lovely," Fiona calls after her.

Charles tuts. "I hope you've remembered what we told you." He says. "Not too much of the chit chat."

"Yes." Isla says. "I remember. Anyway they think I'm not right in the head. I wonder why?" She dares to glare at him. "Oh yes, daddy dear, it's thanks to you!"

"Shut up!" Charles growls. A low growl that others cannot hear. "I'm not your father here, remember?" He grabs her hand. Squeezes the fingers together so hard it hurts. "Just so you don't forget, Isla."

"Did you see the McGinty boys Charles, playing shinty?" James says, intervening before any embarrassing outburst erupts.

"It's so exciting!" exclaims Isla. She will not let him see he's hurt her. "I'd love to play."

"I believe," says James, "there's a Shinty Club somewhere in Rothesay. Perhaps, Isla, you could join."

"And perhaps she could not," says her father. "It's too dangerous. And we don't want her getting injured, do we?"

Isla wonders on this. But then she does get to join in something else. After the displays finish, folk start to gather. The bagpipes play 'Ceol Beag'— rhythmic toe-tapping music that inspires folks' feet to dance. Charles, James, and Isla join a group. Dance the reels. Create the figures.

But then the 'Strathspey' starts. A slower dance for couples. James partners Isla, whilst Charles stands at the side. Watching. Seething.

"I'm enjoying this, James," she says. "I feel special."

"And you are," he replies.

Charles follows the smiles on their faces. Is filled with a jealous rage. So when pipe music for the Gay Gordons begins, he roughly cuts in. Shoves Isla out of the way. Monopolizes James. Isla, jostled by fast stepping, twirling couples, and thronged by so many people without anyone to protect her, flees.

The grass is still slightly wet from some overnight rain. Isla's ballerina pumps slip. And she skids. When she gets to her feet, she sees that a few tiny streaks of green stain the pristine white outfit. She wants to go home. But knows she can't. Not until her father decrees it. They leave at the end of the day when the Games are all over for another year.

As soon as she is in her bedroom, Isla strips off the catsuit. Kicks off the pumps. She's angry. Her father spoils something again. Bundling them up, she shoves them into a holdall at the back of the wardrobe. The holdall she sees in Rothesay, the same day she purchases the catsuit. It's commodious. Colourful. Striped with the colours of the rainbow. Isla buys it. Thinks perhaps one day such a bag might be useful.

But her father does not spoil the Ice Cream Alliance annual conference, which they attend later in the month. It's held in the Pavilion.

"Ooh come and try this," Isla calls when the sampling begins. When they get to try a tiny taste of all the different ice creams. "It's absolutely scrumptious."

Now, it is her father and James who trail behind. Are caught up in her enthusiasm. Taste a teaspoon of this. A teaspoon of that. Not a single argument. No angst. It's just a perfect day. And because her father is in such a good mood this day, it's a perfect night too. They drink whisky. Enact charades. Sing songs as Isla plays the piano.

But this will be Isla's last perfect night. For it is not long before she learns the true cost of her freedom.

Chapter 25

It is the evening. Isla cooks their dinner. The table is set. Ready for when they come in after another long day. She hopes they remember to take off their muddy boots when they do. She does keep asking.

"Yirdit," Mrs McGinty cries when she comes into the kitchen and finds mud all over the floor, which she vigorously cleans.

Isla is not sure whether she is swearing or stating a fact. But she is very fond of Mrs McGinty. And Mrs McGinty is very fond of Isla. When she's not out exploring, Isla helps her. Churns the butter and cheese. Loads the cart if the men are out. Goes with her when she takes the produce to town and some of the outlying villages. She's soon well known. For her sunny smile. Her simplicity.

Mrs McGinty teaches Isla to knit. To sew. How to make simple clothes for herself. And as she watches how quickly Isla masters each new craft, thinks the lassie no less 'reit in the heid' than she herself is. When they go to town, Isla buys needles, pins, scissors, wool, and cloth. Patterns.

Persuades James and her father to give her enough money to buy a sewing machine, which she and Mrs McGinty load onto the cart and bring back to the farm. And when magazines come over from the mainland, Isla buys them. There is a new fashion called the mini. A mini skirt, or a mini dress, will be easy to cut out and sew she thinks.

Suddenly, unbidden, she is back at Oakwood. In the attic. She can see her mother cutting out, pinning, hemming. The dressmaking dummy wearing a raw sample of the finished product. She can see her pink party dress. And something inside her screams.

"Are ye awrite, hinnie?" Mrs McGinty asks as Isla halts, her face ashen, her feet rooted to the spot. And then, remembering what they've been told about her, "Dinna fash. Haud ma airm. Let's awa hame."

And Isla lets her guide her through the streets, back to where Bilbo is tethered. They load the cart and clatter back along the tracks. Sit in companionable silence.

By the time they reach the farm, Isla has regained her composure. Her smile. She runs into the kitchen with her purchases. Plonks them on the table. She can't wait to get started.

"Taphadh leat. Thenk ye," she says to Mrs McGinty as she goes back to get the sewing machine off the cart. Hopes she's remembered it correctly.

A broad beam fills Mrs McGinty's face.

"Nae problem," she says. "Ye are verra kin…Very kind."

"And I'm sorry if I cut your morning short. If you had more to do."

"Och dinna fash yersel!" exclaims Mrs McGinty. "It's eechie ochie."

'Eechie ochie', she's always saying this, so Isla asks James what it means.

"It's neither here nor there," he tells her.

Another favourite saying of Mrs McGinty's is, 'Ne'er cast a cloot 'til May be oot'. But Isla knows what this means because her mother says it. You mustn't put your winter clothes away 'til May is out. What she doesn't know is that it's not the month of May it refers to, but the May blossom.

May seems long ago now. When she puts her winter coat away. The mornings and evenings are chilly again. Her warm jacket is pulled out of its hidey-hole. Along with scarf and mittens.

Now she can hear boots crunching across the yard. Chad flies in first. Pushes the kitchen door open and dashes in to greet her. He's closely followed by James and her father. They're back. And they do remember to take their boots off.

"Dinner's ready," says Isla.

Much to her distaste she cooks a shepherd's pie. She knows the meat she uses is lamb. But her father insists. That is what he wants tonight. With roast potatoes, green beans and mint sauce. All Isla can see as she puts the minced lamb in the pie dish, is the lambs frolicking.

They play games. She watches them. Sees how they gather in their own little flock. Then one will break free and gambol to a chosen place. Then another will break free. Join the first. And so on, until the last one joins them. When they start all over. The lamb in this pie will never frolic or play again.

"You're not eating, Isla," her father says. "All this fresh air and exercise, you should be ravenous." He's looking at James. "I know I am."

"Mrs McGinty and I had a big lunch in town," she lies. "So I'm not hungry."

"It's good, Isla," James says in between shovelling it down. "Very good. Chad will love it."

"Bloody waste," Charles mutters.

Isla puts what would have been her portion into Chad's bowl. Scrapes the pie dish. Empties the gravy jug. And clearing the table when they have finished, places his dish by the Aga.

"We're going in the parlour," her father says. "For a nightcap and a cigar. When you've finished clearing up, why don't you join us. And make sure that dog is shut in the kitchen," he adds. "No open doors!"

Isla takes her time. She does not want to join them. She would much rather stay in the kitchen. Cut out material. Sew. Anything but sit in a fug of cigar smoke and be at their bidding. Perhaps she can take her knitting bag. Sit quietly in a corner. Continue with the jumper she is trying to finish for the winter. Or sneak to her room and read. Learn a few more Scottish words so she can understand Mr and Mrs McGinty when they forget to speak English.

Isla dries the last plate and wipes her hands. She's daydreaming. Dreams of her visit to St. Ninians. Her swims in Ettrick Bay. The long walks across the sands. Standing on Windy Hill. Remembers how proud she is when finally she masters Chad's commands. Even uses him to herd the cows in for milking. Her finest achievement.

All this because of the confidence Scott McGinty gives her. The kindness of Mrs McGinty. The things she teaches her. Things a mother teaches a daughter. One day Isla thinks. When she is free. When she can. She will repay the McGinty's for their devotion to the farm. And her.

"Isla!" her father calls. "What the deuce are you doing? Hurry up!"

The plates, bowls, glasses and cutlery are washed and dried. She's putting everything away now. Slowly.

"Isla?" Another call.

She quickly ruffles Chad's fur. Whispers 'sorry' in his ear. Then picking up her knitting bag, shuts the kitchen door firmly and skips along the corridor, past the grandfather clock, into the parlour.

And freezes in the doorway. Where to look? There is nowhere she wants to let her eyes settle. All she can see is flesh. White flesh with hairs. Appendages.

Her father and James have not a stitch of clothing between them. They are both naked. She has never seen anything like it. Clutching her knitting bag, Isla turns to leave when her father barks.

"Don't go! Come in. Shut the door and take off your clothes."

Does he really say that? No, she mishears. Surely.

But no. "Take off your clothes, Isla. Now!" he orders. "We're both doctors. We've seen plenty of naked bodies."

'And besides I'm a doctor. I've seen naked bodies before.' James's words all those years ago. Her first day on the farm. Her first bath. But she trusts James. She does not trust her father. Not anymore.

Isla removes her jumper, jeans and socks. Stands before them, semi-naked.

"Everything…"

He's watching her. His eyes glint, whilst his hands stroke his penis.

Masturbating, thinks Isla. *My father is masturbating.* She knows what this is. Reads about it in the book on the Human Body that James gives her that fifth Christmas. She even does it to herself. Explores her body. Finds those special spots that bid her touch more. Enjoys the final release. But she would never do it in front of anyone. Especially her own father. That would be grotesque.

Slowly, she removes her bra and pants.

James stares at her small breasts. The nipples pink and pert. The blonde triangle of hair between her thighs. The perfect shape of her. *She is quite exquisite*, he thinks.

"On your hands and knees." Her father orders. He rubs faster. His penis swells. Hardens. "Go on. Get down…Like a pig," he pants.

Isla waits for James to do something. To stop this, whatever it is. But he doesn't. She drops to her hands and knees. Suddenly, feels a pain like nothing she has ever felt before as her father rams into her. He holds her hips up. Thrusts and thrusts like a rutting animal. Panting and grunting. Until he climaxes, crying out, "Mummy! Mummy!"

Isla doesn't cry out. She is mute. Torn. There is no scream big enough to voice such agony. Such humiliation. Such degradation. So she does not give it one.

And then he's asking her to smack him. Hard. To call him a filthy butcher's boy. A bastard. A pig. He's that little abused boy again. He wants to feel the pain. Pain that cannot demean him now. Can only give redemption.

Isla is so scared as to what will happen if she does not do as he asks, that she does. Slaps him with the palm of her hand flat. Hits him with a curled fist. And the more she slaps and hits, the more she vents the anger she has kept hidden.

The pain of the last seven years. Of this life that takes her from her mother. From her friends.

Her father's aroused again. Already. She can see it. And then she hears, "Hurry up James. Get on with it. Roll her on her back. I can't hold on much longer."

Isla is scared. Bemused. Cannot work out what is happening. And now, she finds her voice. Screams. A loud, terrifying scream.

Chad hears her. He flies at the kitchen door. It doesn't budge. So he sits on his haunches, throws back his head and howls. Isla hears his cry. But he can't save her this time. Finally he lays down, rests his head on his paws and shoving his nose against the gap under the door, whines. Whilst James rapes her. Robs her of her virginity. And the last vestige of Isla's innocence dies.

After what seems to Isla like hours, the men are sated. Charles swigs a glass of whisky down. Lights a cigar. He is looking pleased. Smug.

Isla staggers out of the parlour. There is blood on the inside of her thighs. Her bottom feels like a red-hot poker has been thrust up it. Chad leaps back as the kitchen door opens.

"It's alright boy," she says. "I'm alright."

Even though she wonders if she will ever be alright again. It's so hard to walk. Everything hurts. One foot at a time, she thinks. All the way to the bathroom where she turns just the hot tap on. Fills the bath to the top and climbing in, grabs the carbolic soap and scrubs. And scrubs. But no matter how much she abrades her skin, she thinks she will never feel clean again.

James follows her. He's put some trousers on. A vest. But Isla is beyond caring.

"I'm so sorry," he says. "I know it was your first time. I wanted…wanted it to be special for you."

"Why then? Why like that?" Isla submerges. "Because it wasn't!" She splutters.

Through a watery blur, she can see his face swimming above the bath.

Isla sits up. Wrings out her hair.

"I'm getting out now," she says. "I'd like you to go. I think you've seen enough of me tonight."

James goes. But as he starts to close the bathroom door he says, "I'll come to your room later. There are things I need to tell you."

"Isla?" A whisper in the dark. "Are you awake?"

Should she pretend to be asleep? Will he go then? Or should she listen to what he wants to tell her? She can't decide. So James decides for her. He sits on the bed. No light. The dark is the keeper of secrets.

James coughs.

"Charles, your father, er…" Oh this is so hard he thinks. "Well, you know we go back a long way. I had…well I had lost the man I love. The love of my life. Never think I'll meet anyone again. And then there is the war. I meet your father. He's handsome. Charming. Beguiling. Ruthless…Damaged."

Isla is curled up like a foetus. James gropes for a hand and finding one, holds tightly onto it.

"Oh yes, I see it now," he says quietly. "But I don't see it then. All I see is this amazing surgeon. Saving lives. This guy so calm in the face of fire. I do not see the wound that festers inside him. Until…"

How can he tell her? Because when all is said and done, Charles August is still her father.

The sweet sound of Isla's voice dances in the dark.

"It's alright," she says. "I think I know."

"He wants a child. A boy. When Columbine gives him you, he plays the devoted father act to perfection. But I know him. I know all the time he is scheming. This obsession for a son I never can understand. Until that night when he tells us of his appalling childhood. The abuse. The damage it does to a fragile mind."

"That's when I realize too," says Isla.

"When I meet him," James continues. "When I am so in love with him and cannot see clearly…"

"Looking through rose-coloured glasses," whispers Isla.

"Yes, I was. I am. And I'm too afraid to take them off."

"Don't be," Isla says. "I'm not."

"It's too late now." James sighs. "I listen to his plans. Just let him sweep me along. I don't question. I just do. But this…This hurting you…It's just he wants a son so badly."

Isla rolls onto her back. It's sore, like the rest of her. She places her other hand on top of James's.

"But it won't be his son," she whispers. "It will be our son."

"I don't think that matters. He wants to change history. Give this boy a life full of love. Fill it with good food and fresh air. Friends and freedom…"

Friends and freedom. What he takes from her. What they both take from her.

"All the things that he always wants but never gets," continues James. "He's still haunted by that terrified, abused little boy."

"And if I, we, can't give him a son, what then?"

"I fear for him. For us. This dream fills his entire life."

He doesn't tell her that now he sees Charles's façade cracking. That what holds him together is slowly crumbling. That he realizes two people occupy his psyche. A Dr Jekyll, Charles the surgeon, the saver of lives. And Mr Hyde, Charles the murderer, the taker of lives. A man without conscience.

And now James is telling her that his mother is not the first person her father kills. That, without realizing at the time, he already meets Mr Hyde. In the war. Recalls at least five severely wounded patients that Charles operates on. The first is a young German boy. A gunner on a plane shot down their side of enemy lines. Stretchered into the field tent. The lad is in a pretty bad way but he, Charles, Columbine, and Eleanor put him back together again.

The other four are women. Militia. Ambulance drivers getting caught up in air raids. Bombed. Blown up. The rescuers needing rescuing. Charles successfully saves their lives. Only to return in the depths of night and smother them with a pillow. James witnesses this. Fortunately, he is the only one who does.

"Why, Charles?" He feels he needs to know why.

"They're going to die eventually, anyway. Or be severely disabled. Lead a miserable existence. I just save them again," Charles replies. "And some folk just don't deserve to live James. Trust me."

"And I do. I'm wearing the rose-coloured glasses. So all I see is this man I love. A god amongst men."

"But now you know he isn't." Isla strokes his hand. "What if you leave him? What if we both leave? Go someplace else. Be together."

"We can't, Isla."

"Why not?"

"Because he's so close to the edge. And if he tips over it, I know what he's capable of."

"So do I now. But that doesn't mean…"

He must tell her, now, or she will never understand.

"I'm his, Isla. Not yours. He owns me. He will never let me go. I have no choice but to stay, whatever. So please..." He rests his head against hers. "Do it for me. Let us give him this boy."

"No," Isla says. "This can't be how you make a baby. It can't be. It's not right. You're just too afraid of him to admit it."

A glimmer of light keeks through a chink in the curtains. James plants a kiss on Isla's forehead and gets off her bed.

"Best go," he says. "Before the cockerel crows and wakes him up. We'll talk again. When we can."

Chapter 26

But Isla doesn't get to talk to James with such intimacy for many months. And in the ensuing nights her father gives her no choice but to endure the rough sex. The rapes. The defilement of her body. She knows nothing of the meaning of rape. All she knows is that she never assents. That it is nothing like the love making she reads of in her novels. That she does not feel loved. Just used. And there is no-one to save her.

Then one morning, when the trees are almost bare, when migrating birds fly overhead, she wakes up suddenly. Feels very nauseous. No time to get to the bathroom. Espying the pretty flowered chamber pot, which is now just a decorative ornament, filled with dried, scented leaves and petals, Isla runs across. She drops to her knees and holding back her long hair, vomits into it until her guts are spent. The flora floats in a pool of khaki-coloured liquid.

She tries to think, as she empties the pot into the toilet, what she's eaten to upset her stomach so. Is it the chicken they eat last night? The greasy bacon and eggs they eat at breakfast? Yet now, strangely, she feels better. Hungry, in fact. So, Isla dismisses such notions. Makes no mention of her sickness.

But the same nausea assails her each morning. And naïve though she is, Isla thinks she knows. But who to talk to? Her mother. It should be her mother. Isla quietly weeps for what should be. Is frightened for what might be. But cannot, and does not want to, discuss it with her father or James. So one morning when they churn the milk, she tells Mrs McGinty. About the nausea. The tingling of her breasts. A cramping in her stomach.

"And I can't bear the smell of coffee anymore. But I crave coke," Isla tells her. "Not Coca-Cola, but the coke for the Aga. Do you think I could be?"

Mrs McGinty looks at her. Really looks at her.

"A dinna ken ha hinnie, yer awa to skin an' bane. But aye, lassie, yer wi bairn."

Isla doesn't know whether to be horrified, or happy. She chooses to be happy. She is expecting James's child. Surely such news will change her father's behaviour.

It does. But in the event, she doesn't need to tell them. Because that very night when Isla undresses, something she is now resigned to, her father's eyes feast on the imperceptible swell of her breasts, across which thin blue veins meander. A smile creases the corners of his lips. James is looking too. At Isla. At Charles. He sees the moment Mr Hyde leaves. And the persona of Dr Jekyll arrives. But for how long, he does not know.

"When did you last menstruate, Isla?" her father asks.

"I don't," she replies. "Have monthly bleeds that is. I did, to begin with. But then they stopped, so I wasn't sure if I can…"

"Get pregnant? Well, I can tell you, right here and now, you can. You're pregnant!" he exclaims. "A few weeks I guess."

He hugs her. A proper fatherly love. No wandering fingers. No squeezing of a breast. Just the biggest hug ever.

"Thank you," he says. "From both of us."

James smiles wryly. Hugs her too. Rests his head on hers.

"Yes, thank you," he whispers. Yet wonders what this will mean for Isla. For all of them.

****

What it means for Isla is that this baby is her saviour. That now her nights belong to her again. No more hours of enduring abuse, humiliation. The loss of herself. Now they spoil her. Cosset her. Encourage her to eat.

"You're feeding two now," her father says. "You must look after yourself and our son."

"And if it isn't a boy?"

There, she has said it. Asked the inconceivable.

"It will be." He is sure. Certain. His plan. No other outcome possible.

They tell the McGintys the impending news. The whole family is delighted. Mr McGinty says he will make a cradle for the baby. *Out of oak…Oakwood,* thinks Isla.

A poignant memory of her mother beating the cake mixture on that fateful morning. Images of the house and garden flood her mind. Whilst Fiona is telling her that her mother and sisters will knit little jackets, bootees and mittens.

"What colour wool shall we use?" she asks, jolting Isla out of her reminiscing.

"White. Lemon. I don't…"

"One or the other then." Fiona grins. "Or both."

Isla is overwhelmed by their generosity. Their enthusiasm. Her own enthusiasm is somewhat dampened. But as the nausea subsides and she feels the first butterfly kicks, the magic of what slowly, secretly, happens inside her, suddenly dawns.

It's true, she thinks. I really am having a baby. Something to hold. To love. To cherish. But that knowledge of what Charles asserts about her mother tempers the joy she begins to feel. It would mean so much if she could be here.

Yet not all joy is extinguished. Now on her daily excursions James accompanies her. Just James. Which fills her heart with gladness. He tells her something he only recently learns. That Charles has rheumatoid arthritis.

"I never knew," he says. "Apparently he develops it as a teenager. Is in and out of remission. He's on medication, Ibuprofen and Aspirin, I think…"

Isla thinks she does not care what medication he is on.

"But now, with the long days out on the farm," James continues, "his bones are besieged by swelling and soreness. And because it affects him in other ways too, he needs to rest. Charles is not a well man right now."

This, her father he speaks of. The father as a child she adores. The father who always has magic at his fingertips. The father who, now, she can conjure not an ounce of compassion for.

"But he doesn't want you going out on your own. He's paranoid that something will befall you."

"You mean befall the baby!" Isla retorts. "I'm just a vessel carrying precious cargo." She smiles at James. Her once upon a time uncle. Now the father of her child. "And I mustn't sink. That's about right, isn't it?"

James does not answer. Instead, on this late May morning when Isla's 'bump' is prominent, he asks, "May I?"

Isla nods. James spans his hands across her swollen belly. Quietly waits. Isla feels the baby kick. So does James. He can find no words. So, stands in silence. Beaming. Awed.

They go into town. Walk round the castle and then onto the pier, where they sit and eat fish and chips. Isla smothers hers in vinegar, something she never likes until now. She is entranced by the big paddle steamboat with its two striped funnels and huge white paddles.

"Would you like to take a trip?" James asks. "To Glasgow."

"What now? I thought you had things to do."

Isla stuffs the last chip in her mouth. She finds she is always hungry now. Worries she will get too fat. She already feels like an elephant, but with less grace.

"Why not now? There's always tomorrow for everything else. Besides, I have a fancy to go 'doon the watter', as Scott would say."

"OK then." Isla pushes herself up. Puts the fish and chips paper in the bins. And taking his arm for support says, "Let's go doon the watter."

The steamer is called The Waverley. It is beautiful! At least Isla thinks so. It's all polished brass and teak decks. They wander round dining rooms and saloon bars from a bygone age.

When the whistle shrilly blows and she leaves the pier, they go to look at the engine room where gigantic pistons and cranks hypnotically whirr, powering the steamboat out into the sea and through the Firth of Clyde. Isla inhales a rich aroma of steam and oil. And before she can stop it, vomits onto the polished deck.

"You don't tell me you are seasick," James says, concerned.

"I'm not. Honestly." She laughs. "Guess the baby doesn't like the fumes."

"Well, stand back. I'll go and find someone to clean it up."

Isla is embarrassed. "Couldn't we just walk away?"

"What if someone slips in it? No, don't worry. You're pregnant. They'll understand."

In fact, the man that comes with mop and bucket more than understands. Says his wife is just the same. "Always being sick when you don't expect it," he says. "And it's baby number five." And as he swabs the deck with the mop, he chatters away.

A mine of information. And aping a tour guide, proceeds to tell them that PS (paddle steamer) Waverley is named after Sir Walter Scott's first novel. It is built in 1946 because the first PS Waverley, built in 1899, is sunk in the War in 1940 whilst helping to evacuate troops from Dunkirk.

"Thank you," Isla says. "And for your interesting talk. I hope your wife will be fine," she adds.

"Oh she'll be right as rain," he says. "Pops 'em out like smarties." And throwing the bucket contents overboard, off he struts, whistling jauntily. The mop tucked under one arm. The bucket swinging from the other.

They disembark at Plantation Quay. Isla discovers that Glasgow is a large bustling city with big department stores, throngs of people. And so much noise. She is overwhelmed. Looks to James to guide her.

"Don't let go of me, will you," she says.

"I won't," says James. "Promise." And he doesn't.

They ride on a trolley bus which clatters and bumps over the old tram tracks. Get off in the heart of the city, right opposite an enormous department store. It is called John Lewis. Isla's never been in anything like it. She is besotted with the colours. The clothes. The pretty bottles of perfumes. In her excitement, she lets go of James and squibs the testers on her wrist. Sneezes as the heady scents invade her nose.

"Isla," James calls. He's pointing at a sign. 'Maternity and baby care'. "Shall we, whilst we're here?"

They ride up an escalator.

"It's a moving staircase!" exclaims Isla, tripping as it reaches the next floor and department. She has never been on an escalator. Is not sure how to get off.

"Oh look!" She gasps, staring into a magical place full of baby paraphernalia. First her eyes lock on the perambulators. There are several, but she falls in love with a white, deep bellied, pram with big wheels. And a big price. It has a blue hood and blue rain cover. A tray underneath. Isla runs her hands over the cover. Sees the embroidered edging on the hood.

"It's gorgeous," she whispers on a breath. "But far too expensive."

"That's because it's a Silver Cross," says an assistant who, seeing the desire in Isla's demeanour, approaches. A badge pinned to her navy-blue blazer denotes she is Miss Foster.

"Queen Elizabeth has one," she continues. "So, as you will appreciate, they are the best. Manufactured in Yorkshire since the 1800's. I'm from Yorkshire, so I know. You won't find a better, more comfortable, more reliable form of transport for your bairn." Miss Foster smiles at Isla. "Your first?" she asks.

"Yes," says Isla.

"How long have you got to go?"

"About six weeks," James answers. He's also looking at the pram. The price... "Get what you want. The best. Don't stint on what you spend..." Charles's words when James tells him what they will need for a baby.

"We'll take it," James says.

"Really, but?" Isla can't believe it.

"Yes. We will definitely take it. And get everything else you need, Isla. Go mad, Mrs Duncan."

So, Isla goes mad. Buys a highchair. A pushchair. Flannelette nighties. Bibs. Terry nappies. Tiny suits. Coats. Little leather boots. And then...

"You'll need these," says Miss Foster.

She fetches waterproof pants. Big, dangerous looking safety pins. And a bucket...

"It's to soak the dirty nappies in," she explains, seeing Isla's bewilderment. "And the pins are to fasten them." She smiles. "So they don't drop down."

"Of course," Isla says.

"We'll take everything," says James. "I'll pay now. And for shipment across to Bute. I'll be able to collect from Rothesay."

"Certainly, Sir," says Miss Foster.

"That's a very generous dad you've got there," she says to Isla.

The truth and its ambiguity are not lost on Isla or James.

On the return journey, Isla sits on the deck looking out to sea as they steam down the Firth of Clyde, leaving Glasgow and its excitement behind. She listens to the churning of the water as the paddles turn. The steam belching from the funnels. Sees the cragged hills, dark forests and fjord like sea-lochs. A different perspective of Bute. My island. My home she thinks as they approach the pier at Rothesay.

Isla's hair is windswept. Damp with sea spray. Her face is sun-bronzed, glowing. She's tired. Happy.

"That was wonderful," she says as they disembark. "The paddle steamer. The shopping. All of it. I'm glad you persuaded me."

James laughs.

"I don't recall you needing much persuasion. And I enjoyed it too," he says. He doesn't tell her that it's been good to get away from Charles's sometimes overbearing presence. That he's having doubts about everything. But he won't leave Charles. He can't.

******

A week later James borrows Charles's quad cab and drives into Rothesay to collect the cargo. As he and the McGinty's unload it all, the McGinty women 'ooh' and 'aah' at such extravagances. Cannot help their unbelieving fingers running along each item. Everything is carted into the farmhouse, the Silver Cross Pram holding court in the centre of the kitchen. Not one of Mrs McGinty's bairns ever sleeps in such luxury. Isla wonders how something so small and not yet even present, can take up so much space.

That July Isla blooms. Her glorious bump is enormous. She struggles to get about. It feels like there's a cannonball between her thighs. The only time she feels comfortable is in the water when she is buoyant, her limbs weightless.

"Take off your clothes, James."

James looks at her.

"What. Out here? But the bay is open. Anyone can see."

Isla laughs.

"What anyone? There's no-one around."

She begins to strip. Peels off the maternity dress she wears. Pulls off her pants and bra. Puts them in a pile on the sand. And waddling down to the bay's shore where the smallest of waves ripple, wades in.

"Come on, James," she calls. "It's wonderful."

And it is. She takes him to Ettrick Bay. The sun burns down from a beautiful azure sky. Not a cotton wool cloud in sight. It warms the soft, golden sands that stretch right round the bay. Glistens on the calm, blue water. Above, herring gulls circle and screech. Whilst sanderlings skitter up and down the beach.

For a moment James watches her float, belly up, bobbing along like a strange sea creature. The inhibitions Isla comes with have gone. Left with the child she once was. He has never seen her so happy. But is there a cloud on the horizon he wonders as casting off his clothes, he piles them up next to hers and runs into the sea to join her.

Isla splashes him. He yells. Retaliates. And then he swims out whilst Isla floats on her back in the shallows. After, they lie side by side on the warm sand. A slight breeze brews. And fluffy cumulus clouds drift lazily across the azure sky. They make shapes out of them. Isla loves doing this. James sees castles, sheep, and cows. But all Isla sees in every passing cloud is a baby.

Chapter 27

Sweat glistens on her forehead. Trickles between her breasts. Stains the cloth around her armpits. She's taking a tray of cold lemon squash and egg sandwiches to the 'back faulds' as McGinty calls them. Refreshments on this hot day for the men and Mrs McGinty working out on the fields. Another of the McGinty clan, Campbell, a tall lanky laddie, helps now. Charles is still limited as to what he can do. As is Isla now. She struggles along the stony path. A low backache accompanies her. It used to seem such a short walk. Now it seems like a marathon.

It's late July. The baby is due any time. Isla can't wait to get her body back. To let the air out of this enormous balloon she's become. To meet this tiny person who causes her crave coke. Sardines and bananas…together. Kicks her when she rests. Compels her eat a lot. Drink a lot. Go to the toilet a lot. Takes over, not only her body, but her mind. So she's crying one minute. Laughing the next. She's forgetful. Obsessional. And lately can't stop cleaning. Touching and folding the tiny clothes. The nappies.

Nesting she reads. I'm making a nest. Like a bird at the top of a tree…*Rock a bye baby on the treetops. When the wind blows, the cradle will rock. When the bough breaks, the cradle will fall. And down will come baby, cradle, and all.* Isla recites the nursery rhyme. Please, don't let my nest fall, she prays.

Suddenly, there's a gush of water between her thighs. The sanitary towel she wears can't contain the flood. Isla puts the tray down at the side of the path and sits. She's scared. Has she wet herself? Or have her waters broken? Whichever, she is too embarrassed to go up to the fields. And the dull ache in her lower back is now a pain. Unforgiving. Unrelenting. As if at any moment her back might break in half.

Up in the fields, Chad suddenly turns. Stands, poised, head raised to the sky. And sniffs. McGinty calls him. Whistles. But, with a low whine, he suddenly shoots off.

"Whit's the dug aboot?" McGinty scratches his head. Chad never disobeys him. "Summat's nae awright. A'll be reit back," he shouts.

And puzzled, wondering, the others watch as he hurries off. Follows Chad as fast as he can.

Isla tries to get back on her feet. But her bump hides them. And she can't push up from her elbows. So she rolls to her side. A shooting pain cramps her stomach. Isla screams out. Waits for it to pass. Tries again to get up. And stumbling, upends the tray. Sandwiches, lemon squash and glasses tumble onto the path.

"No. Oh no," she wails. What to do? "Help!" She shouts. "Will somebody help me."

A wet nose suddenly thrusts itself against her face. A tongue licks her.

"Chad!" She exclaims, sobbing.

Chad lays by her side. And the minutes tick by. Another cramping pain. Now she bellows like a bull. Feels her belly tighten. Spreads her hands across. It's as hard as rocks. And then, when the pain subsides, she feels it soften. Something moves inside her. Is the baby coming? No. It can't be. It's too quick. Her heart beats fast as panic sets in.

And then a voice pierces it. "Awa, lassie. Dinna feart. Yer awright. Guid dug," he says, patting Chad. He whispers something in his ear. And Chad leaps up and charges back up the path.

Isla babbles. "Aaagh! Aaagh! it hurts. This can't be happening. Not here. Aaagh! Not now. There's no nest. Aaagh. No wind. Aaagh." She sobs wildly. "No cradle."

"Haud yer catter!" McGinty says. "Yer bum's oot the windae."

"No. No," screams Isla. "It's not my bum It's my bump!" She's breathing heavily. Her heart is racing. "Jack fell down and broke his crown…Humpty Dumpty fell off the wall…Little Bo Peep has lost her sheep," Isla recites randomly.

"Yer a barmpot!" McGinty laughs.

"No. No. It's me who fell over. I've broken my baby," Isla wails as another contraction assails her.

McGinty sees her agitation. Hears her fear.

"Awa, lassie. Yer heid's full o' mince. Yer awright," he repeats. "So haud yer wheesht, aye."

He knows animals can become agitated before giving birth. But agitated as she is, he doesn't feel she's ready yet. To drop the bairn. There's still time. And he knows Chad will not fail him.

"Noo, just haud on hinnie," he says. "Gie's yer haund."

He reaches both arms down. Isla grabs his hands. And slowly, carefully, he pulls her to her feet. Steadies her. At the same time, the tractor and trailer, Charles at the wheel, James and Chad riding in the trailer, chug down the track. Charles sees what's happening and pulls to a stop ahead of them. Leaves the engine running.

"That's one clever animal," he admits begrudgingly. "Comes dashing up to the fields like a streak of lightening. Finds James. Circles round him one way, then the other, nudging at his ankles 'til he moves. Herds him across to the tractor," Charles tells them. "That dog doesn't need to speak."

But McGinty isn't listening and James, already out of the trailer, is helping him support Isla.

"Get off me!" Isla suddenly snaps. "What do you think I am, a baby?" The pains stop and now upright, she is mortified by the state of her dress, the broken glass and strewn sandwiches.

"I am perfectly capable of walking on my own."

"No!" Her father's voice. Firm. Decisive. "You're not a baby. But you are about to have one. Sooner rather than later. Do not dance with the devil, Isla. Get in."

Isla hears his tone. Knows he's right and, demurring, lets them help her up into the trailer. James and Chad ride beside her whilst McGinty sits on a bale, chewing on a piece of straw as they bump along the path.

Once in the farmyard, Charles struggles to get off the tractor seat. His knees are unwilling to straighten. Damn this arthritis, he thinks.

"Thank you, Scott," he says, "but we can take it from here…" He notes McGinty's bewilderment. "Before we are farmers," he tells him, "we are doctors. So, she's in good hands. We know what to do."

Two men delivering a baby. And one of them the husband. Truth stranger than fiction, thinks McGinty. He's delivered many a lamb but never one of his own bairns. He doesn't think he could. He doesn't think his wife would let him. It seems to him that Isla has no choice.

"You can take Chad and the tractor back up to the fields, Scott," James tells him. "Oh and if you wouldn't mind, do you think you could clear up the mess on the path. I expect the fauna will eat the sandwiches, but it's the glass I'm worried about."

"Aye," says McGinty. "Nae problem."

****

James manages to get Isla up the stairs and into her bedroom. Charles hobbles behind them. They take off all the bedding. Cover the mattress with towels. Help Isla out of her clothes. She lays down and for a while. Drifts in and out of sleep. Then several hours later, the contractions start again. And if she thinks it is painful before, these are far stronger. The gaps in between far shorter. As soon as Isla relaxes from one, another one is waiting.

They are both there. James and her father.

"Get on your hands and knees," she hears him say. Screams at the top of her voice. "Not that. Not now."

"It'll help," he continues. "And bite down on this…" He puts a rolled-up handkerchief in her mouth. "Whilst the contraction lasts."

Isla stays where she is. And spitting out the handkerchief, growls, "It helps if I can…Aaaagh! Aaaagh! Roar!"

Two hours pass. Still nothing. James wipes her forehead with a cold flannel. Her face and hair are wet with sweat. Maximum effort with minimum reward he thinks. He and Charles are both worried.

"Her waters broke a long time ago," says James. "We need to get this baby out asap."

The cockerel crows and daylight begins to flood the room. It shines on the beautiful carved oak cradle at the foot of the bed. Fine-crafted, the slightest touch sets in motion a gentle, sleep-inducing rocking.

James examines her again.

"I can just see the baby's head," he says as Isla, holding the bed rail, screams through another contraction.

Without flinching Charles takes control. Pulling out Isla's desk chair, he sits on it like the director of a play which is acting out before him.

"Right," he barks. "Here's what we do. We are going to go native. James, put a pile of towels on the floor, then get Isla on her feet. And, Isla," he says loud enough to jolt her out of her torpor, "I know your legs are strong, so I want you to squat. Squat low, over the towels. Hang onto James. And listen to my voice."

159

Isla, almost senseless with fatigue, is on her feet. She squats. Grips both James's hands as if she is about to fall into the abyss. And only he can save her.

"Next contraction, Isla," she hears Charles say. "Push. Bear down as hard as you can."

Isla takes a deep breath in and using its exhale, pushes.

"Come on, sweetheart," whispers James. "I know you're tired. But you're almost there."

Charles hears 'sweetheart'. Looks at James. Wonders.

Isla hears 'almost there'. Waits for the next pain to reach its peak and bellowing, pushes with all her might.

"The head is crowning," James declares. "I can see the top of it."

"Next contraction, Isla," shouts Charles. "Pant. Pant like a dog. Don't push."

Isla imagines Chad, panting on a hot day. She pants. Poof. Poof. Poof.

"Next one, Isla. Just a gentle push."

"Head's out!" Charles cries.

The baby repositions to turn its shoulders.

"Now!" Charles barks. "Give it all you've got, Isla. And James, get ready."

With the last and final contraction, when Isla gives it all she has left, the rest of the baby slithers out into James's waiting arms.

A lusty cry fills the space around them.

Isla cries too. At the relief that it's over. All she wants to do is hold this little miracle which fights so strongly to enter the world.

"It's a boy!" exclaims James. "With a fine pair of lungs. All fingers and toes correct." He is both awed, joyous. And crying.

"A boy!" echoes Charles. "Wait. Do not cut the cord," he orders. "I will do it." James waits. No argument.

Charles, fuelled with adrenalin and suddenly surprisingly agile, gets off the chair. Goes over and picks up the scissors they boil in a pan to sterilize. Then he cuts the umbilical cord between the clamps James puts on. Isla rests down on the towels now saturated with mucous and blood. She leans her back against the bed.

James gently wipes the baby's bloodied head and places him on Isla's chest. "Meet our son," he whispers. And he's not looking at Charles.

An arm, the size of a doll's, lays across her swollen breasts. Isla strokes the soft skin with a finger, and a tiny hand wraps around it. The grip is strong. He won't let go. Isla kisses the top of his head which is covered with a blonde fuzz.

"I'll never let you go," she whispers against it. "I promise." But often it is a cruel happenstance that breaks a promise.

"I need a bath," she says. "And so does this little man. Iain." She smiles at James.

"Iain?" he repeats. And then as it dawns, "Oh. Our son. So that's the name you're giving him."

"No, it is not!" Charles. The words uttered with muted venom. "In case you forget James, this *little man* is *our* son. Yours and mine. And his name will be William Joseph. After the young man who went to war and never came back. The man who should have been my father."

James sees Isla's expectation suddenly clouded by disappointment.

"What about a compromise?" he asks.

"I don't do compromise. You know that."

"I was thinking Williain," says James. "It's almost the same but unique. Special."

Isla, fearing reprisal should she suggest anything, keeps her own thoughts muted.

Charles considers. He likes the idea of 'unique'. He likes the idea of 'special'.

"Williain Joseph it is then," he declares. "It's a strong sounding name."

"Thank you," Isla says. "I like it." But she is not addressing her father.

"And no bath until the placenta comes," he's saying.

Isla knows all about placentas.

"Do I have to eat it?" she asks.

James laughs.

"Yes." Charles, serious. "It will be good for you. Good for the milk."

"We'll have some too," says James as he sees the look on her face. "Why, with some potatoes and vegetables, a spot of gravy, it'll be just like a roast dinner."

Isla is not so sure. But if Angharad, Bethan, Carys, Dwynwen, Elin, Fflur, Glynis, Hafren, and Iona can do it, she thinks. Then so can she.

The roast dinner ingredient arrives without problem. Entire. Disease free. Healthy.

Isla has her bath. She lays, knees bent, the baby on her thighs. Cups the warm water in her hand and gently pours it over him. He squirms, kicks his little legs, splashes the water with tiny hands. But he doesn't cry. Then she sits up and lays him near her breast. Marvels at how he finds the nipple and latching on, begins to suckle. It's a sensation she can't describe. But it's beautiful. Special. Isla Duncan is smitten.

As is her father. He's sitting on the same rickety chair Isla sits on after that first bath. Her first day on the farm. Meanwhile, James burns the bloodied towels in the metal bin, which still sits in the middle of the farmyard. Some things stay the same she thinks. Whilst all around her changes.

That night as Charles and James lay in bed after making love, Charles props up on one elbow and looks down on James's face. Strokes a finger down his cheek.

"I see the way you look at her," he says. "I hear the words you say to her."

He digs the finger into the corner of James's mouth.

"But don't ever think that you can swap camps, James. Or jump ship. Because if you attempt either, I will kill her in front of you. And then I will kill you. Do you understand?"

The intent and vehemence are obvious. His capability undoubted.

"I will never leave you, Charles," James says, wiping the spittle that Charles's words spray on his skin. "I promise." He wonders how, in the event, Charles will explain their disappearance. But as always Charles makes plans.

"And you needn't worry what folk will think or say."

Keep it light, thinks James. No provocation. I am dealing with Mr Hyde right now. He gives a weak laugh.

"Well, I won't, will I? Not if I'm dead."

Charles pays no heed to his attempt at jocularity. Continues. "I believe pigs enjoy a bit of fresh meat." He smiles. "So after they dispose of your bodies, I shall simply say that you and Isla have emigrated to Australia. Are waiting to get settled before you send for the boy." He leans down and kisses James full on the lips. "But of course, you never will."

Chapter 28

But some changes Isla cannot see at first. She is too busy breastfeeding. Winding and burping the baby. Changing and washing nappies. Hanging them out on the line McGinty rigs up. He fixes it above the farmyard, from the farmhouse to the barn. He makes a long wooden pole. Carves an upside-down triangular nick at one end. The line fits in this. When all the washing is pegged, Isla props the pole up. The washing blows high above the dust and chaff that wafts about the farmyard.

Scarcely does she complete one task than it's time to feed him again. Change him. More nappies to soak. Mrs McGinty demonstrates how to fold and pin a nappy for a boy. Isla finds it baffling. So, to practice, she spends an entire morning folding. Has a goodly pile of nappies at her fingertips. Mrs McGinty also shows Isla how to line them with a piece of muslin which catches the worst of a baby's volcanic eruptions. These can be disposed of in the cesspit. Whilst the nappies go into the bucket with the Milton solution. To be scrubbed and washed in the butcher's sink that night.

On top of this, Isla still cooks the meals, clears up. Helps Mrs McGinty. Does the monthly accounts. And any other paperwork relevant to Lochfrein. She knows this will get easier as he grows. But then is sure a whole new set of challenges will present. I am a mother now, she thinks. It's not about me anymore.

The McGinty girls visit three days after Williain's birth. She tells Isla they couldn't wait any longer. They are so excited. Want to hold him. Nurse him. He doesn't cry as Isla gathers him up from the cradle where he lays asleep. Nor when they stroke his face, marvelling at the soft, peachy skin. Exclaim over his tiny toes. Put a finger in the palm of his hand knowing that a reflex will make him grasp it.

After the first two weeks, unless it is pouring down, Isla puts him outside in the pram. She parks it in the farmyard where she can keep an eye on it. Hear him should he cry. But he rarely does. James tells her she must cover the hood in case one of the cats should decide to jump in. Perhaps smother him. Isla finds this hard to believe but nevertheless, fixes a fine laced sheet over the hood. Mrs McGinty and the girls are a big help in these first few weeks.

They take Williain out in his pram, the girls fighting as to who will push it. They have never seen anything so splendid. None of the McGintys has ever slumbered in a Silver Cross pram. Isla takes a little nap. Enjoys a cup of tea and a biscuit without a baby cradled against her, searching for a breast.

The days pass. Williain thrives. It is then she notices that James, her 'husband', the father of her son isn't around much. Not like before, when she waits for the birth. Is he avoiding her? And if so, why? Because her father is around too much. In her face. Controlling. Commenting. Tutting. She finds it disconcerting. Uncomfortable. It makes her clumsy. Forgetful. But however hard she tries to escape his watchful eyes, his interfering words, he finds her.

"I'm taking Williain for a walk," she says one morning.

"Wait. I'll come with you." Her father is already off his seat.

"A long walk," Isla says. "Not in the pram. I've made a sling. So he'll be close to me. Won't wake up and cry."

She knows that when Williain wakes, he never cries. Unless he's hungry. He will lay looking up at the brightly coloured beads and bells strung across the hood of the pram, kicking his little legs. Sometimes, knocking against a bell as his arms reach up with neither direction nor co-ordination. She's sure she sees him smile. He's the cutest, calmest, baby ever. But Isla also knows that long walks for Charles are now compromised. This is the only way she can have some time to herself. Some peace.

In the evening they are all together, so she can't talk intimately with James. But he is always eager to hold Williain To play with him. Bath him when Charles permits. Feed him as the months pass and Isla cannot produce enough milk to satisfy his lusty appetite. He seems to grow overnight.

She hands James a small bowl and a spoon.

"I call it smush," Isla says. "A bit of this. A bit of that. A bit of the other. All mushed up in gravy. It looks disgusting, but Williain loves it. Gobbles it down. He's so greedy."

She tickles his chin, knowing that he will giggle. She just loves to listen. It's so infectious and lights up the day.

In the smallness of time he goes from being fed to attempting to feed himself. He's sitting up now. In the wooden highchair at the kitchen table. Wriggling and banging his spoon on the tray until his bowl is placed before him. Immediately digs the spoon in. But the distance from bowl to mouth is not yet mapped. Takes many directions. The tray. The floor. Chad. Himself. Sometimes, if the bowl is full of porridge or rice pudding, the highchair, and everything else, is covered. It's hard to see his laughing little face. Because Williain is always laughing. As if the world is one big joke to him.

Isla watches the two men with him. Both vying for the baby's attention. Each trying to be a better father than the other. She wishes it were just her and James. Because it's Charles who captains the ship. Makes all the decisions regarding 'their' son.

Isla know better than to make any suggestions of her own. He just swats them away like flies. And somewhere in her heart she fears her father will overcompensate. Give Williain too much of everything, so he grows into a spoilt, selfish little boy. And there is nothing she can do about it. Unless she takes him and leaves.

This idea begins to ferment inside her. Grows exponentially with the passing months. Until it is all she thinks about. Now, it is Isla who makes plans. Pulls out the large colourful holdall from the back of the wardrobe. Begins to secret things away. Things she will need for her and Williain. She always felt that her spur of the moment buy would one day come in useful. And that day has come.

"I can do this. I can do this," she repeats morning, afternoon and evening. Over, and over, and over again. In the hope that one day she will believe it. That one day she will be bold enough. Brave enough. Because the smallness of her world, these last eight years does not enable either.

Chapter 29

Isla is in the parlour with Williain. He is eighteen months old. Walking and running everywhere. Into everything. Avidly curious. A sturdy little lad with blonde curly hair and the piercing blue eyes of her father. They all adore him. He's a lovable rascal with a happy disposition. Nothing seems to faze him.

He calls Isla 'Mammy'. Whilst her father is 'Pappy Choochoo' as Charles buys him a clockwork train and carriages. Metal railway lines that clip together to make a track. And James is 'Pappy Vroomvroom' because he buys Williain a wooden garage and cars. A toddler with, as yet, limited vocabulary. But nevertheless one who knows he has two fathers and makes his own distinction between them.

She sits at her desk. James and Scott bring it down from her bedroom. Now she can do paperwork, the monthly accounts, whilst keeping an eye on Williain. This particular morning he runs round and round her desk as she tries to work. Weaves in and out of the chairs. Shrieks with laughter at this newfound game. Suddenly trips. Isla turns. The Monopoly box lays at the edge of the carpet. It's this that fells Williain. Not that it bothers him in the slightest. He just rolls back onto his feet and continues charging about.

Blonde curls bouncing. Laughter always on his lips. Whilst Isla picks up the box. Wipes the fine layer of dust off the lid. And remembers. Remembers that night of disclosure. Not realizing then that the very word of the game, 'Monopoly', would come to symbolize her father's behaviour. His monopoly of James. His monopoly of Williain.

Her brain, with the toddler's boisterous distraction, won't work. So, she closes the ledger and gets up. The accounts can wait until later.

"Come, Williain," she says. "You seem to have an abundance of energy today. Let's go up to the pastures. See Pappy Vroomvroom. See what he's doing. You'd like that, wouldn't you?"

Williain stops his bustling. "And Mackmack?" He squeals with delight.

"Mr McGinty, yes. And Chad will be up there too. Come on, we'll find you a coat and some boots. I know," Isla says, "how about we take them their lunch, and ours. We can pack a picnic. A surprise."

****

James sees Isla pushing the pram up the path. The hood is down and he can see Williain's blonde head. As they draw nearer, he can also see his son shares space with a large wicker hamper. Isla lifts Williain out of the pram. Watches his chubby little legs propel him the remainder of the path into his father's open arms. James swings him round and round.

"Look!" he shouts. "Williain's an aeroplane."

Williain shrieks with dizzying joy. And Chad, barking excitedly, runs around and around them.

Isla lugs the hamper onto the grass. Takes out a tarpaulin sheet and spreads it out. She's packed sandwiches, cooked ribs, chicken legs, sausages, apples, and biscuits. A flask of tea. Some orange juice for Williain.

"This is wonderful," says James, sitting on the sheet. He calls the others over.

Scott and his sons, Donald, Hamish, Campbell and Cameron join them. As do Mrs McGinty and her daughters, Fiona, Caitlin, Aggie and Donella, who have been picking vegetables and fruit. It's quite a gathering. Little of the tarpaulin sheet can be seen when they all sit their weary bottoms down.

"Me sit, Pappy Vroomvroom," says Williain. He plonks himself next to James. Shuffles up as close as he can.

There's a camaraderie in the gentle chatter. A peace as mouths busily engage in eating.

When the rev of an engine torments the tranquillity.

Charles in the pickup. Isla's disappointment is hard to hide.

They all watch as he switches off the engine, pulls up the handbrake and climbs down from the cab.

"I don't seem to have received an invite," he says petulantly.

"It was a spur of the moment thing," Isla blurts. "Because it's a lovely day. And we couldn't find you."

She knows full well where he is. She hears him tell James he is going into Rothesay.

"Yes, I did go out," he says. "But I couldn't get what I wanted, so I came back. Only to find the farmhouse empty and the pram and my son gone."

They all hear *my* son. Look from James to Isla. Charles is on the tarpaulin now. Carefully avoiding food and feet, he stops in front of Williain. He smiles at James. Glares at Isla. It's a look that says it all. She can't make a scene out here. It would distress Williain who, pleased to see him, stretches out his arms and cries, "Pappy Choochoo."

Reluctantly, Isa relinquishes her place next to him. Moves. Fiona, a puzzled expression on her face, pats the tarpaulin next to her where there is just enough space for Isla to squeeze in.

Williain now flanked by his two fathers, picks up a sausage and holds it up for each to take a bite. Then he picks up another and eats it himself.

There's a change in the atmosphere. An air of disquiet. They are all aware of it, except Williain. But no-one can put a name to it.

After they finish, Isla packs the remains of the feast back in the hamper and fastens down the lid. She beckons to James. He comes across and lifts it up. Puts it back in the pram.

"Walk with me," she whispers, "I'm just going with James," she calls, already walking away before her father can intervene. "He's got something he wants to show me. Williain stay with Pappy Choochoo. I won't be long."

James moves quickly. Is ahead of her now.

"And what am I supposed to be showing you? You know he'll ask."

"Think of something. A rare fungus. A migrating bird. Oh, I don't know. I just want to talk to you without him breathing over my shoulder."

"About?"

"About him. My father. The way he treats Williain."

"He adores him, Isla. You must see this. He would never abuse him."

"There are different ways to abuse," she says. "There's abuse by neglect. And abuse by overindulgence."

"That's very perceptive Isla." He smiles at her. "And you're only seventeen. So, you think the latter is what Charles is doing?"

"Definitely. You don't see it James because you're hardly ever there. It's too much of everything. Too many toys. He's always buying him something. Too much playing. Too much food. Every time Williain asks for a 'bisbis', he'll give him one. I worry he'll grow up fat and spoilt. Unhealthy. Unfit. He'll be teased.

I can see it. Charles never reprimands him. Pushes in if I try to suggest anything. Corrects me when I say anything he doesn't agree with. About my son, *our* son."

Isla takes a pause for breath.

"He's always there. Hovering like a hawk above its prey. Waiting to pounce. I can't breathe, James. I hardly get a look in. It's as if I don't exist. That I've played my part and it's exit left."

"Whoa there." James stops and puts a hand on her arm. "Where's all this coming from?"

"From here." She taps her heart. "I've got to get far away from Lochfrein. I can't stay and watch this happen. I was hoping you would come too. Please, James. I'm not sure I can do it on my own."

"We've been through this before, Isla. Nothing's changed. I won't leave him. I can't. And now, with his ailing health, he needs me more than ever."

So, she thinks, he's made his choice. And it isn't her. Quietly she weeps for that which might have been.

James wipes the tears away with his handkerchief. And suddenly, leaning into her, takes her face in his hands. And kisses her. A proper kiss, full on the lips. Full of a desire which might have been. But can never be.

"I won't say anything to Charles," he says. "And I won't stand in your way. But I will say, make sure you are far away from Bute before he discovers what you've done. Because if he finds you, I can't bear to think of the consequences. He won't harm Williain. But you…"

They can see him now, Williain in tow, looking for them.

"See," she says. "He can't let us out of his sight for two seconds. He doesn't trust us."

"I'll give you some money," James hurriedly says, "to tide you over until you find your mother. I'm guessing that's what you'll do."

If she's alive, thinks Isla.

"Mammy!" Williain points. "Pappy Vroomvroom."

And it's too late for any more conversation. In silence they walk back to join her father and her son. A cloud scurries across the sky. And in that moment the endless dithering, the dread of a decision dissipates. James makes his choice. In so doing he takes hers. So she must make a different choice. And his revelation gives her the resolve to do this. She resolves to leave the island at the earliest opportunity.

"So, did you see what you were looking for?" asks Charles.

James shakes his head. "No. I couldn't find it this time. It's a beautiful and rare migrating bird. But there's still time for it to leave."

Chapter 30

It will be another few months before an opportunity presents. Summer. The summer before Williain's second birthday. He sits at the kitchen table, his teddy bear on the seat next to him, eating toast. Isla is at the Aga cooking what Mrs McGinty calls 'a full English Breakfast'. The bacon spits in the frying pan. Competes with the mushrooms, tomatoes, eggs, and potato thins.

She hears James and her father talk of a livestock show in Rothesay. They want to look at a prize Cloughead bull.

"It's won many awards" James says. "A fine specimen." He whistles through his teeth. "Apparently, it's worth over fifty thousand guineas."

"A bit beyond our means then." Charles scoffs. "But yes, it would be interesting to see the beast that can fetch such a price."

"Do you want to come, Isla?" asks James. "Bring Williain. There'll be stalls, lots of animals. A pets corner. There might even be an air display."

"Maybe next year," she replies. "He's a bit small to thrust into such a big event." It's all she can think to say. She doesn't want to go. Not today. Not ever.

"Nonsense," says Charles. "He'll love it. We can show him off to everyone."

"What, like a prize bull." Isla laughs nervously as she plates up the breakfast. "Anyway I think he's coming down with something. I was up most of the night with him. That's why he's only having toast this morning. To see if it stays down."

James looks at Williain. He looks pink cheeked and healthy. And then he glances at Isla. Realizes. It will be today. She's leaving. He might never see either of them again. But there is nothing he can say or do. He made his choice. But is glad he kissed her on that day of the picnic.

"Very well then," Charles concedes. He doesn't want the bother of a sick child. "Never mind." He ruffles Williain's curls. "Pappy Choochoo will bring a present back for you. Who knows we might even bring back a present for mammy…If she's a good girl."

Isla feigns indifference. But her heart beats faster. There's a weakness in her legs as she contemplates what she's going to do.

"Probably best he doesn't come," agrees James. "It'll be a long day." And then, with a knowing glance at Isla, "We won't be back 'til early evening."

"And make sure you rustle up a decent dinner," says Charles. "After all, you've got all day to do nothing."

Oh, have I, she thinks. Little do you know.

Isla waits 'til Charles's quad cab leaves the farmyard. Listens until the noise of its engine recedes. She must be sure. She gives Williain some left over bacon to nibble on whilst she hastily throws together some food for the journey. She can't find any cold meats, so it's just slices of bread spread with butter and honey. Some morsels of cheese. A couple of apples and a bottle of fruit juice.

A sudden draught of warm air creeps under the kitchen door. The light dims.

Isla grabs Williain and takes him to the toilet. He's out of nappies now. Something less to worry about. A quick brush of his teeth. A flick of a comb through his hair. He grizzles a little as she's hurrying him. But stops when she gets some toy cars out. Sits happily on the kitchen floor pushing them. Making 'vroom' 'vroom' sounds.

Isla's heart is pounding now. She must not waste a moment. Quickly, she gathers all their toiletries together. She doesn't have a washbag, but James does. He won't mind she thinks as she empties it and crams them all in.

A door slams somewhere as she runs up the stairs to her bedroom and finishes packing the holdall. She's glad it's so commodious but, nevertheless, can't take everything she'd like to, since she must carry it. She takes a coat out of the wardrobe. A yellow oilskin with a hood. It's the one where she hides the wad of money in a pocket. The money James gives her when he realizes she is finally brave enough to flee.

Isla takes a last look out of the bedroom window. Remembers. No! Don't! Don't reminisce, she thinks. There's no time. And grabbing the holdall, her booted feet clatter down the stairs.

The last thing she puts in is Williain's one-eyed, slightly bald but much-loved teddy bear. Pooh he calls it. He once belonged to Fiona. Isla has been reading Winnie the Pooh and The House at Pooh Corner to him. She knows Williain will not go anywhere without it.

"Come on, sweet pea," she says, putting his arms into the sleeves of a blue tweed coat. It's his newest, woven from Scottish wool. Will keep him warm and dry she hopes, buttoning it up to his chin. "We're going on an adventure."

"With Pooh?"

"Yes, with Pooh. He's snuggled in the bag. See…" She shows him.

Happy, he lets Isla take his hand.

There is no time to tidy up. She must leave the dirty dishes, cups and cutlery. The greasy frying pan, and the teapot full of cold tea.

"I'm sorry, Mrs McGinty," she whispers.

A gust of wind that comes from nowhere all but wrenches the kitchen door from her hands. It blasts a fat blowfly in. The dry chaff in the farmyard blows every which way. And grey clouds lay heavy on the horizon. Not a storm, she prays. Please not a storm. Not now. But she can't turn back. So pulling Williain along, she heads down the grass sided path toward their freedom.

The bluebottle, now trapped in the kitchen, buzzes round and round before settling happily on the remains of their last breakfast at Lochfrein.

She spies two swans on the loch. They glide hurriedly across the water, as if they know what the darkening skies and rising winds portend. Five little cygnets paddle frantically behind. Isla recalls that first day. When she is nine. When she gets out of the car crumpled and cross. James pointing at the loch. The binoculars. James telling her that they are called Whooper swans. Hanging on tightly to Williain she walks alongside the loch, head down against the increasing gale. Whooper, she thinks. The word 'hope' is enfolded in their name.

Waves now cut across the loch. Big waves. The wind shrieks. Williain is frightened.

"Mammy. Mammy," he cries. Clings tight to Isla.

It's so dark. Yet not even the middle of the day. Isla stops. Only long enough for Williain to do a piddle. He's tired. Raises his arms to be carried. They still have a way to go. For she dare not go the short way, the easy way, in case her father decides to leave the show early because of the impending storm and she meet them on the road.

Carrying a toddler and a large holdall is not easy. She needs to keep stopping. Putting him down to give her arms a rest. She is scared now. Terrified. Cannot see them boarding the ferry this day. Her resolve and their future are scattered to the wind. But she must protect Williain. Keep him calm. Safe. This is not in dispute.

"Come on my brave little man," she says in a light voice. "Not much farther. Then we shall sail on a ship. Go on that big adventure with Pooh."

It begins to hail as they reach Rothesay. Lightning forks across the sky. Onto the straits. Humungous waves, whipped by the spring tide and gale force wind, crash over the quay. Send spumes of saltwater up into the air. The noise is awesome. Mixed in with the claps of thunder is the scrape and creaking of the boats alongside the quay as they strain against their moorings. Some, not tethered securely, snap free. Are forced out into the angry sea. And there, cabins and hulls flooded with her wrath, sink down onto the seabed.

Afterwards, Isla has no idea where she finds the strength. But she does. Picking Williain up, she balances him on her hip and moves back, away from the waterfront. Walks along a path on the opposite side. Eventually, she finds a bed and breakfast and books them in for the night. Wonders what she would have done without James's money.

Once in their room, she drops the holdall and sits Williain on the bed. Pulls the curtains closed against the rage outside. And looks around. Isla has never stayed in a hotel or a bed and breakfast. She has no idea what to expect. But it looks tidy and clean. And on a tray atop a small table there's an electric kettle, some tea and coffee, two cups, sugar cubes and spoons. A little milk in a jug. She picks it up and sniffs. Fresh she thinks and turns the kettle on.

Now, she unzips the holdall and takes out Pooh bear. Sits him on the bed next to Williain. Williain picks him up and holds him close. Watches her through hooded eyes, heavy with sleep.

There are two towels hanging on a rail next to a wash basin. His mammy takes one and lays it across the bed. Then she takes the sandwiches, the cheese and apples and fruit juice out of the holdall and places them on the towel. Pours the fruit juice into a cup. Makes tea in the other when the kettle boils.

"Look, Williain," she says. "It's a picnic for a little boy and a Pooh bear who have a rumbly in their tumbly." She strokes her hand over his curls. "See, honey for his tummy." He watches her lift the corner of a piece of bread up. "But not in a jar," she says, "In a special sandwich." She tickles him.

Williain giggles. And picks up a sandwich. But he only manages a few bites, a sip of juice before the traumatic events of the day overwhelm him, and he falls fast asleep. Isla takes his shoes off and slips him under the covers.

But Isla cannot sleep. After she clears the picnic, she lies beside him and listens to the ferocity of the storm. A backdrop to his gentle breaths. Until, in the early hours of the morning, the noise of the wind and hail, the thunder and lightning, the crashing waves on the front gradually abates. We are alright, she thinks as sunshine floods the room. We have survived. We are safe. She decides they will have breakfast, then leave. Board the first ferry to depart. But someone else waits for that ferry. Someone with no intent to leave.

Chapter 31

That same day Isla packs her bags, Charles and James will return to the farm sooner than they wish. Unpack the produce they purchase at the show. For even as they leave and head toward Rothesay, there is an eerie light out to sea. Dark clouds gather. Menace.

Charles parks the jeep. The agricultural show is in full flow, packed with livestock, farmers, machinery, and marquees. They see the bull. It is indeed a magnificent animal. Wander around the exhibits. The stalls. Charles buys Williain a tartan kilt and sporran for when he is older. A shawl for Isla. James would love to buy her something too but decides Charles would find this unacceptable.

But by mid-afternoon, the first forks of lightning zigzag across the sky. Thunder booms in the distance. And a dry wind, warm and sulphurous smelling, tornadoes across the island. One of the marquees collapses. Bales of straw barrel across the showground. Agitate the livestock which begin to panic. The organisers and sponsors have no choice but to announce the closure of this year's show. Charles and James have no choice but to return to Lochfrein.

Charles drives steadily, cautiously, as driving hail clouds the windscreen and gusts of wind buffet the jeep, threatening to blow it off the road. He's a good, steady driver. Yet, they are both relieved when he finally pulls into the farmyard. All of a piece.

Climbing out of the cab they battle through the flying debris to the kitchen door. Purchases clutched tightly to their chests. They trust McGinty. Know he will have made sure all the livestock are safe. Neither wants to venture out in this.

The farmhouse is uncannily quiet. Strangely tidy. No toys strewn across the floor. No sign of any food preparation. No Chad to greet them. McGinty must have him. But who has Isla and the boy?

"Isla? Williain?" shouts Charles. No reply. Just silence.

Charles throws the presents onto the table which is also strangely tidy. No plates. No knives and forks. No napkins.

"Isla? Williain?" he calls out again.

Nothing. It's so quiet they can hear the coke burning in the Aga. The ticking of the grandfather clock in the corridor. A hollowness echoes through the empty rooms.

The soul has gone out of Lochfrein. The farmhouse now feels devoid of human warmth. We've both lost someone special thinks James. And are steeped in sadness.

Charles climbs the stairs as fast as his arthritic knees will permit. Enters Isla's bedroom. Sees the open wardrobe. The empty coat hangers. The pulled-out drawers.

"BITCH! BITCH! HOW DARE SHE!"

James hears his rants. Runs up the stairs.

"What? Dare what?" he asks. Although he already knows the answer.

"She's gone. Left. Taken our son. How dare she. I'll find her. I'll kill her."

"Not this night, my love. You'd be a fool to go back out in this. The eye of the storm is right overhead. Best we go at first light. Drive to Rothesay. We'll find them." He looks at Charles. "You know it makes sense."

"I can't wait until the morning. I shan't be able to sleep. What if something befalls the boy?"

Or Isla, thinks James. He prays they are safe. He prays they made it to the ferry before the storm engulfed the island. He prays they are on a train, travelling down to Yorkshire.

"Isla would never put Williain in harm's way, Charles. She will protect him. Why don't we have something to eat? Go to bed early. Make love all night. Then you won't have to sleep."

"Why don't we forget the food." Charles, fuelled with testosterone, adrenalin and rage. A lethal combination. "Why don't we just fuck, darling. Go and grab the whisky."

****

Isla waits on the quay. It's a calm bright morning. Warm and sunny. Debris from yesterday's tempest is strewn everywhere. People are already out and about, putting the world to rights. There are a few others waiting for the ferry.

She's anxious. Fidgety. Wishes time could go faster. Williain, after a good night's sleep, is excited. He's awed by the ships. The smells of the harbour.

And then, she sees the blue of the quad cab as it pulls into a nearby car park. He's out first. James trails behind. She can tell by his movements that he's angry. And as he draws nearer, she knows by the look on his face that this is not her father who bears down on them, but Mr Hyde. Isla holds onto Williain because she knows that once the little boy spots his fathers, he will want to run to them. And for now Williain is all she has. She will not let him go.

"Pappy Choochoo!"

He sees Charles first. Struggles to break free. Isla's hand grips his tiny wrist. Too tight. He squirms. Cries out. Isla knows she's hurting him. But dare not loosen her hold.

And as her father, robust in his rage, is almost upon them, she realizes it's too late. She has nowhere to run to.

Williain shrieks now. A high-pitched child's shriek that cuts to the soul. Folk are turning to see where the noise comes from. What the problem is.

"Pappy Choochoo! Pappy Choochoo! Me go. Mammy. Me go."

"Let the boy go, Isla."

He's right in front of her. Yet when she searches for James, hoping he'll do something. Anything. He stands back. A look of anguish etched on his face. His body carved in stone. A statue that cannot move.

"Get away from us!" Isla shouts.

Charles reaches out. Isla kicks him. Williain wails louder. Isla grips him tighter. Charles slaps her cheek.

They have an audience now. Bystanders wearing expressions of concern.

"You're not having him," she yells. "You're never having him. I'll kill us both before you do. I will. I mean it."

The audience watching the developing debacle hear her words. But do not witness the knee he thrusts into her belly. The fist he slams into her cheek. Punches against her head.

Its impetus propels her forward. In that fleeting moment, Isla knows he wins. She can't hold on to Williain, or life, any longer. She tumbles forcibly forward. Bangs her head on the scrolled iron support of a bench. There's a resounding crack. And the world goes black. As black as the Earl of Hell's waistcoat. Then there is nothing. She is back in the womb. Before birth. Before life. Whilst a thin trickle of blood tracks across the quay.

The play ends. Aghast the audience rushes up.

"I'll go and call for an ambulance," shouts someone.

James's façade crumbles. He rushes up too.

"What have you done, Charles," he says.

Charles feigns distress. Drops to his knees and tries to find a pulse. But his once fine fingers, fingers that could deftly wield a scalpel, now twist and knot, their tips devoid of feeling. He can't find one.

"She's dead," he declares. And playing his part to perfection, turns a stunned face to the audience. "You heard her," he says. "I had to stop her." He weeps false tears. "She…She just fell."

"Mammy. Mammy. Mammy," screams Williain over, and over, and over again. James is sobbing too now.

"Take him, James!" Charles, still directing. "Take him back to the jeep. I'll wait here. Until they come for her."

******

The ambulance arrives. Three ambulance men discharge. Each smartly attired in a dark blue uniform. Peaked blue caps on their heads. One asks Charles the patient's name. A telephone number where he can be contacted. A brief recap of the 'accident'. Any underlying problems. Whilst the other two, quickly and efficiently, put Isla on a stretcher and load her into the ambulance. The one taking details, closes the doors with a resounding slam. Turns to Charles.

"Don't worry," he says. "Whatever, she'll be in the best hands."

He climbs into the driver's seat. And blue light spinning, bell ringing shrilly, the ambulance races off. Takes Isla to the accident and emergency department at the Victoria Hospital.

The police also arrive. Take statements from Charles. And some of the onlookers who, witnessing the fracas and its aftermath, feel it prudent to stay. Even though they miss the ferry and will have to wait for the next one.

James remains in the jeep trying to calm a distressed little boy. How can they tell him that his mother is dead? What words can they use for one so young? That she sleeps? Is up in the sky? With God, in heaven? As disbelievers such words would be disingenuous. Maybe, thinks James, take out 'God', and for the time being, 'in heaven' might suffice.

They drive back to Lochfrein in silence. James warms some milk, sweetens it with honey. Pours a tot of whisky in and gives it to Williain. The little boy is traumatised and tearful. But he's quiet now. All screamed out. James carries him upstairs and lays him gently in Isla's bed. Quietly closes the door.

Downstairs McGinty and Chad have come into the kitchen.

"Ahm pure dun in," he says.

His face is grimy. Sweaty. He tells them that all is well. The animals are fine. Lochfrein is lucky. There is little storm damage. And what there is, he will fix.

James should tell him. Now before he loses his nerve.

"Isla's dead," he blurts out.

"Deid?" McGinty's face is a picture of disbelief. "Nae. Yer maun talking oot yer fanny flaps."

"English, Scott," says Charles. "And it's true. She's dead. There was a terrible accident yesterday in the storm. Down by the quay in Rothesay."

"The bairn?" he asks.

"Williain is fine. Not a scratch. He's flat out, tucked up in bed."

"Aw, the puir wee lassie." McGinty is a tough Scotsman. He has dealt with many deaths. But his eyes well with tears. "I maun awa an tell the guidwife. The laddies an lassies." He's embarrassed. Not looking at Charles or James, but rubbing Chad's back, he says, "Cum the morn's morn, we mun keep the heid an' cairry oan'." And with that, head down, he leaves.

"I think he means that tomorrow," says James. "We must keep calm and carry on."

"Well, we don't have a choice, do we?"

"I suppose not. Williain *is* asleep by the way. I gave him a tot of whisky. What are we going to tell him when he awakes?"

"Humph! I don't want to be bothered with that now. Ah, whisky. Now you mention it, I think I will."

He's already picked up the decanter. Is pouring it into a tumbler. The first of many, thinks James.

"She's your daughter, Charles. Surely you must feel something. Some remorse. Some grief."

"Well I don't!" His voice is snarly. "She betrays us. Takes our son. Is going goodness knows where. Blabbing to god knows who. It's better this way." He leers at James. "Three's a crowd my dear."

"Perhaps, she was just taking him to see Columbine," James suggests, trying to appease. "She is his grandmother. And he is her first grandchild. She has rights. A right to see him, don't you think?"

Charles finishes the whisky. Pours another.

"Rights!" He takes a swig. "Columbine gives up any right when she turns to the bottle."

James keeps his counsel. Wonders if Charles can see the irony in his choice of words.

Chapter 32

The telephone is ringing. It's early. Charles snores in a whisky-soaked slumber. He peeps in on Williain. But he too stays fast asleep. Tying the cord of his dressing gown, James makes his way to the corridor where the telephone sits on a half-moon table pushed up to the wall.

"Good morning," says a voice. It has a slight Scottish lilt. "I'm calling from the Victoria Hospital. Could I speak to a Mr Charles Duncan?"

"I'm Mr Duncan," answers James. He's suddenly icy cold. Grips the telephone cord tightly.

"I'm transferring you to Dr Finlay. Bear with me, I won't be a moment."

There's a crackling on the line. James holds his breath.

"Mr Duncan?"

"Yes." He exhales.

"I'm pleased to inform you…"

Pleased, thinks James. *Then it must be good news, surely.*

"The young lady, Isla Duncan, your wife I believe, brought in last night was not dead. She did, however, suffer a severe head injury. The x-ray shows a small fracture. We have stitched the wound on her skull and she's on intravenous medication to reduce any infection or swelling of the brain. Unfortunately, she is in a coma. Your wife, Mr Duncan will remain in intensive care until we know more. The good news is that she is breathing on her own." He clears his throat. "I hope this answers any questions you may have."

James's relief is palpable. He's crying now.

"Thank you. Thank you," he sobs down the phone when he realizes she is still alive.

After he replaces the receiver, he also realizes that they will not have to have that 'talk' with Williain. That disingenuity does not present now. Instead, they will tell him that mammy is poorly and needs to stay in hospital until she is better. And what then he wonders?

The weeks pass and the first signs of Autumn make themselves known. James visits Isla regularly. He takes Williain. Isla is now in a tiny side room off the main ward. Her vital signs are stable. But she does not wake up.

"Mammy's asleep," he tells Williain.

Williain lies next to her. Strokes her face. Sings lullabies to her in his childish voice with its lisp and loosely formed words.

"Wake up, mammy," he says. "Wake up."

But when Isla does wake up, all is not as it should be. She recognizes neither James nor Williain. Does not even recognize herself. Becomes agitated. Violent. Shrieks and screams. Writhes in the bed. They pull up the sides so she can't fall out. Tether her to them. A temporary measure to protect her flaying arms from harm. But it's all too distressing for Williain.

James takes him back to Lochfrein. And as he drives into the farmyard, a heavy weight descends on his heart. What have they done to her?

It's not long after this last visit that James receives another call from Dr Finlay.

They are sitting in the parlour. No lights switched on. Pine logs crackle and spit in the fire grate. Flickering flames cast shadows. The smell of the pine mingles with the smell of cigar smoke. They drink whisky. Muse on the day. Williain is tucked up in Isla's bed. Chad lays on the carpet in front of the fire. He is not eating. His eyes carry a look of sorrow. He's pining for her, thinks James.

"Charles," he says. "I've had a phone call from the Victoria. They are transferring Isla to a hospital at Lochgilphead. It's an asylum. She's upsetting the other patients. Apparently, she has some sort of trauma induced amnesia. They have no idea when, or even if, she will remember what happens before the fall. But they talk of a treatment called Electroconvulsive Therapy. They think it might shock her brain into remembering."

"I don't think we want her to remember, do we?"

He draws on the cigar. Stands and, shooing Chad away, moves in front of the fire, turning so that it warms the backs of his legs.

"And it's too close…" He scratches his chin with his thumb and forefinger, the cigar still in his mouth. "There's a place in Yorkshire. I know the psychiatrist there. A Dr Zircona. It's a quaker run asylum It's reputedly the best in the country." He smiles. "At least it will look like we care…"

Oh but I do, thinks James.

"And of course, it's too far away to visit regularly," he continues "If at all. So, the boy will get used to having no mother. Forget her. We'll have to pay and it's not cheap." He's thinking. Finding a way. "But not to worry, I will sort that out, as a brother-in-law. The money can be transferred monthly from the farm account. You will have to sort Isla out, as her husband. Buy some pretty negligees. Underwear. A nice washbag. You know, women's stuff. You'll be good at that James." He scoffs. "Far better than me."

He is watching him closely. His eyes. His mouth. Somehow James manages to stop his face misbehaving. Betraying him. And keeps his expression impassive.

Charles is already making plans. Plotting the future.

"Tomorrow you will call this Dr Finlay and explain what you wish to do. You will tell the McGinty's that Isla's state of mind does not allow her to come back to Lochfrein. That we are taking her to a place where she will be cared for. Tell Scott that he and the boys are to look after the farm, whilst we are away. Just a few days, that's all. Ask Mrs McGinty if Williain and the dog can stay with them. Voila! The pieces start to fit together."

"And what will you be doing?"

"Me? I will be calling Dr Zircona. Explaining the situation. Putting the wheels in motion. Something in my gut tells me Isla will never be herself again. That she will never remember. And our lives can be just as I have always planned. The two of us…And our son."

"Awrite?" says McGinty when James spots him in the farmyard. Goes out. Recites Charles's spiel. "Och dinna fash," he says. "It's nae problem. Me and the laddies'll tak guid care o' the farm. The wean and Chad'll be awright at hame. The guidwife and lassies will be reit stoked."

James shakes his hand. "Thank you, Scott. Taphadh leat."

Three days later, Charles and James leave Lochfrein. Dr Finlay gives Isla something to keep her calm. Once on the ferry, Charles whiles away the time removing Williain's clothes from the rainbow striped holdall. Artfully places a pretty washbag, some lingerie and the few clothes that James buys into it. The sea is calm. The weather fair. And now they too are set fair.

As James drives down the Great North Road, he cannot help but recall that last time, ten years before. When he drives up. With the nine-year-old Amaryllis drugged and asleep in his steamer trunk. When he wonders how he will cope until Charles arrives. But in the end Amaryllis makes it easy. That goodness which shines out. Not just through her beautiful smile. But through all of her. He will never forget. Williain will fill the hole she leaves. Guilt and remorse will fill the hole left in his heart.

NINETEEN SEVENTY-FOUR

AMARYLLIS

Chapter 33

Amaryllis walks along the road where her father's practice once was. He has rooms, she recalls, in what is virtually a mansion. The road is lined either side with huge houses and their private driveways. Now they stand back and salute the newly tarmacked road. It still has a glean. No more potholes. The children that live here will not jump in puddles. Or hear the glorious crack of ice as it splinters.

She's come back. To the market town she grows up in. Seventeen years since she is abducted. Seven years since she tries to escape and fails. They are staying in a hotel. It sits on a hill near the town's War Memorial. It's nothing extravagant but the rooms are clean. The food edible. And it's affordable.

Eric comes with her. But today, he is going to find a museum. Apparently, the town and its environs has a lot of roman history which he'd like to learn about. He thinks Amaryllis needs space to face whatever she might learn as she retraces her childhood footprints.

And now, her feet take her round the corner. Onto Oaktree Drive. She can see Oakwood now. The porthole window under the eaves. The stepped wall she sits on. Her mouth is dry. Be strong she tells herself as her feet lead her toward the gates of the drive. And then they halt. Right by a turning to the left. Pasture Lane. Something is changed.

She's remembering an open lane, mostly full of weeds, stones, and grass. Roughly fenced, it ran alongside Oakwood's drive, past the vegetable patch, the coke shed, the orchard. All the way down to the compost heap at the bottom of the garden. Another memory. Her and Penelope. They play in that lane. Build dens. It ends at a ranch style gate to a field.

The gate is wide enough to allow a tractor and trailer through. But she can't recall what is in the field. Horses perhaps? Or...Yes, they see what looks like a rickety shelter with a corrugated roof. Think it will make a better den than the ones they make. Climb over the gate and quietly creep up. Two sides have some sort of boarding on them. The rest is open to the field.

The shelter is full of straw. And something else. Something that snores. Amaryllis is back there with Penelope. She can hear it. Smell it. See the roundly mass that pokes out of the straw. It's a dirty pink. Imperceptibly moves with each snore.

"What is it?" Penelope says.

"I don't know." Amaryllis giggles. "Let's find out."

There's a pitchfork propped against the shelter. Amaryllis picks it up. Prods whatever it is. The straw moves. A loud grunt. A loud disgruntled grunt. And a huge boar, angry and tusked, rises out of the straw. Sees the two girls. Prepares to charge.

"Run!" cries Amaryllis.

She grabs Penelope's hand and they race back to the gate. The boar is right behind them. There's no time to climb back over the gate so they squirm and wriggle under it. Just in time! Its fearsome tusks stab through a gap in the slats, narrowly missing them. Snuffling and grunting, the boar makes its way back to the shelter.

Amaryllis and Penelope collapse on the grass with relief. Gulp in huge gasps of air. And now, the danger is gone, laugh. Silly girlish laughter, which once begun, is hard to stop. We 'laugh our socks off', thinks Amaryllis. She wonders where Penelope is now. If she is married? Has children?

Then, the present, where she is, what she tries to delay, intrudes her reverie. It's not a lane now but a road. Still signed Pasture Lane. But the sign is new. Smart. Why turn it into a road? She wonders. Where does it go? And still pondering, Amaryllis turns into Oakwood's drive and with trepidation, walks past the rockery and up the steps. The big iron knocker is still on the porch door. She lifts it up and raps three times. Waits.

A woman comes through the inner door and opens the outer one. It can't be her mother. She is far too young.

"Good morning," she says. "How can I help you?"

Amaryllis notices she wears jeans. A fluffy jumper. Has an apron over her clothes. Her face is kindly.

"My name is…Amaryllis August. I lived here as a child. I…"

"Come in. Come in. My name is Prudence. Prudence Walker."

She ushers her into the hall. The Victorian tiles still cover the floor. The carved banisters are still well polished. But now carpeting covers each stair, end to end. No more edges to sweep with dustpan and brush. Amaryllis recalls Gladys doing this. All the way down from the attic.

"Would you like to look round?" Prudence is asking. "I expect you'll notice a great deal of change."

"No, thank you," Amaryllis replies. "I think I want to remember it as it was."

She can hear a lot of chatter and laughter coming from the lounge. Several youngsters come out and cross the hall. Two more are descending the stairs. Another one is being pushed in a wheelchair.

"You have a large family," Amaryllis comments. "There was only me and my parents rattling about in this big old house."

Prudence Walker laughs.

"Good heavens, no. We have no children of our own. Sadly, we couldn't. So, me and my husband think perhaps we can combine our talents. Buy a large house and care for young people. Some physically disabled. Most mentally impaired. But all from families that cannot cope. Shunned by a society that does not want to. When we look round Oakwood, it is perfect."

Amaryllis pales.

"So, it's an asylum?" she asks.

"Goodness me, it's certainly not an asylum. This is their home. We hope to help them, eventually lead independent lives. Those who cannot achieve this will stay at Oakwood for as long as we can take care of them." She pauses. "It's a hotel you know when we buy it. Hence, all the alterations."

"Then you can't have purchased it from my father, Dr Charles August."

"No, his name isn't August. And he isn't a doctor. The circumstances are quite tragic. Won't you come and sit down. Have a cup of tea?"

"I don't really have the time. I'm looking for someone. But thank you. So could I ask who you did you purchase the house from?"

"Well...Walk Thomas, don't run," she calls to a young boy who suddenly runs through to the dining room. "The doors to the garden are open," she explains. "He always wants to be outside. We have a garden man who helps..."

Garden man remembers Amaryllis fondly. But it can't be Mr Kirby. Not after all this time.

"Working with the soil. Growing flowers. Different vegetables they can cook and eat," Amaryllis hears her saying, "helps their mental state. We also have rabbits, guinea pigs, and chickens…Oh, I digress. No, his name is, um, let me think, Martindale! Mr Martindale. That's right. He's an entrepreneur. The husband of the young couple who buy Oakwood before us. I believe a family had it first for a few years. Then they emigrate and Mr and Mrs Martindale purchase it…

"They wish to open a hotel. So all the bedrooms are given a bathroom and toilet. The dining room is furnished with tables and chairs. The kitchen upgraded with big ovens and all the latest appliances. There's even a laundry room. A drying room. They spend a small fortune. But three years after they open, his wife and child are killed in an automobile accident. He loses heart. Doesn't want to run a hotel on his own. So, he puts it up for sale."

"Me and my husband, we are looking for somewhere. See the photo in an estate agent's window. It's perfect for our needs. So here we are."

"How tragic," says Amaryllis. "Yet out of tragedy comes something good. You find what you are looking for. I wish I could."

"And what is it you look for my dear?"

"My mother, Columbine August."

"Columbine?" echoes Prudence. "Such an unusual name. It could be coincidence but…"

Amaryllis's heart skips a beat.

"We do have a Columbine who helps here. She comes most weekdays." Prudence pauses. "I'm sorry, her surname eludes me. All the kids love her. She's an excellent cook. Makes wonderful cakes. Chocolate cakes. Coffee and walnut cakes. Birthday cakes…"

Her mother in the kitchen with the big brown bowl, beating the cake mixture. The mixture for her birthday cake when she is nine.

"And she brings bunches of fresh roses from her garden." Prudence gives a laugh. "What that woman doesn't know about roses. She's a skilled seamstress too."

"My mother is a dressmaker," says Amaryllis. "I'm not sure about the roses. But I remember her cakes. My favourites were the fairy cakes with the butterfly wings pushed into the creamy stuff. Do you think she could be my mother?"

She's feeling a little sick from an excitement that bubbles inside her. Does not want to get her hopes up in case they are dashed. But she needs to know. One way or the other.

"Well…" Prudence takes a long, hard look at Amaryllis. "She's the right sort of age to be a mother. But she never speaks of a daughter."

"She wouldn't. She believes me dead."

"Ah, that would explain the sad expression that often flits across her face."

"It all fits," says Amaryllis. "Could you tell me where she lives? After all this time, I'm prepared to take a gamble."

"I can. And I will. I'm not going to pry into the circumstances that bring you here. Because I know that should Columbine be your mother, she will tell me in her own good time."

Prudence Walker beckons Amaryllis outside. Takes her round to where a path once lay below the wide bay window and dining room door. She remembers the iron bench. Her father likes to sit there where he can view the whole garden in all its glorious colours. She remembers sitting on this with her mother. They pod peas, which they collect from the row upon row that Mr Kirby grows at the side of the garden. The pea vines are taller than her. She recalls how sweet they taste. That she eats more than she pods.

The bench is gone. The path is now a beautiful stone patio. There are tables and chairs. Big umbrellas to give shade from the sun. The dining room now has two doors which open out onto the patio. But the grass hill still slopes down to the flowerbeds, shrubs. The oak tree. Amaryllis remembers sliding down the grass hill on the metal tray that covers the gas cooker. When the snow turns the garden into a winter wonderland. When once the hill seems so steep. So exciting.

"Now then," Prudence is saying, "do you see that stone wall along the bottom of the garden?"

Amaryllis looks. It runs behind the oak tree, the length of the garden's diameter. The orchard which used to be there is gone. Disappeared behind a wall.

"Does the builder need glasses?" she asks.

"Glasses? Why?"

"The wall's all wonky. In fact it undulates like waves on the sea; but vertically."

Prudence Walker laughs. "A poetic way of looking at it. But the builder is most proud of his wall. A crinkle crankle wall…"

Now, it's Amaryllis who laughs.

"They're mostly found farther south, Suffolk, Norfolk," Prudence explains. "Particularly places that get strong winds as they are stronger than a straight wall.

But a few are creeping into the north. The builder puts it there for aesthetic reasons".

Amaryllis agrees. There's a soothing rhythm in its rolling contours.

"Well, behind that crinkle crankle wall is a cul-de-sac. It's called Acorn Way. You get to it from Pasture Lane…"

"I know Pasture Lane. But when I lived here, it was just that, an overgrown lane that led to a field."

"Well if you go right down to the bottom, you'll see the turning to Acorn Way. There are four bungalows. Columbine lives in one. Rose Cottage, it's called."

Amaryllis hugs her. "Thank you," she says. "It's nice to know Oakwood is in good hands. I think what you do for these young people is amazing. You save them from being locked up in an asylum at the mercy of strangers."

She says it with feeling. From the heart. Because Isla Duncan knows.

"Good luck, my dear." Prudence Walker stands outside the porch and waves. "I hope you find what you are looking for."

Chapter 34

Now, Amaryllis's feet take her along a narrow footpath at the side of Pasture Lane. Remembering, she goes past where the old garage used to be. It's now replaced with a freshly painted dark green one. The coke shed is gone. Mr Kirby's greenhouse and its talking tomatoes is gone. In their place are small vegetable plots. Strawberry beds, the plants under nets. Two rows of pea vines. Rabbit hutches with runs.

There's a hen coop and outside space for scrabbling and pecking, all enclosed in wire netting. She can hear the whistling call of guinea pigs. See two rather overweight girls weeding and watering the vegetables. And tomatoes now planted outside in pots. Their tall stems tied to stakes of bamboo.

Bamboo. She has a bow and arrow made from bamboo. Uncle James, as she thinks him then, makes it for her. He makes one for Penelope too. Because she asks him. So they can play cowboys and Indians. He is kind to her. Fun. She loves him. Why does it all have to go so wrong?

Now she comes to a turning. A sign which reads Acorn Way. The cul-de-sac is as long as the width of Oakwood's garden. It encroaches on the field at the bottom where now two piebald horses munch the sparse grass. Swish their tails to bat away the flies. There's a shelter for them to escape the wind and rain. It's sturdy. With a water trough outside.

Rose Cottage is the first bungalow she sees. All the bungalows have small, well-tended, front gardens. Each has a parking space and garage. A path to the side leading to a gate and back garden. A Morris Minor, dark blue, sits on the parking space next to Rose Cottage. Her mother has a Morris Minor, she recalls. Has she kept it all these years? Too many coincidences. Now, as Amaryllis puts a finger on the doorbell and pushes, she lets the excitement bubble up. Froth over.

There's no answer. She rings it again. Still no-one comes. No, she thinks. I haven't come this far for her to be out. She must be here. She must. So, quietly, she opens the side gate and walks down a path to the back garden. Rose bushes in myriad colours are planted in beds that surround a small, grassed area with a sundial in the middle.

There's a woman on her knees. A slim woman. She's weeding between the bushes. It's hot. She stops to lay down a trowel. Wipes her forehead. She's wearing gardening gloves. Amaryllis can't see her face. All she can see is the back of her head. Her hair is curly. Streaked with silver.

I'm nine she thinks. My mummy has raven black hair. She's round and cuddly. But...

"Mum?" she says softly.

The woman hears. But picks up the trowel and carries on weeding. Does not turn. How many times since that day does she hear her voice? Over the years it progresses from 'mummy' to 'mum'. But when hope fills her heart. When she looks, there is never anybody there.

"Mum. It's me. Amaryllis." She steps a little closer.

The woman drops the trowel. Takes off the gardening gloves and pushing up onto her feet, turns. Gasps. This time there is somebody there. A young woman is facing her. She has long blonde hair. Is wearing a blue, white and green blocked knee-length dress. Long blue laced boots and large, white-rimmed sunglasses. She doesn't recognize the voice. Or her.

"Say it again," she says, slowly approaching until they stand face to face.

"It's me, mum. Amaryllis." Her lips tremble. She's taken off the sunglasses and put them in a green shoulder bag. But now that she stands before this woman, she doesn't recognize her.

Columbine reaches out her hands. Still expects them to pass through thin air. But no, they touch a face. She holds it between them. The skin is soft, subtly tinted with make-up. Her lips are full and fuchsia pink. The eyes are wide and brown, their lids painted a pale green. She is real. Not a spectre. And the more Columbine searches this face, the more she sees the nine-year-old Amaryllis. A child who grows into this beautiful young woman.

"How old are you?" she asks, still remembering when Detective Moulton tells them that their daughter is likely dead.

"Twenty-six," replies Amaryllis, still remembering when her father tells her that her mother has probably topped herself.

"I thought you were dead," they both cry simultaneously. And hug. The biggest hug ever. A hug that embraces seventeen years of hidden hope and sorrow. They cry and laugh. Laugh and cry. Cry because they lose each other. Laugh because they find each other.

"It's you. It's really you." Columbine can't stop touching her. Still thinks it's all a dream. That perhaps she has sunstroke from weeding too long. Is delirious. Hallucinating. But no, when she says, "Shall we go inside. I'll put the kettle on." Amaryllis is right behind her.

Columbine leaves her garden clogs on the step. Slides open a patio door that leads into a kitchen. It's compact with pristine white units and black granite worktops. The glean of stainless steel is everywhere. She bustles about, opening doors, getting out cups and saucers. Taking milk out of the fridge. Lighting a gas ring on which a blue kettle sits.

"Do you take sugar?" she asks. And then sobs. A mother should know such things.

Amaryllis shakes her head. Gazes out at the roses. Wonders how to begin. To tell a story that is not exactly a good read.

The kettle whistles. Its shrill cry invades the awkward silence. The absence of speech. Columbine pours the water into a brown teapot and puts it on the table. She's not sure how to ask. How to start a conversation a part of her dreads the answer to. But she wants to know.

"Where've you been all this time?" There, she's said it. Asked. Columbine pours milk into the cups. Gives the teapot a stir. Waits.

"On a farm." Amaryllis pulls a cup and saucer toward her. "On an island." She can't tell her what they do to her. The Sanctum. Not yet.

"But how? Why? And why don't you call?"

"I can't. I am not allowed. And I'm too afraid to disobey."

Columbine feels a frisson of fear. Her daughter's words. They hide something. Something she does not want to hear. But knows she must.

"Mum," Amaryllis says, before Columbine opens her mouth. "Can I ask you a question?"

Columbine's head nods imperceptibly. Better to be asked than be the one who is asking.

"How well do you know my father. I mean really know him?"

Columbine pours out the tea.

"Well, I know he's a good doctor. I know he wants a son. I know he has a cruel streak." She plops two sugar cubes into her cup. "And I know he doesn't love me." She looks up. "But I know he loves you."

194

Amaryllis looks into her mother's eyes. "Then you don't know that when I am little," she begins to say, "when he baths me, when he sometimes comes into my bedroom at night, he…"

"No!" cries Columbine. "He wouldn't. He couldn't. Not that."

"He tells me it's our secret. That I mustn't tell anyone, especially you. So, I don't."

Columbine gets up. Goes to a cupboard. Fusses choosing biscuits. Arranging them on a plate. Whilst she tries to digest this. But it's the truth. She hears it in her daughter's voice. Sees it in her eyes.

"So do you run away? Is that what you do? But on your special day? Does someone find you. Take you?" she asks, putting the plate on the table.

Amaryllis stares at the pink and lemon iced biscuits she once so covets.

"Are they still your favourites?" Columbine asks, trying not to imagine what Charles does.

Amaryllis bursts out crying. "I wouldn't know," she says in between sobs. "I forget." That isn't true she thinks. "I forget who I am. Because in all this time he tells me I am not Amaryllis August. I am Isla Duncan. He makes me repeat it over and over. Until I begin to believe it."

"Duncan?" Columbine ponders. "Isn't that your Uncle James's name?"

"He's not my uncle." Amaryllis wipes her face on a tissue she plucks from a box on the table. "I find out. I find out something else too. That he's my father's lover. Has been for many years. Do you, did you, know?"

Columbine's eyes well with tears. She nods.

"Oh mum, it must have been so awful for you."

Columbine's teacup chinks on the saucer as she puts it down. Hands reaching out, she entwines her fingers with her daughter's.

"Awful? No. He gives me you my darling girl. And a place to live. Status. When after the war I have nothing. Am nobody."

"Then cruelly takes it all away from you."

"No. No." Columbine squeezes her hands. "It's because he's devastated when you disappear. After a few years he tells me he cannot bear to live at Oakwood anymore. He's going to first sell the orchard. A property developer buys it. Builds the road and bungalows. Charles buys a bungalow for me. I want for nothing. Then he sells the house. A young family buy it." She pauses. "So I hear their children's laughter."

"Don't you see, mum." Now Amaryllis squeezes her mother's hands. "That's cruel too. He's a cruel man."

"A sad man," says Columbine. "He says he's going to travel the world. Forget the war. Forget me. Forget what happens to you."

"But he doesn't."

Amaryllis stirs the tea in her cup even though she puts no sugar in. She can't look at her mother.

"He doesn't travel the world. He comes to the farm. Where James is. Where I am imprisoned. And he doesn't forget me because he uses me to fulfil his dream. Oh, mum." Somehow Amaryllis keeps her voice steady. "Why can't you accept it's my father who writes the music from the day he meets you. From the day I am born. It's my father who orchestrates everything. And because James loves him, he follows every instruction of his baton. It's James who abducts me that day. The day of my ninth birthday."

The look of horror on Columbine's face says it all. She doesn't know. Doesn't suspect. Can't believe.

"But then…Does that mean when you are Isla Duncan, you marry him? A man not much younger than your father. Please tell me you don't."

"I do," says Amaryllis. "And I don't. But I do have a child." She's trying so hard to not lose her composure.

"What? No! No! No!" Columbine almost screams the words. "Not Charles. No. He wouldn't. That's incest!"

Amaryllis gets up from the table and walking round to her mother drops onto her knees and buries her face in her lap.

"You have a grandson mum," she says softly. "And no, he's not my father's. He is mine and James's. But it's my father who incites him. I am scarcely sixteen when…" Oh god, she knows the meaning of the word now. "They rape me."

She cannot tell her how painful it is. How frightened she is. How she dreads every night. How defiled she feels. Nor can she give voice to the terrible things her father makes her do. The terrible things he does to her. These are things a mother does not need to hear. For once heard they can never be forgotten. So, wrapping her arms around Columbine's waist, she quietly weeps.

"There. There. It's alright. You're safe now. I should have been there to protect you."

Amaryllis feels her mother's fingers combing through her hair. Like she does when she is a child and wakes from a nightmare. Comforting. Calming.

"How could you? You don't know where I am. Daddy…" Columbine hears the regression. So does Amaryllis. She coughs. "My father. He makes sure of that. He engineers everything so coldly. And in the end, he has it all. James. The farm. The son he always wants. Happy families. But he doesn't want me now. I've played my part. And in the end, he doesn't even let me be a mum."

Columbine gently peels Amaryllis's arms from round her waist. Lifts her head so she can see her face. Brushes the fine blonde hair back from it. Wipes the tears off her cheeks.

"My grandson," she says, "what's his name?"

"Williain. Williain Joseph Duncan."

"And he's how old?"

"He'll be nine now." Amaryllis can see her mother knows the significance of this. "I haven't seen him since he is almost two."

"Then you don't bring him with you."

Amaryllis is really crying now. Remembering.

"I can't. Because when I try, seven years ago, my father stops me. He takes James. He takes Williain. And he takes my life."

"Ssh! Ssh! Somehow, we will make it right. You cry, sweetheart. I cry an ocean of tears that day and every day on. Trying not to picture all the dreadful things that might have befallen you. Things no mother should have to imagine. So I eat and I eat. Drink more bottles of gin than I can count. Try to lose myself. Try to end it all."

Amaryllis hears the anguish in her voice. Sees her pain mirrored in Columbine's tear-streaked face. She never really thinks how much her abduction affects her mother. But now she knows.

"But you don't," she says, smiling weakly.

"I contemplate it many times," Columbine says. "But no, I don't. Because there is always hope."

Chapter 35

Columbine boils the kettle again. Rinses out the teapot and puts fresh leaves in. Empties the cups into the sink. The first brew is cold. Abandoned in the telling. Now they sit in silence. Sip their tea. Eat all the party biscuits. A guilty feast of celebration. Amaryllis's journey is too convoluted to untwist in these few precious hours. But she has all the time in the world now.

"Can you stay?" Columbine is at the sink now. A pair of yellow rubber gloves on her hand. The sound of running water is soothing as she rinses the cups and saucers.

"Not today, mum. I did not come alone." She picks up a teacloth and begins to dry the china.

Columbine is peeling off the gloves. Wiping down the stainless-steel sink and taps so they shine in the sunlight that shines through the window. "But you said…"

"No, it's not James. It's my fiancé…"

"Fiancé? That means you're getting married. Is it for real this time?" It's all moving too fast for Columbine.

"Yes." Amaryllis smiles. Dries the spoons. "He's called Eric Skeldergate. He's a psychiatric nurse. You'll like him. And you'll like his mum, Doris. She's been so good to me. But I need to find you. I don't believe what my father tells me, that you've probably topped yourself. I am so glad you didn't. And I am so glad I've found you. Because now, I can ask if you will give me away."

"Well, I never." Columbine is smiling now.

"And make my wedding dress…If you'd like to. If you could."

"Just a minute…" Amaryllis watches as her mother leaves the kitchen. Restless, walks around, trailing her fingers across the cool, smooth, granite worktops.

When she comes back in, she's holding a coat hanger. Whatever hangs on it is shrouded in plastic. Columbine rolls up the plastic and there is the pink party dress in all its frills and frippery.

"I made this for your ninth birthday," she says. "Do you remember?"

Amaryllis stares at the sash, the pink bow. "I remember," she says.

"I've kept it all these years. At first, in case you came back, as the detective said you might. But when you didn't, I just couldn't bring myself to part with it. I never thought then that the next dress I make for you will be a wedding dress."

"So you will? Oh that's wonderful!"

Amaryllis goes to her. Touches the dress. It's a bit over the top for her tastes now, but a young girl would feel like a princess wearing it she thinks. And hugs both Columbine and the dress.

"Mum, do you remember my school friend, Penelope? She is always round Oakwood."

"I do. A pair of scallywags you are when you're together."

"Does she still live in the town?"

"Yes. She marries a dentist. Mrs Wilberforce, she's called now."

"And children?"

"I believe she has two. A boy and a girl. The girl is the older, seven or eight, I think. Pretty little things. I meet her in the market one day." Columbine stops. Looks from the dress to Amaryllis. "Are you thinking what I'm thinking?" she says.

"It will make a lovely bridesmaid's dress." They both say together.

"That's settled then," Columbine hangs the dress on a door handle.

"Not quite." Amaryllis is walking round and round the table. "I want Williain to be a page boy."

"And he can't, because?"

"I told you, they have him. James and my father."

"On the farm?"

"Yes."

"Then we'll go and fetch him. I said, we'll make it right."

"We can't mum. It's not that easy. You don't understand."

"Then tell me."

"Not now. There is too much to tell. Tomorrow. I really must go now. Meet Eric back at the hotel. Tell him the good news. We're staying at the Talbot. But first thing in the morning, I promise we will both come round. You can meet him. And we'll talk then." She laughs. "I think I might need his moral support."

Parting is such sweet sorrow thinks Columbine as she watches her daughter walk through the gate and looking back, lift her arm and wave.

She will not sleep this night. Will replay this day over and over. As will Amaryllis, who will not sleep either. Because she still must work out how tell her mother about Isla Duncan. About the Sanctum.

******

It's another lovely day. Amaryllis and Eric walk hand in hand, retracing her footprints of yesterday. She keeps lifting her hand so the sun can catch the diamond in the ring on her finger. Last evening as she walks down the hill toward the Talbot, she sees Eric sitting outside with a beer. Breathless with excitement, she runs up to him. Kisses his lips lovingly.

"I found her. I found her," she repeats. "She's alive. She wants to meet you." She pauses for breath. "And she's going to give me away. Make my wedding dress. I have had such a wonderful day, Eric. Oh this is all so amazing!"

Eric kisses her back. "In case you're interested, I have had a wonderful day too," he says, smiling.

"Sorry. Sorry. Yes. I forgot. So did you find the museum?"

"I did." Eric replies. "And I was told about a roman camp. So I went there too. A feast of artefacts, relics, and information. And I found something else…"

He's delving into pockets. Pulls out a small box. And then, in front of the other guests sitting outside, sipping cocktails, enjoying the last few hours of the sun's warmth, he gets up and drops onto one knee. Opens the box. "I know I've already asked you, but I didn't have a ring then, so I'm asking you again. Amaryllis August, will you marry me?"

Everyone is smiling. Waiting.

"Yes, Eric Skeldergate. I will marry you."

Everyone claps. Cheers.

Eric gets up. Slips the ring on her wedding finger. She gasps. It's beautiful. And very unusual.

"After wandering round the museum and the camp, I take a wander round the town," he says. "See a jewellery shop and go in. It isn't a brand name jeweller, but small and independent. I discover the owner is a woman who designs and fashions all the jewellery herself. I tell her what I'm looking for and she puts a tray of rings on the counter. I see this. It isn't an engagement ring as such. But I think it perfect."

Amaryllis kisses him, long and deeply. There is more clapping and cheering. So, she walks in and out of the tables, showing everyone. The ring is intricately braided, a slim plait of intertwined yellow and white gold. Its statement is one diamond, surrounded by three sapphires, set between what is fashioned to look like the wings of a white swan. The sapphires representing the baby cygnets carried safely therein. Whooper swan she thinks again. Hope.

The following morning as they walk, hand in hand, along the Mount, Amaryllis points out things she remembers.

"This is the road I walk to school along. And see that big house?"

"They're all big," says Eric.

"That one, over there on the left. The one with the statue of an elephant in the garden. Well, that's where my father held his surgery. In two rooms downstairs." They turn now onto Oaktree Drive. "And see that wall up there? Where you can see a porthole window. That's Oakwood."

She tells him of her life there. As they draw nearer, he cannot believe the size of it. Cannot imagine having all those rooms. To be able to change bedrooms on a whim when he sleeps in the same bedroom since his birth. To have a tree big enough to build a tree house in. An orchard. And all the other stuff she tells him. It is a far different childhood than his. But he feels not an ounce of envy. He has always known he is loved.

Down Pasture Lane into Acorn Way, Eric follows Amaryllis to the doorbell of Rose Cottage. This time when she pushes it, the door opens immediately. As if Columbine has been waiting behind it.

"Oh come in. Come in," she says, ushering them along a corridor and into a spacious lounge. Eric takes his shoes off. Amaryllis her boots. And leave them in the corridor, aligned with several pairs of Columbine's shoes. Her mother's feet are small, she thinks.

"You must be Eric," Columbine begins to say and then spots the ring. "Oh let me see," she cries. "You weren't wearing it yesterday." Amaryllis holds out her hand. Straightens her fingers. "Why, it's quite exquisite!" Columbine exclaims. "I don't think I have ever seen one like it."

"And you never will, Mum. Eric only found it yesterday in an independent jeweller in the town. She only makes one of each design."

"I know that shop." Columbine says. "I sometimes have a browse. But never buy. You have excellent taste, Eric. Now, sit you both down. I'm going to pour us all a glass of champagne. I know it's a little early in the day. But I want to celebrate this moment. And then you can tell me how you met." And off she goes. Amaryllis and Eric look at each other and smile.

In the quiet, they hear the POP of the cork as it leaves the bottle and unleashes the bubbles. Columbine returns with a tray bearing a half full bottle of Dom Perignon and three champagne flutes.

"I always knew," she says, "that one day I'd have something to celebrate. And look, I suddenly have three things to celebrate. Finding my daughter. Gaining a future son-in-law. And planning a wedding."

They each take a flute. Clink them together.

"Let's drink to the future," says Columbine.

"To the future," chime Eric and Amaryllis.

"Now then," says Columbine as they sit on the comfy sofas. "You say you will tell me about the farm. Where you are kept."

Eric quietly sips his champagne and listens.

"James takes me there." Amaryllis pauses, the lips of the champagne flute half-way to her own. "That's when I become Isla Duncan. When I cannot be seen. When I am locked in my bedroom until darkness falls."

Columbine does not ask how she copes. "So you don't go to school?" she asks instead.

Amaryllis shakes her head. "James schools me. In fairness, he teaches me so much. I have a bedroom full of every book imaginable. There's a piano in the parlour," Amaryllis says, remembering. "And he teaches me to play both classical and modern music."

So, that's where she learns thinks Eric.

"She's an excellent player," he says. "I can vouch for that."

Columbine remembers the piano at Oakwood. A young lady who comes to the house to give Amaryllis lessons. Amaryllis's fingers running up and down the scales. Playing basic tunes.

"He tells me about the animals," Amaryllis continues, now lost in reverie. "Takes me out round the farm in the dark. I love it." She takes a big gulp of champagne. Hiccups as the bubbles go up her nose. "But all stops when my father arrives. He wants me drugged and locked up again." She laughs. "Until suddenly, when I am sixteen, I appear. Like a rabbit conjured from a magician's hat. And am paraded as James's wife."

Columbine hears in Amaryllis's words the bond she forms with James. The dread she holds for her father.

"Is that where Williain is born. On the farm?"

Amaryllis nods.

"But you don't tell me where it is. Is it near here?"

"The Ise of Bute." Amaryllis watches disbelief track across her mother's face. "I know," she says. "It's a fair long way."

"But not impossible. We could go. Fetch Williain."

"No. You still don't understand. It is on Rothesay pier my father tries to kill me, that day when I try to escape with Williain. He might appear charming on the surface. But underneath, he is a dangerous man, mum. Will stop at nothing to get what he wants."

"Listening to Amaryllis's story again," says Eric. "I agree with her. I'd even go as far as to say, he's a psychopath."

A psychopath! Columbine finds this hard to believe. All she ever saw was the charm. His charisma. Yes, he always expects to get what he wants, she remembers. And yes, he can be cruel. But that? Surely not.

"They are charming," he says. "Pillars of the community. But lack empathy. Have no moral compass. No conscience."

"Well," she says. "I guess that does describe him. But this is a day I want to celebrate. Not a day I want to discuss the character or morals of a man I foolishly fall in love with and marry. So, let us talk of happier things. Tell me how you meet…"

"I meet Eric…" Amaryllis drinks more champagne. Hiccups again. Laughs. "In the Sanctum."

"The Sanctum? But isn't that the?"

"Lunatic Asylum," says Amaryllis. "Yes, it is. And it's where I spend seven years of my life. Locked up for being one," She says it flippantly. But beneath her words, they hear the injustice she still feels.

Eric looks from Amaryllis to her mother. Sees the look of alarm on her face. Appreciates her incomprehension.

"I wouldn't call it that, Mrs August. It's more for those who are mentally impaired. Amaryllis or Isla, as I know her then, has amnesia and an eating disorder," he tells her. "But she's certainly no lunatic."

"Then why? How? And do call me Columbine. After all you're going to be my son-in-law."

"I think only she can tell this." And taking one of Amaryllis's hands, he lovingly holds it.

And so, in between the clink of glass, the sips of champagne, the only other sound to intrude is Amaryllis's voice as she recounts her flight from Lochfrein and what happens on the pier.

"I remember I am screaming. Williain is screaming. Then my father punches me hard. Shoves me. I fall. Hear the crack of my skull. Then nothing. I have no idea how long it is before I become aware. But when I do, I am in a strange bed, in a strange room. In a strange place. And that's where I stay for seven years."

Columbine feels her anguish. Her pain. This is her daughter. The daughter she believes dead. And so, has no idea of her suffering. The foundation she wears cracks as tears track a rivulet down her cheeks. Hurriedly, she wipes them away. Says nothing.

Eric: "I meet her at a hospital dance."

Amaryllis: "He's my knight in shining armour. Come to rescue me from Hannah. The ward I am locked in. Like Rapunzel in the tower," she says, trying to make light of it. "Except he can't climb up my hair." She laughs. "It's not long enough."

Locked up again, thinks Columbine. Wonders how she survives. But does not interrupt. This is her daughter's story. Not hers.

Eric: "I ask the Staff Nurse if she can come with me to walk with the patients that I take round the gardens."

Amaryllis: "And it's so good to be outside. To breathe the fresh air. To feel free. And we talk."

Eric: "We get on so well. We both write poetry. Love music. Laugh at the same things. I take her to my home. See no harm in it at the time. She meets my mum, Doris. And Rafferty, our puppy."

Amaryllis: "We ride on a bus." Her eyes light up. "And I love it there. At the house on Peasholme Green."

There's a Peasholm at Scarborough, thinks Columbine. A park with a lake, miniature railway and booths that sell ice creams, buckets and spades. I take her there on her seventh birthday. We have such a good day. We ride the water splash and get wet. If only I could have foreseen then what would occur two years later, perhaps I could have prevented it.

Eric: "But the establishment finds out. It's not permitted." His face mirrors the sadness that now clouds Amaryllis's. "A relationship that is not professional between a member of staff and a patient. I receive a letter. Go before the Board and am severely reprimanded. I cannot see 'Isla' anymore. So I write her a letter explaining. Say I love her. Want to marry her. And I post it."

Amaryllis: "I get the same letter from The Board of Trustees. And when I read it, I do go insane. Really insane. But then I don't get to read Eric's letter, until after I complete the jigsaw."

"Jigsaw?" echoes Columbine. "I don't understand."

Eric: "She tells me, that first time we meet at the dance, she is doing one in her head. Each piece a memory. And when all the pieces are in place, she will remember all those years she forgets."

"And I do. But first I must endure more treatment." Amaryllis laughs. Finishes off the champagne. Puts the empty flute on the coffee table. "Bolts of electricity shot through my head."

ECT. Columbine has heard of it. She thinks it barbaric. And to imagine her own daughter must endure this on top of everything else.

"And I don't know whether it's that which makes the severed connections in my brain find other pathways," Amaryllis continues. "Or whether I am now brave enough to use the key and unlock that space. Recognize what happens during those years. And confront it. Like your mother tells me to, Eric."

A hush falls in the room. Amaryllis is spent. But she feels calmer. Absolved. Slightly tipsy. Whilst Columbine is both shocked and horrified at what she learns. Watches Eric embrace Amaryllis. Hold her close.

"Well," she says, breaking the silence. "Your father is not the only one who can make plans. I have been making a few of my own." She refills the flutes. Empties the bottle of champagne.

"Amaryllis must stay here. Until the wedding, that is. There is a lot to organize. Dresses to make and fit. A date to decide. The church to book. Banns to be read. Caterers to be organized. Flowers. Oh golly! I am actually planning a wedding! I am going to see my daughter in a wedding dress and walk her down the aisle." Columbine is overwhelmed. "Not in a million years could I imagine this." She raises her glass. "To the future bride and groom."

Amaryllis and Eric hook arms. And laughing, try to get their lips on the brim of the glass. "To us," they splutter.

"I agree, Amaryllis should be with her mother now, not us," says Eric. "She's waited long enough to find you. And I imagine you still have much to catch up on. And a lot to organize. But I need to go back to the Sanctum tomorrow. I have an afternoon shift. I'll come over as soon as I can." He looks at Amaryllis. "Every day off, I'll come." And then, looking at Columbine, "Perhaps, one day I could bring my mum. I know she's dying to meet you. She'll want to help. She loves a wedding. And she's a pretty good sewer herself."

"Perfect," says Columbine. "But you can stay tonight surely? I have another bedroom." She sees their shock. "Well you are getting married, aren't you?" And then she laughs. "Don't worry, it has two single beds. But I guess you could push them together," she adds mischievously.

Amaryllis finds it hard to hear Eric and her mother make plans for her when all her life someone maps her every day. Perhaps it is now time to make plans of her own.

"Sorry, we can't stay tonight mum. We've paid for the room at the Talbot. And for dinner. Eric can leave from the hotel tomorrow. Then I'll come back here. I'd love to stay with you mum. Help plan the wedding. But the first thing we are going to do is go to the Police. I want my father apprehended. Locked up for ever. Give him a taste of his own medicine. And I want my son back."

Columbine notes that she makes no mention of James.

Chapter 36

Amaryllis and Eric walk back to the hotel, arms wrapped around each other. After the dinner, which is three courses, they wander into the snug to enjoy a late-night drink. They sit at the bar on tall stools. The stools swivel. Amaryllis cannot resist spinning round and round whilst the barman, his back to them, opens a bottle of fizz. Amaryllis hears the pop of the cork. The clink of glass as he puts the bottle in a bucket. The banging of the hammer as he breaks up the ice to pack round the bottle. Then he puts the bucket and two glasses on the top of the bar. And teacloth over his shoulder, starts to tidy the tables. Empty the ashtrays.

Amaryllis and Eric swivel their stools until they face each other. "Our last night together," he says. "Already I'm thinking of my next day off." But that is not all he is thinking of. Should he? Would she?

Amaryllis leans across and brushes her lips over his. Smiles into his eyes.

"Does that mean you will?" he asks.

"Will what?" She empties her glass. Feels the fizz bubbling down her throat. "Dance the fandango?" She laughs. "I think I'm too squiffy."

"That depends on what sort of fandango you refer to, my sweetheart." He takes her hand. "Let's finish this," he says. "And go up. I want you all to myself...Naked." He whispers in her ear.

And then she realizes. Her body freezes. Her muscles tense. She is back at Lochfrein. The parlour. Her father and James without a stitch of clothing on. Undressing in front of them. And then...

"What? What is it, darling? You've gone very pale." His voice. Her fiancé's voice. Not her father's. She loves him. Trusts him. Knows he will not hurt her. But then she trusted James, didn't she?

She drinks another glass of fizz. Perhaps if she is drunk, it will be alright. There is no-one left in the bar now. Eric picks her up and carries her to their room. She's giggling. Talking nonsense. Yet as soon as they are in the bedroom, she begins to dance. Spinning and twirling round and round the two beds.

"Look!" she cries. "I'm dancing the fandango. Dance with me, James." She has no idea she says his name.

But Eric hears the slip of her tongue. Begins to wonder. He grabs hold of her and sits her on the bed. Murmurs in her ear, "Take off your clothes…"

"Take off your clothes. Now!" She can see her father masturbating. His swollen penis. Just before he…Every muscle in her body tightens. She waits for Eric to tell her to get on her hands and knees.

But he doesn't. And it's not her father's voice she hears now. It's her fiancé's. The man she loves. The man she wants to spend the rest of her life with.

"Please," he whispers as he strokes the nape of her neck. "For me. I want to make love to you." He runs his hands up and down her back. Feels the tension in her shoulders. "Relax," he says, as he unbuttons her blouse and removes it. "Just relax and let me pleasure you."

Now he is kissing her neck. All the way round. Puts a finger under her chin and tilting her head, locks his lips on hers. His tongue explores her mouth. Amaryllis tenses. Eric pulls away.

"Trust me," he says. And gently lays her back on the bed. He twines his fingers through her hair. Kisses her eyes, her nose. Brushes them over her lips.

Now his hands explore her body. All the while he is kissing her. She closes her eyes and moans softly. Before she knows it, he has undressed her. Now his lips gently kiss her breasts. Nibble lightly on the nipples. She begins to writhe beneath him. Wants more. But she's not sure what of. A draught of cool air wafts across her bare skin. She doesn't open her eyes.

"Eric," she says on a breath. Time pauses. Then suddenly she feels his warm skin against hers. Tries not to think of all those other times when she is naked and feels skin against hers. But it never felt like this.

"Open your eyes. Look at me, my darling," she hears Eric say. But it's not an order. It's whispered on a kiss. She opens her eyes. And looks into his. They are full of love.

"Trust me," he whispers. "I know they hurt you. But I won't. I promise."

His fingers trail round her breasts, down between her ribs, over her stomach, between her thighs. And stay there.

Amaryllis moans. Writhes. She has no idea what he's doing, but she's tingling all over. On fire. Unbidden, she arches her back. And she is pleading.

Panting. Begging. And as Eric enters her, she moves with him, slowly at first. Gently. Until their desire for each other rules everything else out and they climax together. This is like the lovemaking she reads of in her novels, she thinks as she falls asleep, her head on Eric's chest. His arms wrapped around her.

Sunlight floods through the thin curtains which flutter in a gentle breeze blowing through the open window. Amaryllis stretches languidly in the bed.

"Oh, you're awake, sleepyhead."

Eric is up and dressed. She can see he's already packed his bag. A bag with straps which he can put over his shoulders. It's green and made of some kind of canvas.

"A backpack," he tells her. "Thanks to Asher 'Dick' Kelty, known as the Henry Ford of backpacking."

Amaryllis has no idea what a backpack is. But she does know Henry Ford is the maker of cars. Eric bends down to kiss her.

"Alright?" he asks.

"Very alright," she replies and kisses him. And then a sudden thought pops into her head. "Eric," she says, "I won't get pregnant, will I? I mean I want to." She laughs. "I want to have lots of babies with you. But not yet. Not with the trial and the move."

"Don't worry my love. I wore a condom this time." He smiles at her.

"What's a condom?"

"I'll show you." And he pecks her on the cheek. "Next time. But get a move on. They're serving breakfast, so we'd best go down…"

I am still so naïve, Amaryllis thinks, as she throws some clothes on. Quickly brushes through the tangle of her hair. Slips her feet into some sandals.

"Ready!" she says. "Let's eat, pack and go." She picks up the keys to the room. "In that order." She adds, her hand on the door handle.

The dining room is full. She can feel everyone's eyes on them as they make their way to a table by the window. They are all smiling. Do they know.

"Do I look different?" she whispers to Eric. "You look radiant, my darling," he says. "Whilst I could murder a full English breakfast." A waitress is approaching, pad and pencil at the ready.

"Two full English breakfasts please and a pot of tea for two," orders Amaryllis. And then to Eric, "You're not the only one who's hungry," she says laughingly.

Their room is to be vacated by 10 o'clock. Amaryllis packs her few clothes into the holdall. The holdall with the rainbow colours that she buys in Rothesay. The same holdall she packs that fateful day. But she is not going to think on that. Not today when she feels loved. Happy.

"I'm catching the ten fifty-five train to York," Eric is saying as they stand in the car park. "But I'll come over on my first day off. Fetch the rest of your things. Love you." And with a wave of his hand, he is walking down the hill. She watches the green backpack, snug against his back, until she can no longer see it. And then picking up her holdall, makes her way to Rose Cottage and her mother.

Chapter 37

"Can I be of assistance, ma'am?" The desk sergeant is leaning across the counter. Amaryllis and Columbine are the only two people in what doubles as a reception room and waiting room.

"We'd like to see your Commanding Officer," says Columbine.

Uh, oh thinks the desk sergeant. What've we got here?

"Mum." Amaryllis nudges her. "This isn't the army. It's the police."

"Oh yes, of course." Columbine laughs. "Silly me. Well we want to report a crime," she says.

"Well I'm your man," he says jovially. "I just need to…" Whereupon the desk sergeant disappears. They can hear him rummaging about under the counter. A muffled, "Find the incident." Then up he pops, like a jack-in-the-box, with a thick pad which he slams on the counter. Retrieves a biro from behind his ear and hand poised ready to write, looks up at the two women.

Left-handed, Columbine notes.

"Could I first take your name and address," he says.

Columbine goes right up to the counter.

"Columbine August, Rose Cottage, Acorn Way, Pasture Lane, Malton."

Col…the sergeant begins to write. "That's an unusual name," he remarks. "Could you spell it."

Columbine pronounces each vowel and consonant loudly and clearly. Watches him scribble across the page, the incident pad all of a slant.

"You'd do better to put the pad straight," she says. "It might help with your writing."

"Why thank you, ma'am," he says. "And it might not. I'm left-handed see. Got to tilt the paper so's I can write."

"Of course. Yes, I did note that. Sorry."

"Telephone?"

"2404."

"Thank you. And the crime you want to report?"

"Abduction. Drugging. Imprisonment. Rape. And attempted murder."

"That's five crimes ma'am," says the desk sergeant, wryly. He takes his time to write it all down. "Date and time of said crimes?" He waits, wondering now.

"The 21st of June 1957." Columbine falters. It's all coming back to her. "About noonish."

"Beg pardon. Could you repeat that?" Has he misheard?

Columbine repeats it.

The desk sergeant scratches his head. He's got a numskull here. And the other one. Well, she's not said a word yet. She's a tad too pale. But a whole lot pretty.

"I'm sorry, Mrs er…" He glances down at the incident pad. "Mrs August. But that's seventeen years ago. There's nothing we can do now. There'll be no clues or evidence left after all this time."

"I'm quite aware of the time lapse, sergeant. But the abduction *was* reported seventeen years ago. There are no clues or evidence then, except a rose gold watch which a PC finds. It belongs to my daughter. And no, there are no other fingerprints. Just hers. She is never found. The case is closed. I believe you call them 'Cold Cases'?"

"You've been watching too many of them detective programmes."

"Be that as it may sergeant. But we come here today to warm that case up. We have evidence now. And I would really like to speak to someone, um, no disrespect, higher up."

The desk sergeant is still scribbling.

"Well if you can just tell me what this new evidence is, I can log it. And then see where it takes us." Out the door he thinks.

Amaryllis who remains quiet throughout their somewhat comical exchange, suddenly speaks.

"I'm the new evidence," she declares. She now joins her mother at the counter. Holds out her hand to the sergeant. Taking it with his right hand, he shakes it. "And you are?" he asks.

"Amaryllis August."

What is it with these unusual names? Could they be aliens he wonders?

Amaryllis sees him hesitate so, like her mother, spells out each vowel and consonant. Waits until he's laboriously written it and then quite calmly says, "Abducted. Drugged. Raped and almost murdered."

212

The desk sergeant gawps. Could this crime report get any more bizarre?

"And I can confirm." Amaryllis attests. "That the rose gold watch is mine. It's a birthday present from my mother."

He is writing all this down. Trying to keep up.

"The case was in all the papers," says Columbine. "So you must have copies buried somewhere in your archives. A file. Statements were taken at the time. I remember."

"Maybe. Maybe not." The desk sergeant replaces the biro behind his ear. Tears off the top sheet of the incident pad. And waving it in the air, leaves the counter.

"Now don't you go away," he says.

They see him knock on a door. But cannot read the name on the brass plaque screwed into it.

"Come in," says a voice. The desk sergeant opens the door and steps into the room. Behind a desk, sits a man, smartly attired in a black suit. Everything on the desk is arranged neatly. Aligned. Nothing out of place. He's smoking, knocking the ash into a green marble ashtray. There's a name holder perpendicular in front of the leather upholstered chair opposite him. *Detective Inspector Gibson* is typed across it.

"What can I do for you, Sergeant Parker?"

"Got a couple of funnies out in reception, Sir."

"Are they causing a disturbance?"

"Not exactly, Sir."

"Do they pose a threat?"

"Not a threat, Sir, more of a conundrum." He hands him the piece of paper.

Detective Inspector Gibson reads it.

"Not a good advert for a Parker pen, are you, Sergeant Parker," he says, tongue in cheek. "You need to practice your handwriting. It's bordering on illegible."

"Yes Sir."

The detective finishes reading it through. Stubs out his cigarette and stands up. There's an air of excitement about him. He begins to pace. His shoes are black, polished to a high sheen.

"What shall I do with 'em, Sir. Send 'em packing for wasting police time?"

"What you will do, Sergeant Parker, is make sure they get a cup of tea. Politely inform them that the Inspector will see them shortly."

The look of astonishment on the sergeant's face is priceless.

"And then you will get someone to cover the desk whilst *you* go into the basement and look for the files on missing persons in 1957."

"What all of them?"

"All of them sergeant. Hopefully, there will not be that many. Well?"

"Yes Sir. Right on it, Sir." And flummoxed he goes back out into the wating room. The two ladies are still there. Sitting side by side on a hard-backed bench, they quietly converse.

He nods at them and hurries off.

Columbine and Amaryllis watch. Wonder what is going on.

After a short space of time a young female constable appears. She carefully carries a tray on which there is a teapot, two cups and saucers, a twee milk jug, a bowl of sugar and two spoons. She places it on the bench.

"I'm to tell you," she says, "someone, I mean the Inspector, will see you shortly."

The telephone is now ringing relentlessly. She hurries behind the counter and picking up the receiver, begins to write on the pad.

Columbine and Amaryllis can see no sign of the desk sergeant who takes their details. They watch the hands on the big clock, high on the wall, tick slowly by. Half an hour becomes an hour. An hour becomes two. It's almost lunch time they think, stomachs rumbling.

And then a door opens and a tall distinguished looking man walks into the foyer and approaches them.

"I'm sorry for the delay," he says. "But I needed to garner further information pertaining to the incident form my sergeant gave me. I gather he thinks you time wasters. But I don't." He reaches out to shake their hands. "I am Detective Inspector Gibson. Perhaps you would follow me into my office and I can explain."

His tidy desk is now littered with files and papers which he has hurriedly scanned through before calling the two women in. More files are stacked at the side of his desk. There are now two chairs facing his. He invites them to sit.

Amaryllis wrings her hands. She's going to have to go over it all again.

The Inspector looks at her. Glances down at his desk. Reads something. Whilst Columbine is looking at him, the name Gibson going round and round in her head. The kitchen. A different Inspector. The nine constables. And two sergeants. One named Stock something or other. Hill, that's it, Stockhill. And the other, Gibson. Yes, she remembers it clearly. He is the one who goes with the constables to search the countryside. He is the one holding the rose gold watch.

"Are you? Were you?"

"Yes, Mrs August. I was there. A rather green sergeant with the Malton Constabulary then. Just passed my exams. First time on a missing persons case. First time organizing a search. I remember it well. It haunts me for many years."

He looks at her, sadly.

"It haunts us all. We're on our way back to your house, that late June evening. We search everywhere. Find nothing. Then one of the constables sees something glittering in the grass. He fishes. Retrieves a watch and places it in my hand. The strap is small, so I know it belongs to a child. And we all know that should you recognize it, then the news is not good."

"And of course, I do," says Columbine.

The Inspector remembers her cries. Her howls. The lack of any empathy from her husband, Dr Charles August. A cold fish of a man he thinks.

"Yes. Very distressing. I have a daughter. The watch would fit her." It's there on his desk. Sealed in an evidence bag. "I can only imagine how you must have felt then," he says. His voice is deep. Throaty. Yet kind. "But I can't imagine how you coped."

Amaryllis is staring at the bag. At the watch.

"I don't," says Columbine. "Not for a long time." She can see the watch out of the corner of her eye. But doesn't want to look "And then, well, you just learn to live with it."

Detective Inspector Gibson now looks to Amaryllis. She smiles at him.

"We all remember the photograph of you. Your blonde hair. Your beaming smile." The photo is also on the desk in front of him. In colour. Which intrigues them all at the time, he recalls. "And here you are, still with the blonde hair, the beaming smile. All grown up. And I expect," he says kindly, "not looking forward to this interview. Would you have any objection to my recording it?" he asks.

Amaryllis shakes her head.

Columbine decides it is time for her to keep mum. Literally.

Amaryllis tells the Inspector and the whirring tape recorder a shortened edition of her story. A precis. She remembers James showing her how to accomplish this. Giving her chapters in books to precis, whilst she is locked in her bedroom all day. But she never masters it fully. So even now, the telling takes almost an hour.

"So your father, Dr Charles August, tries to kill you," says Inspector Gibson when she finishes. "Is that correct?"

Amaryllis nods.

"Can you say it for the tape please, Amaryllis."

"Yes, it's the truth. My father tries to kill me. And takes my son."

Inspector Gibson turns the tape recorder off.

"Thank you, ladies. I think that will be enough for today. What I would like to do is to take the file and witness statements home tonight. Read them thoroughly. Listen to the tape recording. And invite you both back tomorrow. Say after lunch, 2 o'clock. Would that be convenient?" He shakes both their hands.

"Yes. Of course," Columbine and Amaryllis say together.

As they leave his office, Columbine glances down at his feet. "I remember your boots," she says. "I remember thinking how enormous they are."

He laughs, "What a strange thing to remember."

"I am in a strange place then," Columbine says. "But now your feet don't look quite so big," she adds. And they don't, here in his office, shod in glossy leather loafers.

Whilst Amaryllis turns at the door and asks, "Detective Inspector Gibson, you will get my son back for me, won't you?"

"I will do my upmost, Amaryllis," he answers. "I promise. But we must tread carefully," he goes on to say. "Tiptoe. Lest a journalist gets wind of the story. Because it will be a big scoop for the first newspaper that prints it. And we want to keep your son safe, whilst we find your father and James Duncan. We don't want them running scared before we can apprehend them. But I can assure you that as soon as we have the necessary warrants and manpower, we will be paying a visit to the Isle of Bute."

Chapter 38

The next morning, a Saturday, Amaryllis is up bright and early. She is surprised at how well she sleeps. That the first time in a long time, she is hungry. Wants to eat. Not just eat to live. She fills a bowl with cornflakes. Sploshes milk on top. And whilst she spoons the cereal up before it goes soggy, she writes a note to her mother who is still fast asleep.

Mum, can you pick me up at the war memorial at half one. That'll give us plenty of time to get to the Police Station for two. I got an address for Penelope out of the telephone directory. So I'm going to see her. Have a catch up. And ask her if she and her daughter will be bridesmaids at the wedding. See you later. xxxxx

Amaryllis walks down Oaktree Drive, across The Mount and down Yorkersgate, past the War memorial and the Talbot. All the way to the crossroads and traffic lights. Despite these there is always a bottleneck here when they come back from the seaside, Scarborough, she remembers. Since her father's car is a two-seater, he drives her mother's Morris Minor. Always gets angry. Sits tapping on the steering wheel. Rants. Grumbles when they get stuck in a traffic jam. Sometimes stretching as far back as the level crossing. Sometimes going on for two hours before they can get home.

She waits for the lights to turn red, stop the traffic. And then she's walking up an incline. Old Malton Road it is signed. Passes what looks like a tennis club. She can see grass courts and nets. Remembers playing tennis with Robert Howard when she's at the Sanctum. Not that long ago, she thinks. But it seems like a zillion years.

She is looking for The Old School House. Once where an actual school was but now converted into two semi-detached houses. Penelope lives in one of them.

Number two. They are easy to spot as the high apexes have been retained, along with the pointed eaves at the front.

Number two is clearly marked. There is a square plaque on the wall which reads, G. M. Wilberforce, D.M.D. Neither house has a front garden, but they are set back from the footpath. Amaryllis assumes that their gardens will be at the back where the playground would once have been.

She walks up to the entrance and pulls open the door. It's heavy. Made of solid oak. There's a chiming noise and she's in a waiting room. A woman sits behind a counter which has an old-fashioned phone on it. Behind her are shelves and shelves of files.

Amaryllis approaches the counter.

"Good morning," says the receptionist. "Could I take your name please and the time of your appointment?" She's looking down, scanning a large book open in front of her. Full of names, dates and times. She wears a smart navy-blue suit and white blouse. Is well spoken.

"My name is Amaryllis August. But I don't have an appointment. I'd like to see Mrs Wilberforce please."

"Oh love, you've come in the practice door. The front door is round the side of the house." She looks up at Amaryllis. "But it's early and there's no-one due yet so I can take you through this way. Is Penelope expecting you?"

Amaryllis shakes her head. And thinking of the shock her schoolfriend will have, says, "It's OK. I think I will go to the front door. Thank you, anyway."

The front door is another beautiful oak door with a bell to the side. Amaryllis pushes it. And hearing a jingly tune, waits.

A woman opens the door. She has red-brown hair scraped up on top of her head in a messy topknot. Straggles of escaped hair hang down. A fresh stain, yellowy white, like stale milk, puddles on the shoulder of her short-sleeved knitted jumper.

The two women stand and scrutinize each other. Neither speaks. Amaryllis sees the moment a spark of recognition hits Penelope. Her face blanches. She stumbles. Needs to prop herself up, holding onto the door frame.

"No!" she exclaims. "It can't be! They tell us you are missing. That we must pray for your safe return. And we do. All of us, the Secret Seven. Remember?"

Amaryllis remembers. It's a club they form, seven of them. "I do," she says. "Let me see, it was you and me, and then there was Judy, Rosy, Lesley, Alwyn and, oh let me think and…"

"Jeffery." Penelope laughs. "Poor old Jeffers. He was a bit short in the brain department. We weren't at all nice to him. But I think he did alright. Went back to his parents farm out Settringham way."

"We have our own secret language, don't we?" Amaryllis ponders. "But I can't remember it."

"I think we said things backwards," says Penelope. "And we made up stories. Built dens. Pretended to be cowboys and Indians."

"Yes, that's right. What about the others. Are they still around?"

"Judy, she marries a dishy guy in the upper sixth, Philip, has three kids. Lesley, she emigrates to Australia. Rosy, she doesn't marry, has no kids. And Alwyn, he's some hot shot solicitor with a beautiful wife from somewhere in the orient. Come to think, they live up Oaktree Drive. Gerald plays tennis with them. I do too. When I can. And we have dinner dates. She's an amazing cook. Oh wait 'til I tell them. They're not going to believe it."

"Sometimes I don't believe it myself," says Amaryllis.

"Have you time to come in. It seems silly standing on the doorstep when we haven't seen each other for, what…"

"Seventeen years," says Amaryllis.

"Gosh. Where have the years gone?"

Amaryllis steps through the doorway into a hall. The two friends embrace. Hug each other tight. Just as they do when they are in kindergarten. Then stepping back, they look at each other and laugh.

"But all that praying we do," Penelope says soberly, "doesn't bring you back. And we grow older without you. Sit the eleven plus without you. Go to the grammar school without you. Miss Tong talks to us. Says we must understand that you are likely dead. And every day we walk past your house and remember you."

"And I remember you," says Amaryllis. "Every day when I do my schoolwork. When I am alone and friendless. By the way, is Miss Tong still teaching? I remember her fondly."

"Ha. Ha." Penelope laughs. "Even though she is always sending you out the classroom. You were such a chatterbox."

Not anymore, thinks Amaryllis.

"And yes, she still teaches. In fact, she teaches Hetty. It's weird to think she teaches me and now she teaches my daughter. Oh, you will stay, won't you?" Penelope asks. "There's so much to catch up on. I've just got to…"

The wail of a hungry baby floats out into the hallway. Amaryllis recognizes it. The only cry Williain really makes when he is tiny. She follows Penelope down the hallway and into a spacious lounge. The floorboards are all a warm brown oak. A large geometric rug dominates most of the room. It is patterned with zigzags of orange and yellow. On it sits a small boy surrounded by brightly coloured Lego. An older child, a girl sits beside him. They are building a castle.

"My mum tells me you have two children," Amaryllis says, watching them.

"Yes, I meet her in the market one day. And we have a little chat. I bet she is more shocked than me when you turn up. Or did she know?"

"No, she didn't. And it's only a few days ago that I find her." Amaryllis can't take her eyes off the little boy. Suddenly, there is another raucous cry. It comes from a bassinette tucked in a corner of the room. Before Penelope moves one foot, the little girl jumps up and rushes across to it. And lifts out a swaddled baby. Rocks it. Croons to it.

"As you can see," remarks Penelope, "two becomes three. He is born four weeks ago." She laughs. "Hence the somewhat frazzled look."

Amaryllis traverses the rug and drops onto her knees next to the little boy. Begins to click the Lego together. He watches her. Clicks some bricks onto hers.

"What's your name?" she asks.

"Haydn," answers the girl, carrying the baby across to her mother, so Penelope can feed it. "And I'm Hetty."

"I have a son," says Amaryllis. "Called Williain. He's nine."

"I'm seven and a half," says Hetty. "And Haydn's three. I look after him. And my baby sister, Harriet. Will you bring Williain to play with us?" she asks.

Amaryllis's mind flits. Three children she thinks. The three 'Aitches'.

"Maybe one day," she replies. "But he's with his father, a long way, away."

"Oh." Hetty sits on the floor next to her. Barrages her with questions.

Penelope listens to their chattering as she puts the baby to her breast. Oh she has so many questions to ask Amaryllis. Still cannot believe that her schoolfriend is here. Sitting on her floor. In her house. As if she has never been away. She wants to know all about her son. Her husband. Everything.

"So, where do you go missing then?" she asks casually, putting the baby over her shoulder and rubbing its back. A good place to start.

"Not missing," replies Amaryllis. "Abducted." She carries on clicking bricks of Lego together. So much easier to occupy the hands. Not look at Penelope

220

when she tells the bare bones of her story, always mindful that little ears will hear.

"But if my life had taken a different path," she says at the end. "I would not have met Eric, my fiancé."

"Oh, so this time you're really getting married!" exclaims Penelope. "That's wonderful." She doesn't want to comment on Amaryllis's woeful tale. Not yet. If ever.

"And partly why I'm here." Amaryllis confesses. "Because I'd love for you and Hetty to be my bridesmaids."

"Well as long as it's not in the next few weeks." Penelope laughs. "Look at me. I'm such a frump. Got to get fit. Get my figure back, before I'll look half decent in a bridesmaid's dress. It's not a bad figure until it gets stretched out of shape. I have told Gerald, 'No More'. So it's either I take the pill, or he has the snip."

Hetty looks up. "Is being a bridesmaid like being a princess? And why are you going to snip daddy?" she asks innocently.

Whilst Amaryllis thinks Penelope looks as lovely as she always did.

"It's not that sort of snip sweetie," says Penelope. "And yes, you will be a princess. Now, why don't you take Harriet and rock her to sleep. You're so good at that. I'm going to make Amaryllis and mummy a cup of coffee. Would you and Haydn like some juice?"

"Yes please, yummy mummy," they both chorus.

Amaryllis follows her friend into the kitchen. Haydn abandoning the Lego, trots after them. They can hear Hetty singing to the baby. Her voice is sweet.

Penelope lifts Haydn onto a chair. Pours some orange juice into a beaker. Pops a straw in. "Just a sec…" She pours another beaker of juice and takes it into the lounge. "I'm all yours," she says coming back into the kitchen. "You were saying…"

"I don't think the wedding will be 'til next year. There's a lot to sort out. So I shouldn't worry about getting your figure back. Plenty of time. Though it looks pretty fine now. And Mum has kept my party dress. The one she makes me for my ninth birthday…"

"The party we never get to go to," says Penelope. "And we are all so excited about the magician. And your mum's cakes."

"Well, it's the party I never get to go to either. And the dress I never get to wear," Amaryllis remarks sadly. "But by next year, I think it will fit your Hetty perfectly. She will look like the princess I never am."

"Oh, she'll love that."

And so the two friends chat. Drink coffee which Penelope makes in a machine. Amaryllis contributes little. She's said all that she wants to say. But she listens avidly as Penelope tells her how she meets Gerald Wilberforce on her first day at the Grammar School. They are both in the A stream. How their friendship blossoms. How in the sixth form they become a couple. How the relationship falters when they go to university. Gerald to study dentistry. Penelope to study history. How they meet again when both return to Malton. Fall in love again. Marry.

"And the rest, as they say, is history."

Amaryllis looks up at the clock on the kitchen wall. "Gosh, Penpen..." Unbidden she uses her schoolgirl name for her. "Is that the time. Got to fly. Am meeting mum. We're driving to York. An Inspector calls," she adds mysteriously.

"You'll come again, won't you? I'm sure the others would love to see you. I can arrange something. If you let me have your telephone number. So, I can call you."

"It's 2404. I'm staying with mum. Until after the wedding."

"At Oakwood?"

"No. My father sells Oakwood. She lives in a bungalow nearby. He tells her a pack of lies. Abandons her. She has no idea where he goes. Mum's bungalow is down Pasture Lane. Rose Cottage, Acorn Way."

"I remember Pasture Lane. It's where we build our dens when we are kids. We see it gets tarmacked on our way to school. But we don't know why. And we don't know your parents are no longer at Oakwood."

"Well, you must come. Hetty will need to try the dress on. And you and me will need to discuss your bridesmaid's dress. Because I know my mum will want to make it."

"I will. We can walk it. I mean you've walked here."

"It's quite a walk," says Amaryllis.

"No farther than walking to St. Andrews. Which we do most days. If I'm not running late. I find that the more often we do it, the shorter it becomes."

"Yes, I know," says Amaryllis. "I discover this when I walk round the farm." She watches Haydn suck the last of his juice up through a straw. Hears the shlucking noise it makes. Listens to his giggles. He keeps on sucking. Keeps on giggling. Until Penelope pulls out the straw and bins it.

Amaryllis looks at the clock again. She gets up.

"I've really got to dash, Penpen. But see you soon?"

"You bet. Golly, I still can't believe it. I keep thinking I'm dreaming. That you're not real." Penelope grabs her. "But I'm not dreaming. And you are real," she says, hugging her one last time to be sure. "Maybe prayers do get answered. Even if it is nearly twenty years later."

Penelope takes her out to the back. There is a sizeable garden. Not many flowers and plants, but a swing, a slide, a sandpit, a seesaw. A kiddie's paradise. Haydn goes straight to the slide. And before Amaryllis reaches the gate and waves goodbye, Hetty is there at the bottom. Ready to catch him.

Hurrying back to get to the War Memorial in time, Amaryllis thinks of Williain. Wishes he could have a life like theirs. And then her mind leaps, as it's often wont to do. And she is thinking of Miss Tong. That perhaps she will call at the school. Give her a shock. Then invite her to the wedding.

Chapter 39

"Good afternoon, ladies," says the desk sergeant amiably. He picks up the phone, pushes an extension button. "They're here, Sir." They hear him say. "Very well, Sir." He gets up and comes round the counter. "Come this way, please."

Columbine and Amaryllis follow him down a long corridor. There are doors with names on, but they go past these until they come to four doors at the farthest end. Two at each side of the corridor. Each marked 'Interview Room'. The desk sergeant opens the door of Interview Room 3.

Amaryllis is uneasy. Are they now suspects? Are they going to be interrogated?

Inspector Gibson and a Police Sergeant sit behind a table. In the middle is a microphone. Apart from the table, four chairs and a tape recorder, the room is sparse. Clinical.

"Thank you for coming," says Inspector Gibson. "Please sit down." He looks at Amaryllis. "Don't be alarmed," he says. "This is not an interrogation. It's just a casual interview to hopefully clear up some discrepancies I find between the original statements taken at the time of your abduction and yesterday's tape recording."

Amaryllis shuffles her bottom in the chair nervously.

Columbine is uncomfortable. She thinks she might know what these discrepancies are. Something that bothers her that night, after the Inspectors, Sergeants and Constables leave Oakwood.

Inspector Gibson turns the tape recorder on.

"For the benefit of the tape, the date is Saturday, the 24th of August 1974. Time at fourteen hundred hours. Present, are Detective Inspector Gibson, Detective Sergeant Bogue, Mrs Columbine August and Amaryllis August. This is a reactive interview in the light of new evidence pertaining to a cold case, The Disappearance of Amaryllis August on the 21st of June 1957."

"Now, Amaryllis." And so it begins she thinks. "In your taped account, you say you are abducted by your Uncle James, who is coming to your birthday party as he always does. Is this correct?"

"Yes."

"And that he's expected about lunch time. So, you wait for him on the wall. You then describe in detail the car he arrives in. Because it's not his usual car. It's an…" He looks down at a written sheet. "MG-YB Saloon in a shiny bronze colour. And this is the car he abducts you in. Is this correct?"

"Yes. He says we will go for a spin."

"Does he often take you for…a spin?"

"Yes."

"So you feel no reason to doubt him?"

"No."

"Because, at the time, you are not aware he is not your father's brother but his lover."

"That's correct. I only find this out when I am at Lochfrein. When I become Isla Duncan."

"So, you feel no fear. Not even when he parks the car and walks you through a wood and up a farm track to where there are just derelict buildings?"

"No. He makes me believe we are going to a farm to look at puppies. To choose one for my birthday present. I don't know that there is no farm. And then it's too late." Amaryllis sees her mother jump. Slam her hands over her mouth.

"Thank you, Amaryllis," the Inspector says. "That's enough for now."

He now looks to Columbine, who rubs her teary eyes, smudging the mascara. Wipes her nose yet again. The red lipstick she painstakingly applies before they come has wandered off. She knows what is coming.

"Now, Mrs August. In your statement, taken by Sergeant Stockhill on the 21st of June 1957, there is no mention of a James Duncan. Nor is his name mentioned in the witness statements of a…" He glances down at the sheet again. "Mr and Miss Kirby."

Garden man and Gladys thinks Amaryllis. Now why?

"But he is there," says Columbine. "I will swear on the bible if need be. He arrives in a fluster with not much time to spare. Joins my husband who organizes a search of the local houses and outbuildings."

"Can you recall the time?"

"Well the party is at 4 o'clock, so probably a half hour before?"

"Is that usual, for him to be late?"

"No. And, in hindsight, he's expected around lunch time. I send Amaryllis out to wait for him." She trembles. Takes a deep breath in. Tries to stay calm. "It's the last time I see her."

"And do you notice the car he arrives in?"

"A mere glance Inspector. I am too distressed. I do notice it's not his usual two-seater convertible, but bigger. Yes, a saloon. But Amaryllis is the one who's mad on cars. Knows them all." She is thinking back. "But I do recall my husband comments on it. And they chat. James asks him what he thinks of the colour. Tells him it's called, er, let me think, Sunbronze. It's a metallic brown.

That's it! I'm sure that's what he says. But, at the time, I do find it all a tad odd that my husband discusses cars with James when his daughter has vanished. And that James is called away before daylight breaks, for an emergency at the hospital. Because although I am close to the telephone, I do not hear it ring. And that he appears as if by magic, all packed up and ready to leave."

"Can you tell me the name of the hospital, Mrs August?"

"Yes. The Northern General in Sheffield. He's an Orthopaedic Consultant."

"So why is none of this mentioned in any of your statements?" asks Inspector Gibson.

"Because my husband, Dr Charles August tells all of us that we must make no mention of James's arrival or departure. Or the fact that he is here at all. That it's better he goes back to Sheffield. That he will be of no use to the police. My husband, Inspector, is a very persuasive man. And not one you would wish to disobey. And of course, the Kirby's are loyal to the bone."

"So, he threatens you?"

"Yes."

"Thank you, Mrs August. This must all be very distressing for you. But now, at least, we can tie up Amaryllis's account of events with yours. And we will investigate this Dr James Duncan a little more closely. See if he is what he pertains to be."

Whereupon Amaryllis suddenly speaks out.

"Inspector Gibson," she begins. "Could you please let my mother leave. There are things I need to tell you. And yes, they are pertaining to the case. Sorry, Mum." She smiles weakly at her.

"For the benefit of the tape," the Inspector says, "Mrs Columbine August leaves the room at fifteen hundred hours."

Amaryllis waits as Detective Sergeant Bogue escorts her mother out of the interview room. At the door, Columbine twists her head and looks to Amaryllis. With the black mascara that streaks down her cheeks and the smudged red lipstick, she looks like a character in a horror film. Amaryllis mouths, 'Don't worry. It's alright.' And the door closes.

"Can I speak freely, Detective?" asks Amaryllis. "What I am about to tell you, I have never spoken of before. I do not want my mother to hear it."

"Of course."

"Dr Charles August murders his own mother."

"And you know this because?"

"He tells us. Me and James. One night when he is drunk. He murders her because she is going to disinherit him. Swaps her insulin dose. Drowns her in the bath when she is too sleepy to fight. She is very poorly. No-one suspects."

Inspector Gibson rubs his chin thoughtfully. "This will be difficult to prove now."

"And he murders a few patients in the War. James sees him do it but never tells. They're mostly women. But there's a German soldier, shot down and wounded. My father operates on them. Saves their lives. And then smothers them in the night."

"Again, Amaryllis, this will be difficult to prove."

"James will corroborate all of it, I'm sure. If he were to receive a more lenient sentence."

The Inspector wonders if perhaps there is more between her and this James Duncan than she lets on.

"Oh and I can tell you," she adds. "That at Lochfrein, in one of the barns, covered with straw, is the car James abducts me in. The registration is JDZ 777. I remember it at the time…In case it proves important. James says he doesn't want to part with it, so I'm sure it will still be there.

There's a trunk on the back seat which he puts me in. When he drives up to the farm. And upstairs, in the farmhouse, you'll find a bedroom where one wall is covered in cars. It's mine. Where I am when I cannot be seen. It's all evidence, isn't it? And ask Scott McGinty about the sudden appearance of Mrs Isla Duncan."

"Thank you," the inspector says. And then, "For the record, this interview terminates at fifteen thirty hours."

He stands up and pushes his chair back. Amaryllis listens to the squeaky scrape of its legs before she too stands. Her legs feel like jelly. She is light-headed. But oh so glad it's over. That now there is a real possibility her father will be brought to justice. As for James, uncertainty still clouds her thoughts. He is and always will be, Williain's biological father.

"You should also look into my father's past. Before the war. Before he marries my mother. I believe he practices at a hospital in London. Perhaps there are other deaths of patients he treats and who suddenly and unexplainably die."

"Now, why didn't I think of that," the Inspector says. There's a twinkle in his eye. "Scotland Yard's criminal investigation services are, as we speak, looking into Dr Charles August's past. I do believe, Miss August, we'll make a detective of you yet." And with that, he opens the door and ushers her through.

She can see her mother. A cup of tea and some biscuits in front of her. Her face is pallid. All traces of mascara and lipstick gone.

Columbine gets up. Goes to Amaryllis and embraces her. "I won't ask," she says. And then to the Inspector, "What happens next?"

"I will present this new evidence to the Chief Superintendent. Ask him, in light of what you tell me, if we can re-open the case. Start a re-investigation. I'm certain he'll give a thumbs up. He's big on solving cold cases. After all, it looks good for the Police."

"And what do we do in the meantime?" Amaryllis is wondering how long this is all going to take. How long before she can hold Williain. How long before she knows her father is where he belongs. Locked up.

"Nothing," says Inspector Gibson. He shakes their hands. "I'll be in touch. Once we've carried out the preliminary investigations."

******

Columbine shifts the gear down as they climb slowly up to the top of Whitwell-on-the-Hill. Amaryllis looks at the panoramic view across the Vale of York. To the right she can see the river Derwent and the railway line which goes into Malton Station. There's a big blue diesel train pulling a long line of goods carriages, heading out towards the way they come from. She wonders where its journey ends. Thinks, I've never been on a train. And then remembers. She has. Just that once, on her seventh birthday, when her mum takes her to Scarborough.

But this not a diesel train. It is a great beast of a thing that chunters into the station. It is smelly and noisy. Hisses and belches steam as the great pistons that power its wheels grind to a halt. Amaryllis sees the red glow of fire from the furnace.

"It's where they feed the engine," her mother tells her.

Not an engine thinks Amaryllis. But a dragon. A dragon with fire in its belly. Belching smoke from its nostrils. Amaryllis holds tight her mother's hand. Stares up at the huge wheels. They are taller than her. They sit in a compartment. The seats are hard. A whistle blows. It wakes the dragon. Roaring, it slowly leaves the platform. She looks out of the window as it picks up speed. Watches the scenery fly past as they clatter and rock on the rails. Beasts and dragons forgotten. Just the seaside to look forward to. Amaryllis chatters and prattles. It's all so wonderfully exciting.

There is no chatter or prattling now as her mother concentrates on getting the old Morris Minor to the top of the hill. Then it's a winding descent down to York Road and the top of Yorkersgate where the spire of St. Leonard's church is easily seen. It's large clock face beneath the spire, a timely reminder to Columbine that she's almost home. Neither women speak. For all the words spoken this afternoon, all the sentences, paragraphs and pages which tell a story, are said. And now they must be patient. Something Amaryllis, as a child, never is but learns to be.

Chapter 40

"Why, it's stunning!" exclaims Columbine, staring up at the majestic edifice that is Selby Abbey. "I've been to Selby before but never really taken much note of the Abbey."

"This is where I walk one day," Amaryllis tells her. "I find peace within the haven of its walls. And I find the vicar. He tells me he is the Reverend Canon John de Vere. Mum, I want to get married here. And I want Vicar John to marry us."

"But don't you have to live within the parish. And if you don't, attend services for at least six months?"

"Perhaps not," Amaryllis replies mysteriously. "I have a plan. As you say, it's not only my father who can make plans." She snorts. "But mine, unlike his, are not of evil intent."

They enter through the magnificent doors. Columbine gazes up at the huge ornate columns and arches.

"You can't believe how they build such a glorious place monument to God without today's modern machinery," she whispers reverently. There are flowers everywhere. Bouquets of Gypsophilia, tied with green ribbons hanging off every pew. Baby's breath. White Gardenias and Snow Pixie Lupins. *A wedding,* she thinks.

Whilst Amaryllis is thinking that this is exactly how she envisages her wedding. Here in the Abbey. With Eric by her side.

Suddenly, a man comes out of the sacristy near the High Alter. He is robed in the Abbey's vestments. As he walks down the red carpet of the main aisle towards them, Amaryllis recognizes his face.

"Vicar John?" she says. And waits.

"Well. Well," he says. "I find you here again, my child. It's Isla, isn't it? Isla and?"

"My mother, Columbine August. And it is not Isla," she says. "That day when I pray to St. Benedict to make me and my friends whole. Well, he answers me. I find myself. I remember who I am. My name is Amaryllis August. And I do leave the Sanctum. And now, I'm engaged." She holds out her ringed hand and he sees the white gold swan harbouring her cygnets.

"Selebiae," he says. "The three swans." And he remembers why she comes that day. When he finds her in the Abbey, dirty and dishevelled. But this woman is neither of these. "So your jigsaw, it is complete?"

"Yes. And Vicar John? I want to get married in Selby Abbey. To my fiancé, Eric Skeldergate. And I would so love it if you would marry us."

"I told her," says Columbine. "It's not that easy. But she doesn't listen. Says she has a plan."

The Reverend Canon John de Vere remembers the determination of her. To walk all that way just because she reads the story of St. Benedict of Auxerre. And believes. He also remembers the sadness in her eyes. Now, when he looks at the young woman before him, he still sees that determination. But the sadness is flown. And he knows she will jump any hurdles that present, so her plan can reach fruition.

"Well Amaryllis," he says smiling. "When you are ready, come and see me again. I will be honoured to marry you. But now I must ask you to leave as that's what I am about to do…" He glances at a watch on his wrist. "In approximately half an hour. Join in holy matrimony two parishioners I have known since their birth."

As they leave, Amaryllis says to him, "Thank you, Reverend Canon John de Vere…And I forgive you."

He knows precisely what she alludes to.

****

Eric. "C'mon, Amaryllis, let's take Rafferty for a walk. Look at him. He's going to have everything on the floor. Mix the patterns up. Oh and the pins!" Amaryllis is standing on a chair, the white silk under bodice and skirt of her wedding dress being tacked together, the hem pinned up. She's been standing straight for ages. Her back aches.

"Yes, off you go," says Columbine. "That's enough for today. I can see where it is going. So, Doris and I will get on with the bridesmaids' dresses…"

Bridesmaids, thinks Amaryllis. Penelope, Judy, and Rosy. She meets them all. At Penelope's. A reunion of friends parted too soon. They have a giggly, girlie night in. Watch a film, The Wizard of Oz. Drink too much wine Penelope brings back from France. Something new to Amaryllis. Eat too much ice-cream. But it is so good to all be together again.

"Because I'll be busy the rest of this week," Amaryllis hears her mother saying as she helps her out of the stitches and pins. "Prudence and Christopher Walker are organizing a short holiday for their family. So, they need all hands on deck. I'll be overseeing Oakwood and the garden, whilst they are away."

Amaryllis hears the pride in her mother's voice. That she is trusted. Valued. Wanted. Carefully, she steps down gets off the chair. Unabashed that now she wears only her bra and panties. Her jeans and jumper, well sniffed and foraged in by Rafferty, lay in a heap on the sofa.

They are all there, filling Rose Cottage with their bodies and belongings. From the very first time Eric brings his mother to meet Columbine, they take to each other. Soon become firm friends. Enjoy discussing gardening. Knitting and sewing. The wedding. Try to avoid discussing the forthcoming trial which Columbine knows will happen and which she and Amaryllis will have to attend. Even Rafferty treats Rose Cottage as his second home. And those 'supposed' allergies Columbine suffers from? Not an itch or a sneeze. Another of her father's ploys, thinks Amaryllis.

Eric grabs his lead. "Ladies," he says, "we're going for a walk. Take ourselves and Rafferty out from under your feet."

Doris and Columbine, engrossed in stitching the sleeves of a dress, barely look up.

"I'm so glad your mum and my mum like each other. Have become such good friends," says Amaryllis as they walk down Pasture Lane. "It would make life awkward if they weren't."

"Well, I always thought," says Eric, trying his best to stop Rafferty leaping about at the end of the lead, "that my mum loves you like a daughter. And your mum is so like you. So it's obvious to me they will like each other."

Amaryllis kisses him.

They walk up the Broughton Road until they reach a green lane. It's a bridle path right out in the countryside. Nothing about. Eric unleashes Rafferty so he can sniff beneath the hedgerows. Eat horse manure. Roll in fox droppings and other noxious smelling particles. All perfume to him.

"Eric?" Amaryllis begins. Stops. Go on, ask. A voice in her head. If you don't ask, you'll never know. Fine, she thinks. Just go for it. "How much do you like your job? Say on a scale of one to ten?"

"A strange question to ask," he says. "I love my job. But I wouldn't say it defines me. So maybe an eight."

"Would you ever consider pursuing a different career?"

"Such as?" Where is this leading, he wonders?

"Farming." There she has said it. Time to find out if he will be onside. Yet in her heart she has already decided that if his answer is 'no' she will pursue her plan alone. Stand up for what she believes is the right path to follow.

"Farming," he echoes. "I don't know the first thing about farming."

"But I do. I know quite a bit about the life of a farmer. And what we don't know, we can learn as we go along."

Eric notices she says, 'we'. So, he thinks, she already assumes that he will be a farmer too.

The whinny of a horse interrupts. Quickly Eric whistles Rafferty to heel. Puts his leash on. They stand back against the hedgerow. Watch as two beautiful piebald horses canter past. The riders, in tweed jodhpurs, helmets and long boots, raise their crops in acknowledgement. Then as fast as they appear they disappear. Rumps bouncing. Tails swishing. Churn deep hoofprints in the soft ground. A declaration of their transient presence.

"So when you say 'farming'," Eric begins after dwelling on her suggestion. "Does that mean you want to return to Lochfrein?"

Amaryllis grabs his hand. Swings his arm.

"Good heavens no! Beautiful though it is on the island, there are too many memories."

Eric breathes a sigh of relief. "So where then? And why?"

"Hear me out, will you." She stops. Turns to face him. Eyes to eyes. Hers full of excitement. His full of apprehension.

"I want to map my own destiny, Eric. Remember I tell you about Vicar John. How me and mum go to Selby Abbey. And he says he will marry us. But he can't, not until we live in the parish for at least three months. Well, I reckon, it's going to be a good six months before the trial is over and by then, well, we could be living on a farm somewhere near Selby. Like Monk Fryston."

"And Monk Fryston because?"

"There's a farm just outside the village. It's called Mistletoe Farm. And it's for sale. I mean it hasn't been farmed in a while but the buildings, machinery and farmhouse are well maintained. And the owner is dead. She dies intestate. Has no known family. It's perfect. And big enough for us all to live there. You, me, mum, Williain, Doris and Rafferty. A family."

"I assume they know nothing of this plan of yours?"

"Well, I am thinking."

"You've been doing a lot of that lately, love. Thinking."

"Yes. But if you agree. Between us, I believe we can make them see, it makes sense. And since Williain grows up on a farm, it may help lessen the shock when he loses his home. And the only parents he knows."

Yes, Williain, he thinks. A boy who has two fathers. And probably does not want a third. How will he cope? Thrust into a family with a man, a stranger to him, and a woman, albeit his mother, after seven years likely a stranger too.

"And this farm," he says. "How do we pay for it? I'm not exactly a millionaire."

"Well…" Amaryllis takes a deep breath. "I am thinking that if my mum and your mum sell their properties we would easily have enough. And I've, er, sort of put in a provisional offer based on their agreement. Please don't look at me like that, Eric. I had to. I don't want to lose this opportunity. It's through my school friend I learn of the farm. She marries a solicitor. So, he can sort all the paperwork out for us. And Alwyn, that's his name, tells me he will be glad to get it off his books. So…"

Eric grabs her and his lips, warm and soft, explore hers. He kisses her. Deeply. Passionately. "I love you, Amaryllis August," he says when they come up for air.

"Does that mean?" She leaps at him. Wraps her arms around his neck. Her legs around his waist. Kisses him over and over again. "Thank you. Thank you. Thank you."

Eric untangles her from him. Puts her down. "It means," he says. "We'll see what the matriarchs have to say. Rafferty, drop!" He suddenly shouts. Rafferty has a very big, and very dead, pheasant in his mouth. He does not drop it. Carries it proudly along the bridle path to the very end. Only deigns to abandon it when they come out onto the road and Eric puts his leash back on.

"No roast pheasant tonight then," says Amaryllis. And hugging each other, they laugh.

"That's the school I go to," she tells him as walking down the road from Castle Howard, they pass a large red brick building. "Penelope tells me my teacher is still there. I loved Miss Tong. So, when the wedding date is set, I'm going to pay her a visit and invite her."

"Now, that you are Amaryllis," says Eric, "you are certainly a different person to know than the Isla I meet at the Sanctum."

"Oh. What does that mean then?"

"It means that I love the both of you. Will go anywhere with you. Will do anything for you." And then he adds, somewhat drolly, "But I won't go as far as murder."

****

"Live on a farm!" Columbine exclaims. "When you say you have a plan Amaryllis, I never envisage this."

"I don't understand," says Doris. "And you agree with this, Eric?"

He nods his head. They sit round the table in Columbine's kitchen. She cooks sausages and mashed potato with onion gravy and apple sauce. Amaryllis tries to block the memory of that first night at Lochfrein when James cooks her this. When she is led to believe her mother tells him it's her favourite. That she will be seeing her soon. When obviously she never does.

"Why don't I let Amaryllis explain it to you as she did to me. Just listen," he says, spooning apple sauce on top of the onion gravy.

And so Amaryllis paints a picture of a hard but worthwhile life. A life full of animals. Of unconditional love. And by the time the last morsel of sausage is wiped round the plate, cleaning up any residual gravy, mash, and apple sauce, her plan is sold. Her mother and Doris are on board. An air of excitement and anticipation buzzes around the table as Columbine gets out the fizz. Filling four glasses, she raises hers and toasts, "To Mistletoe Farm and the future."

"To new beginnings," chorus the others, clinking their glasses together.

Columbine knows she could have said this. But she remembers the last time she hears these words. Mendacious words from Charles's lying mouth. When he sells her home from under her. Puts her in a bungalow and leaves. When in her despair, she scatters the sleeping tablets on the table. Is about to swallow them. End it all. But now, she rejoices that she doesn't. And hopes this toast to her new extending family will come true.

235

Chapter 41

Detective Inspector Gibson stares at the gleaming automobile he uncovers in the barn. It's just as Amaryllis describes it. A MG-YB Saloon in a bronze colour, number plate JDZ 777. Considering how many years it languishes here, he thinks, it has been lovingly kept. He takes photographs. Then opens the back door, where he sees the steamer trunk on the back seat. Lifts the lid. Sees the padding. The pillow. There is a fusty smell. He wonders if any hint of opiate lingers?

Finds it hard to believe that the young woman who comes into his office is once a child, drugged, stuffed in this trunk and transported all the way up here. She must have been terrified. And to think his own daughter could fit in it. The thought horrifies him.

"Sir. Sir." One of the sergeants they bring is calling. He runs into the barn. "Detective Sergeant Bogue says to tell you he's looked in the bedroom. And the wall *is* covered in cars. And he says, it looks like a child still sleeps there. Yet, there's some clothes at the back of a wardrobe that would fit a teenager. But it's all like she says, Sir. And yes, Sir, he has photographed everything. Logged it all."

Inspector Gibson smiles. Her story is panning out. "Where is DS Bogue now?" he asks the sergeant.

"He's talking with a woman in the kitchen, Sir. A Mrs McGinty. Says her husband is out with Charles Duncan and his brother James. But she's got quite a Scottish twang and is difficult to understand."

"Thank you, sergeant."

So, thinks DI Gibson, Charles August calls himself Charles Duncan here. It all seems so innocent. Two loving brothers. One, unfortunately, with a wife who has already had one head injury and then suffers another. Must be taken somewhere to help her get better. Disappear again. And voila, just as Amaryllis tells him, they have what they want. Each other. A son. And no-one any the wiser. Until now. When Isla Duncan reincarnates as Amaryllis August and the seedy undercurrents of this case come to light.

As he walks round the farmyard, he hears the squealing of pigs and walks to investigate. There's a young woman in the sty, tossing the straw. Filtering out the soiled chaffs. She hears him approach and turns. Now, she can see uniformed men poking about in the barns and outhouses. Flashing cameras. She's worried. What are they looking for? Has something bad happened?

"Detective Inspector Gibson," he says, holding up his ID card. "And you are?"

"Fiona McGinty," she replies. "What's going on?"

"We have a warrant, Miss McGinty, to search the house and outbuildings of Lochfrein Farm, concerning the disappearance of a child in 1957." He flashes it in front of her.

"In the name of the wee man!" Fiona exclaims, a look of horror on her face. "Ye dinna ken she's deid and buried o' the farm?"

"Do you remember an Isla Duncan?"

"Yes. Poor Isla. James's wife. We're told not to talk to her much because she's not right. But me and my mum find her sweet. Kind. Quick to learn stuff. She loves the farm and the animals. She loves James. But she's feart o' him."

"Who? Who does she fear, Miss McGinty?"

"His brother. Charles Duncan." There it is again, he thinks. The duplicity.

"Does this Isla have a child?"

"Yes. A wee laddie, Williain. Oh he's a reit bonnie bairn. He's nine now. Goes to school in Rothesay. Isla adores him. We all do." She pauses. "Such a shame she dies when he's just a babby."

"Is that what they tell you? That she's dead?"

"It's what they tell the bairn. But we knows different."

And Fiona McGinty tells the detective that Isla is sent away to an asylum. Because she tries to kill herself and Williain. That she's insane. "But we're all sworn ne'er to tell Williain," she says. "And we dinna. Sorry, and we don't."

"Thank you," says Detective Inspector Gibson. "You've been most helpful."

And he can tell from her voice, her demeanour, that she has no idea that Isla Duncan is Amaryllis August. Or what really happens to Isla Duncan that day on the pier.

A few hours later Scott McGinty drives the tractor into the farmyard. Charles August and James Duncan, along with some of the McGinty lads, sit in the trailer it pulls.

The Inspector approaches them with caution. His uniformed men are strategically hidden in case of any trouble.

"I am Detective Inspector Gibson," he says, approaching. "Charles August…"

He notes the glance between the two men. They know.

"And James Duncan. You are, singly and jointly, under arrest for the abduction of Amaryllis August. For the unlawful use of opiates on a minor. For the imprisonment of Amaryllis August. For the rape and sodomy of Amaryllis August. And for her attempted murder. You do not have to say anything, but it may harm your defence if you do not mention when questioned something which you later rely on in court." He takes a breath. "Anything you do say may be given in evidence."

A shock wave rolls across the farmyard. Horror and bewilderment etches on each face. There's a stunned silence. Until Charles, inflated with outrage, shouts, "THE BITCH! That lying conniving daughter of mine…"

A daughter? Where? And Amaryllis August? Who is she? And what about Isla Duncan? The McGintys glance from one to each other. From James to Charles. They always feel uncomfortable around him. His charm belies an ire with a short fuse. Whilst James is easy going. Likeable. Always the same. But what does all this mean for them?

"She tells you a pack of lies and you believe her. Over me!" Charles continues to rant. "Well, you're not arresting me on some trumped-up charge. She's mad. Always was. Now, if you don't mind, *detective*, I'll be going to pick up my son from school."

"I'm afraid not, Mr August. One of my officers will collect him. You and Mr Duncan will be accompanying myself and Detective Sergeant Bogue back to York, where you will be held in custody until a trial date is set. Williain, who we know is not your son but James and your daughter's, will be taken to a hospital to be checked out, and reunited with his mother as soon as possible."

Mrs McGinty and Fiona, hearing the fracas, have come outside. They catch some of the conversation. Mrs McGinty is as stupefied as her husband and the rest of their clan. They are calling Charles Mr August, not Duncan. So, he is not

James's brother. Who is he then? And where does this Amaryllis fit in? Isla is Williain's mother. This they do know. But the rest is a mystery.

Charles August implodes. "NO!" he yells. Spittle flies from his angry mouth. "You can't do this. You can't take the boy."

He is already clambering out of the trailer.

"James," he cries. "Tell them! Tell them he's ours. That we never harm a hair of his head."

A sergeant runs out of one of the barns and grabs hold of him before he can reach his quad cab. Charles punches him in the face. He falls backwards. Two more dash up and fell him. Roughly put his arms behind his back. Snap handcuffs on his wrists.

James remains in the trailer. Immobile. Shocked at the final performance his partner puts on.

"Charles August," says the Inspector, walking round the trailer, where Charles struggles against his restraints. "I must caution you that you are now under arrest for the assault of a police officer. Also for the murder of your mother, Victoria Elizabeth Ann August and pending enquiries, the deaths of vulnerable women, later to be named in court, who were patients in The Royal Free Hospital when you were a doctor there. And I would remind you again that you do not have to say anything, but it may harm your defence if you do not mention when questioned something which you later rely on in court. Anything you do say may be given in evidence."

"Lies!" shouts Charles. "More lies." He struggles. "She betrays us, James. The little whore betrays us! Tell them, James. Tell them it's not true. None of it. It's all in her head."

James watches the disintegration of this man he loves. This man he gives up everything for. And taking off the rose-tinted glasses he's worn so long, finally sees him for what he really is. Egotistical. Controlling. Possessive. And yes, a murderer.

James comes to a decision. Standing up in the trailer, he proclaims for all to hear, "It's true. All of it. Exactly as you say. And I, James Duncan, plead guilty. I plead guilty to everything. But I will not plead guilty to the sodomy or attempted murder of Amaryllis. I could never do that to her. To Williain's mother. That's all Charles's doing." He sobs. "It's all Charles's doing."

And suddenly the huge weight that anchors him. The weight that sits on his shoulders since he meets Charles in the war, is lifted. And all he can feel is immeasurable sadness. And relief. Even when he puts his arms behind his back and the handcuffs are snapped on.

"TRAITOR!" screams Charles. "BASTARD! PIG! You betray me too!" He's crying now. Crying crocodile tears. "I know you love the whore. I should have killed the both of you when I had the chance and taken the boy. Some people don't deserve to live."

His words, his admission is heard by all and duly noted. Defiant to the last, Charles August is bundled into the back of a police van. The McGinty's, shocked at what they witness, what they hear, listen to the resounding noise of the doors as they are slammed shut. Whilst James, quiet and unresisting, is put in the back of another van.

Detective Inspector Gibson addresses the McGinty's.

"It's the wishes of Columbine August, Charles August's wife and Amaryllis August, his daughter, that you continue to manage the farm until after the trial. And in the event of their conviction, that the deeds of Lochfrein be transferred into your names, Mr and Mrs McGinty. For perpetuity."

"Isla, she dinna want tae cam hame?" asks Scott McGinty, still baffled by the turn of events.

"No." Inspector Gibson shakes his hand. "She says there are too many memories. But she tells me how much you and your family help her despite everything. And since Isla is really Amaryllis, it's both their way of saying thank you."

"Och, she's aye a verra kin bonnie wee lassie," Scott says, wiping a tear away from his eye, just as a police car pulls into the farmyard. There's a young boy sitting on the front seat next to the officer. Inspector Gibson opens the door.

"Hello," he says. "You must be Williain."

Williain is indeed a beautiful child. He has the curly auburn gold hair of his father. The big brown eyes of his mother. He runs up to Mrs McGinty.

"I rode in a police car!" he exclaims. "All the way from school to home. Everyone is watching. And the policeman let me put the flashing light and siren on. I can't wait to tell my daddies."

Inspector Gibson quietly approaches. He is glad, at times like this, he has his own children. It makes it easier to relate to them. So, he drops down to the boy's level.

"About your daddies," he says. "I don't want you to be scared, Williain because there's nothing to be scared about. They are both alright, but they've done something naughty, so we must take them away for a while. And you are to come with us, Williain. We have found your mummy…"

"Mammy's dead," cries Williain. "I don't have a mammy. Just two daddies. And my Ginty."

"Your mammy isn't dead, Williain. She is very much alive and so wants to meet you. All this time she misses you. And now she'll look after you until you can be with your daddies again." He's not sure this will ever happen but doesn't want to distress the boy any more than necessary. "How about you ride in my car? You can sit in the front again. Can you do that?"

Williain nods.

"Afore ye go," says Mrs McGinty. "Will ye no huv a wee refreshment? The laddie's lookin a tad peely-wally. Aw can soon put some scran together." She beams broadly at the Inspector.

"What my mother means," Fiona McGinty intercedes. "Is that Williain looks peaky. And she can soon rustle up some food and drinks before you leave."

"That's most kind of you, Mrs McGinty," says Inspector Gibson. "I'm sure my men will appreciate it. And the use of the bathroom if we may," he adds.

Whilst they gather in the kitchen and partake of fresh bread, cheese, and ham. Swallow it down with glasses of pear cider, Fiona finds a suitcase. Fills it with day and night clothes for Williain. Puts a few of his favourite books and toys in. And as she drags the case down the stairs, the weight of it matches the weight in her heart. She has known Williain since his birth. They all have. And Fiona McGinty knows that they will likely never see him again.

One hour later, on this balmy late summer's evening when the sun drops in the sky, tinging the cloudscape with orange and pink, the cavalcade leaves Lochfrein and makes its way to Rothesay. There the two police vans and two police cars drive onto the ferry, which the Argyll & Bute Police have commissioned to take them across the straits to Wemyss Bay. There are no other passengers.

Then it's the long drive south down the Great North Road to Yorkshire. Most of the coaching inns are gone now where large stretches of the old road are paralleled with the new A1, which is dual carriageway and bypasses some of the towns and cities. A much quicker route than in 1957 when James Duncan drives north to Glasgow and the Isle of Bute with a nine-year-old girl shut in a trunk on the back seat of his car.

Chapter 42

Columbine kneads flour and lard in a bowl. She's making pastry for a steak and kidney pie. The telephone rings. Wiping her floury hands on a tea towel, she hurries across to the phone and picks up the receiver.

"2404," she says. "Who's calling?"

"It's Detective Inspector Gibson, Mrs August." He clears his throat, whilst Columbine pushes the receiver right up to her ear and holds her breath. She knows they were going up to Bute. To the farm Amaryllis tells them of. Is this the news they wait for? Oh, she hopes so.

"We've got them," he says. "Charles August and James Duncan are in custody. They are being held at York Crown Court. At their arraignment James pleads guilty so he will not stand trial but can be called as a witness. Charles pleads not guilty. Very vociferously, apparently. I believe the trial is set for Monday, the 20th of January 1975. But you will receive written confirmation in the post. Where it is being held. How to get there. What facilities there are. So, don't worry. And no bail is being offered."

Columbine lets out a huge sigh. "And Williain?" she asks.

"Yes, we have Williain too. He's been checked out at the hospital." He hears a sharp intake of breath. "Williain's fine, Mrs August. He has been well looked after. And before you ask no, there are no signs of abuse. But he's distressed and confused as you can imagine."

"Then he needs to be with us, not strangers," says Columbine. "We can take care of him."

"Are not you and your daughter strangers too?"

Columbine ponders this. He's right, she thinks. Williain will not know them.

"So what happens now then?" she asks. "When *can* he come to us?"

There is a pause on the line. Inspector Gibson does not want to be the deliverer of bad news. He knows neither Columbine August nor Amaryllis will like what he is going to tell them. Particularly Amaryllis who has waited so long. And now must wait even longer.

"The Custodial Court deems that in view of the forthcoming trial and the media attention it will attract," Inspector Gibson begins to say, "and the fact that you are in the process of relocating to Monk Fryston, another big upheaval, it would be in Williain's best interest if he is put in short-term foster care, until everything quietens down. I'm sure you'll both be able to visit in this period of his adjustment."

"I can see the sense in the arrangement Inspector," Columbine says. "But Amaryllis will be so upset. She thinks she'll see him in a few days. Oh dear, I don't know how to tell her." And thanking him for the call, she quietly puts the receiver down.

"Tell me what?" says Amaryllis.

She's come out of the bathroom and is towelling her hair as she walks into the kitchen.

"And what will upset me?" Then she freezes. "It's Williain, isn't it? Does something happen to him? Oh my god, mum. Tell me."

So, Columbine tells her.

****

Over the next few months there is a flurry of activity at number 11 Peasholme Green and Rose Cottage. Both properties sell within a week of being put on the market. There is a lot of packing and organizing to do. Eric hands in his notice to the Sanctum's Board of Trustees. He finishes his last shift on the 25th of October. And whilst his mother, Columbine and Amaryllis sort out the houses, he supervises the building work and decorating at Mistletoe Farm. Even does some of it himself.

"It's looking good," he tells them. "I don't know about being a farmer, but I'm a dab hand at the do it yourselfing stuff. The builders say they will be finished by the new year. The decorating is all but done. And so," he adds, "we should easily be able to move in before the trial."

"That's wonderful!" exclaims Amaryllis, hugging him.

"Well, I think Christmas is cancelled this year," announces Columbine. "As far as decorations go," she explains. "There's no point putting a tree up just to take it down." She laughs. "But we will eat, drink and be merry. Of that, you can be sure."

But halfway through November, a grey and mizzly month, the front doorbell rings. Amaryllis ploughs between the boxes and cases to open it.

"Amaryllis August?" asks the woman. She has a slight Yorkshire accent. Is neatly attired. A pleasant enough face. Amaryllis nods.

"My name is Sarah Blythe. I'm from Social Services. May I come in?"

Amaryllis opens the door wider.

"I'm sorry about all the chaos," she says. "But we're in the process of moving. I expect you know. To a farm. Williain grows up on a farm," she adds.

"He looks very like you," Sarah Blythe remarks.

"Does he? He was only a toddler when I last saw him. His hair was auburn gold with curls."

"It still is, Amaryllis. What I am here for today is to tell you that it has been arranged with the foster parents, a Mr and Mrs Grice, for you to visit Williain. Get to know each other. And see how it goes..."

"Mum!" shouts Amaryllis. "There's a lady from Social services here. Can you put the kettle on?"

Amaryllis takes a box off one of the chairs so Sarah Blythe can sit. Balance a cup and saucer on her knees. In between carefully sipping the tea, she tells them what Williain has been told and what he hasn't. Gives them the address where he's at. It's 23 Audus Street.

"They're expecting you on Saturday," she explains. "For lunch, about twelve-thirty." She smiles at Columbine, who she knows is Williain's grandmother. "I'm sure you're dying to see him too, Mrs August. But I think the first visit should be just his mother. Is this OK with you?"

"Whatever it takes," replies Columbine.

"I also understand you're getting married, Amaryllis."

She puts the cup and saucer on the floor.

"So perhaps, three visits initially leading up to Christmas. One on your own. One with your mother. And one with your fiancé. Give Williain time to take it all in. It's a lot of changes to cope with. And then if all goes well, after the trial, he will be able to join you at your new home. Mistletoe Farm, isn't it?"

"Yes" Amaryllis and Columbine say together.

And with that, Sarah Blythe departs. Her instincts tell her that Williain will be loved and well cared for in this extended family unit.

Chapter 43

Amaryllis finds it hard to be patient. To wait for Saturday. She can drive now. The time spent at Rose Cottage she takes driving lessons with Frank England, a local instructor. Picks it up quickly and passes her driving test first time.

"Before you ask," her mother says. "Yes, you can borrow the Morris. Don't overrev her though."

"Oh mum!" Amaryllis hugs her. "Thanks. And I'll drive carefully. Promise."

23 Audus Street is a large, terraced house. With some trepidation Amaryllis knocks on the door. There is no bell. She waits. Knocks again. When it finally opens a frazzled looking woman stands there.

"Sorry," she says. "You're Amaryllis, Williain's birth mother?"

"Yes."

"We're expecting you. But these terraces go back a long way. I was in the kitchen, getting the lunch ready. Please come in. We'll have a little chat. And then I'll call Williain."

"Have you fostered for a long time?" asks Amaryllis as she follows the woman down a long corridor that leads to a large kitchen diner looing out onto a garden. It's all fenced in. Safe. She can see a trampoline. Football posts. A netball or basketball hoop. Not much in the way of flora.

"About eleven years. We couldn't have kids, so it works for us. Usually, only have one or two at a time. We might adopt one day. My name is Alice by the way. And my husband is Frank. He's not here right now."

"How has Williain been coping?"

"Rather distressed at first. Crying for his daddies a lot. Not sleeping. Not eating. Pretty normal stuff when the kids first arrive. We give them time. Space. Rules. And we talk. Let them talk. Williain's not what you'd call a chatterbox. But he loves football. Frank plays in the garden with him. And I think he's quite excited at meeting you, although his memory of you is hazy. That's an unusual bag," she comments, looking at the holdall on Amaryllis's shoulder with its rainbow stripes.

"I bought it in Rothesay," Amaryllis explains. "I had it with me that...Well, anyway, I thought it might spark a memory. I've got something special in it. Special to Williain, I mean."

"I'll go and fetch him. He's upstairs reading." She laughs. "He's a big reader. Quite a clever little chap."

Amaryllis smiles. Remembers the bedroom at Lochfrein with its shelves of books. Expects Williain has also read them all.

When Alice Grice reappears there is a boy with her. Her fears that Charles would indulge him too much, that he would be overweight, spoilt, laugh in her face. A face that mirrors her own. Large brown eyes. Cute button nose. And smiling lips. He is small and slim, with hair exactly like his dad's, auburn gold and curly. He's just like she remembers. She just wants to grab him. Hug him. Never let him go again. But she doesn't. One day, perhaps.

Whilst Alice starts to plate the lunch, sandwiches, crisps and fruit, Amaryllis and Williain sit at the table. He is shy. Reserved.

"Are you really my mum?" he asks. "My daddies told me you are dead."

"Yes. I am really your mum. I was poorly, Williain. I had to go away. I lost you and I couldn't find you. But now, I have."

Amaryllis rummages in the holdall. Pulls out the one eyed, one eared, slightly bald bear. And sits him on the table. She has kept him since that evening, the evening she meets Eric. She is in her cell on Hannah, getting ready for the patients' dance. When, pulling the white catsuit out of the holdall, a tatty old bear drops onto the floor. She has no idea where it comes from. Or its significance.

Alice comes to sit at the table. Pours apple juice into three tumblers. They both watch Williain. He is staring at the bear, his brow furrowed, his lips moving as if he's trying to speak. Then, of a sudden, he cries out, "Pooh. It's Pooh Bear!" And grabbing him off the table, he holds him tight. Just as he used to.

"I kept him for you, Williain. I know how much you love him. Fiona McGinty gives him to you when you are born."

"Fiona," echoes Williain, wistfully.

"Right then, Williain," interjects Alice. "Why don't you offer your mum a sandwich."

"Would you like a sandwich? Mrs Grice makes really nice ones."

He doesn't say 'mum'. Not yet. But he's polite. Someone has been a good influence on him. She suspects it's not her father.

The first visit passes too quickly. Mr Grice, Frank, comes through the back door. He leaves his muddy shoes on the step. Alice introduces him to Amaryllis.

"So, you're his mum." He looks from her to Williain. "Two peas in a pod," he says. "Which is where I've been. At the allotment. Williain likes to help me, don't you, lad? But not today, eh? He has a knack for growing stuff. Nice to meet you Ama…Williain's mum. Just going to scrub up. Don't eat all the sandwiches!"

But Amaryllis is leaving now. And there are plenty left. They arrange the next visit when Alice tells Williain his grandmother will be coming too. Williain shows interest. His friends have grandmothers. But he never knew he has one too.

The next two visits go well. Columbine has a way with children and Williain takes to her straightaway. He is more reserved about Eric. Says little. He's not ready for another daddy yet. But when Eric takes him outside to kick a ball about, he begins to open up. And before the visit ends, he is telling Eric all about Lochfrein, the animals, the school he attends. His friends. Amaryllis watches them through the window. *It's going to be alright*, she thinks. And knows the perfect gift for Williain when he joins them at Mistletoe after Christmas. After the trial.

And at that last visit, as Alice opens the front door to let Eric and Amaryllis out, a body comes hurtling down the corridor and wraps its arms around Amaryllis's waist. It's a hug. A big hug. And she fancies she hears the word 'mammy' which is what he calls her at Lochfrein. But, of course, it could just be wishful thinking.

Engrossed in getting to know her son, Amaryllis is unaware that her father is taken down to Scotland Yard. The criminal investigators have been digging. Resurrecting old patients' records at The Royal Free Hospital for the time that Dr Charles August is there. Patients who are doing well and then suddenly and inexplicably die. Over a period of time, they find six women, for each of which Charles signs the death warrants. These record death due to incorrect dosage of medicine.

Dr Charles August is a charming, well respected, member of the hospital Board. He cannot fall under suspicion. It would not look good for the hospital should one of their eminent doctors be found guilty of such catastrophic errors.

So, the blame falls on a junior nurse. She is brought before the Board. Given no chance to defend herself. And sacked. Her career over.

But the criminal investigators delve deeper. Inspector Gibson has told them of Charles's boastful confession to murdering his mother, Victoria Elizabeth Anne August. And strangely, they discover that each of the six women who die mysteriously has a forename of either Victoria, Elizabeth, or Anne.

Charles never believes that anyone will make a connection. But when interviewed, his ego dictates he boasts of his cleverness. And he is summarily charged with the murder of his mother and the six patients once in his care.

However, none of this is admissible at his forthcoming trial since it would bias the jury towards him. He is taken back to York with no-one the wiser.

Chapter 44

The letter informing Amaryllis of the trial arrives. Its formality gives her a sense of vindication. A chance to get justice. But also fills her with apprehension for the unknown.

It's Monday, the 20th of January 1975. York Crown Court. Amaryllis and Columbine sit outside the courtroom, waiting until they are called. Called as witnesses for the Crown Prosecution. Amaryllis will be the first witness to take the stand. She's nervous. Fidgety. Swings her legs back and forth. Tries to control the riot that breaks out in her stomach.

"Do you think we are doing the right thing?" she asks quietly. Columbine takes her hand. Holds it tight.

"Yes," she says. "Your father must answer to his actions. And as for James, well, he should never have gone along with it. But love can blind you." She snorts. "It certainly did me."

Inside the court, the usher calls, "All rise!"

The Judge, wigged and robed, sweeps into the courtroom, and goes behind the bench, a raised wooden podium that puts him above everyone else.

"Be seated," he orders. And the court is filled with the shuffle of bottoms getting comfortable. The last blow of a nose. The last cough. The rustle of paper.

"This trial," the Judge addresses the court, "is about the abduction of Amaryllis August on her ninth birthday, the 21st of June 1957. And what happens to her in the seventeen years before her sudden reappearance. It is your job, as jurors, to decide whether the defendants, Charles August and James Duncan are guilty or not guilty of the charges brought against them, based on the evidence presented to you in the court proceedings. This court is now in session, and I would ask the Prosecutor for the Crown to give his opening speech."

The Crown Prosecutor stands. "Charles August and his lover…"

Someone sniggers.

"James Duncan are singly and jointly charged," he begins, "with the premeditated abduction of Amaryllis August. The use of drugs to sedate her. The loss of her liberty by imprisonment. The brutal and continuous rape of her. Begetting a child by her. And the attempted murder of her."

He passes a copy of the indictments to the jury.

There are a few horrified gasps.

"At arraignment," he continues, "James Duncan pleads guilty to all charges except attempted murder. I shall, therefore, be calling him as a witness for the prosecution."

At this point he turns to the Judge, "My Lord," he addresses him, "before I call my first witness, I would like to play to the Court a tape recording taken by Detective Inspector Gibson on the 24th of August 1964 at the York Constabulary. This is Amaryllis August's personal victim statement. It initiates the re-opening of this unusual and complex case in the light of new evidence, Amaryllis August herself."

"Very well," says the Judge. "Proceed."

It's so quiet they all hear the click of the tape recorder as it's switched on. The rasp of the reel as it turns. Then Amaryllis's voice speaks out. And they listen, whilst the court stenographer taps the keys on his machine. A machine which records the proceedings in shorthand.

"Now," says the Crown Prosecutor when the tape finishes, "I would like to call Amaryllis August as my first witness."

Amaryllis hears the creak of a hinge as a door opens and a court usher comes out. "I call Amaryllis August," he says. Amaryllis stands up. Her legs are like jelly. Her mother gives her hand one last squeeze.

"Walk tall," she hears her say. "You can do this. I know you can." And then she is walking with the usher through the doors and into the courtroom.

Amaryllis has been told what to expect. Where everyone will be seated. But nothing prepares her for the sheer magnitude of the place. The pomposity. The polished wood. The fustiness. Her mother's words ring in her ears. And standing tall, walking proud, she somehow stops her legs from collapsing. And takes the witness stand.

To the left of her, she sees the red robe of the Judge. His short curly wig. It's slightly askew. She wants to laugh. But doesn't. Her eyes dart round the courtroom. She can't see her father or James. Even though she knows they will be called at some point, it's a relief.

A relief she will not have to describe what they do to her with their eyes condemning her. But she feels the scrutiny of twelve pairs of eyes. The eyes of the jurors. Ordinary looking folk in ordinary looking attire, waiting. Ears open. Lips shut. But they are not ordinary thinks Amaryllis. They will decide the fate of the defendants. And consequently, hers.

For a few moments she stands frozen in time. Silent. Glances to where the public are seated. She can see Eric. Can feel his love flow into her. Doris sits next to him. Penelope's there with her husband, Gerald. She sees Judy and spouse, Philip. And there's Rosy, alone, yet enveloped by them all. And last, but not least, Alwyn and his exotic wife. She's from Japan. Tells Amaryllis when they all get together, her name is 'Sakura'. It means cherry blossom. Cherry blossom is small and beautiful. So is Sakura. And before she begins to recite the oath, she espies Detective Inspector Gibson and Detective Sergeant Bogue. All here to support her.

"Amaryllis?" A voice intrudes. It belongs to the Crown Prosecutor. "Are you ready?"

I can do this, she thinks and places her hand on the bible. "I swear that the evidence." A slight almost indiscernible pause as suddenly she spots Miss Tong in the public gallery too. How did she miss her? She has hardly changed. Her hair is still tightly curled. Only the odd streak of white. "I shall give," she continues, "shall be the truth, the whole truth and nothing but the truth."

"Can you please state your name for the Court."

"Amaryllis August."

"Amaryllis," he addresses her, "I would like you to tell the Court, in your own words and in your own time, what happens that day, the 21st of June 1957. The day of your ninth birthday when you disappear. And afterwards. Until you reappear in a police station."

Amaryllis knows that this will probably be the last time this story will be told. That this is her chance to put in all the emotions and feelings that she and Isla never truly acknowledge. The tiny details. Prior to the trial she is told by her barrister to stay calm. To speak clearly and slowly. To watch the tap, tap, tap of the court reporter who will be sitting at a desk adjacent to the witness stand, recording the proceedings. Ensure he keeps up.

She knows that in the public gallery, reporters from the press are poised ready to write their own account of the trial for the newspaper they represent. Each one vying for the best story. The one that will sell the most newspapers.

Meanwhile, a court artist draws quick sketches of faces. Before the day there will be many. But it's the face of Amaryllis which will stand out. She is told to turn that face to the jury when she speaks. To look at them, but not stare. To engage with them so they believe in her.

And so Amaryllis begins.

"He has a new car. This one has a roof. And it sparkles in the sun. I remember the number plate, JDZ 777."

The court clerk presents to the Judge the photographs that Inspector Gibson and Sergeant Bogue take that day at Lochfrein. Of the car. The farm. Her bedroom. Now labelled as Exhibits A, B and C. The Judge then gives his permission for them to be passed to the jury. Exhibit A clearly shows the car and number plate.

"I think I am going to get a puppy. For my birthday. I am so happy. But then we get to this derelict, empty farm. I'm afraid. And then there is nothing. It's dark. I am trapped. Terrified. I scream and scream. But no-one comes."

Taking a deep breath, she continues with her story...

"And then suddenly someone is pulling me out. It's my uncle. I think he has come to take me home. But he doesn't. I must climb in a big trunk on the back seat of the car. I seem to be in it forever..."

The jurors can see from the photographs, the trunk she speaks of.

"He puts a needle in my arm, and I am calm. Sleepy. He says he won't close the lid. But he does. I'm sad. I want my mother. My friends. But I realize I'm lost to them. And they are lost to me."

She tells the court about the farm.

"I am locked in my room with a small window, books and a chamber pot..."

Exhibits B and C are shown to the jury as evidence.

"I am told I am no longer Amaryllis. Amaryllis is gone. I am Isla. Over and over. And over again I must say it. If I get it wrong, he slaps me. I am afraid. Confused. But I am a good girl. Bad girls get punished. So, I become Isla. And lose my true self."

Looks of disbelief pass between the jurors. The people in the gallery. Such a cruel thing to do. Strip a person of their identity.

"I am not allowed to be seen. I am only allowed out in the dark."

Recalling the nightly walks around the farm, she is encouraged to continue.

"At first, I do everything in the dark. Even learning to cook."

The jurors smile.

"I am happy out on the farm. I am happy with James. He's all I've got." And she describes those first few years.

"But then, just before one Christmas, my father arrives. He ruins everything. I am locked up again. Drugged. Until suddenly, one morning, I can be seen. But mustn't be heard. He puts rings on my fingers. Tells me I am married to James."

Her voice wobbles. She takes a sip of water from a glass that sits on the stand. Breathes. *I can do this*, she tells herself.

"And then, when I am going on sixteen, he rapes me."

Someone gasps.

"I'm on the floor like a dog. I've no idea what's happening. Only that the pain is like nothing I have ever felt. Then James rapes me. Every night they do this. It only stops when I am pregnant."

There are horrified glances from juror to juror. Some wipe tears from their eyes.

But now Amaryllis nears the end of her testimony. She has recounted it all. Everything. No loops left. All the way to its bitter end...

"And then he, my father, Charles August, hits me so hard I fall. I don't want to let go of Williain because I know he'll take him. But I do. I fall. The world is dark. When the light appears again, I am in an asylum. I don't know who I truly am. I have no past. No future. Only the present. I am imprisoned there for seven years. Until I find myself again. When I find Amaryllis August."

There, she has done it! A theatrical performance. Packed with emotions. Every person sitting in that court empathizes with her. And her mother has not had to listen to one single word.

"Does the Barrister for the Defence wish to question the witness?" The Judge asks.

There is a momentary hush before...

"No questions, My Lord."

"Thank you, Amaryllis. You may step down."

Amaryllis goes to sit behind the table for the plaintiff where her barrister, the Crown Prosecutor is. He smiles encouragingly at her.

"I now call James Duncan as my next witness."

Amaryllis, upon hearing his name, wonders why he is being called to the witness stand by the prosecuting barrister and not the defence barrister.

There is a short pause in the proceedings, whilst an usher carries some written questions from the jury to the Judge. These he quickly reads then instructs him to call James Duncan to be brought from the holding cells into court. Upon hearing his name, Amaryllis's heart begins to gallop. Eight years have passed since she's seen him. But in less than eight minutes he's there, in the courtroom, standing in the dock, a prison officer beside him. Labelled a criminal. Yet still, the father of her son.

Oh god, she thinks. *He is still beautiful. The years have advanced, but he remains the same.* Once, he was all she had. But now she has so much more. And she doesn't love him. Not anymore. This she does know.

James is sworn in. On oath, he confirms that he was indeed at Oakwood for Amaryllis's birthday on the 21st of June 1957.

"What car were you driving Mr Duncan?"

"An MG-YB saloon. Registration JDZ 777."

"Please show Mr Duncan Exhibit A."

James looks at the photograph.

"And is this the car you abduct Amaryllis August in?"

"Yes."

"And can you confirm that you were no longer a consultant at Sheffield Northern Infirmary, which is what the household is led to believe. That you do, in fact, leave that post in August 1953. To become a farmer."

"Yes."

"Can you tell the Court then, where you do actually go when you leave Oakwood in the middle of that night. And why."

"To the derelict farm at the end of Oaktree Drive." He looks at Amaryllis, but she will not acknowledge him. "To retrieve Amaryllis from the hogshead barrel I put her in."

Looks of abhorrence rest on the jurors' faces.

Someone shouts out, "Bastard!"

Another, "Lock him up."

Someone else, "Throw away the key."

"Silence in Court!" calls the Judge. His voice is weighty. Authoritative. Silence descends.

"And why must you do this?"

"It's part of the plan. Charles's plan."

"So the abduction and all that ensues is premeditated?"

"Yes."

"When did you meet Charles August? And can you explain to the Court what the entirety of his plan is."

"We meet in the War. And we fall in love." A snigger from the public gallery can be heard.

"Poofters! Perverts!" someone shouts.

"Silence in Court!" The Judge reiterates.

"We know it's a crime, punishable by imprisonment," James continues when all is quiet again. "That's when Charles devises his plan. A plan for us to be together. At the end of the War, he will marry. Just to appear respectable. In the meantime I am to find a place. Somewhere remote. A place where we can be together. Where he will adopt my surname and we will live as brothers. I already have a considerable amount of money left to me by my parents. So I sell my own home. And use the funds to purchase the farm, Lochfrein, on the Isle of Bute."

"Please show Mr Duncan Exhibits B and C."

James is shown the photos of the farm. Amaryllis's bedroom.

"Is this the farm?"

"Yes."

"So, you have your remote place where you can live together as, I quote, 'brothers'. Could you tell the court why then you need to abduct Amaryllis August?"

"Because Charles wants us to have a son. He's obsessed at having a son."

"And of course," says the Crown Prosecutor, "Columbine August only gives him a daughter. So, how does he propose to do this? She is only nine years old."

Now James takes them to that day, the 21st of June 1957.

"I do, in fact, arrive early that morning. Drive to the derelict farm Charles tells me of. I poke around. Discover the hogshead barrel. Amaryllis is small. I know she will fit in it. I tape an empty milk bottle to the inside. I've filled this with juice, and sedative I steal from the hospital before I leave."

Speaking the words out loud, listening to them himself, he wonders how he could ever be so callous.

Something everyone in the court now thinks.

"I put a straw in the bottle, knowing if she's thirsty she'll drink. And sleep. Will not cry out if the police are searching for her. Then I drive back down Oaktree Drive, round the marketplace and back up. I stop outside Oakwood. Amaryllis is sitting on the wall, waiting for me. I know she'll want a ride in my new car. I make her hide in the footwell so no-one will see her. She thinks it's a game. Charles tells me of a vacant house with a hidden driveway. We park there and walk to the farm. That's when I inject her with a barbiturate." He coughs to clear his throat. "And put her in the barrel."

"And then you leave Oakwood in the early hours of the morning. Retrieve Amaryllis from the barrel. Put her in the trunk. And drive to Bute. Is this correct?"

"Yes."

"And when you arrive on the island, no-one questions why you have a nine-year-old girl with you?"

"No. Because she is hidden until she is sixteen. When she becomes my wife. When Charles decides it's time to get her pregnant."

"Amaryllis states that until her father arrives, you take good care of her. Teach her. Quite a lot it would appear as she is intelligent and articulate. Is this part of your remit?"

"No. But she's funny and smart. Eager to learn. It's something I enjoy doing. Until he comes. Two's company. Three's a crowd," he says wryly.

"And when, Mr Duncan, do you begin to question yourself. Your involvement with Charles August. The things you've done?"

"When I begin to fall in love with her."

So, she wasn't mistaken, thinks Amaryllis. And almost smiles.

The jurors, wearing grim masks, listen carefully to what ensues.

"When we are playing Monopoly and he tells us that he murders his mother when she threatens to disinherit him. When he rapes Amaryllis. When as soon as Williain is born, he tries to break the bond between them. When I remember the broken people in the War he puts back together and think how marvellous he is. Only to see him smother them in the night…"

"How many, Mr Duncan? How many does he dispose of in this way?"

"At least five. He tells me he is saving them from a life of pain. And I believe him."

It's so quiet in the courtroom, that should a pin drop, it would be heard.

"We, Amaryllis and I, talk of wearing rose-tinted glasses. I think I wear mine too long. I still love him. I love Amaryllis. I love my son. Believe I can have it all. Until that day when I finally take the glasses off."

"And that is the day that you witness Charles August try to murder his daughter, Amaryllis August?"

"Yes."

"Mr Duncan, you claim to have had no part in her attempted murder. Yet you were there, that day, on Rothesay pier when this event occurred?"

"Yes."

"Can you tell the Court what you witness?"

"I hear him, Charles August, yelling at her to give him the boy. Our son, Williain. I see him slap her. I see his knee thrust in her stomach. Still she holds tight to the boy. And then I see him punch her. Shove her so hard she falls, banging her head on some iron. She's lifeless. I hear him call out, she's dead. And I believe him."

"Why do you not intervene? Try to save her."

"Because I'm a coward. I'm weak. And I'm afraid for us both. He knows how I feel about her."

So, he did mean what he said, thinks Amaryllis. And yes, he was a coward. But he's not one now. He's a hero.

"Now, I see what he is," continues James. "This man I give up everything for. Egotistical. A beguiling bully. Controlling. A man without empathy. With no moral compass. Because he always tells me that if I ever try to leave. Go with Amaryllis and take our son away, he will first kill her. Then he will kill me. And feed us to the pigs. Tell everyone we have emigrated and when we are settled, will come back for Williain. But, of course, we won't. He has everything worked out. He always does."

Amaryllis wrings her hands. This is the first time she hears this.

"Thank you, Mr Duncan. No further questions. You may step down."

The Barrister for the Defence has no questions. James has turned Queens evidence. Said it all. As the prison officer takes him back to the holding cell, he turns to see Amaryllis looking at him. He smiles. He has done this for her. For their son. She smiles back.

And now Amaryllis hears her mother being called to give witness. Watches her being led into the courtroom, slim, pretty. Confident.

"I swear," she says from the stand. Her voice is clear. Firm. "That the evidence I shall give shall be the truth, the whole truth and nothing but the truth."

"Please state your name," says the Crown Prosecutor.

"Columbine August."

"And you are married to Charles August?"

"Yes."

"When was the last time you saw your husband?"

"Just before Christmas, 1961."

"So you haven't seen him in…" Quick calculations are being made by everyone. "Fourteen years."

"That is correct."

"And can you tell the court where you believe him to be in all this time?"

"Travelling. He tells me he wants to travel the world. Everywhere. Except Europe. But now, I know the only place he travels to is to the farm on the Isle of Bute. To be with James Duncan and my daughter."

"And can you confirm, Mrs August, that James Duncan, contrary to statements taken at the time, does come to your house, Oakwood, on the 21st of June 1957. That he arrives in a new car. This car." He shows her photo Exhibit A.

Columbine tries to remember. "It sort of looks like it," she says.

"I need a 'yes' or a 'no' Mrs August. Take your time."

Columbine stares at the photo.

"Yes," she says. "He says it's a sunbronze metallic colour. Like that car." She points at the photograph. "I remember now."

"Thank you, Mrs August. And is it true that you, the gardener and maid, are told not to mention this to the police. That your husband threatens you."

"Yes." Columbine confirms.

"So, until your daughter suddenly appears at your home, last year, you have no idea what happens to her, where she is? Whether she is alive or dead?"

"No. But I believe her dead. Because nothing is ever found. Except the watch I give her that day, her birthday."

"And is this the watch, Mrs August?" The rose gold watch, tagged, bagged and labelled Exhibit D, is shown to her and the jury.

"Yes." Columbine affirms. Tries not to let her mind go back to that day, the day after, when a young sergeant places it on the kitchen table at Oakwood.

"No further questions."

"Does the Barrister for the Defence wish to question the witness?"

"No, My Lord."

"Thank you, Mrs August. You may step down."

Columbine goes to sit with Amaryllis. Amaryllis finds her hand under the table and holds it. Both have decided to stay until Charles is called.

The Crown Prosecutor addresses the jury.

"You have heard the evidence given by Amaryllis August, both in her personal witness statement and her testimony. You have heard the testimony of James Duncan. You will note that each testimony corroborates with the other. You have also heard Amaryllis's mother's account of that day. You will note that this also concurs with the dates and facts.

I put it to you, the jury, that the two defendants, Charles August and James Duncan do indeed premeditatedly and deliberately abduct Amaryllis August. That they deprive her of her liberty for seventeen years. The right to be seen. The right to be heard. The right to attend school. Have friends. The right to choose. That they constantly rape her to satisfy Charles August's desires.

You already know that James Duncan pleads guilty to these crimes. But after deliberation and re-reading the list of indictments in your possession, I trust you will find both the defendants guilty on all counts. Give Amaryllis August the justice she deserves. That," he says, "is the case for the Crown."

The Judge thanks the Crown Prosecutor. Addresses the court.

"James Duncan will remain in custody at Her Majesty's pleasure until sentencing. Which will be dependent on whether the jurors find him guilty or not guilty on the single count of attempted murder."

It's been a long morning. The members of the jury and the public have sat for three hours, listening to harrowing testimonies. Stomachs are rumbling. Those desperate for a caffeine fix, a cigarette, glance at their watches. It's 1 o'clock.

The Judge stands. They await to hear him call a recess for lunch. But instead he announces, "This Court will now adjourn at thirteen hundred hours. And reconvene tomorrow morning, Tuesday the 22nd of January at ten hundred hours. When the Barrister for the Defence will present his case." He now turns to the jury. "May I remind the jurors that in the meantime, they must not discuss the case with anyone."

Chapter 45

As soon as they are outside the courtroom, Amaryllis gets separated from her mother. Is besieged by reporters who jostle her. Fire a barrage of questions at her. The experience is frightening. She does as she's been told. Keeps her head down. Says nothing. So, deprived of juicy gossip, they turn their attention to Columbine and pursue her. Bombard her with questions.

"I have nothing to say," she tells them.

Suddenly, a voice rings out. Strong arms elbow the reporters out of the way. Eric. Her knight in shining armour. He blocks them.

"Gentlemen," he says. "Would you please allow the ladies to get past. I'm sure Amaryllis will give you a statement when she's ready. In the meantime, please give her and her mother some space and some privacy."

With that, he steers them safely through to the car park. Where he hugs Amaryllis. Kisses her. Columbine and Doris look on and smile.

"You did good darling," he says. "I think the jury have already made up their minds. I know everyone in the public gallery has."

"I wish I could have heard her testimony," says Columbine. "And James's. But I wasn't called to testify until after them."

"She put some good words in for James. Despite." Doris tells her. "And probably best you didn't hear it all. Amaryllis threw everything at them, didn't she, Eric?"

"Everything," he agrees. "Even the kitchen sink. And it wasn't easy listening. Now, who's for a strong coffee and some sandwiches before we head back to the farm? Give those reporters time to retreat, eh?"

The farm. Mistletoe farm. Our farm, dreams Amaryllis. They move in on the 10th of January. All the building alterations are finished and some of the decorating. There is still a lot to do, but they have four pairs of hands now, that can all pick up a paintbrush. A roller. Amaryllis wants it all finished before Williain comes to join them. She's already chosen a room for him. Painted two walls, the door and window frames. Then when she discovers that Rosy is an artist, asks her if she will paint cars on one of the remaining walls and trains on the other. Planets on the ceiling.

"That's amazing," she says when Rosy finally puts her paintbrushes and paints away.

"I really enjoyed it. I don't get to do many wall murals. Hope you don't mind but I took some photos which I can show to clients. Maybe I'll branch out. Do less paintings. And more murals."

Amaryllis hugs her. Slips a cheque in the pocket of her overalls, a multi-coloured statement of splodges and smears.

"I think you'll be great," she says. "Make sure you empty your pockets before you wash those," she adds, pointing at them.

That evening they are all quiet. Doris and Columbine go to check on the few chickens they now have. And feed the two pairs of breeding pigs which have aluminium shelters on a field of mud and scrub. "I want to call those two," Amaryllis says pointing, when they come snuffling and shrieking out of the truck, "Boris and Betty. And shall we let Williain name the other two?"

Eric shrugs his shoulders. "Don't ask me," he says. "I didn't know you give pigs names. And I'd be useless at choosing them."

The morning comes too soon. As they approach the Crown Court, microphones are thrust in front of Amaryllis. Light flashes with the click of cameras. She's again barraged with questions. But remembering what they tell her, she keeps her head down, says nothing, whilst Eric, his arms around her pushes them out of the way.

This morning Doris and Columbine travel together. So far, the media does not know of Mistletoe Farm. Only her friends, the police and the barristers do. And they are not going to tell. They arrive and leave in separate cars. Always make sure they are not followed.

Inside the courtroom as everyone reassembles, it's like a re-run of the morning before. Everyone going to their appointed place. Except…

A sudden feeling. A shiver down her spine. She looks to the dock. It's not empty. An old man with white hair sits there. A prison officer stands at either side. So, the old man must be…She looks more closely. He is staring at her. No, not staring, she thinks. Glaring. Her father! Yes, it must be. Outside the courtroom she would not recognize him. For, unlike James, the years have not been kind to him. Amaryllis glares back. He will not intimidate her again.

"All rise!" calls the court usher. And the Judge enters. Amaryllis notices that his wig is no longer askew.

She's talked it over with her mother. And they decide they want to be in court to hear what, if anything, Charles will say in his defence. They know he pleads 'not guilty' at his arraignment. They also know that the Crown Prosecutor will cross-examine him. Amaryllis hopes he will crumple and reveal the real Charles August. Surprisingly, she finds herself quite excited.

The Judge reminds the jury of the salient facts. Then calls the Barrister for the Defence to give his opening speech.

He stands. Clears his throat.

"I am going to prove to you, the jury, that my client, Charles August is, in fact, the victim here. That contrary to what Amaryllis August says, she goes willingly with James Duncan because she's afraid of her mother. That it's her mother who abuses her, not her father."

"That's utter poppycock!" shouts Columbine. "It's him she's afraid of. As we all were."

"Silence in Court!"

Columbine. He recognizes her voice. Charles looks down. Can't see her. There's a woman sitting next to Amaryllis watching him. A loathsome look on her face. A pretty face. She's slim, Attractive. Elegantly dressed. Is that her?

His last memory of his wife is an overweight, lank haired woman who cries all the time and matches his alcohol intake, glass for glass. But yes, it is her. Like she looked in the war when she nursed alongside James and himself. So, he thinks, she doesn't drink herself to death or top herself. What a pity. He meets her gaze. Smirks. Shrugs his shoulders.

"That Amaryllis August is aware of the relationship between her father and James Duncan," the Barrister for the Defence continues. "That she purposely encourages James. Convinces him that it's she he loves, not her father. And that when she bears his child, she persuades James to leave the island with her and Williain. Thus, abandoning her father and leaving him to run Lochfrein. Something she knows he is not capable of. A man who suffers from rheumatoid arthritis and degenerate heart disease. I now ask Charles August to take the witness stand."

The prison officers help Charles to his feet. It's obvious that the rheumatoid arthritis, the excessive quantity of whisky he imbibes over the years, the strain on his heart, have all taken their toll. He breathes heavily. Coughs.

"You may remain seated as you testify, Mr August," says the Judge.

Charles drops heavily and awkwardly back onto the seat. Amaryllis prays the jury will not feel sorry for him. Believe the lies which she knows will pour out of his mouth.

But already he disrupts the court. Will not take the oath.

"Why should I swear to anything," he says. "You're my barrister. I've already pleaded 'not guilty'. That's the truth. It's up to you to prove that I am."

"Nevertheless, Mr August," the Barrister for the Defence says, "the trial cannot proceed until you have taken the oath. It is a rule of the British Judiciary."

"Fuck the British Judiciary!"

"Charles August," calls the Judge. "May I remind you that you are in a Court of Law."

"I don't need bloody reminding where I am. I'm not stupid. I was a brilliant surgeon once. Until look at me now..." He lifts his hands with the swollen twisted joints. "Can't even dress myself properly. They were supposed to look after me." He snarls. "But no, they bugger off. But not her. I don't let her."

The Barrister for the Defence interrupts. He is afraid his client is about to incriminate himself.

"Charles August, if you do not take the oath, you will be taken back down to the holding cell. This will prolong the trial for you and everyone else. If you take the oath, we can proceed, and you will get your chance to present your defence to the jury."

Charles sees the bible. Refuses to put his hand on it. "Bloody god-fearing folk." He spits. "My mother was one of them. Put the fear of God in me. But tables can be turned around," he says. "Just like lives." And much to his barrister's relief, he takes the oath.

Amaryllis and Columbine, the jurors, in fact everyone in the court is on edge. There is an air of disquiet. A foreboding. Even the Judge feels a sense of unease. A sense that Charles August is like a grenade. That when someone takes the pin out, he will explode.

"Mr August," the Barrister for the Defence begins. "I understand that your father, William Joseph August, a foot soldier in the Alexandra Princess of Wales's Own Yorkshire Regiment, is killed at the first battle of Ypres in October 1914."

"Yes," says Charles. "Dies for his country, a fine man. A hero. But even though I carry his name, he's not my father. Well, he couldn't be, could he?" He snorts. "Since I am born in 1917. It's the pretty-faced pig boy who is."

"I also understand that your mother, Victoria Elizabeth August, abhors the man who sires you. And since she sees a resemblance of this man in you, she abhors you too. Consequently, you endure a distressing childhood…"

Charles snorts. "You could say that."

The Barrister for the Defence pauses. Looks at Charles. Tries to gauge his client's demeanour. He is quiet. Listening. Decides that perhaps now, is the time to gain some sympathy for him. Swing the pendulum back in his favour.

"Would you tell the court, Mr August, what your early life is like. Help us understand."

And Charles does. He has an audience now. A captive audience. He has no idea that Amaryllis and James already tell of those years and what the consequences are. The jurors listen avidly. But their faces remain impassive.

And the more Charles opens his mouth, the more his ego inflates.

"You wouldn't treat an animal like she treated me. I couldn't wait to get away from her. That's why I chose to go to medical school. I wanted to help people. Care for them. Things I never had. Oh and I am good! I have power at my fingertips." He looks ruefully down at his hands. There is little sensation at the tips of his fingers now. "I can choose who lives. And who dies. And I do."

Horrified, his barrister tries to hush him. But Charles will not be hushed. He's on a pedestal. He's a god.

"It's so easy," he says. "I have the means. And I use them. No-one ever suspects."

"Thank you, Mr August." The Barrister for the Defence finally intercedes on his client's behalf. Before he buries himself deeper in the hole he digs. "Let us move on to your time at Lochfrein when James Duncan marries your daughter and they have a child. A boy. Williain Joseph, I believe."

Another lie, thinks Amaryllis. *We never marry.*

She sees her father's lower jaw protrude. He's biting down on it. Hard. She knows he's angry. Simmering under the cold, unfeeling, monologue he gives to his audience.

"Beautiful child," he says. "Just like his mother." There is no warmth in the latter statement.

"And you wish them to remain with you at the farm where you can participate in your grandson's upbringing…

Woops, thinks Amaryllis. He won't like that. As far as her father is concerned Williain is his son. His and James's.

But Charles appears calm. The only indication that he is about to boil is the tap, tap of a finger on the bible. The shuffle of his bottom.

"Give him all the things you never had as a child," continues the Barrister for the Defence. "And that contrary to what has been said, you do not try to murder your daughter. But believing she is going to harm herself and Williain, you are in fact trying to save her. When she slips out of your grasp and falls."

"Yes, that's about it. That's how it was."

"And furthermore, I would advise the court that Charles August, upon realizing the extent of his daughter's injury, takes her to the best sanitorium in the country, the Sanctum at York. Where he pays for her treatment for the seven years she remains there. I, therefore, put it to the jury that the allegations against my client, Charles August, are based on hearsay. That they are spurious and without proof. And you should, therefore, find him 'not guilty'. That," he says, "is the case for the Defence."

"Does the Crown Prosecutor wish to cross-examine."

"I do, my Lord."

Now the fun starts, thinks Amaryllis. Her father hears 'cross-examine'. He is all of a fidget now. About to come to the boil.

"Charles August, is it not true that the real reason you plan the orchestration of your daughter's abduction is that you want a child. A son. Then you can play happy families with your lover, James Duncan. But, as a doctor, you are aware a baby born out of incest could inherit unwanted traits. Yet, you want your genes to be passed on. So the progeny of James and Amaryllis is the perfect solution. And once this is achieved you have no further use for her?"

Charles turns the bible round. One way, then the other. "Not true." His voice is almost a hiss.

"I also put it to you that had the child been a girl, you would have continued the brutal rape of your daughter until a boy is produced. To satisfy *your* desire. Regardless of the consequences to her or her offspring."

"Not true."

"And that because your partner realizes he loves her…"

"Thinks he loves her," says Charles. Tap. Tap. Tap. "But he'd never leave me. He wouldn't dare."

"And we all know why. Your partner, James Duncan, tells all. And we also know what you would feed to the pigs should he dare."

The tapping of his fingers stops. There is a momentary lull. Then the first piece of Charles's façade crumbles. He tries to get up.

"He lies! It's all lies!" he cries. "I do it all for him. For us."

The Judge ignores the outburst. Allows the Crown Prosecutor to continue…

"But there's nothing to stop Amaryllis and Williain leaving, is there? And we know James Duncan gives her the wherewithal to do this. Even suggests the day. The day you both go to the agricultural show in Rothesay."

"Bastard!" cries Charles. "He betrays me again. I should have killed him too."

He's agitated now. The thump, thump, thumping of his feet on the base of the stand joins the tap, tap, tapping of his fingers on the bible.

Again the Judge does not intervene. Although he must remain unbiased. Ensure every person gets a fair trial. Direct the jury so they can reach their own conclusion. There is a sense that this defendant, if allowed to continue, will dig his own grave. And the case will be concluded.

"But no-one expects the storm, which ravages the island and delays her escape." The Crown Prosecutor again. "So you find her the following morning, waiting for the ferry. She has Williain. A large holdall. They are leaving you. And I put it to you, Charles August, there is no way you are going to allow this. So you stop her. Hope you have done enough to kill her. And when you find you have not, ship her to an asylum. Out of the goodness of your heart. Which I believe you do not, and never have, possessed."

"Why would I do that?" Charles says, sneeringly. "She's my daughter. I love her."

Amaryllis would so like to believe this. Once, a lifetime ago, she thought him the best father in the world. They shared a secret. But as she grew, so did the secret. And so did her fear of him. He never loved her. He just used her.

"Why don't *you* tell the court why, Mr August."

"I already have." His voice is snarly.

"Then why don't you tell us again. In your own words."

The last of Charles's façade drops off. And Dr Hyde enters the witness stand. And erupts. An overflow of lava pours out. Everything. All the plans he makes.

268

The deeds he commits to achieve them. There is no remorse. No guilt. His ego will not allow this. It is almost too much for his audience to take in but take it in they do. Until the last expletive leaves his mouth. And there is nothing left. The mountain sleeps.

"No further questions," says the Crown Prosecutor.

The two prison officers, one on each side of Charles, take an arm and escort him off the witness stand. And with legs dragging, he is frogmarched down to a cell.

The Judge reminds the jury of the case, so it is fresh in their minds when they go to deliberate. Gives final instructions.

"Should any one of you have the slightest element of doubt, you must record a vote of 'not' guilty'. Have you elected a foreperson?"

A man stands. He wears a tweed jacket…

Amaryllis remembers the tiny tweed coat Williain wears that day. The last day she sees him.

"My Lord, I am the elected foreman," he says. The Judge gives the court usher the verdict form. He passes it to the foreman to be completed when the jury reaches a unanimous decision. The jury retires to the deliberation room.

Standing, the Judge announces, "This Court is now in recess. You will be recalled when the jury reaches a verdict. In the meantime, please make yourselves available of the facilities."

****

Hardly has there been time to grab a sandwich and coffee and consume them, when the foreman alerts the court, and all parties are called back into the courtroom. Less than two hours have passed.

Because Charles has been firing a verbal volley of bullets at James, ranting and raving in his cell, it's decided to have one defendant at a time in the dock. James is brought into court first.

"Will the foreperson for the jury please stand," says the Judge. "Have you reached a verdict?"

"Yes, my Lord."

"Will the defendant please stand."

Amaryllis looks at James. Smiles reassuringly at him.

"On the count of attempted murder, how do you find the defendant, James Duncan?"

"Not guilty."

James breathes a sigh of relief. As does Amaryllis.

"James Duncan," says the Judge. "I believe that intrinsically you are a good man. Nevertheless, a weak and easily led man. That you were drawn too deep into Charles August's depravity to see a way out. But you admit to your crimes. Show remorse and in your defence, Amaryllis August has submitted a written testimony. So I therefore sentence you to five years imprisonment. You will be taken from here to Full Sutton Prison near York until your release."

James is escorted from the dock. Five years. It could have been worse he thinks. Perhaps Amaryllis will visit. Bring Williain. All in good time. He's not sad. What he, what they did, was wrong. And five years out of a life is nothing in comparison to the seventeen years they stole from her.

Now, it is Charles's turn. Surprisingly, this morning he walks into the courtroom unaided, albeit stiffly and with stooped back. Stands arrogantly in the dock. There is no sign that he believes the verdict will be anything but 'not guilty'.

"Has the jury reached a unanimous verdict?" the Judge asks the foreman.

"Yes, my Lord."

"Please read the verdict out."

"We find the defendant, Charles August, guilty on all counts."

Charles grips the polished edge of the dock so hard his knuckles go white.

"Charles August," the Judge addresses him. "The heinous acts you commit with impunity and for which you show neither guilt nor remorse, speak of a man who is larger than himself. A man who is a danger to family, friends, and society.

For I can now inform the jury that in a prior court, Charles August inadvertently admits to the murder of his mother, Victoria Elizabeth Anne August and six other women. Women who were loved. Had families. Families denied of the truth at the time. I would now like to name these women. Give these families the resolution they deserve. Elizabeth Arundel, Elizabeth Chantry, Victoria Nelson, Victoria Swift, Anne McAllen, and Anne Collinson."

The reporters for the of the press write frantically. As does the court stenographer. Whist the jurors, the barristers, the court usher, members of the public, the bailiff and the police officers bow their heads in a moment of respect.

"Charles August," continues the Judge, "I therefore sentence you to two life sentences. You will be taken from this place to Broadmoor Psychiatric Hospital, where you will be detained until your death."

Amaryllis and Columbine look at each other. They never expected this. Their eyes smile. Amaryllis looks up to Eric and Doris. They give a thumbs up. Then she looks directly at her father. And smirks. She has never smirked before. But oh, does she enjoy it now. Broadmoor. A far worse place to be imprisoned than Lochfrein.

Charles folds. Crumples like an airless accordion. Life. All he does and achieves gone. He will never see Williain again. A life not worth living. And he knows that as soon as an opportunity presents, he will end it.

The Judge thanks the jury. "You may go home to your families, safe in the knowledge that justice has been done this day." And then, unexpectedly, to Amaryllis, "Amaryllis August, your endurance is stoical. I wish you well for the future. A future you have fought for and deserve. This case is now finally closed. Court dismissed."

So this is it, she thinks. Closure. She watches the Judge depart, his red robe and wig standing out from all the polished brown wood. And then Amaryllis August is hugging everyone. Her mother. Eric and Doris. Her friends who come down from the gallery. Anyone. Even the Crown Prosecutor.

"Thank you," she says. "No, thank you," he replies. "You made the case easy for me."

She finds Inspector Gibson. Hugs him too. "Thank you for believing in me."

Taken by surprise, all he can think to say is, "You are very easy to believe. And I'm glad you've got the verdicts you sought."

Outside, Amaryllis no longer keeps her head down. Arm in arm with Eric, she stands tall. Beams for the cameras and the reporters who will relay the verdicts to their respective newspapers.

Now, she will go home and start that future. A future with Williain and her new family. And she vows to herself, she will make it as happy and fulfilling as she can.

Chapter 46

Three weeks later there is a telephone call. It's Sarah Blythe.

"We believe he's ready," she says. "You can collect your son, Amaryllis. I've seen the papers. Quite a headline case. But you won. I'm pleased for you. It will take time. For both of you. But I know you'll get there. Good luck."

Amaryllis places the receiver back in the cradle. A huge sigh escapes her lips. As if the past breathes out in all the air she has. But then she takes a huge breath in. And begins…

First, she finds her mother to tell her the news. Columbine is making sure their little flock of goats have not been eating the washing. They have all decided not to have sheep at Mistletoe. Amaryllis has read that goats milk is kinder on the digestion and helps with eczema which she is prone to suffer. They will make goats cheese and sell both the milk and cheese locally.

Most of Mistletoe's acreage is arable. So, she plans to grow root vegetables. Peas and beans. Lettuce and salad vegetables for the summer. There are pear and apple trees. So she thinks to produce a local perry and apple cider.

Apart from the farm, she also needs to find a primary school in Monk Fryston to register Williain. There is only one, which feeds most of its pupils into Selby High School. The headmistress is very obliging and listens as Amaryllis tells her all about Williain's circumstances. And there are still last-minute details for the wedding to plan. A date is now set, her birthday, the 21st of June. It's a Saturday. So many plans, she thinks. Hopes she is not turning into her father.

"Eric's driving me over there," she tells her mum. He has bought a car. A Ford Cortina. It's blue and roomy. A family car. "Can you make sure his room's all ready."

"I don't think I need to," says her mother. "I know you've made sure it's perfect." She gives Amaryllis a quick kiss on her cheek. "Off you go then. Sooner you get there. Sooner you'll be back."

"Williain settles into Mistletoe surprisingly well. He likes his room with the painted walls. He likes his school where he is a popular pupil. The teachers like him because he is polite and diligent. A bit quirky. The girls like him because he is good-looking, clever, funny. And does a mean Scottish accent. The boys like him because he's good at sport. Is always ready to join in with a kick-about at play time. Will help a friend struggling with their homework."

"You mark my words," Columbine says. "That boy of yours..."

"Your grandson, Mum," Amaryllis reminds her. Just in case she's about to say something bad of him. But you can't say anything bad about Williain. He has a wonderful aura. She can't believe how confident and adjusted he sems to be. Although sometimes she glimpses him sitting very quietly, staring into space. A dreamy expression on his face.

"Will break many a heart," Columbine finishes. "He'll be a ladies' man. And a man's man," she adds as an afterthought.

Amaryllis grins. "He already has. Broken some hearts. There's a few girls in his class that have shed a tear or two over him."

Williain stops asking about his daddies. He knows they are in prison. But not what for. Amaryllis will tell him one day. When he is ready.

"We might go and visit PappyVroomvroom," she tells him.

Williain giggles. "That's a silly name," he says.

"Well, it's what you called your daddy James. When you were a baby. Daddy Charles was PappyChoochoo."

Williain considers.

"I like PappyVroomvroom best," he whispers. "PappyChoochoo can be a reit crabbit."

I know, thinks Amaryllis.

Over time, a fatherly bond begins to grow between Eric and Williain. Precipitated when Eric discovers the boy's love of trains, cars and anything mechanical. Often the two of them can be seen together in one of the big sheds, the doors open, muted chatter drifting out as, heads bent, they take something apart. Look for the problem and then, working it out, fix it. Put all the pieces back together again. And Eric plays football with him. Takes him to the Railway Museum in York, which Williain loves.

But what really helps him settle into his new life is the puppy that Amaryllis takes him to choose. She learns of a family in Monk Fryston whose bitch, a beautiful golden Labrador, has a litter. There are eight puppies. Williain sits on the floor, whilst still clumsy and uncoordinated, they try to climb on him. He picks them up. But they wriggle and squiggle to be put down. Except one. One that is content to be held. And falls asleep in his arms.

"This one," he says. It's a little girl. They can collect her in three weeks.

"I'm going to call her Fiona," Williain says on the way home. "If it'd been a boy dog, I'd have called him Chad."

Chad…Oh Chad. Amaryllis is back at Lochfrein. That first day when she is sent upstairs, so she is not seen. When Scott McGinty and his dog come into the kitchen. When James tells her terrible things about him. All of which she discovers are not true. They both save her in their own way.

"I remember Chad," she says. Fears what is coming.

"He died," Williain says. "Last year. But he was a jolly good age. Scott has another dog now. A girl dog. A black and white collie, called Sky. We were training her up. Scot's a whizz with animals. And mum…"

He finally says it. Out loud. A tiny word but big in its meaning. A word she has been longing to hear.

"I'm going to train Fiona tae be a reit guid dug."

All this is said with the prosaicness of a nine-year-old boy who grows up on a farm. Has an intrinsic yet pragmatic view of animals. And one day will, probably, be a farmer himself.

****

Amaryllis August marries her knight in shining armour, her Prince Charming, in Selby Abbey on Saturday the 21st of June 1975 at two-fifteen in the afternoon. Her mother, resplendent in a navy and lemon suit, a wide brimmed navy hat with lemon bow, walks her down the aisle to the alter where Eric awaits her. Behind, Penelope and Hetty hold the outer edges of the lacy train. Both wear pink, Penelope's dress is pink lace over pink satin. It is fitted below the breasts and has puff sleeves.

Penelope has lost all her baby weight and looks amazing. So does Hetty in the party dress Columbine makes for Amaryllis's ninth birthday. It fits the little girl perfectly. As do the silver ballerina pumps. Between them Williain in a navy and white page boy suit holds the middle of the train.

The dress Columbine sews for this, Amaryllis's special day, is less frivolous than the party dress. Simply cut, dove white, its long floaty silk fabric is embellished with tiny translucent pearls that catch the light. She looks almost ethereal.

The Abbey is bedecked with flowers. All those Amaryllis sees when she and her mother call upon The Reverend Canon John De Vere. Bouquets of Gypsophilia tied with green ribbons hang off the end of the pews. There are Baby's Breath, white Gardenias and Snow Pixie lupins everywhere.

And there he is, the very man himself, robed and ready. At the alter facing Eric and the congregation. A somewhat small congregation. It hardly fills two pews.

Doris is there. Penelope's husband, Gerald. Alwyn and Sakura. Judy and Philip. Rosy. Miss Tong, who Amaryllis calls on at St. Andrews and surprises her by giving a written invitation. And there are three other women sitting together. Amaryllis knows them all. She's overwhelmed.

Doris. Doris with her talent of tracing people. How she does it, she doesn't know. How she's kept it secret, she doesn't know. But she has found them, Caro, Bea and Staff Nurse Magdalena. Three people from the past who were, and are, important to her. Three people she can't wait to catch up with. But right now, she has something more important to do. Marry Eric. Oh and not trip over her train.

And as she walks slowly down the aisle, accompanied by Handel's Water Music to join Eric at the altar, Vicar John smiles at her every step.

The music stops. Penelope lifts the veil from her Amaryllis's face. Williain stands proudly to the side. He has the rings in his pocket. He knows what to do. And in the vastness of the Abbey, The Reverend Canon John De Vere's melodic voice rings out…"We are gathered here together…" Until finally, "I now pronounce you man and wife."

Eric turns to his wife. And kisses her. A long, loving kiss.

At the same time, three swans fly over the Abbey and alight on the river. In 1069 Benedict of Auxerre has a vision from God. He is called by St Germain to build a new monastery at the place where three swans will appear to him. Benedict takes his vision on a long and winding journey, across sea and land, until, resting, he sees three swans alight in a bend on the river Ouse. 'Selebiae'. There he builds the new monastery.

A monastery which, over the years, will grow and become Selby Abbey. A magnificent and glorious monument to a man's vision. And a fitting place to end a story. The long and winding journey of Amaryllis August and Isla Duncan to find a place to build a future.

The End